The author is a former teacher who specialized in English and History. She is married with two sons. Felicity was brought up in Worcestershire and now lives in Yorkshire. She is an avid reader who always had an ambition to write. Her other interests include travelling and antiques.

CARENZA'S JOURNEY

Felicity Knight

CARENZA'S JOURNEY

AUSTIN MACAULEY
PUBLISHERS LTD.

A CIP catalogue record for this title is available from the British
Library.

ISBN 978 14963 447 2

www.austinmacauley.com

First Published (2013)
Austin Macauley Publishers Ltd.
25 Canada Square
Canary Wharf
London
E14 5LB

Printed and Bound in Great Britain

Acknowledgments

I would like to thank my husband for his patience in living with Carenza on a daily basis and his meticulous research on the historical aspects of the novel. I also thank my two sons for their constant support throughout the project.

Finally, I must say thank you to my sister, Judith Milne, for her creation of the front cover which shows Carenza in her Worcestershire environment.

Contents

Part 1: Sept 1939- The Start of the Journey

Chapter 1

It had not been the best of days for Hannah. The world seemed a drab place at the moment with the East End looking grey with rain battering against the window pane and people scurrying about their business, heads bent against the relentless winter storm. The day had not started well with her husband, Ray, shouting about every wrongdoing under the sun and there was to be no appeasement to lighten his mood. His problem had begun with the fact that there was no money in the old tin tea caddy that stood high on top of the kitchen dresser.

'There must be some money in this house,' he had shouted at the top of his voice. 'Find some for me.'

Hannah had witnessed these moods before and they usually heralded a tide of abuse in the physical sense.

'There's nothing here. I've told you,' she retorted cowering back into the shadows expecting the inevitable. 'Perhaps if you were to find a job…' She knew that she had said too much.

Ray turned to face her, a look of thunder etching his features.

'What did you say?'

But before she could answer his hand struck high across her cheek bone leaving a welt on her already bruised skin.

'Please don't,' she whispered but to no avail. Another crashing blow sent her reeling backwards onto the floor before she heard the back door slam closed in sheer temper.

Rising from the floor she stumbled, before steadying herself again. At the stone sink she turned on the single tap from which a gush of cold water flowed. Picking up the grey cloth which sat in its customary place on the pine draining board, she placed it under the tap and having wrung out the excess water dabbed it over the bruise that was beginning to form on her face.

'Dear God,' she exclaimed at the pain. She was beginning to learn to live with her regular beatings. The rest of the day had progressed slowly with life's humdrum chores being accomplished through sheer physical effort. There was no sign of Ray who would have found someone to buy him round after round of drinks at the pub and would roll home in another drunken stupor in time to fall into bed with no knowledge of the day's events.

Hannah sat by the window in the living room staring into oblivion as the grey, depressing clouds scurried across the sky. The early twilight of the winter's day only contributed to her already despondent feelings. Like many other people she wondered about what uncertainties this new year of 1939 would bring. The political outlook was bleak she thought, although others around her varied in their degree of optimism or sense of foreboding. But Hannah was not just reflecting on the storm clouds of war. There was no solution to the strife under her own roof without dwelling on the troubles of the world. However, this house was where she should have some control over her own destiny and that of her daughter, Carenza, but Ray's regime dominated events.

'My beautiful girl,' she murmured to herself in the gathering gloom.

Her features softened momentarily when her thoughts drifted towards her daughter. How high her hopes had been all those years ago when she had held the tiny bundle in her arms for the first time and contemplated the brilliant future that she had planned for her child. It was to be a future full of promise for the whole family. Hannah smiled at her own sense of ideology. It was a wry smile full of cynicism owing to the emotional baggage that she had acquired over the years and she could never shed while she was married to Ray. How she wished that she could move forward with her life, perhaps to begin again with her daughter, to move out of the constant darkness of fear into the light of hope, expectancy and happiness. Ah, happiness, that most elusive of emotions that she had once possessed in abundance all that time ago. The dream had been there from the beginning. Had it gone completely or was there still a ray of hope that times would improve and they could touch the stars and feel the thrill of anticipation on course for a brighter tomorrow?

The dream had been to improve the quality of their drab existence and transform it to a world of richness and glamour that would carry them from the dreariness and hardship of the East End, far away where Carenza could grow physically and emotionally. Hannah had spent much of her spare time at the moving pictures where people loved the razzmatazz of a luxurious life. Her mother Doris did not hold with this dreaming.

'Sort yourself out my girl. All that day dreaming stuff and nonsense is no good for you. Is it Frank?'

She would refer to her husband, who was a man of few words and he would nod his silent agreement and continue with his workload or read his paper when the luxury of time permitted.

'Let her get an education,' Doris would continue sagely.

Doris was not quite sure how they would accomplish this but she knew that educated people had a different expectation from life. Education was the key to a brighter tomorrow. She was in awe of educated people. Words meant wisdom. Her knowledge of the professions filled her with inhibitions that she could not explain. Their poverty was a shame that she could not condone but they worked hard as a family apart from Ray. Often they found difficulty putting food on the table and there was rarely enough money in their pockets for luxuries. They were not the only family who suffered in this way. The streets teemed with children in rags begging for money.

'Give us a penny mister.' This rang through the streets.

Children often sat despondently on doorsteps with nothing to do. Washing still hung across the streets and boys played football dodging the billowing laundry to score a goal. Theft was rife. Pickpockets were adept at taking your hard earned money. If richer people strayed along the streets they became a prime target for theft or beatings. Such was the hardship of the people, but there was much pride which raised you beyond poverty. There was a community that pulled together when times became tougher, ready and willing to support others suffering distress, and there were those that could break free and begin a life away from the distress and poverty.

So the dream continued. Carenza would receive the best of educations that their money could buy and live the life that her forebears had had to earn through hard work. They had even christened this child of their heart, Carenza, a more exotic name than most children in the East End had ever heard before. It was a name that was meant to make Carenza stand apart from other children and prepare her for this journey into the future, a journey on a path paved with gold. Hannah thought about her parents who had persisted that the name was not fair on the child.

'What do you want to call her by such a fancy name for,' Frank had asked. It seemed nonsensical to him. 'People gonna laugh at such airs and graces.'

'Don't be stupid Dad,' Hannah had replied. 'We need to better ourselves.'

'Good hard work is the answer. Don't get anywhere without neither.' That was all he would say on the matter. Frank was not a great talker but he thought deeply.

But at that time Hannah and her husband Ray had been as one in thought and deed and were committed to this course they had mapped out for themselves - their destiny. But Hannah now had to acknowledge that her mother had been right. Her child had suffered the teasing and torment from families who thought that they were rising above their station. Such aspirations were not part of the accepted code of conduct nor was it apparently to be part of theirs either for here they were, twelve years on from Carenza's birth, still living in a two bedroom Victorian slum which had hardly changed since the day it was built except to become more run down.

The twilight had turned into the blackness of a midwinter's night. The cloud cover allowed no moonlight or a myriad of stars to twinkle enthusiastically in order to enhance the blank darkness.

Hannah was still sitting by the window deep in thought. There were no lights lit in the sparsely furnished room and there was a dampness and chillness permeating the atmosphere as her thoughts drifted towards Ray, her husband of thirteen years. He had been the light of her life all those years ago. He had stolen her heart even against her mother's better judgement. His looks had been dashing with his piercing blue eyes and dark, well cut bryl creemed hair which parted neatly on the right hand side of his handsomely shaped head. He was dapper in appearance with fastidiousness about his clothes allowing only the best suits which he could afford to clothe his athletic frame.

He had romantically courted her and bought her presents which had taken her breath away. She had been in love and felt loved in return. Whilst in the security of this all-consuming tide of emotion they had evolved the ideas for their glamorous future. Two young people, both good looking, who would go forward hand in hand allowing nothing to go wrong.

'I love you,' Ray had whispered romantically into her ear. 'There will be nobody else for me.'

'I love you too,' she had responded and had snuggled even closer into his embrace watching films at the pictures where love had triumphed over evil.

They could not fail to live the dream together. They were invincible. Even now she had to acknowledge that her mother had been right. As the months turned to years Hannah had papered over the cracks of her failing marriage not wishing to recognise that there were severe problems. The truth was that at seventeen she had been too young for marriage and did not have any experience of life to deal with what lay ahead but she had been pregnant and it was the only way out of the situation; to marry Ray who had promised to stand by her. Together with the baby the dream persisted for a while but began to fade after time.

Her reverie was sharply interrupted by the banging of a door followed by a vibrant presence in the room. Carenza stood before her with a glowing face which told Hannah that her daughter's world was a happy place this once. Carenza's cream toned complexion shone against the ebony colour of her hair, so like her father's, as it fell in a glossy sheet down her back. She was tall and graceful for her twelve years, again following Ray's imposing height. But there the similarity ended. She had inherited Hannah's brown eyes, which when they were happy, danced and sparkled with a life of their own. Those times were much fewer these days.

'How's your day bin, my precious?' Hannah smiled her greeting uttering the endearment that she had used so often during her child's life. Her arms were thrown wide to embrace this treasured daughter. Carenza slid easily into her mother's embrace and kissed her cheek.

'Ma, let's put a light on in here before I tell you. It's cold. Let me light the fire.' Carenza disentangled herself from her mother's arms and moved towards the fireplace shivering as she went. The box of matches, kept in the old soap dish on top of the mantelpiece, was removed from its container and Carenza adeptly lit the rolls of folded newspaper which lay ready in the grate for lighting. The fire soon sprang to life while the flames fluttered and danced, adding an extra glow to the dreary room. Carenza held out her hands to the heat to breathe life back into her cold body before turning to her mother to commence her tale.

'Ma, we have had a fair day today. I've been a teacher and I have decided that's what I want to do when I'm older. What do you

19

think me dad will say? Mrs Watson had a headache and by this afternoon it had got so bad that Mr Jones had to send her home with instructions not to come back until she was fit again. He didn't have anyone to take her class so he asked me an' Sylvie to go and stop with them 'til it was 'ometime. He said that we were by far the most sensible of our class to do such a job and he was putting great faith in us.' Hannah laughed, a rare enough event these days.

Carenza barely paused for an intake of breath before continuing.

'We read them story on top of story. Little Maisie Betts fell asleep and only woke up when Mr Jones popped in to see that all was well. He even said that we would make good teachers one day,'

'Well that's bin a fair old day today. Let's be hoping that Mrs Watson is better tomorrow. Otherwise poor Mr Jones will have too much to do and you will be teaching again.' Hannah smiled softly at her daughter's enthusiasm.

'You didn't tell me what me dad would say about me being a teacher. I know it would cost to educate me but I'll work really 'ard to make you proud of me an' I'll pay you back double the cost or even treble.'

Hannah smiled again and remembered the dream. Was it too late even now?

'Your dad would be proud of you love. You know he wants you to do well,' she sighed hoping to convince her daughter that what she said would be the truth. There was no knowing what would happen now.

The old Ray would have been proud but the new Ray had changed beyond all recognition in thought and appearance. His frequent out bursts of violent temper coupled with the loss of his looks to the ravages of smoking and drinking to excess had contributed to their lack of funds. The fine suits had disappeared and the care with which he had groomed his appearance was a thing of the past. His hair had premature streaks of grey around his temples and it had grown longer due to infrequent visits to the barber now that money was in such short supply. Hannah knew that talk of college and the struggle that would ensue to send Carenza there would send Ray into a new frenzy. Any mention of it would make him witless with rage and see his tall frame stride down to the school to see Mr Jones, the Headmaster, and revile him for putting fancy ideas into his daughter's head. She did not want the gentle, caring Mr Jones to become another of Ray's victims. Carenza did not deserve the whispers that would pursue such actions from people who thought that the Dodds were now on a downward spiral. Neighbours were well aware of the violent streaks of which Ray was capable. Some of them had been on the receiving end of his temper resulting in physical consequences. Ray had been fortunate that he had not been in more trouble but his peers were frightened of his aggressive nature.

Hannah turned to Carenza with what appeared to be a carefree smile and said.

'Shall we keep it to ourselves for the moment love and tell your dad when he is less tired?'

Carenza smiled her reply. She knew what was going through her mother's mind. She nodded her head knowing that the euphoria that she had felt on her return home had evaporated and the dream had died before it could even have chance to begin.

*

The school that Carenza had attended since she was five stood in the middle of Travis Street. It was a grey coloured building which on dank winter days gave an impression of gloom. It had been built at the end of the previous century and many memories abounded both good and bad in the minds of the older generation whose families had inhabited the East End for years, but thanks to the care and the hard work of the staff the children loved to attend school which often became a sanctuary from the problems and deprivation felt at home . Considering the hardship of the area there was a good community spirit where the unwritten law was that people would help each other in times of trouble. Mr Jones' strength lay in the fact that he believed in communication instead of physical violence. His only arrogance lay in the fact, of which he was immensely proud, that he had never administered the cane. Generally, the population at large agreed except for some of the tougher fathers who regularly gave their errant offspring a clip around the ears without such a course of action entering their thoughts as something they should not do. Violence was often a reaction to the frustration and daily grind of their lives.

The interior of the school building was dark and gloomy allowing only a small amount of sunshine to penetrate even on the brightest of days. It was here that Carenza's fertile mind was sharpened and honed and where Mr Jones recognised that her keen intelligence required nourishing way beyond the sterile environment that was called home. On many an occasion he had taken Ray Dodds to task when he had set foot in school to complain about the amount of homework that Carenza received while other children had next to nothing. Eric Jones had tried in vain to explain that Carenza was a bright child who could have a favourable future ahead of her but Ray was more concerned with life in the present.

'But Mr Dodds,' he addressed the bullish man standing before him. 'You have a very intelligent daughter who could have a successful future ahead of her. She could win a scholarship to grammar school.' He did not add his innermost thoughts of, if you could see further than your nose end.

'That does not put food in stomachs now or next week, does it,' Ray banged a desk to emphasise his point.

He viewed Carenza as an additional pair of hands which made life easier in the long term. While she sat for hours poring over her work there was no time for Carenza to help her mother at home or run the numerous errands which he did not want to undertake mostly because he was often incapable of doing so in his almost continual inebriated state. Ray Dodds' belligerent manner had not intimidated the headmaster who had explained his reasons for the work load which had been heaped upon Carenza with the best of intentions.

Ray had not received an academic education. His roots were firmly entrenched in the traditions of the East End like his father before him. It had never crossed the minds of the different generations of the Dodds family to have ambition and to find a life that would be conducive to all members of the family. Ray's brief flirtation with ambition and success had only lasted a matter of months but the hasty marriage followed closely by the birth of a daughter had been too much for him. He loved the idea of opportunity and wealth but hard work combined with the responsibilities of marriage and enforced parenthood were soon to become an anathema to him.

At first he had been quite taken with the idea of a baby which enabled him to stand tall amongst his peers but his disappointment at the birth of a daughter had not changed over the intervening years. He was not prepared to be told that his daughter's intelligence needed fuelling to such a degree that she would have airs above her station in life and could possibly become a threat to his own vanity, knowing that she could possibly stand taller in society and look down on him. Ray's already fragile ego could not possibly cope with that. The East End had been good enough for all his family in the past and would be in the future. He had long forgotten the dream that he had planned with Hannah. His ambition lay these days in imbibing in the local public house, The King's Arms, with like-minded people. Work was not always easy to find but he never bothered looking for it anyway.

Ray had first seen Hannah down at the market shouting out at the fruit stall that she ran with her father and mother. She had been as pretty as a picture with her strawberry blonde hair shining in the spring sunshine and her brown eyes dancing with humour as she laughed at the jokes the regular customers imparted. Her strong, young arms lifted the boxes of fruit and vegetables with ease and she refilled the empty spaces on the stall where fruit had been sold. It was this picture of Hannah which had drawn Ray like a magnet to the stall and had engaged her in light-hearted banter. The attraction had been mutual and it was not long before they had started walking out on a regular basis. Hannah's parents had not objected at first, seeing the happiness that Ray had brought to their daughter. His smart appearance had been noted and they had felt that he was a cut above the other boys that Hannah had brought home. He had worked in a men's outfitters shop up in the West End. This had given Ray his debonair attitude to life. There had been a time that he could have had any girl that he had wanted but he had been flattered by Hannah's attention and flirtatious manner and to be honest had enjoyed the fact that Hannah was totally in awe of him, particularly his physical attributes. But as time went on Doris and Frank (Hannah's parents) had observed the other side to Ray's character. Regularly he would appear at the market stall at various times of the day when he should have been at work. He had taken so much time off that eventually he was dismissed. He had married Hannah promising to begin afresh but had only found casual labour at the market generally humping boxes and driving to pick up goods which the stall holders found useful at first, saving them time with their own businesses but eventually it became irksome when Ray was often late in returning. But Hannah was blind to all the problems. Her infatuation was such that she could find no fault and when her condition was discovered everybody turned a blind eye to Ray's attitudes because he was prepared to stand by Hannah.

She had lived for months in her idealistic state when she had longed for the evenings so that she could be in his arms alone out of the way of parental observation. This state of affairs lasted for an idyllic six months until the horror hit Hannah that she must be pregnant because she had not seen her monthlies for quite some time. A quick calculation made it three. This realization sent the alarm bells ringing and a raging sensation of anxiety numbed her senses. The ecstasy which had been hers during these past months began to subside when the full impact of her situation hit her with such a force that she felt physically ill. She knew that something had to be done quickly. Ray's promise to stand by her had given her hope once more and the support of her parents had swept her away on a euphoric tide of emotion which was to last long after the birth of Carenza.

When Hannah could bring herself to think dispassionately she did not see Ray as the best husband material but both had a strong physical attraction for the other. And so it was that Ray and Hannah were married in the church where she had been christened less than twenty years before and they had started out on one of life's adventures with an optimism that was soon quenched.

Chapter 2

The late summer sun shone through the back kitchen window offering the only cheerfulness to be found in the stuffy atmosphere of baking and dirt as well as the late heat of the day. Hannah's hair stuck to her head in unflattering waves as she regularly wiped her forehead with the back of her hand. She had been up since 5.30 a.m., initially to hasten to the fruit and vegetable stall at the market where she still helped Doris and Frank and then along to Mrs Potter's house down at the bottom of Travis Street not far from the school to help with the cleaning. Mrs Potter worked in the shop alongside Mr Potter. The Potters had owned the grocery store all their married lives. They had been unable to have children of their own and enjoyed the end of the school day when many of the children came into the shop to spend the odd halfpenny when there was one to spare. They had engaged Hannah as a cleaner when Mrs Potter felt that she could not cope with running a home and helping out in the business. They had taken to her straight away for her hard work and engaging honesty. It had also been known for Hannah to take over in the shop at times. Her knowledge of a business and the fact that she could relate to the customers was a useful asset. But after her two hours stint she returned to the market to work alongside her mother, Doris and her father, Frank.

There had been hopes that Ray would enter the family business with a view to taking over when Doris and Frank were near retirement but Ray had had other plans which did not involve a great deal of work. Most days were spent at The King's Arms, the pub which lay at the end of Bentley Street. This was where the family's money for life's little luxuries was spent. Regularly he was drunk, often emerging at closing time or when his quota of money had run out. Ray's violent streak, which had lain dormant for years, reared its ugly head at regular intervals and was triggered by the most trivial of things . It could begin by Hannah making a throw away comment about their apparent lack of funds. Ray's fist would lash out and knock her off balance. There was the pinning her arms tightly to her side which developed finger bruises. She had to wear long sleeved blouses which hid the tell tale marks away from her mother's suspicious gaze.

But Doris had had her suspicions for quite some time. She kept her eyes peeled before she would make any accusations. Her sharp eyes watched Hannah's relationship with Ray and the impact this had upon Carenza and their daily lives. Carenza displayed wide-eyed fear, which was there only when her father was at home and the affection and protective instincts which surfaced when she had her mother all to herself. Doris observed her daughter, once so pretty and outgoing in her personality, now struggle with her appearance and her confidence. The once so fair hair which had shone like burnished gold in the summer sun, now hung in greasy strands around her drooping shoulders and the bright brown eyes which had danced with humour and the love of life were regularly downcast and filled with fear. Frank had not noticed any of these things. He loved his family without question but the long hours at the market were beginning to take their toll on his health. He no longer possessed the stamina that he had had five years before. But the family needed his hard efforts in order to put food in their mouths and clothes on their back. He, too had witnessed Ray's time at the pub and the lack of extra money, which would have made life easier but he no longer wished to spoil for a fight. He did not have the energy and secretly he was afraid of Ray's temper and what he might do to any of them if he could not have his own way. Ray was aware of the hold he possessed over the entire family. It was this fear which empowered him and kept him fuelled with funds to promote his drinking habits. He had received frequent warnings from the doctor about the state of his health and the damage he was doing to his body but he heeded nothing and continued with his normal routine of self destruction.

One late evening, in the middle of August when Hannah was about to douse the coal fire, which had warded off the chill of a cloudy evening, there came a fervent knocking on the front door. This was unusual because ten o'clock was not a customary time for visitors. She shivered from the chilliness of the cold room as she moved towards the door straining her ears for noises which might indicate who was there. It was too early for Ray's return from his boozing sessions and he would have woken the whole neighbourhood if his way was barred into the house. There was no noise until a more impatient knock came and an unknown voice called through the door.

'Mrs Dodds are you there? If you are I need to speak to you urgently. It's PC McArthur. It's about your husband. Mrs Dodds are you there?'

Hannah moved silently towards the door taking a deep intake of breath. She paused momentarily not knowing what to expect. The knocking and the voice came again, this time more agitated than before.

Hannah pulled back the bolt which creaked, in desperate need of oiling. She always kept the bolt across the door until she knew that Ray was about to make his entrance. It gave her an opportunity to steel herself for any of his mood swings.

She turned the key and lifted the latch which made a protest almost fitting her reluctant mood. As she pulled the door open a fraction she caught a glimpse of an outline of a man's body. Her eyes travelled down towards his feet vaguely registering a uniform in the gloom.

'Mrs Dodds?' he repeated gently.

Hannah nodded struggling to raise her voice but finally producing a croaky:

'Yes.'

'Can I come in please? I have something urgent to speak to you about,' the constable answered and at the same time took a small step forward slightly pushing open the door.

His presence made Hannah recoil partly in fear but also to allow him to enter the uninviting kitchen which was now cold and with only one lamp lit to welcome Ray home. There was little money to burn needlessly.

'What is it?' she found the courage to ask.

'Are you Ray Dodd's wife?' The constable asked the obvious at the same time taking note of the layout of the room and the poverty which was all too obvious to see.

Hannah nodded again, a light of dawning realization appearing in her eyes. Had something happened to him? Was he at the hospital? Had he had an accident? The questions were there but her lips could not form them and she waited for the next piece of information to be imparted. Momentarily there was silence before PC McArthur coughed, looked alarmed but decided that he had no choice but to continue. He kindly took her arm and steered her towards one of the kitchen chairs which was placed next to the fireplace and encouraged her to sit down before he continued with his unwelcome news. Any remaining heat from the dying embers would be crucial to warm her cold body before he began. He looked around to find some coal or kindling to reignite the flames. In the side oven he found some yellowed newspaper lying side by side with some sticks. These he threw on the reluctant fire, watching it struggle to warm the chilled space. His eyes wandered around the room noting the poverty which never failed to touch his heart. He turned to her observing the dread in her eyes.

'It's your husband, Mrs Dodds. He has met with an accident,' he paused to allow that knowledge to penetrate her already fearful mind.

'I am afraid that it was a fatal accident. He had left the public house early tonight. He was on his way home when he stumbled out into the road and was knocked down by an oncoming car. I am afraid that he died instantly. It wasn't the driver's fault. He had tried to brake but your husband did not see him coming. He walked straight into the road. There are several witnesses who will bear testament to that. They said he had been drinking heavily all evening. I am sorry Mrs Dodds, really sorry.' He hated this part of his job. It never became easier no matter how many times he did it.

The constable felt her go limp in his grasp but she had not fainted. Shock had set in almost immediately owing to her already heightened nervous state.

Hannah gasped and her hand flew to her mouth while the colour drained from her face. She sat in the chair, slumped sideways as if the life force had been taken from her. It took several moments for her to gather her wits and to force herself to make eye contact with the constable who looked very unsure about how to handle this very difficult situation.

'Did he suffer?' Hannah now had recovered a little to question the constable about the last minutes of Ray's life. 'Tell me he didn't suffer too much.'

The constable regarded Hannah for a few minutes before answering.

'No, he did not suffer. It was instantaneous,' he repeated. He was not sure how much information she had heard.

He possessed a little knowledge of the Dodds' family, particularly Ray who over the previous few years had been known to the local constabulary for his drunken behaviour and bullying tactics within the neighbourhood. It had also been common knowledge that Ray also used domestic violence at home but nothing could be done about this. It was with this knowledge that he looked at Hannah with fresh eyes wondering how the victims of violence could still hold a candle for the people who hurt them most. Ray had not died immediately but had been lying semi-conscious while the ambulance had been called and the police had arrived to take control of the situation. PC McArthur had remained with Ray until the ambulance had arrived by which time he had lapsed into unconsciousness and had suddenly stopped breathing. There was blood everywhere and there had been little hope of a chance of survival. The constable could not allow this poor woman to suffer any more. He took a deep breath and plunged straight in.

'No, he did not suffer. Death was instantaneous', he lied. 'They have taken him to the hospital but he was declared dead at the scene of the accident. There was a doctor who witnessed the accident on his way home from a call. Here, let me make you a drink of something. Tea maybe or have you something stronger?'

'Over there in the dresser cupboard,' she pointed across the room. 'I never touch the stuff usually.' The constable was not surprised that she did not touch alcohol. There was a child he knew and one alcoholic was enough in any family.

'I think you need it at the moment,' he moved quickly across the kitchen to complete the task grateful to have something practical to do. He poured a large measure of brandy into a tumbler he had found next to the bottle in the cupboard. He returned to Hannah's side and held the glass while she took it unsteadily from him and then put it to her lips to sip the strong liquid. The first mouthful had the desired effect. It sent a rush of warmth to the back of her throat and then down into her body. A few more sips saw the colour slowly return to Hannah's face and with it the courage to ask what was in her mind.

'What time did he leave the pub? Why had he left early? He was never home before eleven any day of the week.' The questions came thick and fast, tumbling from her lips as her brain lost the numbness it had felt since the onslaught of the news.

'Steady now, one question at a time. The landlord told Ray to leave the pub. Apparently he had had far more to drink than normal and was in a particularly aggressive mood. He was picking quarrels with anybody who spoke to him. He even threatened to thump someone over some sort of disagreement. The landlord was not prepared to put up with any more and several men threw him out into the street before a brawl started. He lay on the pavement for a few minutes before wandering out in front of a car. The doctor had been out on call and saw what happened. He said that nothing could be done for Ray.'

'What will happen now?' asked Hannah, her future in turmoil. She had not relied on Ray for emotional or financial support but he had been a fixture in her life for so long that it was difficult to visualise him not being there. She no longer had feelings for him. They had long since died. Her only luxury in life had been to love and protect Carenza who was her single purpose in life

'Well there will have to be an inquest as a matter of course but that should only be a formality. It was an accident through and through. The doctor will bear testimony to that. After that the body should be released to you for burial. Look, I really do think that you have had enough for one night. You should have some rest. Is there anybody I can fetch to be with you?' The constable was concerned at leaving her on her own but he could not stay much longer. It was nearly the end of his shift and his own day had been traumatic.

'I shall be all right,' she whispered but already the tears were beginning to form and trickle down the side of her face.

He shook his head.

'No I insist. You must have someone with you. Can I call a neighbour or relative?'

'My mother lives just four doors down. She'll come.'

The constable looked relieved and opened the door into the street in search of Doris.

*

Two weeks later Ray's body was released for burial which was to take place at St. Winifred's at a quarter past eleven. It had witnessed the marriage of Frank and Doris and Ray and Hannah and numerous family christenings over the years. But this was the first family funeral for decades. The church was filled with strong, scented lilies which had been donated by market stall holders who had known and liked Frank and Doris most of their lives. They were not thinking of Ray as they sat at the back of the church. Ray had possessed little charity in his soul towards others but their hearts went out to his widow who sat in the first pew erect and dignified surrounded by Doris, Frank and Carenza. Ray had had no other family or friends which made the presence of these few people so poignant.

The happenings were surreal to Carenza who could not relate to the coffin containing the body of her dead father which lay just in front of them. She did not justify this time as a time of mourning but as a kind of release from the mental anguish that Ray had inflicted upon the family. It was as if a burden had been lifted from their shoulders and at last they were free to allow their spirits to soar and take hold of the dream once more. She had not found out about his death until the morning after it had happened. Doris had hastened to Hannah's side as soon as she had received the news from PC McArthur. Between them they had come to the decision that there was little point in waking Carenza when the situation could not be reversed. Morning would be soon enough to impart the tragic events of the previous night. Doris had stayed with Hannah until the dawn came offering little comfort but a touch of reality that life still had to go on. There was too much living to be done. Doris could not mourn Ray. She had regarded him as a pariah inflicting too much emotional damage on the people she loved most. Even the slow demise of Frank's health had not gone unnoticed which she laid at Ray's door. Gentle Frank did not deserve to lose his health in such away. All that had become a legacy from Ray's sordid regime.

*

Carenza had risen early and found the two women huddled in coats for warmth sitting at the kitchen table with their hands holding two steaming mugs of tea, sweet and sickly to counter balance the shock which their bodies still suffered. They had not been to bed but had watched the night slip into a late summer dawn holding onto each other. No words needed to be spoken. They both knew what the other was thinking and what might have been if everything had turned out differently.

Hannah had risen from her chair without being asked and poured another mug of tea stirring two full teaspoons of sugar into it. Without a word she handed the mug to Carenza who sat down with the two older women never questioning the strange events of the morning. It was as if she already knew that a momentous event had occurred in her short life leaving no time for adolescence but she was about to spring board into adult life and assume a role that had arrived too soon.

'I have something to tell you Carrie,' Hannah had begun. She looked at her daughter's face which appeared different in the morning light as if she had already some knowledge of the previous night's events.

'I know, Ma,' she replied flatly,' I heard it all last night. He's dead and is never coming back again ever. That's fine by me Ma. He was no good and you know it. You won't have to suffer the beatings any more. We're free to live our lives the way we want now.'

'Oh Carrie you must not think that way. He was no great father to you but at the end of the day you were born out of love. There were good times as well as the bad, my love.' Hannah could not find the heart to scold this object of that unstable love but she felt that it was only natural to grieve for a father whatever he had done. She regarded the wistful face before her and great feelings of tenderness overwhelmed her for this daughter who had grown overnight from being a child into a young adult. She rose to her feet taking the child in her arms and together they shared a sorrow that contained feelings of genuine grief mingled with guilt and ran the full gambit of emotions that only they could share.

Doris, touched by the scene before her, rose stiffly to her feet and felt that it was time to leave mother and daughter together for a while to work through their grief. They knew that she was there for them as long as she could be. Doris smiled momentarily as the phrase 'blood is thicker than water' passed through her mind. She closed the door quietly behind her passing into the deserted street as she headed for home and Frank. Another day had dawned and life had to go on and a crust had to be earned. Doris took control of her emotions ready to steer her family through the traumas of life with as much gusto as she could muster.

*

Carenza returned to the present abandoning her reverie having felt a dig in the ribs from her grandfather who was rising to his feet with difficulty as he emanated a massive sigh. The organ was already playing the opening strains to 'The Lord is My Shepherd' .

The Reverend Blackman had finished his discourse on Ray's brief sojourn on earth and had placed himself at the head of the coffin in readiness for the end of the service. His great baritone voice soared into the solemn atmosphere of the church followed after an interval of only seconds by the voices of the small congregation. Hannah blew her nose into her handkerchief while her free hand sought that of Carenza's. They held tightly to one another, each possessing different pictures in their mind's eye of the dead man before them. Hannah had wiped away years and had returned to the man of her youth who had filled her heart with dreams. Carenza had not experienced those moments and could only picture her father beating her mother black and blue after a drinking session. The only emotions left in her heart were hate and overwhelming relief such moments had passed.

The last notes of the psalm died from the lips of those present allowing the coffin bearers to rise and now finish the job they had begun. The coffin was being lifted onto shoulders to be carried to the churchyard where it was to be buried alongside members of Hannah's family who had lived in this part of the East End for decades. Doris and Frank had been more than dubious about this but Hannah had insisted that Ray had been her husband and there was little else to say on the matter.

The family followed the coffin into the strong light of day to Ray's final resting place. The coffin was finally lowered and the soil was thrown onto the lid with a dull thud as the Reverend Blackman said the final words and the coffin would be obliterated from view forever. The mourners' heads bowed turned towards the vicar with the inevitable words of thanks and walked away to begin a new day in an increasingly uncertain world.

Chapter 3

Ray was barely cold in his grave when Carenza left childhood far behind. Hannah had descended into a deep depression that left her sitting staring into space for hours on end. Her love for Ray had gone long ago but she could not pull herself from the dark abyss that her mind had fallen into during the days that followed the funeral. Days slid into weeks and then months. Carenza had assumed the adult role by rising early to light the kitchen fire and making breakfast for herself and her mother before she helped her ageing grandfather down at the market to arrange the stall. Doris was too stiff first thing in the morning with her arthritis to leave the house. She took her time to rise these days but she knew that it was her lot to help Frank as soon as she was able. He was also feeling the pain in his joints but retirement was not an option now that Ray had gone. Those far off plans to pass the stall onto Ray and Hannah had dissipated when it became apparent that Hannah could no longer look after herself let alone this child who was proving beyond any doubt to be worth her weight in gold.

Doris could not help but smile with abundant pride when her mind drifted to think about Carenza. She was everybody's future but her eyes darkened momentarily when she contemplated the pressure that they now were placing on such young shoulders. But Carenza had gained in confidence since Ray's death. The constant fear of what might happen next had been removed and had been replaced by a sunny disposition. But there was still the worry over Hannah but she posed no threat and Doris had intervened to assume a maternal role once more.

At this point Doris knew that she had to make decisions to protect this jewel that shone so brightly in this dull world. Britain was at war with a country that could invade at any time despite all of Mr Chamberlain rhetoric regarding 'Peace in our Time.' Although many people were declaring it to be a phoney war fighting still persisted in Eastern Europe. Little was happening to involve the flower of youth who had joined the forces in a moment of ideology to fight for king and country. The young were restless to see action, to achieve immortality for their brief moments of valour for a justifiable cause. Everywhere in London the young had a conscience to do their duty either on the home front or in the wings waiting with the impatience of youth. But Doris knew that there was little glamour associated with war. She had lost two brothers in the Great War on Flanders Fields. They had acquitted themselves honourably but they had perished nevertheless and their sudden demise had left a trail of misery for the families who were left behind. Nobody actually disclosed the distress felt by families who were bereaved. Mothers and fathers never recovered from the loss of sons, and wives had to instil pride into their children for their dead fathers' heroics. Children felt guilt for the loss of a father that they could not remember but future generations would not forget the sacrifice that was made on the field of battle to set the world free.

Doris, who felt frail more often than she allowed herself to admit, knew that she had to use her wit and wisdom acquired through the greatest educator of all – Life - to control a family which was falling apart at its very heart. She knew from past experiences that it was only a matter of time before the German war machine would come and vent its venom even more virulently than during the Great War. The future of her family had to be secured and the future lay with Carenza. It was a future which could not carry or embrace any form of weakness. Emotions were not to be involved and she knew that she and Frank were embarking on borrowed time. Their health was impaired and Hannah had a fragile hold on her mental state. This was to be Doris's swan song for the child who lay near to her heart. She had to have the future that her name suggested. This was not to be a vain hope but a reality which was to be planned with such precision that nothing could go wrong. Sacrifices would be made and emotions which were aroused in the process were of little consequence to the final result which would be Doris's legacy to Carenza. Little did Doris know how fate would play its own hand.

Chapter 4

May Faithful woke with a feeling of misgiving but could not quite understand why. There had been no great disasters in recent days to justify her mood. In fact she was one of the most placid natured of people. She knew that very little ruffled her feathers and this was the general consensus of opinion in the small village community she inhabited. Most of her life had been spent working for the village. She had taught all her adult life at the village school, including being headteacher for a number of years. She loved her job administering to the needs of the children whose parents mostly worked on the local estates of the financially endowed surrounding the village and the scattered communities. But circumstances had prevented her continuing her job when her mother had become increasingly frail. It was the general decline into old age and the loss of memory of her mother which had catapulted May into making a decision which she knew would be inevitable before too long.

As the only surviving child of Cynthia and David Faithful she knew that it was her lot to look after her ailing mother who was virtually bedridden.

'It's not right that you should give up your career,' Cynthia had admonished her daughter.' We could employ somebody to help out.'

'Fiddlesticks,' came the reply. 'It is not a problem.'

May had loved her gentle mother, who was now so weakened by pneumonia and chest problems, which she had suffered in the latter years of her life, that the doctor was concerned about the state of her health and saying that she required constant nursing.

May's father had died twelve years before of a heart attack. He had been warned on numerous occasions to take life easier but he had been a workaholic all his life making his fortune in the firm his father founded before the end of the nineteenth century. His father had established a secure business but it was nothing compared with his son who became the confidante of the wealthy families in the area. By the time of his death he had made enough money to leave his widow and daughter comfortably provided for. His only son Thomas had died in the Great War fighting for his country. He had worked with his father but the onslaught of war had deprived the business of its future and David had to assume a heavy workload until Thomas's two sons were old enough to take their place beside their grandfather.

'Come home early tonight,' Cynthia would plead.

'I can't,' he would answer, 'there is just too much for me to do.' Consequently David had paid the ultimate price.

Aaron and Seph, Thomas's sons were quite happy to enter the law firm after their studies at university. The firm was thriving. They were young, enthusiastic and happy to enjoy the wealth which had been created for them. David was proud of both grandsons who shouldered responsibility but also took guidance when times were tough. David was concerned though on many accounts. The first major trauma was his health but he had always been driven by his job. He had also had to admit that he could not continue to work at the same pace as he had in the past. He thought that Cynthia was right but did not like to admit it out loud.

If anything happened to him he felt committed to ensure the future of the firm by offering his long time friend, Peter Masters, a partnership. It was this trust in Peter which should secure the continuity of the practice until both young men had acquired the wisdom that generally came with age. David's foresight paid off when the inevitable did happen.

'Keep their noses to the grind,' he had said to Peter slapping him playfully on the shoulder.

'You're being pessimistic,' Peter had teased but as he looked into the face of his friend he knew that something was wrong.

David, a generally wealthy man in his own right, had left his share of the partnership to his only grandchildren but he knew the rest of his estate would be left jointly to his widow and daughter. Neither would want for anything and after Cynthia's days everything would go to May. He had no worries about May who had been the apple of his eye all her life. She had never needed to work but her fierce independence had driven her into a teaching career and given her a personal freedom which few young women ever achieved. If she had married Archie Booth, whom she had met through her father and brother before the last war, she was aware that she would be forced to give up her job like other young married women of the time. They had decided to marry but the swift onslaught of war had prevented the marriage taking place.

Archie had been pronounced missing presumed dead. Eventually the telegram had arrived saying that he had been killed in action. May's grief was genuine but she had always been a stalwart character and her philosophy had always been that life had to go on no matter what happened. She had resolved that she would never marry but dedicate herself to her career. Her only regret was never having a child of her own. This fact had gnawed at her over the years and she had filled her spare time working with local groups of children as a substitute for the emptiness that she felt within.

May's mother had been dead now for three years. The dementia that she had lapsed into so violently near the end of her life had become a draining force upon the whole Faithful clan. Cynthia's illness which had been physical at the outset was now coupled with the mental anguish of the dementia. Her long time memory was acute.

'We've had a lovely day today, Nanny,' she would say to May.

'Of course we have,' came the reply, as May stroked her hand to help her to sleep. Now her mother did not know who she was. It had been quite difficult for May to understand at first but as time moved on it became a game to play the person who was inhabiting her mother's mind.

'I could have been a thespian,' she mused, 'a career on the stage. But you had to be an actor to become a good teacher.' And the thought amused her. It had been May's endeavour to see humour in most situations. Even now there were amusing moments to be enjoyed with some of the things her mother said.

May had made the sacrifice in giving up her career to nurse her mother and now she was left with a huge void which had to be filled. At first she had made her home her project. It was the home she had shared all her life with various members of her family but now it was entirely her own.

It was a sizeable property for a lonely spinster to occupy but she had no desire to move to another house in the village. She had inherited a considerable fortune which she would use to improve the house and to enrich her life. Her list of personal requirements was modest. Clothes had never interested her. They were purely functional.

'May,' she could still hear her mother say, 'shall we go shopping for a new spring wardrobe for you? I need a new dress too.'

'Not for me Mother,' she would reply, 'but I will come with you if you like.' David, her father, liked Cynthia to be accompanied on her excursions. Cynthia often wished that her daughter loved clothes as much as she did but that was not something that they shared.

May envisioned lightness in the house, eroding the darkness of memories of death and disaster which had encapsulated so many lives of the people who had lived there over time. But the furniture which she had inherited with the property had age and character and held too many memories for her to throw it all away. Instead she looked at the garden and decided that would be her next project.

'I'll plant more bulbs for the spring,' she had told her young friend, Jeannette, the vicar's wife. 'And I think the rose garden needs some new bushes. I remember my father's gardener planting some of these when I was a small girl.'

'The garden has always looked a picture,' Jeanette said glancing around her. 'Perhaps you can come and give me some advice on the vicarage garden. Edgar has never enjoyed gardening. I had also wondered if some of the big children would come and help me plant some vegetables now that we have to dig for victory.'

'What a good idea. I could come and help supervise. Some of those big boys can be silly sometimes,' May had said, walking to the gate to wave her friend off.

The house was a gloriously comfortable home reflecting her mother's taste for the best of everything. It was a sizeable property which needed a family living within. The house had originally belonged to May's grandfather and when May was very young her father had suggested that their family came to live with him as he had been ill for several years. She had remembered two servants who lived on the top floor and she had occupied the nursery with her nanny. Over time the servants had left and her mother had a daily help to support her with the heavier work. It was a large house to run but eventually the top floor had been closed up and used for storage. As time passed her nephews' children came to stay regularly breathing life into it again.

'Let's play hide and seek,' they would shout at the top of their voices. And the walls resonated with their excitement and happiness.

Her neighbours and friends came to visit regularly and she walked the lanes of her beloved Worcestershire enjoying the freedom after the years she had spent working and nursing her mother. The luxurious countryside around her village lay in the shadow of the Malvern Hills which acted as a theatrical backdrop as she played out the everyday drama of her life.

May at last, could say that she was content, not devastatingly happy but there was a level of peace now that she was entering the late summer of her life. She was picking up the pieces after her mother's death, filling the void left to her with pleasures that she had not had time for in earlier days. It had quite often been the lot of the spinster daughter to look after aged parents, to make sacrifices so that the rest of the family could conduct their lives selfishly without a backward glance. May had not felt this. She had maintained a fulfilling career but now her time was her own.

She had friends, who were loyal, some of whom had been family friends over the decades. They lived in the surrounding area giving support to each other during times of disaster or family misfortune. May also had friends from her brief heady college days when she had experienced a sense of freedom and lack of responsibility, before she had once more returned to the bosom of her all consuming family. These long ago friendships had stood the test of time although communications were often limited to hastily written letters and the briefest of visits at certain times of the year.

'We must meet up soon,' friends would write but daily life would take over and another year passed.

The rumblings of another war sent shock waves of horror through May. She remembered too vividly the loss of loved ones in the trenches in the Great War. Many men had returned broken by the experiences that they had endured. Life would never be the same for them again. The relationships they had had with their loved ones had been changed forever. Wives and sweethearts never quite understood the gamut of emotions that their menfolk had endured seeing mutilated bodies without limbs and men left to die before anybody could help them. The constant sound of gunfire and exploding shells left men emotional wrecks. The mind took longer to heal than the body's physical wounds. But they were the bonds which glued the soldiers together come what may, enduring shared experiences they could never relive or did not want to relive with their womenfolk. They were still bound to their comrades in arms down the years.

'I cannot bear the thought of another war,' the older women would say. 'We have seen the suffering before.'

'But young women will have their role to play in the offices, in the fields, just as before. Even we can play our part in helping wherever we can,' the reply came.

May had some inkling of these emotions. The caring side of her nature had sent her to help some of the soldiers amongst the ranks or even some of the commissioned officers during their convalescence. They needed to be loved and people to write their letters home when injuries were too horrific for them to do it for themselves. She did not flinch but felt that by doing this she was closer to understanding why Archie had died as he had. She had no intention of becoming emotionally attached to anyone again. The price to pay was too great but she had developed friendships for however short a time these soldiers spent in recuperation, some of whom did not live long after receiving their injuries.

Life for country children still continued in much the same vein for quite some time after the beginning of the war. There was talk that it was a phoney war and it would be over before it had begun but in the cities parents were being organized to evacuate their children to the country to keep them safe. Even some teachers were prepared to accompany these children to the countryside to provide continuity of education or to take the place of others who were determined to do their bit for king and country.

May had felt that it was her duty to become part of the organising body that would be appointed to place the evacuees in homes within the area. Her vast knowledge of village and farming families lay in her long association with the village school. It would be May's tact and her standing in the community that would persuade families to take on the responsibility of these children who were often dirty with lice infected heads and had little regard for the little niceties of life in the form of good manners and basic etiquette. These children were homesick for the hardships of their own lives in deprived areas of the country's inner cities where barely enough food was placed on tables particularly since food rationing had been introduced.

Nether Haydon, in the heartlands of rural Worcestershire, was due an influx of evacuees whose arrival was imminent. The committee, which had been hastily appointed to sort out these new problems, consisted of Dolly Parsons, a farmer's wife and Jeanette Stringer, the vicar's wife. Dolly's organisational skills were poor. However, her zest for life and boundless energy were equal to none. Jeannette maintained a calming influence on any village event and her immense common sense prevailed when others failed to think clearly. May Faithful chaired this small committee with all the tact that she could muster and had sent out feelers to the community at large to see who would be prepared to take on the responsibility of these children. Some families, particularly the farming fraternity, saw the evacuees as an extra pair of hands to work on the land now that young men were joining up before they were eventually conscripted into the armed forces.

May knew that she would have to use as much tact and discretion as she could muster to place these children, who were to be sent for their safety. Their parents had let them go on the condition that they would be cared for and this also included their emotional wellbeing. The impending arrival was due in less than a week. This meant that May and her committee had much to do to place thirty children from the East End of London into suitable homes. It was a momentous task that May and her committee knew would take the greatest of tact. If the rumours of evacuees in other rural areas were anything to go by the problems could be enormous. But May with her experience of children and her practical skills pushed negative thoughts to one side in order to continue the planning of this operation.

'Have we enough homes to place these children yet?' Jeannette asked the two older women.

'Yes,' said May, 'but it doesn't hurt to have a few extra offers just in case anything goes wrong. Not all the children will be happy in their billet.'

'I assume that we will have to have constant checks until we are happy with the whole situation,' Dolly said sagely.

'Of course but it might take some children a time to settle down if they are homesick.'

'It will not be the easiest of tasks to undertake but we must do our very best.'

*

Doris for all of her sixty two years was displaying an inner strength which even she had not believed she possessed. Ray's early demise had taken its toll on the whole family. Frank's health had visibly deteriorated over the last few months. The early starts at the market with long days spent in conditions open to the elements gave him a grey colouring. He was physically exhausted by the demands on his time and the worry which accompanied the whole family's problems. The pallor of his skin had never changed even in the heat of summer. His constant smoking produced a hacking cough which racked his thin, bent frame. Doris was by his side constantly keeping up a cheery banter with regular customers who had come for years to buy from their stall. Nothing could lift Frank's spirits except for the presence of Carenza.

'Hello Granddad,' she would say at the end of a school day when she had run all the way to the market.

'Go and sit down for a bit,' she would order as she tidied the stall and swept the detritus of fruit and vegetables into a place near the wall where the great wagons came to collect rubbish at the end of the day.

'Just for a minute,' he would answer, grateful to be able to take the weight off his legs and he would light a cigarette which gave him time to reflect on everything he did not want to think about.

Hannah had become reclusive with all but her family. After the funeral she had left her own home, with Carenza, and had returned to her childhood home to live with Doris and Frank. It had been an easy decision for her. She no longer wished to relive the unhappiness that she had experienced with Ray. If she had spent most hours on her own she would have become more introspective than she was. Instead of a weight being lifted from her shoulders in the light of Ray's death, which had released her from a physical and mental torment, her state of mind had swung like a pendulum the other way plunging her into a pit of despondency and gloom from which she could not drag herself no matter how much anybody tried to help. Doris had donned the mantle of parent and confidante to Carenza who had blossomed since her father's death. The violent life style she had experienced throughout her young life had been eradicated, replaced now by the love she received from her grandparents. She was aware of her mother's mental frailties but she had returned to a more light hearted childhood within the constraints of her family's poverty.

Carenza now developed friendships with people of all ages. She had become popular amongst her peer group who enjoyed her sense of fun and her strong intellect. Her personality had been transformed. Doris quietly witnessed this happening with immense pride. She was the only member of Carenza's family to do so.

'What's for tea,' she would ask her grandmother when she returned from the market.

'Fruit and vegetables,' she would answer and then both of them would laugh their heads off. Nobody else could share the silly joke for they were too immersed in their misery.

Frank was too worried about his diminishing health to notice. Hannah had dug her own deep pit of despair from which she could not release herself and Carenza had given up on her mother. She had inherited her grandmother's indomitable spirit and she could see beyond the confines of the suffocating walls of the old fashioned, terraced house and the grey streets of the East End.

Towards the end of March it suddenly became a reality that some of the East End Schools would be closing on a temporary basis. Although the war had not fully materialised as it had been thought there was still talk that this was the calm before the real storm. As many children as possible would be evacuated to rural parts of the country. Even some of the teachers were prepared to go in order not to interrupt the education of these young people. Rumour had been rife for a number of days amongst the local community but nobody had actually confirmed the possibility in so many words. Finally the news came, hitting the community hard. Opinion was mixed. Some parents took the news calmly believing that the safety of the children was paramount while others did not want their children to go because they would miss them. The children heard the news at the beginning of their daily worship when Mr Jones announced that letters were to be sent home at the end of the school day to explain to the parents what would now be happening.

'I dint want to go,' some of the children whispered in small groups. 'Can't make us.'

'They can,' some of the older boys said, enjoying the fear which spread across the younger faces.

Reality struck home to Carenza that she could possibly be one of these children and her nerve failed her. Her young life had already been one of turbulence and she did not want to leave her grandparents' security or know that they had to cope with problems which lay beyond their capabilities. She found herself offering up a silent prayer that she might not have to go and even bargaining with God that if she could stay she would be more understanding towards her mother and carry even more responsibility than she was already been doing. As the school bell rang heralding the end of another school day she slipped out of the gloomy building into the sunshine of a spring day.

Doris had heard the news down at the market that the school was now definitely going to close and the children were to be evacuated to the country as soon as the arrangements could be finalised. Frank had made no comment when he had heard the news. His own common sense told him that it was the best thing possible for the girl. When the bombs started dropping nobody would be safe. He did not worry for himself because he felt that his days were numbered but his loved ones were a different matter.

Carenza had returned home from school with the news. She had panicked first of all as she walked home taking the longer route so that she could mull over what Mr Jones had said. Part of her felt excited about experiencing pastures new but she was soon dragged back to the present remembering all the family problems. As she entered the back yard she saw her grandmother through the kitchen window. She burst open the door of the back kitchen and stood momentarily watching her grandmother's slightly bent form as she prepared the family's evening meal. Doris looked up and knew immediately that Carenza had heard the news by the telltale dirty tears, which she had smudged hastily with the back of her hand hoping to disguise her feelings of desperation. Her hawkeyed grandmother would notice any changes in the demeanour of her granddaughter.

'You've heard then?' she said lifting her eyes from her preoccupation with peeling potatoes that had seen better days.

'Mr Jones told us this afternoon. I don' t have to go do I Gran?' she replied looking at her grandmother's face which was totally devoid of emotion although her stomach churned with the thought of losing precious months without the companionship of this child.

'It would be for the best love. You know that them bombs will be coming before you know it. This war has to start afore too long or else it will end afore it's begun.'

'But what about you all Gran? How are you going to cope without my pair of hands? Ma is useless and me granddad is poorly. And you Gran are not getting any younger.' This torrent of words rushed out in hiccupping sobs.

Doris put the half peeled potato back in the water in the bowl and dried her damp hands on the edge of her apron. She moved forward and in a rush of all consuming love she encircled the fragile frame of her granddaughter in her arms, hugging her for quite some time.

'But we will manage my love,' she cooed tenderly rocking the child backwards and forwards as she had done all those years ago when Carenza had been a small child and had needed reassurance.

'There really is no choice Carenza. You just have to go. You know that there are people who will look out for us. There is Willie for one. He won't be called up with his bad leg and your ma will have to shake herself out of this nonsense she has sunk into. Self indulgence I call it.' Doris wiped a tear away from the corner of her eyes before her granddaughter had a chance to suspect that she was not quite as composed as she appeared.

Doris had made the decision. There was nobody else who was able to do so. She shook her head in despair when she contemplated her daughter. Once so vibrant she had become an empty shell without a purpose. Even this beloved child failed to inspire and give direction to Hannah's life.

'Carenza listen to me. There is a new life out there away from the East End. Use your spirit and find out for me what there is. Seize the moment my child. Do it for me. I never had the opportunity to see other places and probably never will. But you have your whole life before you. One never knows what is round the corner. Anyways we can come and visit you. It can't be so far on the train.'

Carenza looked at her grandmother and hugged her tightly not quite knowing what she meant but somehow Doris's strength seemed to pass to Carenza who knew that she would love this woman all the days of her life.

'I love you Gran,' she whispered, stroking the wrinkled cheek of the old woman whom she hugged tightly.

Chapter 5

Nether Heydon was basking in the warmest sunshine of the year so far on this late April day. The last of the spring daffodils were swaying gently and the bright colours of the tulips joined in unison lifting any feelings of gloom there might have been regarding the state of affairs in Europe. This was England at its best. May was determined to spend some of the afternoon in her garden enjoying the sunshine before the onslaught of tomorrow's influx of evacuees who were arriving after lunch. She felt satisfied that she and the rest of the committee had done the best they could for these children in finding them homes for the duration of their stay. There had been a meeting in the school where May had spelt out the do's and don'ts of what was expected. She realized that some of the instructions would fall on stony ground but there were some families who would open their homes and hearts to the children to make them welcome. Those families whom she suspected would need watching would be visited regularly by both herself and the committee to make sure that all was well. It was going to be a tough few weeks until children were settled and the worst of the anticipated homesickness had passed.

May strode with purpose down the long path at the back of the house until she reached the garden potting shed where the door stood slightly open revealing a well ordered array of garden tools which dated back to the time of her father, another keen gardener. Some empty pots had fallen over during the winter winds making the area around the shed look untidy and uncared for. She bent her portly frame and began to tidy the area placing the fragments of pot in the wheelbarrow nearby. When that job had been completed she opened the door of the shed wider enabling her to enter but the hinges creaked and sighed making May make a mental note that they needed oiling soon. To the right of the door she spied the real purpose of her quest. She reached out for the fork and garden rake, which were to be used on the garden borders at the front of the house. Some of the autumn and winter leaves from the beech and silver birch had blown into the corners and crevices and required attention. May's tidy mind would not allow such clutter now that spring had arrived and new life was bursting out around her.

She raked vigorously at the leaves until the last vestiges of the winter had been collected into a pile ready to be burned at the end of the day. The flowerbed by the wall, which bordered onto the road, attracted her attention. She propped the rake against the tree and picked up the fork, which she used to turn over the soil where she was going to put some new bedding plants as soon as the night frosts had ceased. From a distance May heard the sound of the telephone ringing. She placed the garden tools safely against the wall and hurried indoors.

'Hello, Nether Hayden 237, May Faithful speaking. How may I help you?' she was breathing heavily after manoeuvring her bulky frame into the house at speed.

'Hello May,' Dolly Parsons breathy voice replied. 'I was just checking that all the arrangements for tomorrow are in place. We wouldn't want anything to go wrong at this late stage.'

'No we wouldn't Dolly but as far as I know everything is fine. If anything goes wrong it will be unexpected. So don't worry. I will see you as planned tomorrow. The bus is ready to pick up the children and the two teachers outside the station. It will bring them to the church hall where the people who have agreed to billet the children will collect them. Our main job is to see that this runs as smoothly as possible without causing the children to be any more homesick than is necessary.'

'I'm sure that you are right May, but it is quite a responsibility that we have undertaken. Anyway see you tomorrow. Bye for now.'

With that the line went dead and the telephone lay in May's hand. Dolly, kind hearted in the extreme but disorganised as well, was commonly known as a great worrier. She had never had to lift a finger to organise her own life, for her larger than life father had spoilt this only child, born in the autumn of his life and had spent time bringing Dolly up mostly on his own owing to the death of his wife in childbirth. Dolly had adored her father, Tom, and it was with great reluctance that she had agreed to marry the son of her father's best and oldest friend. Jonah Parsons had been thirty- five when he had begun to court Dolly. He had had an interesting youth when he had sown his wild oats throughout the county but it was the death of his father, Adam, at the premature age of sixty that had pulled Jonah up short to reorganise his life before it was too late. He knew that it was time for him to assume a more responsible role and take over the running of the farm, a huge task, considering the immense organisation and legacy that his father had left. He did not want to do this on his own but needed a life partner who would be there for him and to arrange the domestic side of life, as skilfully as his mother had done for his father.

As a result he had turned his back on the frivolous women who had occupied most of his spare time and had looked nearer home to acquire a wife who would be used to the ways of country life. He had not had to look far for right under his nose was Dolly, the daughter of his father's oldest friend. It was this that had set him about pursuing Dolly with a passion that swept her off her feet and within six months they were married.

The gossips had talked viciously but time was to prove that it was not a shotgun wedding. Tom had been shell shocked at the speed of the romance. But he was pleased to see Dolly married which would cushion her against anything untoward occurring. Dolly was now pampered by the two men in her life and led a closeted and protected existence.

'What a worrier she is,' May mumbled. 'Never stops.'

She replaced the telephone receiver in its cradle and smiled to herself. Trust Dolly to be worrying. She did too much of that. But it was a good fault after all. May was confident that everything would go to plan but there were always the unforeseen incidents that it was not easy to legislate for.

The afternoon sunshine beckoned May back to her domain in the garden. She knelt at the flower border clearing dead foliage and leaves that she piled every now and then at the side of the house where there was a wide driveway. This area was designated as the place where she burnt the garden rubbish, well out of any contact with other houses around. This was the perfect day to establish her bonfire. There was little or no breeze to send clouds of smoke billowing out to annoy neighbours in the vicinity. She busied herself fetching matches from the kitchen drawer and returned to the pile of garden rubbish which she lit with quiet satisfaction knowing that the great summer tidy up had begun but she was unsure when time would permit her to continue this pastime. She mused to herself on forthcoming events with a little trepidation wondering if Dolly's anxiety might have some justification. She was not usually a worrier being too pragmatic but these were unprecedented times. Her thoughts drifted to local events as she continued her toil of raking the leaves and sweeping areas of the paths to bring order to the proceedings.

She mused that the war had taken its toll on the local community. The family business had been hit by Aaron joining the army as soon as the rumblings of war had started. Seth had wanted to do the same but his health was not as robust as his brother's. He had had a heart murmur since birth that had not handicapped him unduly but it did restrict some areas of his life. So it was that Seth stayed at home and ran the business tackling a crippling workload with as much help from Lily, his wife of seventeen years, as she could give after focusing her time on home and family. The local community was bereft of its work force. Men of fighting age had left families behind. Women were taking on more and more of the workload especially on the land and in the munitions factories where they worked shifts to help move the war machine forward towards victory. This newfound freedom would have an impact on the youth of the future. Girls had been drafted from far and wide to fill men's shoes on local farms. Every spare piece of land was used to grow vegetables. It was a time when young and old had a common objective and could pull together. In some ways May felt saddened that possibly the world would never be the same again but she knew that was being maudlin and inwardly cursed Dolly and her anxieties. But her mood did not lighten.

Her thoughts drifted towards the village school, which was run by two young women teachers who struggled with the boys whose young lives were dominated by the thrills of war and playing out dramas that had been seen on newsreels. The absence of a father figure led to problems in and out of the school playground. Discipline was found to be lacking on many fronts. Women were stretched to the limit with lives that were now going in different directions. May saw many of these problems and with as much tact as she could muster had used some of her spare time to help in school, enjoying the familiar atmosphere but without the responsibility that she had once experienced. It was at this time that the news came that there was a possibility that evacuees could be sent to Nether Heydon from London. Villagers were not too happy about any more changes in their lives. There had been enough of that in recent months with young men going off to war.

'Why do we want evacuees?' the older generation asked. 'We have enough problems as it is.'

'To help the war effort and keep our children safe. We don't want Jerry to have it all his own way,' came the more reasoned reply.

But many did not want children with their town ways upsetting a country way of life. There was little that could be done because everyone was expected to do his or her bit. May realised that somebody had to take control of the situation and so had given herself the responsibility.

She continued her task for a little while longer before taking a break. She rested on her rake enjoying the late afternoon sunshine. Her mind was once more at peace as she contemplated her surroundings. The mellow stone of the local cottages looked peaceful and quiet. Somewhere in the distance she heard the sounds of farm animals in the fields and the church clock chimed the hour. With a wry smile she knew that this tranquillity would not last much longer but every moment was to be grasped as if it was to be the last.

With that thought she collected the tools to return them to the potting shed and her next project was to boil the kettle for afternoon tea, a task that she undertook daily at the same time unless more exciting events were pressing. She half expected this to be the case for the near future until the arrival of the evacuees became a distant memory. She knew that country areas did not take kindly to change and with that thought in her head she smiled a secret smile and walked briskly along the side of the cottage until she disappeared from view.

Chapter 6

That early morning at the end of April Carenza and her grandmother were waiting on the station platform with all the other children and adults who were accompanying them on this adventure which was to last days, weeks or even months. Speculation was rife because nobody could forecast the duration of the war. The emotions of apprehension and excitement walked hand in hand. Bewilderment was patently obvious on the faces of the children who looked like bundled parcels with a label tied to them bearing details of their identity and destination in case they became lost. Everybody carried a gas mask in a brown case slung across his or her body in various fashions. Some children cried mercilessly clutching parcels and suitcases containing the bare necessities of their forthcoming visits. One or two of the children stood impassively not fully understanding the enormity of the occasion. From some of the tatty parcels they held tightly to them, the well worn ear of a dilapidated toy stuck out giving the smaller children some semblance of comfort. The teachers travelling with the children from Travis Street School began to herd them together like cattle as the train steamed into the station. There were wails from children whose mothers had come to see them off. They clung together as if they shared the same skin. Carenza was no exception.

Her mother had not shown any emotion when Carenza had kissed her 'goodbye' that morning but it was to Doris that she clung in the dying minutes of their wait. Doris had remained dry eyed not daring to show any excess of emotion in order to maintain some dignity and a semblance of calm. She knew that all her emotions would surface later when she had time to herself and she could think more lucidly. The teachers' voices dramatically rose above the babble of noise aware now that they had to show their authority and organisational skills. Doris gave Carenza a tight squeeze and pushed her towards the impatient form of Miss Lightbody who was beckoning frantically in their direction. There was nothing else to say for it had all been said. Doris had uttered that if it was at all possible she might be able to visit Carenza but it was not a promise. She knew that she could not promise anything with her responsibilities but she had said that Carenza must give her visit a fair time before Doris would even contemplate her granddaughter returning home unless of course fate intervened and the war ended before it had properly begun.

Steam belched from the engine, the noise sounding like a sigh in readiness to undertake the journey with great impatience. The teachers shepherded the children onto the train. They had been instructed to seat three children together because the train was full to capacity with soldiers and other service personnel who were going on some journey either on leave or returning to base unsure of what the future held for them. Doors slammed along the length of the train. The railway guard lifted his flag and his whistle was blown giving the signal that the train was ready to depart. It slowly began to move along the edge of the platform while a surge of bodies in unison moved forward to make the final wave before the train was lost to view. Each face told a story of its own but the common denominator, which linked each person, was the uncertainty of the future. People lingered for a moment watching the vanishing train. Faces told their own stories but there was nothing left to be done but to return to their own lives. Doris followed the drift of bodies into the noisy London streets. The one feeling that she harboured most of all and cut her to the quick was whether she would see her granddaughter again. She was fearful that London could be bombed killing the family but the greatest fear lay in the fact that she and Frank might not live long enough to see Carenza into adulthood. Hannah was no use to anyone including herself.

Doris stopped abruptly in her tracks. A young man, rather debonair in appearance wearing a dark brown suit, bumped into her. Confusion and embarrassment overcame him but good manners conquered the moment allowing him to doff his hat.

'I'm so sorry,' he said in his embarrassment. 'I didn't see you there.'

'It dint matter,' she responded.

But Doris appeared oblivious of the situation. She was busy delving into her ancient handbag looking for her handkerchief to dab the remnants of tears from her eyes. Her face gathered composure once again as she walked in a sprightly fashion along the street becoming lost to view amongst the noisy melee of people on the London pavements.

*

Carenza sat on the train wedged on a seat by the window of the compartment looking out onto the mayhem of the station. People scurried in all directions. Others kissed locked into an embrace that would last them for months ahead or perhaps for ever. Two small-undernourished boys looking like two peas in a pod sat next to Carenza wriggling with excitement.

Carenza regarded them with distain.

'Can't you sit still,' she said through her obvious distress. They ignored her but continued giggling.

All the seats were taken and many adults stood. Miss Lightbody and Miss Fellowes had completed their organisational task with great aplomb, a credit to their teacher training of a few years before.

'I'm glad that is over until we reach the other end,' Miss Lightbody sighed.

'Me too. Boys behave yourselves,' Miss Fellowes had caught sight of the two boys annoying everybody around them. She clapped her hands and they settled when they saw her stern look.

'I don't know what country people will think of these townies,' continued Miss Lightbody. 'Most of these children haven't been out of London before.'

'Well look at these two. They can't contain themselves and poor Carenza is so ladylike in dealing with them,' Miss Fellowes said feeling annoyance rearing its head.

'I'll go and sort them. I'll separate them. That should do the trick.' It did not take long to diffuse the situation. One of the boys was moved to sit between two girls further down the carriage.

But inside both young women were harassed beyond comprehension on the journey into the Midlands. Both were Londoners by birth and did not have great enthusiasm about leaving the capital but the women felt that the city held little for them at the moment since their sweethearts were somewhere in Northern France but that was all that they did know. They had decided that this was one way of serving the war effort. Somebody had to educate the next generation but they had not undertaken the task lightly. What they had not realized was the level of responsibility that they had to shoulder. There were so many conflicting emotions that surfaced on that journey. The very young sobbed uncontrollably and would not be comforted. The teaching skills of these young women did not extend quite as far as adopting maternal qualities but Elsie Lightbody did take little Lucy Betts onto her lap and tried to cuddle her hoping that the wails arising from her small body might cease before too long. But a number of the boys including Dan Betts, Lucy's older brother had suddenly realized that some of the constraints that were apparent at home were no longer there. It was unlikely that they would get a cuff around the head from the teachers like they did at home, particularly when fathers returned from the pub in a drunken stupor. They enjoyed a rough and tumble fight in the seats and only quietened down after repeatedly being spoken to. They became transfixed by the views that they saw through the windows of the carriages after they had left the built up areas of the London suburbs. They saw fields which were green and bright in the spring sunshine. There were farmers ploughing in readiness for spring planting. There were trees with leaves bursting forth into life and the oddest thing of all was the presence of new life amongst animals in the fields that these children had not seen before in the flesh. They might have seen them in books or heard about them but they gazed in awe and wonder.

'Cor blimey Miss. Have you seen them animals?' Dan Betts shouted to nobody in particular.

'Look at them moving,' said Sam Allen, pointed at lambs gambolling along behind their mothers.

'What are them?' other children could be heard shouting as they pointed at the phenomenon before them.

Both teachers exchanged looks and secretly smiled knowing that the experiences they were to undergo would be worth a million even if there was some heartache along the way.

'This is an education in itself,' said Miss Fellowes.

'We couldn't have recreated this in school,' Elsie Lightbody exclaimed.

Lucy Betts had wriggled free from Elsie Lightbody's lap and had wormed her way into Carenza's seat in order to find a better vantage point to view the countryside as it passed. The children's curiosity in their surroundings gave the teachers some respite and they found themselves visibly relaxing for some of the time. But they knew that this interlude would undoubtedly be short lived.

The ticket collector walked through the carriages looking for new passengers who had recently got on at the different stations. Again this was a new experience for the children who watched him clip the tickets with precision and authority.

'Any more tickets now,' he shouted on his journey through the carriage.

'That's what I want to do when I'm growed up,' said a small voice lost in the hubbub of the noise of the train.

'Me an'all,' came a chorus.

There had been so much to entertain them that all feelings of homesickness had subsided for the time being. The train continued relentlessly on its journey stopping now and then at small rural stations allowing the ebb and flow of passengers to continue. It whistled and continued to belch steam into the atmosphere.

Minutes later someone was sick.

'You dirty thing,' a child shouted. 'Them's all I have to wear.' The problem was promptly sorted but the odour lingered.

More than two hours later the train edged its way along the station platform into Foregate Street Station in Worcester. The platform was busy once more but with porters humping heavy cases and people pushing in an attempt to board the already full train.

'Let them get off first,' a sensible voice shouted.

'In your dreams,' a wag retorted and the mayhem continued.

'Stay in your seats children,' Elsie Lightbody's voice was just audible above the din of the passengers as they struggled with luggage eager to remove themselves from the confines of their seats. Miss Fellowes had elbowed her way along the aisle and out onto the platform to receive her charges as they descended onto the platform.

'Over here,' she gestured as the first few followed instructions to look for her. They gathered with their partner to form an orderly crocodile, slightly forlorn as they were in a strange place.

Annie the youngest began to cry.

'I want me mam,' she wailed at the top of her voice. An older girl with a tender heart put a gentle arm around her.

'Hush,' she said, 'we all do.' But the wailing continued.

The children's patience had worn thin during the journey. Their cramped conditions had led to petty quarrels and physical debacles, which had not gone unnoticed by the teachers and the public at large. It was one of these spats, which attracted the attention of Dolly and May as they stood on the platform in readiness to fulfil their task. May smiled to herself remembering playground disputes during her teaching days but Dolly's associations with children was limited and May could physically feel her recoil. Her trepidation and worst fears were beginning to come true.

'Come on Dolly, best foot forward,' she urged. 'It won't be that bad.'

'Are you sure,' she breathed heavily. She had never known how May had managed all those years teaching unscathed. Her admiration knew no bounds.

May put a determined hand beneath Dolly's elbow and steered her towards one of the opening doors of the train. Elsie Lightbody had positioned herself near the carriage door in order to shepherd her charges onto the platform as quickly as she could hoping that their behaviour would improve away from the confines of their seats. She caught May's eye momentarily and their gaze locked and recognition dawned on both faces simultaneously.

'Travis Street School,' May mouthed to Elsie Lightbody who nodded in reply visibly showing signs of relief that they had at last made contact with their billeting officer.

'Good to see you, er?' she replied not quite sure whom she was addressing.

'I'm May Faithful and this is Dolly Parsons who is another billeting officer.' May held out her hand to shake that of the younger woman.

'I am very pleased to meet you,' Elsie replied holding out her hand towards May.

May clasped the hand of the young woman in front of her and felt the strength in the hand shake. She felt that she could make a fair judgement of character by this simple gesture. Elsie had strength of character that would prove May right because she was rarely wrong on such matters.

Elsie nodded in Dolly's direction but her attention was suddenly directed towards a wail somewhere behind her. Dan Betts had accidentally stepped on his sister's foot in the melee of bodies that were pushing forward in one surge towards the open door. May easily returned to teacher mode in order to direct proceedings. She took control of the children as they disembarked from the train and soon had them in an orderly line away from the dangers of the platform edge while Elsie Lightbody and Nancy Fellows brought up the rear with Dolly following in their wake wondering what she had let herself in for. But she struggled with her conscience knowing that everyone had to do their bit towards the war effort. She knew that she had been spoilt over the years and it had left her timid.

'I don't know that I can do this,' Dolly had said when May had asked her to help with the evacuation committee. 'I am not very good at making decisions.'

'But I need your help Dolly,' May had been determined that Dolly would come out of her shell at last.

The crocodile of bodies bemused by the newness of their circumstances wound its way out of the station, down the steps onto the pavement of the outside streets and into the blinding sunshine of a spring day. Parked near to the station was Ashthorpe's bus which belonged to the local garage owner in the village. It had been rarely used lately since the introduction of petrol rationing but Bob Ashthorpe had managed to gather enough petrol coupons together for this important event. The children were quiet now as they were herded onto the bus and were allocated places which enabled many of them to sit by the windows to watch the phenomena of the countryside that was to feature so prominently in their new life.

The young teachers placed themselves at intervals amongst the children on the bus. Dolly took refuge on the front seat huddled into the corner half wondering why she had become involved in such an enterprise but May was in her element. She had taken full note of Dan Betts whose antics had drawn her attention to him. She had placed her sizeable bulk next to him pinning him against the window of the bus so that he could not move in the seat to cause any more mayhem.

'What's that un there?' He pointed to a lamb following its mother.

'And that 'un?' He indicated a fat pig sliding in the mud of its field followed by its young.

'And that…?' The lack of a question hung heavily in the air.

'I think,' began May, pinning him even closer to the side of the bus, 'that you are going to have to look all these up in the books in school. There will be plenty of those.'

'I don't read good,' he said with obvious embarrassment.

'Then you are going to have to stop messing about and learn.'

Dan turned his head and looked May directly in the eye. He wondered who she was and if anyone had been telling tales about his behaviour. At least she had not hit him. He knew his Dad would have because he was fed up with the nonsense.

The constant bombardment of questions had been silenced allowing the seven mile journey to pass peacefully until they reached their destination. Many of the children were quiet mostly for a variety of reasons. They were bemused by the sheer momentum of what was happening. Most of them had not moved out of London in their young lives. Many had not travelled by train, such was the poverty of family circumstances. Many had not left family before. These were traumatic times for young and old alike.

Chapter 7

The bus drew up outside the village hall which set the scene for much of the local community's village life. It was here that the home guard had gathered to put together a hastily arranged force of volunteers of all ages to defend the area from any threat of invasion. So far their training had not been put to the test but it did not diminish their zeal or enthusiasm for defending the local population. May and Dolly had used the premises to hold the billeting meetings in order to organise the evacuees. Many women gathered there twice a week to organise knitting parties to provide blankets, gloves and warm jumpers and others garments to allow the soldiers some luxuries from home during the long days they spent away at the front.

But on this late April day many adults had gathered outside in the sunshine and stood gossiping about forthcoming events but with the arrival of the bus a silence descended on the group in anticipation of what was going to happen. Bob Ashthorpe drew the bus very closely alongside the kerb which made the waiting group of people take a step backwards onto the pavement before the bus door swung open. May left Dan Betts behind in his seat catching a swift movement in the corner of her eye as he swivelled round to engage the boy sitting behind him in some token of mischief. Her sigh spoke volumes as she walked to the front of the bus to climb down the steps acknowledging the onlookers with her cheeriest of smiles before she started the proceedings of allocating the children to different adults. Dolly moved swiftly after her only too glad that the journey had been accomplished safely and would soon come to a rapid conclusion.

The children sat quietly on the bus surveying the sea of faces below them. They felt dry mouthed with apprehension hoping that they would be billeted with a family who genuinely liked children. None of them wanted to be separated from their siblings and they clung to them like glue, all thoughts of petty quarrels long forgotten in this new adventure.

Lucy and Dan Betts were the first of the children to alight onto the pavement and were immediately caught up in a surge forward by some of the women eager to take them. Lucy Betts' angelic face belied the demon inside her but May and Dolly motioned them towards a youngish woman who was holding precariously onto a wriggling baby. The child was desperate for sleep and the mother displayed signs of agitation, only too eager to take the baby home. She nodded acknowledgement to May and then without a backward glance strode off in the direction of home. Lucy and Dan followed her demurely along the street holding on tightly to the few possessions that they had brought with them and in seconds were lost to view.

'I hope they don't need rebilleting. The boy's a little monster,' said Dolly.

'She's a young woman with energy.' May was determined that there were to be no problems.

The other children descended from the bus steps and gradually they too disappeared with the different adults who took them eagerly or with a certain amount of indifference. Carenza's face was crumpled in her unhappiness. She had not been able to obliterate the image of Doris on the station platform in London. She had been trying desperately to balance her emotions until her granddaughter was out of sight but Carenza knew her grandmother's kind heart better than anybody. Carenza, a deep thinker at the best of times, could not help but believe that this might be the last time that she saw any of her family again. This all-consuming emotion had haunted her for the duration of the journey and she had cried quietly into the handkerchief that had been well laundered. She had blanked out the quarrels and the hubbub of the compartment but on the bus journey her thin body had been racked by sobs. The handkerchief had been stuffed into her mouth to prevent the sobs from filling the air around her and preventing her being the butt of Dan Betts' jokes. Elsie Lightbody, who was the oldest of five children herself and had often been a surrogate mother to her siblings, recognised the unhappiness of this generally bubbly girl and slid onto the seat beside her to offer some comfort and silently prayed that her charge would settle into her new life as quickly as possible.

'Cheer up Carenza,' she had said. 'It's not going to be that bad.'

'It is,' came the reply. 'I might never see my family again.'

'Don't be so silly. They might come and see you and you never know we might not be here too long.' Elsie tried her best but was not fully aware of all of Carenza's problems.

Elsie had stood on the pavement with her arm around Carenza's shoulders watching the departure of the other children. People had looked at Carenza's face and had sensed problems that they did not want to deal with knowing that they had enough to do to take on the evacuees as it was. There was now only one couple left who did not look too happy at the undertaking that was destined for them. Sarah and Eddie Dunwoody were older than some of the adults who had agreed to take on the evacuees. They had two sons who had signed up for the army at the beginning of the war, thankful to be away from parents who allowed them little freedom to be themselves. They were suffocated by their mother's possessiveness and the fact that their father was dominated by her. The war had come at the right time for them to escape into a wider world and know that they would not return to the parental home chance what the future held. Sarah had not forgiven them for the glee that they demonstrated on their departure.

'You're ungrateful wretches,' she had yelled at them, 'after all that we have done for you.'

'Don't keep on Ma. We would have been called up anyway.' They had tried to placate her but had failed.

Their absence had left an empty void which nothing could fill, least of all Eddie who had taken to spending his free time with his cronies at the Fox and Hounds in the village only to return home when he knew that Sarah was more than likely to be asleep. Sarah had grasped at the opportunity of taking on an evacuee to replace her sons. She had not bothered to discuss the matter with Eddie but delivered it as an ultimatum, which was not up for discussion. Eddie had not bothered too much because he spent little time with Sarah and the situation might well generate more freedom for him if Sarah's time was taken up with the child.

Elsie had observed the sour faced couple who looked bemused at the sight of Carenza's hysterical sobbing.

'Do really want a problem like that,' Eddie had hissed at his wife. 'I told you that we want no more problems.'

'Shut up,' she hissed through gritted teeth. 'They're all listening.'

'I don't care,' he replied. Sensitivity had never been his greatest attribute.

Elsie had hoped that they would show enough compassion towards the child until she had settled into their home and routine. Perhaps this was a situation that required monitoring closely in the next weeks she had mused. Carenza was too amenable to be treated badly.

She managed to catch May's eye. May put on her brightest smile to encourage the situation but her attention was engaged suddenly by the other members of the committee. At this Elsie drew Carenza even closer to her and whispered something inaudible into her ear. Carenza looked up and smiled a watery smile through her tears before walking towards her surrogate family who acknowledged her with a curt nod and a twist of the lips which passed as a smile and together they turned to walk away.

Eddie had made one gesture at gallantry by picking up Carenza's few possessions as they turned to walk crocodile fashion towards home. As they departed Carenza looked backwards towards Elsie who waved and smiled reassurance. Elsie's heart went out to Carenza knowing her so well and wishing fervently that she would be treated with compassion.

Both of the teachers watched the last of their charges disappear knowing that they would be reunited with them on Monday morning when a new school week would begin. The small village school was to be the focal point of the first meeting of the new staff and their pupils but only one class could be absorbed into the old Tudor building which many generations before had been a dark beamed farmhouse. In Victorian times two wings had been added, one either side of the building in order to turn it into a school.

One side of the building housed the infant and junior children while the other end was where the older children were educated until they left school at fourteen. But the more able children passed to the grammar school in Worcester and wore their uniform with pride. The old village hall had been delegated for part of the week to be used as an overspill classroom and the rest of the week the same children were to work in the school hall sharing the space with their sister class. Both Elsie and Nancy had been made aware of the circumstances and were less than happy but knew that they had to make the best of it because it might only be for a short time.

Elsie Lightbody and Nancy Fellows lingered to talk to May and Dolly. The relief that everything had gone to plan was etched on all faces. Dolly's face was a picture of radiant happiness as if the sun had appeared for the first time in days. May, noting this transformation, beamed beatifically herself and felt light-hearted. She had not realized that she had been so traumatized herself.

'Well that went well enough,' May trilled lightly to everybody and nobody in particular.

'For the moment anyway,' Dolly replied not completely letting go of the underlying thoughts of doom and gloom which permeated her thinking.

Her face had clouded again as if some anxiety was passing through her mind but she was not prepared to share it with anyone else. May chose to ignore the thunderclouds. She had had enough for one day. Brief thoughts of getting old passed through her mind but they were pushed away as quickly as they had come.

'I think that this calls for a little celebration before I take you two young ladies along to your billet.' May ignored Dolly's comment and beamed at the young teachers fully admiring their courage in relocating to a new area and in such circumstances.

'Thank you Miss Faithful. We would like that,' Elsie answered for both of them.

'Well follow me ladies,' May replied in a business-like fashion and without further ado she picked up one of the bags and walked along the High Street, turning into Birch Green Lane where she stopped outside her cottage.

She rummaged in the pocket of her waistcoat which she was renowned for wearing all year round as the large pockets housed many of the everyday items that she wanted to carry and needed. Her tenacity was fully rewarded when she promptly displayed a key in front of them and without another word led them along the front path admiring the work that she had accomplished yesterday but making a mental note of more jobs that she must consider doing before this spell of good weather broke.

The key turned effortlessly in the lock allowing May to shepherd her guests and their luggage into the front sitting room, which was filled with sunlight. The vase of daffodils on the occasional table in front of the window was a blaze of colour contributing to the brightness of the room.

'Do come in,' she invited, 'make yourselves at home.'

'I'll put the kettle on.' Dolly was very familiar with the layout of May's kitchen. She disappeared.

'Please make yourselves comfortable. You must be tired after all you have had to do today.'

'Oh what a lovely room,' Nancy exclaimed. She turned round to take in every facet of its splendour which was so different from her rooms in Percy Street in the East End. She observed the long case clock in the corner, which ticked rhythmically lending a solid air of security to their environment. The arrays of chairs were covered in a well-worn chintz covered fabric, which oozed quality but had seen better days. There were a number of occasional tables which were adorned with May's clutter of books and tapestry. The whole room exuded comfort and taste but most of all homeliness.

'Thank you Miss Fellows,' May smiled her delight at the compliment.

'Please call us by our first names. I'm Nancy and this is Elsie. I'm sure we will be seeing a lot of you during our stay here.'

Yes, I'm sure we will and we must become good friends. By the way call me May. Most people do. I can't do with standing on ceremony. Come to tea properly one day when you are settled. Now where is that tea?'

With quick movements despite her size May disappeared leaving her guests to seat themselves politely on the edge of their seats. May returned with a tray filled with blue and white cups and saucers displaying her favourite willow pattern. It was a service that she had inherited from her parents and she treasured it dearly only allowing it to be used on the more special occasions, which were few and far between with the onset of war. But she regarded this as one of those rare times. Dolly followed close behind carrying the matching teapot and then bustled about moving occasional tables nearer to their guests. Inwardly May cursed Dolly, although a good friend, she was hopeless at making small talk with strangers and she was fussing so that she did not have to contribute to the conversation. It was still a legacy from her sheltered childhood which had made her diffident with people until she knew them better.

'Well, here we are then. This is a much-deserved cup of tea. Dolly dear pass around the cake please,' May smiled sweetly around her. This was a way of making things easier for Dolly to become sociable.

'That cake looks wonderful,' Elsie drooled. 'We cannot make cakes easily in London these days because of the rationing.'

'Well this is the country my dear and we all help each other out. My nephew's wife Lily has turned part of her garden over to digging for victory, as the poster says, and keeping chickens. They have a large garden and some fields. She is overrun with eggs, which is most fortunate and Dolly here lives on a farm which in itself is a blessing because we can make use of anything that she and Jonah don't need. Is that not right Dolly?'

'Quite right May,' Dolly smiled her gratitude at May's skilful way of weaving her into the conversation.

'We miss a lot of things in London,' sighed Nancy. 'Life can be difficult. It is the waiting which is worse though, the not knowing when we will be bombed. The not knowing how our sweethearts will fare in the war'

'It is hard my dear but we must make the best of things and just pray that the war does not last too long,' May added as her mind drifted back to the Great War and the anxieties that she had personally suffered but she pulled herself up sharply knowing that it was the present that mattered now and the people who were alive and could suffer today.

'I was very impressed at how smoothly it all went,' Elsie said bringing the conversation back to the present. 'The children did have such a mixture of emotions. I thought they coped well considering all the turmoil.'

A look of pride floated across Dolly's face and suddenly she had found her confidence now that the ice had been broken with these two young women.

'It's all down to May's organisational skills. She was the village headmistress for many years and the school still misses her very much,' she enthused.

'Dolly you will make me blush,' May smiled awkwardly at nobody in particular. 'But we only did our part of the job don't forget.'

'Well I never. You worked at the school here,' Elsie exclaimed. 'We will know where to come if we have problems.' She accepted another small cake from the plate that Dolly proffered her.

'I try and help out when I can because I miss the children but I must not interfere. That is one rule I made for myself when I retired and I have tried to stick to it. Would anyone like another cup of tea?'

'No thank you Miss Faithful. You have been most kind but I think that we had better be getting along now,' Elsie answered for herself and Nancy.

'May, remember to call me May.'

'May,' Elsie repeated, 'of course.'

'You have done enough today May. I will show them to Oak House and then Jonah will be waiting for me,' Dolly said rising from her armchair. May smiled at Dolly only too glad that her friend's shyness was beginning to recede.

'Thank you Dolly, how thoughtful of you.'

Elsie and Nancy rose reluctantly to go. They had enjoyed May's hospitality which had been a welcome interlude after the pressures of the day. The whole ambiance of the May's lovely home exuded a comfortable atmosphere combined with elegance and luxury, which had been missing from their young lives. Elsie hoped that Oak House would provide them with at least some of the trappings of comfort which she had noticed here in May's home.

The young women picked up their luggage. They shook hands formally with May and thanked her profusely for her hospitality. Dolly kissed May lightly on the cheek following the habit of the many years of their friendship. The handle of the front door yielded to her touch and the three women walked down the path to the lane and turned to wave. May followed them at a slower pace, examining the plants and exclaiming at the number of weeds around her. She pulled up some that she had missed placing them in a tidy heap in readiness to be removed when time permitted.

Dolly led the way along Birch Green Lane onto the High Street where she walked a little way before stopping outside Oak House. It was quite an imposing building, constructed in red brick and had been built in the middle of the previous century. Latter years had seen a change in the fortunes of the two sisters who had inherited the property from their father some twenty years previously. The outside needed painting and in some places the paint had begun to peel off windowsills leaving a neglected air. The garden surrounding the property was large but there were signs of work having been started after the constraints of winter neglect. From the other side of the hedge a head popped up startling the group of women. But Molly Redfern had heard the group approaching. If she was honest she had taken to working in the garden to await the arrival of her new lodgers.

'Hello there,' She drawled at them brandishing a hoe in one hand and managing to look fairly wild at the same time. Dolly knew Molly and her older sister Edith well.

'Lovely day Molly, I've brought along your two ladies.' Dolly could not bring herself to say lodgers. It was a little too common for her gently brought up ways.

'Lovely to meet you,' Molly stuck a grubby fist over the hedge in the direction of Elsie and Nancy.

'And you too,' they replied politely wondering what it was going to be like living in such a place.

'Come along in then and meet my sister. We have been waiting for you. Good journey?' The last comment did not require an answer as she moved across the lawn towards the gate to open it for her new house guests. 'It always sticks, such a nuisance.'

'I'll see you another day,' Dolly said remembering that the afternoon was swiftly moving into early evening. She now wanted to return home to Jonah. Her heart skipped a beat. Even after all these years he still had that effect on her.

'Righto,' Molly nodded absently. Her thoughts were fully directed towards the young women who would bring a diversion into her dreary routine. It was their lack of funds which made life difficult.

'Thanks for everything,' Elsie said.

'Yes. Thank you very much. We could not have done it without you.'

Dolly blushed at the praise. 'It was lovely to meet you, too. Let us know how you manage or if you require anything else.'

'We will. Bye.'

Elsie and Nancy waved as Dolly turned back before she had reached the end of the street. They felt slightly apprehensive now that they were somewhere unfamiliar. Elsie felt ashamed of herself when she recalled the events of the afternoon and how the children had been taken like lambs to the slaughter and here she was feeling the same way and she was an adult who should know better. She glanced at Nancy but her face remained masklike under the close scrutiny of the much older woman.

Molly led the two young women into the house. The interior was dark and gloomy despite the brightness of the day. The walls were decorated in a brownish colour, which was partly because the house needed a complete overhaul in decoration and refurbishment. What they didn't know was that May had approached Molly and Edith only a day previously to enquire whether they would be prepared to put up two lodgers. She had done it partly out of charity because she knew that the two older women needed the money desperately. It was a way of achieving this without them losing face in the community, thus keeping their pride intact. She knew that the girls would be well looked after although Molly and Edith appeared a little daunting at first.

Nancy felt her heart sink as she entered the house and witnessed the state of the interior. She glanced at Elsie but did not manage to catch her eye. Molly opened a door into a sitting room at the rear of the property. This room proved to be a little brighter than the hall. The furniture was sparse but what there was appeared to be old but of a quality that had known the grandeur of another era. Nancy began to relax feeling that things might not be so bad. She appraised Molly whose attire was shabby and unfashionable but like the furniture her clothes had once been expensive. She was quite a plain woman, tall and very thin. Her grey hair was screwed up under a headscarf with a knot tied on the top. Nancy concluded that she had dressed for the garden.

'This is your sitting room ladies. You will not be disturbed here and you may bring your friends providing that it is not too late,' Molly turned to them with a slow smile. Nancy noticed the lines, which creased her face making her look older than she was.

'Right then, I'll take you upstairs and show you where you will be sleeping.' She turned to leave the room. At that moment Elsie and Nancy's eyes met and locked momentarily before they followed Molly up the stairs, still carrying their luggage which had been with them all day.

They were pleasantly surprised when they entered the bedrooms, which were stylish from days gone by. Molly relaxed knowing that this part of the house was in better order than the downstairs. For much of the year the furniture in these rooms had been covered by dustsheets. Nobody came to stay any more as they would have done in Molly's parents' days. Elsie had counted six doors off the main landing and there was another less imposing staircase leading up again possibly to what had been servants' quarters. She wondered how two women could live in such an enormous house. It was made to have children living and playing within its walls.

'I'll leave you to unpack but when you are ready come down and meet my sister Edith. Supper will be at seven o'clock.' And with that Molly took her leave.

Both young teachers disappeared to their respective rooms only too glad to have time to themselves. Molly had half run down the stairs and turned the handle of the library door where she knew that Edith would be sitting eagerly waiting for news of their paying guests. The library had only been brought back into use in the last few weeks because it was too expensive to heat during the worst of the winter. Edith sat by the window as she did most days looking out onto the road watching village life pass by. It was her greatest form of entertainment along with reading and the knitting she attempted for the war effort. Experiencing a horse riding accident in her early twenties had left her paralysed. This accident had traumatised the whole family at the time but after their parents' death the full responsibility for Edith's wellbeing had fallen on Molly's broad shoulders. Her dependence on Molly or close friends to wheel her outside in better weather had been hard to bear at first but over time she had become accustomed to her lot.

Molly had had too much to do with the imminent arrival of the young teachers to give much time to her sister's needs and Edith had had to remain impatiently indoors entertaining herself. But she had witnessed the arrival of the evacuees and their teachers. Edith's sensitive heart had gone out to these children who were bewildered and alone. They had looked a motley crew in their odd clothes, some of which were so obviously hand me downs. She had observed the body language of the villagers who had arrived to collect their new charges and pitied some of the children. She remembered the girl who had not wanted to leave the teacher and had clung for all she was worth to her. And as for Sarah Dunwoody that conniving woman, she thought to herself, she would have to be watched.

Edith made a mental note that she would mention it to the young teachers when she had grown to know them better. She would make this her project for the foreseeable future to check on the welfare of the child and do what she could. She had decided not to mention it to Molly because she knew that she had enough to do without extra problems thrust on her. But Edith smiled ruefully to herself believing that life would become a little more interesting now.

Edith looked much younger than Molly although she was the elder by three years. Molly had borne the brunt of anxieties after the death of their parents. Their father, Jack Redfern, had been a prosperous businessman owning a string of shops in the area. He had inherited these from his own father at the turn of the century. But Jack had become addicted to gambling, unbeknown to their mother, Sophie, who enjoyed the prosperous lifestyle which she led now and had grown accustomed to when her own father had invested money wisely. But on their demise Molly and Edith, who had never married, found there was little money left when they had paid off all the gambling debts incurred by their father. It had been David Faithful, May's father who had handled their affairs in his capacity, as family solicitor and it became his lot to have to inform them of their penurious situation. As a result it had fallen to Molly as the able bodied member of the family to take over the purse strings and to earn a living for which she was ill prepared. Her education had been limited. As a small child she had been educated with her sister and a group of friends locally but when she was a little older she and Edith had been schooled at a boarding school for young ladies in Shropshire. But Edith's accident had put an end to both girls' education away from home.

Sophie Redfern felt that she could not cope on her own and Molly had to make the sacrifice to stay at home to appease her mother and look after her disabled sister. Molly had been blessed with a fertile brain, which needed nourishing. Once she had been ambitious to make something of her life and perhaps to follow her friend May into a profession or even follow her father into the business, particularly as her two brothers had perished in the Great War, but it was not to be. Instead she became her sister's carer. She had not felt any animosity towards Edith for the circumstances in which they found themselves but occasionally over the years she had felt it would have been preferable to have some control over her own destiny.

Molly was an avid reader and this was how she occupied her mind on the rare occasions that she had free time. At times she let out the spare rooms to provide the extra income that they needed just as she had done now to Elsie and Nancy. The large garden that Molly tended also provided them with the fresh fruit and vegetables that they required. One of the local farmers rented the two paddocks and the stable, which lay behind the orchard. This additional income was of great significance to both Molly and Edith. With her head buzzing from all the events of the day Molly poked her head around the library door and smiled at Edith knowing that her narrow world needed an injection of excitement. It was on such occasions that Molly took the inevitable guilt trip about wishing for freedom. But she knew that she would not swap places with Edith for all the tea in China. She entered the room with her quick bird like movements and took the chair next to her sister.

'Only five minutes Edith to catch up with the news and then I must go and make supper for our young ladies.'

The two women's heads bent close together in confidentiality not allowing anybody to hear what was said.

Chapter 8

Carenza had followed Eddie and Sarah Dunwoody along the High Street and then they had turned into Church Street. The road was deserted. The church clock struck the half hour as they passed by but as they came level with the vicarage Jeannette Stringer, the vicar's wife, shouted to them in greeting. She waved her hand to them but it was obvious from her body language that she was not going to engage them in conversation. She was feverishly sweeping the driveway and paths free of winter debris. Jeanette had very little spare time to sort out her home circumstances, as she was involved totally with village life and supporting her husband in everything that he did. She had embraced an opportunity to carry out her chores on the home front and although her outgoing nature would not allow her to be rude she did not want to engage the Redferns in conversation. She had never had a lot of time for them but her conscience as a clergyman's wife would not permit her the luxury of avoiding them. Her husband, Edgar would not have approved of such behaviour in his parish.

'We are all God's children,' he would have said pompously in his Sunday sermon but Jeannette knew he was not like that at all.

Sarah and Eddie had returned a curt nod in Jeannette's direction but continued on their way with a miserable child following in their wake. Jeannette paused momentarily making a note of the child's misery and pitied her having to stay with the Redferns. For a moment she was annoyed with herself at her uncharitable thoughts but common sense prevailed and she knew that she was right on this occasion. She made a mental note of visiting all the families who had taken an evacuee under their wing but her mind made a special note of visiting the Redferns fairly soon to see for herself what it was like for the child. The sound of the telephone ringing from the depth of the vicarage diverted her train of thought. She opened the front door to answer it knowing that she was unlikely to finish her jobs that day.

Sarah and Eddie had not spoken a word to Carenza since they had picked her up at the village hall. This was not personal to Carenza but they were used to great unbroken silences. It was the way they operated. They now had very little to say to each other and when they did it was invariably to argue over petty matters. They walked the full length of Church Street but at the end they turned right into a narrow lane which was little more than a dirt track that ran for a short distance but suddenly finished at the entrance to three farm cottages. The cottages were the property of Home Farm where the Appleton family had farmed for several generations. Eddie had worked on the farm since he had left school. Despite his quietness he was a good worker and generally enjoyed farm life. The wage he was paid was a pittance, much to Sarah's chagrin, but Eddie loved the outdoor life and working the land in all the seasons. He was a tall, wiry man with a rugged, weather beaten face acquired from his life out of doors. His rough working hands were clever at mending the farm machinery and he could turn his hand to many jobs. Often he was asked to mend small machinery and this helped to supplement his farm labourer's wages.

He and Sarah had spent their entire married life living in the cottage. They had met twenty-five years before when they had both been twenty. Sarah had arrived in Nether Heydon the year before to live with her invalid aunt whose husband had died. Her aunt could not cope on her own which meant that Sarah nursed her for the six months that she lingered on eventually dying and leaving her homeless. It was during this time that Sarah had met Eddie and they had fallen rapturously in love. Sarah had been a beauty in her youth with flowing fair hair and a haughty manner, which turned the heads of the local youths, but it was Eddie who had won the day and they had married in Nether Heydon Church on a crisp autumn day.

Their union had not been blessed by children for quite some time. Sarah, who had been an only child and had experienced a hard, poverty ridden childhood had hankered for children of her own and was beginning to feel that there was something wrong with her when she fell pregnant, but lost the baby almost as soon as she had found out. Her mood changed in that short time. She blamed everything for the loss of her child despite the doctor's reassurance that it was quite common for a new mother to lose a first baby. Eddie could not do anything right after that. Her mood was only to mellow somewhat when she became pregnant again and this time she was determined that she was going to look after herself and this child. Her expanding body became the centre of her universe. Eddie was neglected emotionally and they began to drift apart. But their first son Jon was born, followed swiftly by Jake. Sarah had no need for Eddie now except for him to provide for the little family.

Again Sarah had a gripe towards Eddie. She was ambitious to continue the lifestyle that she had experienced whilst living with her aunt. Her own upbringing had been one of poverty and lack of love but her mother's sister had married well and had not wanted for anything. It had been Sarah's mother, Sonia, who had suggested that Sarah should look after her aunt and possibly inherit her wealth. But this had not transpired. The money was divided amongst her numerous godchildren and her husband's nephews and nieces. She had not entirely forgotten Sarah or her sister Sonia. They received a very small legacy each but not nearly enough to change their lives. This had left Sonia bitter and twisted but Sarah was in the first full passion of her love for Eddie and had not cared. Her small inheritance and her love for Eddie meant that she had escaped the poverty of her own childhood and in so doing had become mistress of her own destiny. But as time moved on she aspired to greater things particularly regarding her children. Eddie was content with his working life and had few ambitions beyond keeping his job and enjoying the tranquillity that went with it. This had never been enough for Sarah.

They turned into the garden of the first of the three cottages. It was a small black and white cottage, which had been well cared for over the years and the garden was maintained to a high standard. There were fruit trees displaying pink and white blossom clustered together at the bottom of the long narrow strip of land. To the rear of the garden was a well dug plot, which showed evidence of spring planting. Eddie loved his garden and the produce that he grew supplemented his income. Sometimes he could sell part of his produce to a small clientele who returned to him year after year. This money he kept for himself and it funded his nights out with his cronies in the pub. He was determined that he could hold his head up with the next man because he was adamant that he would not go cap in hand to Sarah who controlled the purse strings.

Sarah opened the front door.

'Here we are then,' she said.

She never locked the door except at night feeling confident that nothing would be stolen. She had inherited a few valuable trinkets from her aunt but other than that there was little of value in the cottage. The interior of the house was neat and tidy. Eddie had no quarrels with Sarah on this score. She had always been a good housekeeper taking pride in the home as it reflected her skills. They rarely had visitors but this did not deter her in her efforts to keep the home respectable. Carenza followed her inside. Her face was blotchy from crying although the tears were now spent.

'Take your coat off love,' Eddie said kindly. 'Let me show you your room and then you will feel more at home.'

Carenza smiled a watery smile at him and followed him upstairs where three doors led off a tiny landing. He pushed open the door of the smallest bedroom and deposited her tiny case on the bed. She looked around her taking in every detail of the room. There were animal models carved out of wood along the windowsill. A small bookcase showed titles of boys' adventure books and there were other indications of the room having been used by a boy.

'This is my son Jake's room. He joined the army right at the beginning of the war and is probably somewhere in France at this very moment. He would be pleased to know that you were looking after it for him,' he smiled at Carenza showing rather yellowed teeth.

'Thank you,' she mumbled allowing her eyes to meet his for the first time.

Eddie felt embarrassed. He had had very little to do with girls over the years and particularly ones that blubbered.

'Right ho then. I'll let you get sorted and then when you are nice and ready come down and have a cup of tea. Mrs Redfern will have the kettle on right now. She likes her cuppa any time of the day.' Eddie smiled at her feeling nervous in a situation where he had little confidence.

Carenza thanked him again. Eddie turned to leave the room but had a backward glance before he passed through the door. Carenza had moved to the window and was staring into oblivion. Her thoughts had left Eddie far behind and had returned to London and what might be happening there. It could have been weeks since she had left but it was only hours. Eddie left the room quietly closing the door behind him. He felt sorry for the child who was obviously missing her family but he wondered what they had taken on. He and Sarah had enough problems of their own without taking on the responsibility of other people, and then there was the war. Nobody was very sure of anything these days. He thought about his own sons at the front. A wave of despondency swept over him. Might he ever see the boys again? Eddie was not a sentimental man or very demonstrous with his feelings but he swept an unshed tear from his eye before he moved on to do battle with Sarah once more.

Carenza could hear an impatient voice calling which brought her up sharp.

'Are you coming girl? The tea has been on the table for the last twenty minutes. Are you day dreaming?' Sarah's voice wafted up the stairs.

Carenza recognised the cutting edge to it.

'Yes. I'm coming,' she shouted.

Pulling a comb through her hair, she blew her nose very loudly before descending the stairs into the waiting arms of complete strangers. Eddie had fled as soon as he could up to the farm on the pretext that he still had jobs to do before dark. Sarah poured Carenza a cup of tea from a large brown pot, which had been her mother's. There was also a plate of bacon and eggs, which she had been keeping warm on the range. The kitchen was just large enough to house a table and four chairs. Carenza was amazed at the plate of food placed in front of her. She knew all about rationing and had assumed that this would still be the case in the country. The expression on her face brought a smile to Sarah's lips.

'Bacon and eggs,' Carenza had murmured as if gold dust had been placed in front of her.

'We have better living here in the country than them in the town but there is still lots of things we are short of. Get stuck into it now before it goes cold,' she said.

Carenza nodded and attacked the food with relish. All thought of food had slipped her mind during the agonies of the day and now she realized how hungry she was. She wiped her plate clean with the last of the bread and wondered when she had last eaten so well.

*

Elsie and Nancy had finished unpacking their few possessions. Elsie wandered along the landing towards her friend's room and knocked gently on the door.

'Come in,' Nancy called as she turned around to see who was there.

She smiled her response as Elsie entered and wandered over to where she was standing by the open window, which looked over the back garden. The blossom was out on the fruit trees in the orchard and in the distance there was a man unharnessing a horse after its day's work.

'Well Nance, what do you think?' Elsie asked her friend.

'It could be worse Elsie, I suppose. But I think that I will miss the bustle of London. Everything is so quiet here but once we start teaching again we will be so busy and tired that we might like the quiet after all. You never know there might be some young men as well,' she laughed lightly at her optimism.

'I really don't know how you can be so flippant Nancy with your Jim out there fighting the Jerries.' Elsie made a face at her friend showing her disgust and disapproval at such a thought.

Nancy laughed out loud partly at Elsie's disapproval but knowing that her reaction had been one of nerves. She felt that she lived on a knife-edge these days and the stresses of the day had taken their toll on her. Suddenly she burst into tears and she wept unreservedly. Conscience overcame Elsie who immediately put her arms around the younger girl and held her tight until her tears were spent. Molly's voice from the ground floor interrupted these proceedings announcing that their evening meal was ready.

'Come on girl we had better go down. Splash some water on your face to cool it down. If we are lucky we might get a good night's sleep and then the whole world will look heaps better in the morning.'

Elsie pushed Nancy in the direction of the jug and basin on the wash stand while she decided to return to her own room to run a quick comb through her own unruly mop of curls.

*

May sat in her sitting room as the early spring evening turned to dusk. This was a part of the day that she had always enjoyed more than any other. It was a time for reflection on recent events. She had done this for most of her adult life. It had been useful in her days as a teacher when problems had to be thought through and resolutions found. Old habits died hard with May. It had been a hectic day but it had been concluded without disaster. She rose and moved towards the sideboard where the cut glass decanter stood containing the sherry she allowed herself. A glass or two was permitted at this time but no more. She had witnessed at first hand what drinking alone could do to a person but this small luxury she permitted herself without a feeling of guilt. Pouring herself a generous measure she returned to her seat, a little smile of self-satisfaction and the enjoyment of sheer self indulgence playing about her lips. There was so much to think about and she did not know where to start. Her mind drifted towards the two young teachers and how well they had carried out their responsibilities. An idea sprang to mind that she would hold a small party to introduce them to a few local people to ease them into country society. Dolly would help as she enjoyed such things.

Chapter 9

Spring and summer had a way of making life feel better. The days were lengthening and the sun smiled down benignly on the world. Doris was feeling happier about the events of recent weeks. She had received two letters from Carenza describing her new way of life on the farm and the day to day events that had occurred in school. Her passion for school and her thirst for knowledge were insatiable. The school now had five classes but the old school building could only house four classes at one time. The village hall had been requisitioned for part of the week when it was not being used for the war effort. Often the afternoons were free to the older children who were gainfully employed with a deluge of homework, which was completed in varying degrees of satisfaction. Many of the boys used this new found freedom to run wild or to earn extra pocket money now that summer had arrived. Sometimes havoc was created between the local boys who were vying for supremacy over the evacuees. Dan Betts remained at the fore front of these spats just as he had in the playground of Travis Street School but as the weeks passed life was slowly returning to some kind of normality. The teachers were sighing with relief believing that the adjustment they had made to a new community and its people had paid off more than they could have dreamed.

Carenza eulogized in the letters to her family about country life and the emotions that it evoked in her. This was a whole new experience for her as it was for the rest of the evacuees.

'I love country life more than I thought I would. There is so much to see and do. There are lots of animals to see and walks in the woods. The other day I saw a woodpecker and a squirrel …' and so her letters progressed.

She described her day when she would rise early to complete set tasks before the onset of the school day. School remained her favourite part and she gushed about new friends she had made in the local community both old and young. Doris was disappointed by the lack of detail Carenza omitted about her new guardians, the Dunwoodys. Her reference to them was vague but despite her original unease Doris was not unduly worried but she did miss Carenza dearly.

At home in the East End life remained much the same. Frank rarely left the house any more but sat by the fire ruminating on times past, or more recently warmer days had inveigled him into the back yard where he soaked up the summer sun which did wonders for his spirit and his old bones. He avidly read the newspapers but the news was rarely good. And he tried to create harmony by rarely commenting on what he had read. Doris, who was his mainstay in life, had enough weight to carry on her fragile shoulders without having to digest every morsel of life on the front line. Her energy levels were low as she worked hard to keep body and soul together for the three of them. She had become his lifeline to the outside world. Only rarely did he see old friends from his working days.

Sometimes he would say.

'Who have you seen today, my love. How is Willy doing? Is there anything that I could do to help?'

And the reply would be the same most days.

'Not much news to report Frank. Willy is a godsend as usual. You sit there until I get us summat to eat. Come along Hannah and help me.'

Hannah was still lost to them in the depths of her malaise and perhaps she always would be for a long time yet. Her life had little purpose now that Carenza had gone away. Doris would read Carenza's letters out to them but the two people she had relied upon now inhabited different worlds and were lost to her.

Doris tried not to think too deeply about the problems which manifested themselves in all aspects of life but the burden of carrying so much on her fragile shoulders was taking its toll. Willy and the other stallholders witnessed the effects daily but did not know what to do except support the little family as much as they could. The East End was renowned for such generosity of heart.

*

Carenza's homesickness had not entirely abated but she used as much common sense as she could to overcome it by immersing herself into life in the village community. School was her greatest joy. She had fitted in well with the other children of a similar age and often Elsie Lightbody selected some of the more able children for separate tuition. There was the possibility that some of these children might be capable of moving on to grammar school in the town. The rest of the group would have to stay on at the village school until they were fourteen. This did not open up huge opportunities for them. Local jobs were more than likely to be the only ones available unless they could take their place in apprenticeships with some of the local firms. The war effort also provided employment until they were old enough to join the armed forces.

May Faithful arrived at St Aiden's, the village school, for one of her numerous visits. She and Dolly had been very anxious to see that the children had settled into their new homes as well as into school life. Some of the fights in the school playground had taken several weeks to suppress but now peace and harmony reigned supreme. Elsie and Nancy had worked hard with the fighting factions to make integration possible between both town and country children. Fledgling friendships were emerging and growing stronger.

'It is a relief to know that everything is working out. It could have been a lot worse,' Nancy had sighed one evening when they had returned home after a particularly tiring day. All they wanted to do was to put their feet up and enjoy the rest of the summer sun until bedtime.

'It has been hard for us all but I do believe that our efforts are now being rewarded. I don't think that we could have done any of it without May. She has been a trouper from the beginning,' said Elsie.

'I couldn't agree more Elsie. What shall we do tonight to celebrate?'

'I don't think that I have the energy to do anything more than sleep tonight. We could do something at the weekend. We could go to the pictures in Worcester.'

'Let's do that and treat ourselves to afternoon tea. I think that we deserve it.'

May strode purposely into Class Four where the oldest children were seated, heads bent in deep concentration. Elsie sat at the teacher's desk, pen poised above a pile of exercise books which demanded most of her attention but she cast a suspicious eye around the class at some of her miscreants who worked demurely in front of her but experience told her otherwise. Her head rose at the noise of the opening door and her eyes locked onto those of May.

They held each other's gaze momentarily before smiles were etched on both faces. Dialogue was unnecessary for both women understood the other well. A strong bond had developed between the two over recent weeks since the arrival of the evacuees. Elsie would often walk to May's cottage in the late afternoon as the school day ended. The afternoon sunshine often found them sitting on a garden seat drinking a cup of tea discussing the events of the day. Occasionally Nancy joined them but her preference was to stay behind to tidy up for the next day. She liked to be organized unlike Elsie who could make decisions quickly and enjoyed the freedom that evening would bring.

May watched the children as they worked on an English exercise in their exercise books. It amused her to witness the different expressions on their faces as each one told a different story. Dan Betts, the newest troublemaker in the school, showed impatience at being constrained indoors when all he wanted was to be outside causing trouble with Archie Douglass who had ruled the roost as the naughtiest boy in school before the arrival of Dan. Both boys had been drawn to each other like magnets, having recognized the same qualities each possessed. The safest option was to join together.

May slid along the bench beside Dan, whose eyes returned to the text in front of him, while his demeanour returned to angelic. May's long years of experience knew precisely how to diffuse a potentially volatile situation which could explode into chaos.

'How are you getting on now Dan?' she asked remembering their conversation on the bus the day that the evacuees arrived.

He gave her a sideways glance and began to fidget knowing that this could be an awkward moment for him.

'Awright Miss,' He hoped that the conversation was at an end.

May looked down at the badly formed letters and misspelt words in his jotter. The page was covered in ink blots which would not be there had his scholastic skills been better. He was hurrying to finish his work so that he did not have to stay inside on a day such as this.

'Is your reading improving?' she asked the squirming boy.

'I fink so miss,' he replied.

May had the measure of him and Dan knew it.

'Would you like to read a few pages to me before playtime?'

'No thank you Miss,' he said honestly. May had to admire that quality in him.

'I will let you go out to play on time,' she conceded.

Dan looked at her with more respect.

'You will?' he said in amazement.

'Yes,' she said, 'because all I want to do is help you with your work. The more practice you have the better you will become.'

He capitulated and read from his book in a stuttering fashion hardly able to sound out the words. The subject material within was related to a child of five or six and the obvious embarrassment that he felt was one of deep humiliation. It had not been May's aim to make him feel this way because she genuinely wanted to help him. She knew that once he could read he would feel better about himself and his behaviour would improve.

'Thank you Dan,' she said to him kindly, 'I would like to come and help you again.'

'Awight Miss and fank you,' he smiled his gappy smile feeling for the first time that someone had taken a genuine interest in him. May melted inside as she watched him bask in her ray of sunshine. All children needed to be loved she thought.

The bell rang heralding the beginning of morning playtime. Books snapped shut and bodies rose in unison stampeding towards the door, which led into the playground.

'Off you go then,' May kept her promise.

'Ye mean it?' he asked in surprise.

'Of course I do. I only want to help.'

'Cor, fanks miss,' and he left at the speed of light.

Dan Betts and Archie James were the first to reach the freedom of the yard. They, more than most, needed to remove themselves from the constraints of the classroom to romp and run off excess energy. May rose to her feet, her bubbling sense of humour never far away as she giggled to herself at this display of antics. How many times had she witnessed these before she mused?

Elsie put her pen down, her face expectant with anticipation now that the children had vanished.

'How did you find him,' asked Elsie.

'He requires a lot of help but I don't mind coming in to do that if that is all right.'

'It would be marvellous May. He would learn more if he wasn't so naughty.'

'I would agree but sometimes inadequacies in their class work can lead to such low self esteem that the naughtiness covers the real problem.'

'I hadn't thought of that,' confessed the young teacher. 'Your experience May is of so much value to us.'

'Well I suppose I'm an old war horse really having done the job for so long,' she said, slightly blushing at the compliment.

'The real reason that I have come in is to see how Carenza is doing.' She continued. 'We are several weeks into the evacuation and I wondered how she had settled,' May enquired.

'She is thoroughly enjoying her work. She is a bright girl and I have hopes of her passing to the grammar school for the autumn term. I think that it will be the thirteen plus as they call it,' Elsie answered. 'She is too bright to leave school at fourteen. Heaven only knows what will happen if she has to go home. Her family don't have much money although want the best for the child.'

May nodded thoughtfully. 'I can see that she is able but I am quite worried about her at the Dunwoodys. She appears unsettled and they are not the best at keeping peace in the home. Jeanette often sees her dawdling on her way back from school, a sure sign that she is not anxious to reach there.'

'Give her time,' Elsie began. 'The tears don't flow as often as they did. She often comes to chat, which I encourage her to do. But she never mentions life at home.'

'Perhaps I am being too sensitive about her but she has worried me unduly. Time will tell how things will turn out.' May sighed with feeling. She stood up stiffly collecting her large, brown leather handbag from the desktop. Rubbers and pencils scattered in all directions in her haste to depart.

'Oh dear,' she exclaimed.

'Don't worry about that,' Elsie said. 'What are classroom monitors for?'

May smiled in her embarrassment

'Thank you,' she said.

She turned towards the door but remembering something she glanced back

'I shall see you later Elsie. I am becoming a fusspot in my dotage. I think that I have been with Dolly too much lately. She fusses terribly.'

Elsie smiled.

'Not really. This is a job where we have to care about what we do and most of all about the children. Once you have done the job it never really leaves you. If there are problems they stay with you until they are resolved.'

You're right,' May nodded in agreement. Her next thought was how she was going to cross the playground at her own peril. She stood at the yard door for a moment watching, remembering and thinking about times past. Perhaps she should give up visiting school if the yard gave her a nervousness that she had never experienced before and then the thought occurred to her that there were far more children in the school owing to the presence of the evacuees. She wondered what it would have been like to teach in city schools like these young teachers and she felt huge admiration for their courage. Taking her life in her hands, she crossed the playground dodging the chasing bodies of children and passed through the gate into a more tranquil world.

*

Carenza was finding life at the Dunwoodys' difficult. The atmosphere was unpleasant when Sarah and Eddie were at home together. They quarrelled endlessly, even in front of her, and it was worsening as the weeks passed by. Often Carenza would lie in bed at night with the pillows wrapped about her head to blot out the noise from downstairs. Eddie by now was drinking heavily. Most nights he rolled home drunk from the village public house, The Fox and Hounds, in a belligerent mood, always ready to antagonize Sarah. Her lack of common sense was apparent when she waited up for him to stumble through the door, armed with a string of grievances about his behaviour.

Once or twice Eddie, not renowned for a violent temper, had lashed out at her targeting her head. He knew that she had better language. The rows would rage for hours sometimes denying Carenza chance to sleep until the early hours of the morning. This impacted on her health. Large shadows spread beneath her eyes and her school work began to suffer. She was constantly stressed by the entire situation. A wave of homesickness often engulfed her but she knew that it was impossible to go home. History seemed to be repeating itself again. It was so reminiscent of her parents' behaviour not long before Ray had died. She was not sure how long she could endure it but did not know what to do about it or where to go. On their own, Eddie and Sarah treated Carenza reasonably well. Sarah had given her jobs to do about the house and outside in the garden when the weather was clement so that she could enjoy the fresh country air. One particular day when she was alone with Sarah she had wandered into the kitchen where the older woman was chopping vegetables.

'Have you always argued so much?' she asked and wondered where the courage to voice such a matter had come from.

Sarah's brow furrowed.

'What's it got to do with you? Don't stick your nose into someone else's business,' she snarled menacingly at the child standing before her.

'N-n-n-nothing,' Carenza backtracked and ran from the room without waiting to hear more. She had the feeling that Sarah was going to lash out at her. Was this history repeating itself?

Her cheeks felt hot from her temerity to speak out of turn. She kept her distance from Sarah for some time.

During those early weeks Eddie often took her up to the home farm where she could feed the hens and pigs. It was food waste from the cottage but there was also food supplied by the farm allowing the animals to be adequately fed. She would return to the cottage with a supply of eggs for Sarah to use for baking. Carenza had filled out during her time living in the country. The skinny town child had disappeared. She had eaten better than she had ever done in her life. Even before the war and the start of rationing, money had been tight for Ray and Hannah.

A few weeks later during a Friday lunch time Carenza returned home from school to find Sarah lying on the kitchen floor. She wondered if the older woman had fallen and banged her head on the corner of the table for there was a huge blackening bruise developing on her temple and her body lay still. Carenza threw her satchel aside as she rushed to see how the older woman was. She looked as if she might be dead. Her fertile imagination was apt to run away with her. These were not new feelings. It had often occurred to her in the past that Ray could have killed her mother and in these circumstances it could be Eddie who was responsible for what had happened. Kneeling beside Sarah Carenza stroked her wrist to soothe her and find a pulse point but the shallow rise and fall of her chest indicated that she was still alive but there was no reaction when she tapped Sarah's arm.

'Eddie, are you there?' Carenza shouted.

There was silence. Eddie as usual was nowhere to be seen but Carenza guessed that he had been responsible for Sarah's injuries. The biggest dilemma lay in the fact that Carenza knew that it would be useless to fetch Eddie. It could even make the situation worse. An idea occurred to her that Jeannette Stringer might be at home. The vicarage lay on her route home from school and as she had passed she had noticed a bicycle propped against the wall of the house.

Sarah moaned quietly but did not regain consciousness. This spurred Carenza on to fetch Jeannette. Her legs carried her swiftly over the rough terrain of the lane into the pebbly driveway of the vicarage. The front door was fractionally ajar.

'Is there anybody at home?' she called urgently. 'Can you come and help?' She beat the shiny, brass knocker hard to gain attention.

Jeannette pulled the door wide open, her face displaying a puzzled expression at the urgency of the summons. Not far behind her Edgar Stringer appeared, equally puzzled by the commotion and wondering if this lunchtime intrusion was for him. He received visits from parishioners at any time of day. Jeannette looked in anticipation at Carenza's over anxious face.

'What's up?' she asked abruptly as Carenza could hardly regain her breath from her sprint along the lane.

'It's Sarah Dunwoody,' she gasped, 'I thought she was dead.'

'What do you mean that you thought she was dead,' Edgar asked as he pushed past his wife into the sunshine and stood facing Carenza.

'She's lying on the kitchen floor and she won't wake up,' Carenza stuttered her response. Relief flooded her features now that she had passed on the responsibility of Sarah's and Eddie's problems to an adult.

'Wait here with Jeannette,' he said pushing her kindly but firmly towards his wife.

Edgar walked with a determined stride down the lane towards the Dunwoodys' cottage, already feeling anxious about one of his parishioners. Jeannette steered Carenza into the safe haven of the vicarage, leading her into the bright, homely kitchen where a meal for two was set at the pine scrubbed table. The kettle boiled cheerfully on the kitchen range. Jeannette warmed the teapot with water from the kettle before lifting down the tea caddy from a shelf just above her head, and frugally spooning a small amount of tea into the pot before topping it up with water. Carenza sat on a chair at the table allowing tears to fall in a deluge as the strain of the past minutes and weeks paid its heavy price. Jeannette placed her arm around the child's shoulders as she pulled the cup of sweetened tea towards her to try and ward off further shock.

'Drink,' she ordered kindly but firmly.

*

Edgar reached the cottage where he found the door wide open indicating Carenza's hasty departure. He entered the front lobby, passing into the small sitting room and onto the back kitchen where Sarah still lay where Carenza had found her. Her shallow breathing of earlier had eased to a steady rhythm. Touching her on the arm, Edgar noticed her eyelids flutter open and then close. Sarah moaned quietly while her hand reached out to touch her bruised temple. Feeling that she was beginning to regain consciousness, he pulled out his well laundered handkerchief and moved to the cold water tap at the sink. It ran for a few minutes before he placed his handkerchief underneath the flood of water producing a cold compress to ease the ache that throbbed in Sarah's temple. She had fallen asleep again.

Edgar left her as comfortably as he could before returning to the vicarage. His bicycle rested against the wall where he had left it earlier. Minutes later he rode steadily in the direction of the doctor's house, occasionally lifting his hands in greeting as he passed members of his congregation. Doctor Fulbrook answered the door himself wafting a half-eaten sandwich in greeting at the vicar's presence. Doctor Fulbrook, a man in his early fifties, lived alone except for his son who spent most of the year away at boarding school. His wife had died many years before leaving her two men folk to lead a bachelor existence. The doctor lived in a chaotic state owing to the nature of his work and the long hours that he kept in order to maintain the health of the village. Every so often his sister visited to take pity on him, spending hours sorting out the muddles which had occurred since her previous visit.

'Hello Edgar,' the doctor held out his hand to him. 'What can I do for you?'

'Not for me John. But we have just found Sarah Dunwoody unconscious on her kitchen floor. You're needed I'm afraid.'

'Just a minute, let me fetch my bag.'

Chapter 10

Jeannette took Carenza into the garden at the back of the vicarage where she felt the serenity of this much loved place might do the child some good. It was a large, mature garden which Edgar kept immaculately tidy, aided by Jeannette when she had the time. At the end of the garden which overlooked ripening fields of golden corn, was a wooden seat that Jeanette had used often during her marriage to Edgar when she wanted to think or have time away from the many visitors who came regularly to the vicarage to seek Edgar's advice. It was to this place of refuge that she brought Carenza.

Carenza sat down on the seat. Shock had kicked in and she was visibly shaking now from the experience of finding Sarah alone and hurt.

'It's all right,' Jeannette tried to reassure her. 'Tell me about it. It's better to share a problem. Everything will seem much better when you have told me'

Carenza sat silently at first, and slowly but surely the tears began to flow and trickle down her cheeks. She brushed them away defiantly at first but the floodgates opened. Hiccupping she buried her face in the older woman's ample chest. Jeannette, forever patient, held the child to her waiting for the storm to pass, which slowly it did. Suddenly Carenza broke into a torrent of words and the whole story unfolded. The older woman sat listening without interrupting feeling quite outraged that a child had to endure so much in such a short life.

'They just keep arguing and Eddie is nearly always drunk. Sarah won't stop going on at him. It was like my mam and dad were like in London. They just won't stop.'

Jeannette pulled Carenza closer to her to comfort her.

'Ssh. You won't have to endure it much longer,' she promised.

*

Carenza's emotions were spent now. Exhaustion had engulfed her and sleep was the only option. Kind hearted in every way despite the fact that she had no children of her own, Jeannette steered the weary child upstairs to a spare bedroom in the rabbit warren of a vicarage. Maternal longing had been part of Jeannette's complicated nature during her sixteen years of marriage to Edgar. But nothing had happened and her husband's parish had filled the empty space left in her heart. She knew that Edgar had wanted children too but both partners were resigned to the fact that they were unlikely to have their own after so long. The parish had become their subsequent child and their lives became dedicated to the needs of others.

Edgar had not returned from the Dunwoodys' cottage but Jeannette had made the decision without consulting anybody. Carenza could not return to live with Sarah and Eddie on any account. If Eddie was violent towards Sarah how would he react towards Carenza if his temper rampaged? The dilemma was inconceivable. Her removal from their care was an urgent priority. The two people to consult were May and Dolly as the billeting officers. Although she was a member of the evacuee committee, Jeannette knew that she could not make a decision on her own. The only option open to her was to ring May. Dolly would panic but May's calm manner and her experience with children would find a simple solution to the problem.

May was at home just about to eat her lunch. The morning at school had been a pleasure but she was relieved to find herself in the tranquillity of her own home. Sometimes she wondered how she had managed to teach for so many years because children were so exhausting in vast numbers. She ruminated on such facts but decided that she must be getting old and perhaps maudlin when she had so much more time on her hands to think so deeply.

The ringing of the telephone prized her from her reverie. With a heavy sigh she heaved her considerable bulk from the chair at the table, making her way into the hallway where the telephone stood on an occasional table. May lifted the receiver and mechanically put it to her ear.

'Nether Heydon 235,'she spoke into the receiver wondering who could be calling at such an inauspicious time.

'Hello May,' Jeannette's breathy voice spiralled down the phone. 'I'm afraid there's an urgent problem that I need to speak to you about. It's about Carenza who is here at the moment. Do you think that you can come over?'

May rolled her eyes in frustration. She was rarely bad tempered but she just wanted a little time to herself. The past few weeks had been exhausting.

'Can you tell me now?' She could hear an edge creeping into her voice however hard she was trying to remain patient. After all she had been concerned about the girl's welfare. But she immediately relented knowing that Jeannette never made demands and gave so much of her own time to the community at large.

'It's all right Jeannette. I'll be with you as soon as possible.'

'Thank you May. I knew that I could rely on you.'

May heard a huge sigh emanate from Jeannette which had a huge impact on her own conscience. Guilt was a horrible feeling coupled with the fact that she was now realizing the enormity of the problem. Maybe there had been some justification in her anxiety over Carenza.

Lunch completed and the debris in the kitchen tidied away, May found her large, leather bag where she had left it when she had returned earlier in the day. Double checking that she had locked the front door she strode purposefully down the front path which led onto the lane. Further down the lane her eyes alighted on Delia Prendergast, meandering slowly towards her displaying the amount of time that she had on her hands. This now became a dilemma for Delia Prendergast was renowned for her long, protracted conversations which she had developed into an art form for extracting as much information from a person as she could; which then would be passed on to her cronies as gossip during the regular coffee mornings that she hosted under the pretext of aiding the war effort.

Well practiced in the art of subterfuge which she had learned and honed while dealing with irate parents at the school gate, May bent her head in a determined fashion and completely changed direction.

'I haven't lost my marbles yet,' she chuckled to herself and made her way towards the fields at the other end of the lane.

This meant a circuitous route which crossed the fields but as she neared her destination she had to climb the stile which bordered the road by the vicarage. May did not glance back but if she had she would have roared with laughter to witness the dumbfounded look which was broadly etched on Delia Prendergast's face. The younger woman stopped in her tracks observing May's volte-face. Her intrigue to know where the older woman was going and the purpose for so doing was more than her innate curiosity could stand. When Delia turned to retrace her steps she had discovered the very person with whom to discuss May's strange behaviour.

*

When Edgar had returned from his unsuccessful quest to find Eddie, Doctor Fulbrook had managed to send a message to the district nurse, Edna Knight. By sheer coincidence there had been a knock at the door of the Dunwoody cottage by two of the children from the village school who wanted to walk back with Carenza before afternoon lessons began. Fortunately, Edna had arrived home from her morning duties only minutes before the children arrived. Their rather garbled message from the doctor made her gather her bag in order to set off once more on her bicycle down to Home Farm cottages. Edna had rarely ventured to the cottages but had occasionally had to visit the farm house. She knew Sarah Dunwoody by sight but had not encountered her often except when she visited the village shop and they would nod in passing.

The front door to the cottage stood ajar and from within she heard mumbled voices but could not quite make out what was being said. Knocking on the door, she walked inside following the direction of the voices. She closely observed Sarah lying on the sofa with her eyes closed and the two men deep in conversation, the tones of their voices muted to keep their discussion away from Sarah's ears.

Doctor Fulbrook acknowledged Edna's presence with a curt nod. She was not put out by this reception because she had known the doctor in a professional capacity for several years and he treated everybody in the same way. But Edgar greeted her more warmly as was his way.

'How are you Edna,' He greeted her putting out his great paw of a hand to take hers.

'I'm fine Edgar. How is our patient Doctor?' she asked looking at Sarah.

'She will be fine once her headache has worn off but I would like you to stay with her for a while to make sure that she fully comes round,' the doctor addressed the nurse formally.

'I will indeed Doctor,' her eyes twinkled as she glanced mischievously at the vicar. Edna busied herself by opening and closing cupboards looking for the ingredients to make a sweetened cup of tea. After the kettle had boiled she placed the cup and saucer into Sarah's hands. She was now sitting up on the couch in the little sitting room and moaned at the pain in her head. Edna stroked Sarah's hair back from her temple and witnessed the blackening bruise. Sarah was now more lucid than she had been but not forthcoming about how she had acquired her injury.

'How did you do that, Sarah?' Edna asked quite shocked by what she saw.

'I must have walked into the door,' she blustered. The three visitors looked at each other incredulously.

'Are you sure? It is a much worse type of wound,' the doctor asked. Sarah continued to moan. There would be time to ask questions later.

'I will talk to you later,' Fulbrook spoke to Edna, walking towards the door followed by Edgar. The two men stood by the gate in the lane.

'This needs sorting out before it happens again,' Edgar said. 'I'll come back later to speak to Eddie. He can't go into hiding for too long. We must inform our local constable.'

'You could Edgar. They won't do anything because it's a domestic dispute. But the constable could speak to him and frighten him a bit.'

The doctor continued. 'I'll be back a few times to see Sarah before I am satisfied that she is better. We'll speak again on the matter vicar.'

'I'm sure we will as we both serve the community.'

Edgar raised his hand in acknowledgement as the doctor placed his medical bag in the car and drove away.

*

May had reached the vicarage but her walk over the fields had left her breathless. She had walked at quite a pace in her hurry to reach her destination. The detour had taken slightly longer than she had expected but it had been better than encountering Delia Prendergast. The vicarage door had been left open in anticipation of her visit. May knocked and entered in her usual manner just as

Jeannette appeared offering her cheek to be kissed. Edgar had returned home only minutes earlier but his wife refused to divulge Carenza's story until May had finally put in an appearance. Now the catalogue of events unfolded as Jeannette divulged all the horrors of Carenza's time living under the Dunwoodys' roof.

May sat in an armchair quite flummoxed and rendered speechless, a rare enough event her friends would vouch to the fact.

'So you see May, she can't possibly return to the Dunwoodys,' Jeannette was on the defensive, not quite sure how May would react and May held the final decision on the billeting of the evacuees.

'You're absolutely right Jeannette,' May cooed, noticing now how anxious the younger woman appeared. 'She can never return to Sarah and Eddie. But the point is where are we going to place her because all the possible vacancies have been filled?'

Edgar and Jeannette looked at each other, their faces smiling the secret smile of a married couple whose thoughts and minds were in tune.

'She can stay here for the time being,' Edgar said hoping that his wife would not become too attached to the child for when the war was over she would return to her other life in the East End of London. His concern for Carenza was obvious but his chief anxiety was for his wife whose tender heart would break if she was to lose her.

'That's a relief then as long as you truly understand what you are taking on,' May smiled her approval but she knew too that it was not the final solution to the problem. 'I don't know what we will do if we have any more problems with the evacuees. An old spinster like me might have to do her bit. Where is Carenza now?'

'Upstairs sleeping. We can arrange for her things to be collected as soon as Sarah is showing signs of improvement,' Edgar replied.

'Who will explain everything to her?' asked May.

'I will. It won't be a problem. I do such things a lot in my job.'

'I know. Keep me informed of what goes on. Well I'll be getting back then but we can have a chat about this soon,' May, all smiles collected her handbag from the nearby chair, rose stiffly and kissed Jeannette once more on the cheek. 'Good luck then.'

In a flash she had gone, wondering which was the best route to take home in order to avoid a possible ambush from Delia

Prendergast. Oh the delights of village life, she thought to herself and chuckled, rather relieved that the problem had been sorted so easily. Nothing could go wrong with the child now that she was in the care of her kind friends. She knew that Jeannette would have made a wonderful mother if only she had had the chance.

Chapter 11

The late summer days in London were dry and unbearably hot. In fact they were stifling. Frank had had to stay inside the house. His old bones could not suffer the strength of the sun's rays any longer. Opening windows within the house was not enough to allow a through draught for the air was still and unrelenting. But he soldiered on hoping for the onslaught of autumn, which would perhaps bring some respite to the scorching heat. Much of his time during the day was spent on his own. Hannah and Doris were lengthening their days at the market to make more money but the extra workload was taking its toll on the older woman. Life was little better than it had been months previously. Doris still carried a great weight of responsibility on her shoulders. Hannah's mental health had steadily improved over the weeks but there was selfishness about her that Doris could not account for. As much as Doris prompted her to share the burden of work Hannah resented the fact that she had to do anything.

'Can you not help out a bit more love?' Doris would ask patiently.

'Of course, Ma,' Hannah would reply but the status quo remained the same. 'Let Willy do the shifting. He can carry the heavy weights.'

'Willy can't do everything Hannah. He has his own stall. If I ask him to do much more we will have to pay him and I can't afford to do that.'

'Then ask me dad to do more. All he does is sit in a chair an' gaze into space or read the newspaper.'

'That is a wicked thing to say. You know how ill your dad has bin with his cough and all.'

Hannah just shrugged and would disappear for an hour or two without saying where she was going.

'You will have to be firmer with her Doris,' Willy did not mind saying what he felt.

'I know Willy but some days I don't have the energy to argue after seeing to Frank and coming down here.'

'You're too good for them all my girl. They put on you. It will send you into an early grave and then what will they do?'

'I don't know what will become of us,' she said, her face a picture of misery as she dwelt on their problems.

Doris was still worrying about Frank. He had grown thin, almost shrivelled over recent weeks. The doctor had visited a number of times but could do very little to quell Frank's downhill journey into old age and subsequent death. He was nearly seventy but would easily have passed for eighty. Doris, although, several years younger than Frank felt her own advancing years increasingly and wondered how long she could carry on, but much depended upon her alone. Her physical aches and pains were too numerous to count but she had to ignore them as long as possible.

It was during the early hours of these hot, airless August nights that Frank woke with a dramatic pain in his chest as well as numbness in his left arm. He moaned in response to the pain. Doris turned in her restless sleep, but promptly opened her eyes becoming all too aware of Frank's laboured breathing. Instantly she became fully awake and stretched out a hand to touch him. There was no effort to reassure her that he was fine.

'What is it Frank?' she asked but he did not respond.

'Frank, are you awake?' again she asked.

Her senses were alert now. She felt his pain as if it was her own.

'Hannah!' she screamed. 'Come quickly. It's your father.'

Hannah awoke with a start. Her sleeping pattern had improved with time and now she was sleeping more deeply. But the urgency in her mother's voice had penetrated through her somnolent state as it had been carried on the still night air.

She sat up in bed, and then padded her way across the landing in the direction of her parent's bedroom. She had not bothered to put on her old flannel dressing gown which hung over a chair.

'What's up?' Her state of mind had not registered the urgency in her mother's voice.

'It's your father. I think he might be having a heart attack. Go and ring for an ambulance.'

Pulling herself together Hannah returned to her room to throw some clothes over her nightwear. She fumbled with a loose coat which buttoned up to her chin, before running down the stairs into the kitchen and drawing back the bolt on the door. Running to the telephone box which was at the end of the road she dialled the emergency number and waited for the voice to ask her which service she required.

Frank lay still, looking white and gaunt against the sheets. Doris held his hand, talking reassuringly to him and mopping his brow every now and then. Hannah had already returned and stood awkwardly in the open doorway of her parents' room.

'It should not be long, they said,' she mumbled. She did not know how to respond to her father lying like death in the bed her parents had shared for more than forty years. She had never been good around illness and her reaction to Ray's demise had made her ill too.

'Go and get dressed properly. I will too,' Doris instructed her as calmly as she could. At this moment Doris felt that Hannah should take some responsibility while she was left to comfort her dying husband. She could not see any way back for Frank to full health. His time was nearly up she thought gazing into his grey face but she could not shed a tear. That would come in time when he was no longer there.

When the bell of the approaching ambulance was heard, both women were dressed and waiting. The front door of the terraced house was open to hasten the path of the ambulance personnel to the room where Frank lay. Joe, the biggest of the two ambulance crew, felt for a pulse but it was weak.

'Steady on there old fellow, we'll get you help as soon as we can,' he spoke reassuringly to his patient.

Defying their stature and size the two men lifted Frank carefully and gently onto the stretcher, covering him with a blanket despite the heat. Frank was strapped into the ambulance. Joe sat in the back with his patient while Doris held his hand murmuring encouragement allowing the tears of anguish at last to fall. Hannah remained behind. She could not face the hospital and the possible death of her father. Her mental state had improved but in some respects still remained fragile.

*

Carenza's happiness had increased tenfold over the following weeks. Jeannette's skill at bringing stability to her life had worked wonders on the child during the time she had spent living at the vicarage. The school holidays had been fun with walks in the countryside and helping Jeannette with chores which had not been a burden. Childhood had returned with a vengeance. The anxieties that had affected her during her life in the East End had dissipated. The long summer days were filled with a freedom that she had never known. She was growing into a country child enjoying a carefree existence. The tears, which had heralded her arrival in Nether Heydon, had vanished as if they had never existed. A sense of happiness and wellbeing had taken control.

'I have never seen her so happy,' May had exclaimed one day when she had called to have a cup of tea with her friend.

'I know. She is really enjoying her life at the moment. I'm also enjoying her company too. She can be quite funny when she wants to be. Edgar treats her as the daughter that he has never had.'

'I think that's wonderful and long may it continue. Did you know that she has a grammar school place for the autumn?'

'That's splendid.' May was genuinely happy for the child.

'I just hope that it will give her a secure future,' Jeannette continued. 'A good education is important but if she returns …' The sentence remained unfinished.

'I know what you are thinking but don't. We will cross that bridge should it ever come.'

'Does she hear from her family?' May had wondered about this for quite some time.

'Oh yes. At least her grandmother writes. I gather her grandfather has been quite ill recently. Occasionally she shows me snippets of news. But she does worry about her mother. She has had some mental health problems I gather.'

'Oh dear,' said May. 'Does it run in the family?'

Jeannette smiled, 'No of course not. There was some family trauma ages ago which affected her mother. But things seem a little better.'

Jeannette also felt fulfilled by her new life and was grateful to use her maternal yearnings in a useful way. A close bond had developed between child and mother substitute. Edgar had observed what had happened between his wife and Carenza. The love that had grown was mutual but he was concerned about his wife should the unthinkable happen.

But one morning late in the summer holidays a telegram, addressed to Jeannette and Edgar, had been delivered to the vicarage. Jeannette was filled with trepidation but Edgar, ever the optimist was positive in his attitude as he tore open the envelope. But the news was not good.

Doris, in her wisdom, had had the foresight to send the telegram addressed to the adults although its contents was news for Carenza.

'Not more bad news?' Jeannette enquired anxiously.

Edwin covered Jeannette's small hand with his own.

'I am afraid so my dear.' He passed the telegram across the breakfast table to his wife. She took it from his grasp and perused it.

She looked questioningly at Edgar.

'What shall we do? This will upset Carenza all over again. But we must tell her soon. I suggest that you take her out for a walk and break the news gently.'

Jeannette pulled a wry face. She knew that Edgar was not getting out of doing the deed himself for his day was already preordained with visits and meetings taking him into the early evening.

'Let her sleep in if she is tired and take her out after lunch. You know her favourite haunts and then tell her everything. Let her read the telegram.'

'All right, but just think that she can't even go to the funeral to say good bye to him.'

'May be it's for the best. Her grandmother is a wise woman. Returning to the East End might not be the best thing at this time. Too depressing by far I would say. Her grandmother obviously doesn't want her upset again.'

'I know, oh Edgar, the poor child.'

*

Frank had died on his journey to hospital. Doris had held his hand all the way there without realising that he had drawn his last breath. He had passed away peacefully in his last sleep. All the pain, which had been etched on his wizened features, had been replaced by an aura of calm, even a serenity that Doris had not witnessed for many years. She thought that the last time must have been during Hannah's childhood when she had been the apple of his eye, his darling girl who had vanished after her sham of a marriage to Ray. There was nothing more that Doris could do for

Frank, the love of her life, but to arrange his funeral to the best of her ability and then leave him in peace for eternity.

Hannah had withdrawn into her shell once more leaving all the burden on her mother's shoulders. Doris worked silently through the problems in her tearless grief. There was no time to grieve. That luxury would come later when there was all the time in the world.

Frank's last resting place was to be near Ray in the little churchyard amongst long dead members of the family. It had also been Doris's decision to leave Carenza in the emotional safety of Nether Heydon. Doris knew that at last she was happy and nothing in this world would induce her to upset this applecart of happiness which now surrounded her beloved granddaughter. The child needed stability in her life above anything else.

Frank was laid to rest after a short service attended by the few family members who remained in the East End and friends that had witnessed most of the events in his life both good and bad. It had been a fitting send off for a man who had lived his life to the full with few regrets, except for his only daughter's marriage to Ray Dodds; otherwise he had been happy with his lot. Doris looked down at his coffin and wondered morbidly when it would be her time to join him.

'Goodbye Frank. I love you but I will see you soon. I don't think that I am for this world much longer.'

Doris lingered for a while longer looking down into the open grave. She picked up more clods of earth and threw them onto the coffin and as she did so the tears began to fall down her grief stricken face.

'Goodbye my love,' she said again and turned towards home allowing the grave diggers to do their job.

*

Jeannette was surprised how resilient Carenza had become. She had been upset at her grandfather's death, but for a child of twelve years old she had amazing courage and resolution in her response to the news. Edgar had used the word 'stoic' to his wife. The funeral had been a fait accompli and she had accepted her grandmother's reasoning for refusing to allow her to attend the service. But during the days and weeks that followed Carenza's solace lay in her frequent visits to the village church where she sat, a solitary figure, in the tranquillity of its embrace while thinking of her grandfather and her overwhelming love for him. Sometimes Jeannette would find her there on her mission to change the church flowers but she would not interrupt the peace but would allow Carenza to sit enjoying the sunlight steaming through the stain glass windows sending a cheerful rainbow of colour into the heart of the church.

Gradually these visits grew less as she came to terms with her grief, beginning to pick up the threads of her life once more.

Chapter 12

The Phoney War was now at an end. The cold, stark reality of conflict had manifested itself in September 1940 when the sustained bombing of London and Britain began on the seventh day of the month. The relentless battering of the capital occurred day and night to wear down the spirit of Londoners but in effect it had the opposite reaction. London life carried on. The indomitable spirit was forever present among the population. Sirens wailed the length and breadth of the country over highly populous cities and ports heralding the approach of the Luftwaffe, reducing buildings in many areas to rubble but despite everything life and relationships continued to function.

The emergency services battled the darkened streets, fire and crumbling buildings. Hospitals were stretched to capacity to relieve the suffering of the injured. The indomitable spirit of Londoners never wavered. They were resolute.

There was camaraderie in the East End which had lifted Doris's spirits. She missed Frank with every fibre of her being but was relieved that he had not had to experience this new phase of the war. But she was not able to let go of him completely yet. Barely a day went by without her visiting his grave to talk to him about all that was happening around them, their family and friends but also the country at large. This closeness to Frank gave her some form of comfort which was unavailable in her relationship with her daughter.

Hannah lived with her mother in the physical sense but it did not extend to a spiritual closeness where they could really care about each other. Her need for the comfort of another person had died when her relationship with Ray had begun to fall apart. Her emotions were dead inside. Doris felt that it was time for Hannah to take up the reins of her new life and find a job where she had to take responsibility for herself and relate to others. Her feelings that this was the right thing to do lay in her thoughts that if anything happened to her Hannah would not be able to look after herself properly, let alone her daughter when she would inevitably return home. The market made little money for them and funds were running low so now was the right time to move on.

Hannah had taken some time to find a new job but she had become lucky one autumn day in October when she had crossed London into the West End. Although money was short she had felt that it was time to buy something new even though there was clothes rationing amongst everything else. She had seen a dress that she thought might fit her. It was in the latest style where there was little fullness in the skirt now that everything including material was in such short supply. She had the correct number of coupons for it. Doris's clothing coupons had lain in the dresser drawer for weeks, unused. Hannah had believed that Doris had little use for them. But it did not occur to her to ask her mother for them. She had slipped them into her handbag with her own. Without telling Doris where she was going she had headed for the tube.

Now she stood in front of the shop window looking at the dress. In a corner of the window she noticed an advert for a shop assistant. Without hesitation she opened the shop door and walked in straight to the counter.

'Can I help you?' the woman asked.

'Yes. I saw your dress in the window. Could I try it on?'

'Of course, if you would like to go into the changing room I will bring it to you.'

The shop assistant retrieved the dress from the window and took it to Hannah in the fitting room. Hannah had already made up her mind that the dress would fit her knowing that over recent months she had lost weight. The dress looked as if it had been made for her. She pranced in front of the mirror admiring her reflection and suddenly made a decision. Without changing out of the dress she flung open the curtain of the fitting room and flounced to the counter where the assistant stood writing labels for new stock that had been delivered that day.

'I see that you have an advertisement in your window for a new assistant. I would like to apply.'

Hannah was appraised by the woman before her. In her new dress she looked more than passable to work behind the counter in front of any prospective clientele. Her hair was clean and tidy along with her finger nails and she spoke reasonably well. It was not always possible to have all these accoutrements in one candidate.

'Well it could be your lucky day love,' the assistant replied.

'Really,' Hannah looked pleased.

A hand reached across the counter towards her.

'My name is Sophie Bartlett and I am the owner of this establishment. I have not had any response to my advert. You look the ticket my dear and if you want the job, it is yours.'

'Wonderful,' breathed Hannah.

'I expect you to be here before we open at 9 o' clock and to cover for me if I have any business meetings. You may keep the dress and choose one other but not an expensive one. You will wear these dresses for work so that you keep up the standards for which I am known. I will deduct the price of the garments from your wages over the next few months. Is there anything else you want to know?'

Hannah was rendered dumbfounded at the speed that the whole matter had been conducted.

'Thank you,' was all she could say.

Hannah had been overjoyed at how easy it had been to acquire a new position. She was jubilant at not having to stand in the market square in inclement weather any more. Her new position enabled her to take a step up in the world now and suddenly she did not want to return to her mother in the East End. It even occurred to her that she could rent a room or a flat somewhere in town but reality sobered these thoughts with a vengeance to enlighten her that she did not have the money to do such a thing, at least not yet. Hannah had not thought that her new job was meant to release her mother from the responsibility of putting food on the table or making her life easier.

Sophie Bartlett was a business woman through and through. Although there was rationing and the introduction of coupons the shop managed to function and survive. The clientele were not rich but came from the middle classes who could afford to buy new clothing and to have clothes adapted and repaired to lengthen the life span of any garment. Dresses were often restyled to suit the minimum amount of fabric required. Sophie used all her resourcefulness to make a living. She had owned the shop since the middle of the twenties when she had set up in business after inheriting a legacy from her maternal uncle who had never married. Sophie's own marriage had ended acrimoniously in divorce when her husband Harry had left her for his mistress of many years who was now carrying his child and hopefully his son and heir. This had been the catalyst which had turned him against his wife who had not conceived during the fifteen year duration of their marriage.

The demise of the marriage had left Sophie with little to do except meet her vacuous stream of friends for luncheon or visits to the theatre. She wanted more out of life to fill her day and to give her a purpose. Remarriage was not an option. She never wanted to be possessed by a man again. But her business acumen was brought to the fore. Excess money from her divorce settlement and her inheritance were ploughed into this new business venture. If it failed her very existence did not depend on its success because she was financially secure but her pride did not understand the word failure. With the onslaught of war she had used her wiles to adapt her business to the 'make do and mend' slogan. But it was still aimed at people who had a comfortable life style in order to pay people to alter their clothes. In just a short time business was booming again. Word had filtered through to the upper classes who did not want to lose face with their peers about shortages of money but were prepared to have their clothes altered to remain in fashion as the times dictated.

Sophie had employed Hannah to front the business. She had been quiet and pleasant but really there had been little choice. Nobody of the calibre that Sophie would have employed before the war was available. But she felt that Hannah had potential and could be worked upon to reach Sophie's high standards. Hannah had been clean, quiet and polite. All this could give her a level of credence with her customers. If Hannah did not work out Sophie had the option to employ someone else if that occasion should arise. She had no qualms about other people's emotions. Business was black and white to her with no shades of grey.

The journey from the East End to the West End was not the easiest for Hannah or other Londoners who had similar daily sorties across the capital. During the onslaught of autumn into winter and the approach of darker days, Germany relentlessly bombed the city. The wail of the sirens sounded night and day. It disrupted daily life. But somehow life carried on trying to retain a façade of normality. The underground became a refuge for many. People who worked in the city did not see their homes as much as they would have liked. Hannah with her range of problems coped and grew in confidence. Her quality of life was improving. She felt that she was going up in the world mixing with the hoi polloi of London society albeit on a business basis. Doris was becoming a nuisance to her. She dreamed of moving up in the social world but Doris would pull her back to her roots more than she wanted. She dreamed the dream that she experienced during the early years of her marriage to Ray. Could it still be a possibility?

Doris worried about Hannah's safety on a daily basis. She tried not to become paranoid but now that she had left the market time weighed heavily on her shoulders. But she would be forever grateful to the people who had taken Carenza in and kept her safe.

'You will be careful, my love,' she would say to Hannah.

'Oh Mother stop fussing will you? I hear the sirens and then I seek shelter. That is all I can do. It's all anyone can do.'

'Yes of course,' she replied, but like anyone of her age she was nervous about life nowadays.

Hannah's new found confidence was a wonder to her. Her daughter had changed over the weeks. Her East End accent had been hidden under a pseudo poshness that she could not place. The fact that she called her 'Mother' instead of 'Ma' was another turn around in her ascendancy to a higher eschalance. Doris could not help but wonder what would be next in this succession of events.

*

Carenza was happy for the first time in months. The new people in her life remarked between themselves that the change was incredible. Jeannette had been responsible for this transformation. Edgar, too, had to take credit for his part in the venture but Jeannette possessed a serene personality which had transformed Carenza's life after the turbulence she had experienced at the hands of the Dunwoodys. It had become common knowledge that Sarah had left Eddie after the events of his assault on her. She had found a job as a live in housekeeper nearby but spent her life avoiding her husband who had been spoken to by the village constable and this had had a chastening impact upon him. Dolly had been full of the news. Generally she was not a gossip but one afternoon May had invited her for afternoon tea along with Jeannette.

'It is unbelievable what you have done for her,' Dolly enthused to Jeannette. 'She seems to be a different child altogether.'

May smiled because she was just quoting what she had been told. Dolly had no experience with children and if she was honest was rather frightened of them.

'She is different now. I'm just glad that she is so happy. Even the news of her grandfather's death she dealt with in a very adult way. I will miss her when she returns to London.'

'That won't be for some time with all this news of the bombings,' May chipped in. 'Have you read the papers about the number of casualties?'

'Quite frightful, I think we are so lucky to live here in the country. I wonder what we would do if that awful Mr Hitler landed here. It doesn't bear thinking about.' Dolly always made reference to the German leader in a formal fashion.

'Hopefully it won't happen,' said Jeannette. 'We must pray that it doesn't.'

May looked at Jeannette in a perplexed manner. Although Jeannette was a vicar's wife, she had never been very religious and May had not heard her speak that way before. Jeannette smiled at the older woman but said nothing.

'Have you heard about the Dunwoodys?' began Dolly.

'Dolly I do believe that you are gossiping,' said May quite amused by this sudden transformation in her friend. Dolly had the grace to blush and they all laughed.

The autumn had been a time of peace in the countryside. The outside world of bombing and war could be a million miles away for the community and the evacuees. The changing seasons, which could only be witnessed so vividly in the countryside, had filled Carenza with wonder. School was a new adventure for her now that she had made the transition to grammar school at the beginning of the new term. Her academic success had given her such a thirst for knowledge and self improvement that she became voracious in her pursuit of it. Her mind flew in directions that she could never have considered in the East End. Perhaps she could become a teacher or something even more important but it would be her educational prowess which would ensure her success. Jeannette and Edgar gave her the space and peace to prove herself as well as their complete encouragement.

A few weeks after her afternoon tea invitation, Jeannette was also happy. In fact she was ecstatic in her deep joy. She had felt that Carenza's presence in their lives had fulfilled the maternal side of her nature so much so that this deep contentment had caused the inner glow that she felt at this very moment. Her glance at the clock on the mantel piece told her that Edgar should be home soon. Her stomach had flipped over in her excited and nervous state. Apprehension also played a part in her constantly changing state of mind. What would he say when she told him her news. The front door opened and clicked shut followed by the sound of Edgar's feet moving over the tiles of the hallway. He did not make for the kitchen but walked to his study to drop his load of papers onto his already untidy desk which Jeannette refused to touch in case of disturbing his unusual filing system.

'I'm in here, darling,' she called to him. The butterflies in her stomach were surfacing again. Her voice came out in a squeak as she endeavoured to sound normal. Edgar's head appeared around the dining room door.

'Are you all right?' He asked puzzled by the high pitched nature of her voice.

'Yes, of course' Her voice had returned to normal again as she smiled uncertainly at her husband.

Edgar nodded at her before disappearing again.

'I won't be a minute,' she heard him shout from the depths of his study. He returned only minutes later to sit opposite her at the table which had been laid for afternoon tea. She had waited until this time to divulge her news. It was his favourite time of day when they could spend a little time together.

'Carenza not home yet,' he stated the obvious noting that her chair was empty.

'She will be late today as she is having extra tuition. She can have her tea when she comes in.'

Edgar nodded as he reached for a sandwich.

'How was your day?' Edgar enquired.

Jeannette beamed at him.

'A good one,' she said. He looked at her taking note of her facial expression. It was one of pure radiance. Suddenly she giggled and could not contain herself.

'Out with it,' he smiled too. Her happiness was infectious.

'I went to see Doctor Fulbrook today.'

'And what's the matter with you?' An expression of concern drifted across his normally composed features.

Jeannette fussed with pouring her husband a cup of tea before handing it across the table to him.

Edgar's patience was wearing thin

'And?'

'And I'm pregnant' It at last came out in a rush. Jeannette smiled in confusion knowing that Edgar was least expecting this piece of intelligence after a long childless marriage. His face portrayed a myriad of emotions. Jeannette did not know how to react but his features broke into a gargantuan smile. Visibly she relaxed as he stood up outstretching his arms for her to slide into the strength of his embrace. He kissed her gently on the top of her head.

'Wow! When?' His mind had moved on to gather more information. 'When is it due?'

'In about six months. I've waited until I was fairly sure before I told you.'

'At last our prayers have been answered.'

Jeannette raised her eyes. Edgar could not see her face. She knew that she did not have Edgar's deep religious conviction but it was not an appropriate time to make a comment now that they felt so blessed.

Jeannette drew away from her husband. Her eyes drifted towards the clock on the mantlepiece where an ominous brown envelope was half hidden behind it. She stretched out to retrieve it before handing it to Edgar.

'This came this afternoon and I didn't know whether to open it but it is addressed to you. It's the second telegram in only such a short time. I also feel afraid Edgar.'

Edgar took the envelope from his wife turning it in his hands in a hesitant fashion but he tore the envelope open reading the contents quickly before handing the piece of paper to his wife. His facial expression was grim. Jeannette's face turned white as she digested the piece of information.

'Not again,' she said.

Chapter 13

Two weeks after Edgar had received the telegram, Carenza's only recently settled world was once more in turmoil. She felt rootless and insecure, which had been a frequent state of mind during her early childhood. The news of Doris's and Hannah's deaths had come as a great blow to her so soon after Frank's demise.

The rows of terraced houses where Doris and Hannah had lived had been flattened during one of the night raids over the East End. Many East Enders had fallen victim to the Luftwaffe's relentless bombing of the capital. Hospitals all over the city were full to capacity with the injured and dying. Hospital leave for the working personnel was cancelled and exhaustion sat on everybody's shoulder like a mantle. All off duty policemen, firemen and ambulance workers were recalled to duty to deal with the daily bombardment. There were emotions of euphoria if people were dug out of the rubble alive. Citizens carried on with their lives stoically making the best of some of the worst situations possible. Comforting pots of tea were brewed by millions who had known that to be the immediate answer to all things.

Doris's home had taken the full impact of one of the bombs. Searchers recovered the bodies of those foolish enough not to have sought shelter in the underground or in the Anderson shelters. Many bodies had been discovered huddled together under the stairs or even in cellars where they had taken refuge from the bombing. Two of these victims had been Doris and Hannah. Once the authorities had identified the bodies, the next of kin were then informed. In some cases they were relatives serving in the armed forces. However, Carenza, as the only living relative of Hannah and Doris would have to be informed through the records held by the school and the evacuation authorities.

*

Carenza's behaviour, although understandable, was highly unpredictable. Too much trauma had happened to her in her short life which had left her lodged somewhere between hysteria and depression. Even the counselling by professional help had little impact upon her mental state. The best advice had been to try and understand her and allow the trauma to work itself through until she had reached the other side. All involved agreed that this was the best course of action. But it was Jeannette and Edgar who bore the brunt of her everyday living. Edgar, who was infinitely patient by nature, found great difficulty in coping with the bereaved child. His compassion was a quality that was at the core of his calling to the ministry, but he was secretly reaching the end of his tether. He had dealt with many bereaved people during the course of his work but it became a different matter when it was under your own roof and there was little he could do to lessen the child's suffering. He was consumed by guilt about his inability to help her. Jeannette was also suffering greatly. For a while Carenza had been kept home from school but May had advised them otherwise.

'Are you sure that it is for the best to keep her at home? Would she not be better keeping her mind occupied in school?' She was sitting in the large vicarage kitchen drinking a cup of tea.

'We don't know what to do May. Edgar is at his wits end with worry and feelings of guilt.' Jeannette let her head fall into her hands and sobbed her heart out.

May reached out to take the younger woman's hand squeezing it in sympathy.

'Please don't take it to heart so much my dear. We will do our best to sort it out. Keep you pecker up.'

May rose to go. She felt desperate for her friend but she needed to think. 'This child has had so many problems since she has been here,' she thought to herself as she closed the front door behind her and made her way home.

Edgar's greatest concern now was for Jeannette and the precious baby which had taken so long to be conceived. She could not afford to lose this baby but as time went on Carenza did not appear to be making the mental progress that had been predicted. Edgar had thought that adopting Carenza might be an option to help her stability as well as the fact that as a couple they truly loved her. But as the days progressed he was seriously dismissing this as a possibility. Something had to be done before disaster struck. His conscience was in turmoil but he knew the ultimate decision was his and his alone. He spent time in the church praying for guidance but it was not quite as simple as he had hoped.

It was a cold November day, when Carenza had not coped well again. The tiredness from her pregnancy meant that Jeannette was not feeling rational enough within her own persona to draw on strategies to calm the troubled waters of Carenza's mind. Edgar had witnessed the whole episode which had erupted out of trivia. Whatever he tried he never seemed to find the solution to the problem. On this particular day Carenza had rampaged in her grief leaving Edgar worried about her sanity. Jeannette was beside herself with her own jangled emotions and now sobbed bitterly at all that was happening.

'Go to bed,' Edgar said not unkindly to his wife. She fled from the room as if the devil himself was chasing her.

'Carenza I want you to go to bed as well. Sleep will make you feel better by tomorrow.' He could see that the current storm had blown itself out. The child made no answer but left the room.

Edgar sat in silence looking into the flames of the log fire wondering what to do. He knew that the only person he could speak to was May. She possessed more wisdom than anyone he knew. Even his prayers for guidance had not been answered this time. After checking that the house was quiet he donned his coat and scarf and left the vicarage. He had decided to walk to try and clarify his jumble of thoughts.

*

May Faithful had drawn the curtains early against the grey November afternoon. She had lit the fire in her drawing room and was enjoying the cosiness that only this time of year could bring, particularly in England. Quietly in the background music from the wireless played, the volume of which was turned low. On the occasional table near her chair was a book of sonnets by Keats. This was her time when she could lock the world and its troubles out as if they did not exist. She smiled to herself at this thought. How foolish she was when the world was at war she mused but at this moment in time she would enjoy her solitude while she could. Later she was to return to that thought wondering when she would enjoy such tranquility again.

A little later May heard urgent knocking on her front door. She rarely had visitors in the evening unless she had issued a special invitation. The lights in the cottage were diligently switched off before she pulled back the blackout and looked through the window to ascertain who it could be. She was never fearful about opening the door to unknown visitors. Her life had been spent serving the community for so long that most families were known to her, sometimes even several generations of the same family.

In the darkness she could just make out the size of a large human shape but it was not clear if it was male or female. She was puzzled at first. The rain was teeming down. The figure was shrouded in a mackintosh and hat to keep the inclement conditions at bay. May replaced the blackout and felt her way to the front door. She half opened the door.

'Who's there?' she called.

At the sound of the front door opening Edgar's tall form turned towards May.

'Sorry to bother you on such an awful night May. I need your advice.'

'Oh Edgar, do come in at once. What a frightful night.' She half pulled him into the house wanting anxiously to shut out the rain which was blowing into her hallway but she also wanted to redraw the blackout.

Edgar stepped into the blackness of the house as May switched on the lights beaming happily at her unexpected guest. She extended her hand to take Edgar's outer garments in order to hang them over the chair in the hallway where it stood solely for that purpose. The sitting room exuded its own warmth and welcome on such a chill evening.

'Please sit down Edgar. Warm yourself here.' She indicated a chair near her own next to the hearth. 'What can I do for you?'

Edgar smiled ruefully. It was unusual for him to seek advice when he was usually the one who gave it. May was all ears sensing his diffidence.

'This is not easy to broach May. I feel so guilty about what I am going to say. I have prayed for guidance and what I am about to request is my only solution to the problem.'

May leaned forward in her chair a frown etching her face.

'Go on.' This was not like Edgar at all.

'Jeannette is pregnant, May.'

Her face lit up with pleasure at this piece of information.

'Yes I know.' Said Edgar.

'We haven't made it common knowledge as yet in the village. As you well know there have been so many problems over the years with trying for a baby that this could be our last chance.'

May nodded sagely but the smile never left her eyes.

'You know that Carenza lost her mother and grandmother only weeks ago. Well she has been traumatized by those events. It seems that she has no other living relative. She is all alone in the world.'

'I know because Jeannette has told me. I have been trying to find a solution to the problem. Go on,' she said realizing that there was more to come.

'Well, it's Jeannette,' he continued, 'she cannot take much more of Carenza's moods and histrionics. We love Carenza as if she was our own but we are also afraid about the stress placed upon Jeannette while she is in her condition.'

May looked at him for a brief moment taking stock of what she had been told.

'You want Carenza moved to a more suitable environment?'

Edgar looked at her and nodded. The misery and failure of the situation were etched on his face. May reached out and squeezed his hand in sympathy.

'Another move will have a devastating effect on Carenza. She has been pushed from pillar to post as it is. But you and Jeannette have a right to this baby of yours without any more upset.'

'We just thought that you as billeting officer would be able to find her a new home.'

May shook her head in dismay.

'There is nowhere else. Everywhere is full. I cannot make people take on a child with these emotional problems.'

May looked thoughtful for a moment before looking up at her guest. The cogs of her mind had been turning to find a solution.'

'She must come here. I have plenty of room and experience with children. That's decided then.'

May rose from her seat suddenly, taking hold of Edgar's two hands and held them.

'Tell Jeannette not to worry. It is wonderful news about the baby. I will be over first thing in the morning to see her. Now off you go and worry no more.'

She gave Edgar a playful push towards the door of the sitting room making light of how she felt inside. As long as she had known Edgar, she had never seen him so downcast. He did so much for others that she had felt it to be only right that he should have something back in return. But it did not prevent her misgivings from surfacing. Edgar's face radiated happiness now that a solution had been found. The front door clicked softly behind him as he once more disappeared into the darkened streets.

May went back to her sitting room. Sitting in her chair by the fire, watching the dying embers she mused over the events of the evening knowing that she had made a commitment that she had to keep for years to come. The poor child had no family left and no home to return to after the war was over. Nobody knew when that would be. She shook her head in desperation.

'What on earth have I done,' she whispered to herself before going to bed to face one of the worst nights of her life.

Part 2: Summer 1948

Chapter 14

It had been a happy summer for May and Carenza. Carenza had been at home more than she had been in the last two years. They had both enjoyed their time together in the sunshine and catching up on missed opportunities that had not been possible to do over previous years. The clatter of post onto the hall tiles brought May from the breakfast room in a hurry. She was rather breathless in her haste making her note that it was time to lose weight. Her old navy dressing gown hung loosely around her thickening waste. It would not do up any more as much as she tried. It had seen better days. Part of it was faded and frayed but she could not make herself throw it out. The war had left a legacy of not wanting to waste anything. Make do and mend had been the slogan that had been seen everywhere on posters across the country. She often thought that she would be like that forever but she knew that most of her age group were conditioned into being that way too.

She bent and picked up the wad of envelopes shuffling through them like a pack of playing cards. Many of the envelopes contained bills. There were letters from people she had not seen for a while owing to the war years and other circumstances. But there it was, the letter for which they had waited and waited. It was addressed to Carenza. If she could have opened it herself she would have done. But she knew better than to interfere. Her anxiety had to be curtailed until Carenza came downstairs. She had made a promise to herself years ago that she and Carenza were entitled to privacy and space in order to make their relationship work. But her stomach was now doing back flips with nervousness. She so wanted Carenza to have done well.

By the time Carenza appeared an hour later May had dressed in her habitual attire of a jumper and skirt with her trusty waistcoat over the top. She could not change the habit of a lifetime carrying everything she needed in her already bulging pockets. Old habits die hard, she mused looking in the mirror in order to comb her snow white hair.

When had that happened, she thought, smiling ruefully to herself? Her face was unlined. Often people who did not know her could not believe that she was sixty eight years old.

The letter was now resting on the mantelpiece waiting for Carenza to find it. May had not had the heart to wake Carenza but she still could not subdue her impatience. In recent days Carenza had been feeling tired after her return home from college where she had worked hard to achieve what the letter was about to divulge. She ambled into the sitting room, her face flushed from sleep and the warmth of the summer sunshine which flooded through the French windows that led into the garden. May sat demurely in her chair next to the occasional table which was where she had sat most of her adult life when she was at home. She was also enjoying the warmth of the lovely day that lay ahead. She read her correspondence willing Carenza to see the long, brown envelope.

'Morning my dear,' May grinned at Carenza.

'Morning May,' Carenza moved across the room to plant a kiss on May's soft furry cheek, as was her custom.

'Who are your letters from?' Carenza's voice was as casual as she could make it.

'One is from Dorothy and the other from Bessie.'

'Oh,' Carenza replied flatly, 'nothing for me?'

May had already caught the timbre in Carenza's voice. Her anxiety was tangible. May's eyes travelled in the direction of the mantel piece. Carenza's gaze followed this movement and saw the envelope. Her face had lost its rosy hue. The time had come to know where her future lay. She snatched up the envelope and flew out of the room to open it in peace. May's eyes followed her retreat. Underneath the volume of papers in her hands she crossed her fingers on both hands while she waited for a response.

Carenza had wandered into the garden while she perused her letter. A smile turned the corners of her lips as she danced in circles and then started to run, her black bob flying in a cloud around her rapturous face. May had heard the noise in the garden. She too smiled, needing no telling as to the contents of the letter. But she still jumped when Carenza put her head round the side of the French windows trying to show a face of contrition, but she failed. May's face beamed. She was not going to be caught out by Carenza's mischief. She had been a victim of this many times before.

'You have done it then.' This was a statement of accomplishment.

Now Carenza could not contain herself. The excitement bubbled forth in screeches of delight.

'I've done it,' she screamed jumping up and down. 'I am a fully fledged teacher.' She could not contain the euphoria she felt. May looked at the girl who stood in front of her now - how happy and bubbly she was. At twenty Carenza was beautiful, poised and confident, a complete contrast to the child who had come to her all those years ago.

It had been a struggle to visit the vicarage after Edgar's visit but she had never been one to renege on a promise. She was made of sterner stuff and knew that she would carry out her promise to Jeannette and Edgar. It was impossible to see that poor girl possibly lose her baby owing to Carenza's behaviour. May had arrived when Carenza's tantrum was in full flow. Jeannette looked troubled and the evidence of this was etched on her strained features. Her hands covered her extended stomach as if protecting its contents. Her knuckles were white and strained with the tension of the scene. She was frightened of giving birth then and there as Carenza rampaged.

May witnessed this with a feeling of trepidation. She had been used to naughty children at school but Carenza was not being naughty. She was genuinely traumatized by what had happened to her over previous months. Her entire family had gone in a short space of time and there was nobody permanent in her life that would be her anchor amongst the living. This undertaking that May had made was a commitment forever. Naughty children could be sent home at the end of the school day but she and this child were joined at the hip.

'Go and wait in the sitting room,' May spoke firmly to Jeannette. She hesitated. 'Go on now.' May's voice was determined. Jeannette met her eyes. They locked on together. May looked very stern. It was an expression that Jeannette did not recognize in her old friend. She fled as quickly as she could.

May then turned her attention to Carenza. Her shouting was turning into gulping sobs but slowly she was calming down. May waited until the storm passed. She led the child up the stairs and ultimately to her bedroom.

'You cannot go on like this my dear,' May spoke kindly to the child. 'Let's get your things. You are coming with me.' Her soft hand cupped Carenza's chin turning her young, tearstained face towards her own. 'This will be your last move I promise. Life will be better from now on.'

Carenza looked into the blue pools of May's wise eyes and registered compassion but she did not reply. She no longer knew what to feel. Her whole crumbling world was built on shifting sand.

In Carenza's bedroom in the vicarage they sorted through her possessions packing what was necessary for a few days. May knew that Edgar would bring the rest over as soon as he could. Carenza was led firmly by the hand down the stairs and made to wait in the barn of a hall. The sitting room door was slightly open. Jeannette had heard all that had gone on. May's head had appeared around the door where she saw her friend sitting in a chair not wanting to speak.

'All right Jeannette? I'll see you in a few days. Can you ask Edgar to bring round the rest of Carenza's stuff for her.'

Jeannette nodded her head. She was too full of conflicting emotions to answer. Her worst fear was that she had let Carenza down and she was ashamed of how she had been unable to cope. May closed the door quietly behind her, picked up Carenza's few possessions which had been packed in a small holdall and took the child's hand.

That had been the beginning of a relationship made in heaven, not immediately but over time. Carenza had taken to her life with May. It was a calm, structured and orderly existence. May would not put up with nonsense but she was kind and thoughtful. Her maternal side which had lain dormant all her life suddenly reared its head. She did not try to take the place of Carenza's family but it was the beginning of a new dawn for both of them. They just became a part of each other's lives as naturally as if it was meant to be.

May steered Carenza through the pain barrier of losing so many members of her family until she had reached the other side and had felt capable of picking up the threads of a normal life.

'Let it all out,' May would say when Carenza had a bad day. 'They will get better.' And slowly over a period of time Carenza was able to cope with her emotions and as she began to grow up she saw and understood what May had done for her. She had given her the stability to be herself. They had talked and talked until her problems had become bearable and they had receded but not forgotten.

As the war in Europe was nearing its end May began to panic. Some of the evacuees had begun to go home. There was nowhere for Carenza to go. May could not envisage a life without the child. They were now so much part of each other that she had to put this relationship on a more permanent footing. It was to her nephew's legal firm that she had made overtures in those days to sort this possibility into a reality. She had consulted Carenza every step of the way. Both of them were as eager as the other to make this happen and by late 1944 Carenza legally became May's daughter, adopting the surname of Faithful but neither demanded that May become 'mum' or 'mother'. It remained the same as before. May was still May.

Chapter 15

Over the intervening years May had made sure that Carenza maintained a close relationship with Jeannette and Edgar. Carenza regarded them as an extension of her family. This closeness had helped Jeannette forgive herself for the inadequacy and guilt she had felt in her failure towards Carenza. Now their relationship was more like two sisters. Carenza had become a surrogate aunt to Helen over time and now that she had teacher qualifications she would be even closer to the child when she took up her teaching post in the autumn here in the village school.

It had been a matter of good fortune that a vacancy had become available for September. Both of the young teachers who had accompanied the evacuees during the war had remained at the village school long after the war had finished. They had adapted to country living and had never wanted to return to life in the capital. They had loved their time there during the War feeling as if the turmoil around the world had had little effect on them.

That was not completely true because everyone was affected in some way or other but their sojourn there had given them more security than it would have done in London during the Blitz. The two young teachers had lost their young men in the fight for freedom at the front. Now they were facing happiness again. But Elsie Lightbody had been the first to marry a fellow school teacher from the neighbouring town of Dalton. She had given up her job to become a housewife when her young man had been demobbed from the army. Nancy Fellowes had continued living with Molly and Edith. All the women had formed a close bond and Nancy had been eager to settle in the village but eventually find a home of her own. She wanted to make a family of her own as her parents had died and her only brother had been killed overseas. It had been only in the last few months that her wish had come true when she had met Simon, the son of a local farmer. They had both come to the relationship in their middle thirties and had felt that it was time to tie the knot as soon as possible.

The wedding was to take place as soon as the school year had ended thus establishing a vacancy in the school. May had felt that it was a good beginning for Carenza and had persuaded her to apply for the job.

'Teaching can be a hard job at the best of times,' she said one day as Carenza was considering her future. 'City teaching can be tough. You know what Elsie and Nancy have said.'

'I want to stay here. I can't even think about going to London or any big city,' Carenza said.

'Well that's settled then.' The subject was closed.

May had looked at her daughter for a moment wondering what had made her think this way. The thought of her East End roots and the loss of her family might have been the reason behind her decision but May was tactful enough to say nothing. It had been quite some time since Carenza had mentioned her blood family. The subject was never swept under the carpet but was discussed openly if it was ever raised although May never instigated the topic.

Carenza had been the successful candidate subject to her passing her examinations. Now that this was a fait accompli Carenza was excited about the way her life was going but deep down she wanted more out of life in the future. The teaching job was only the beginning of the road. It would make her financially independent of May. She loved May beyond any doubt but May had given her so much over the years that she did not want to be a burden to her more than she had to be now that she was getting older.

The security and love that May had bestowed on her over the years had made her into the person she was today. The poverty trap of her life in the East End was now only a remote memory. She had lived comfortably in recent years enjoying May's generosity and had found that she enjoyed being regarded as a member of the middle class, but this had never gone to Carenza's head. Her feet were firmly rooted in terra firma. May had made her sole heir. The bond that had been forged in the early days of their relationship was tight and nobody could ever come between them. There were no hidden secrets but Carenza wanted to show that although she had May's backing and blessing she was able to make something of herself through her own efforts. There was much that she wanted to prove to herself. Her independence was like a shining beacon which would always be there. Into all these longings was the desire to create a blood family of her own, though marriage was not on the cards for the immediate future.

Returning from Manchester where she had done her teacher training was no great hardship for Carenza but she had widened her horizons beyond village life. She had also made firm friends with people of her own age and her new status. She rarely divulged her early childhood to recent acquaintances. This had nothing to do with snobbery but it was too painful and complicated to explain, but she did reveal her adoption by May and left the rest to chance hoping that nobody would delve too deeply into her background. She was not ashamed of her humble origins but the tragedies she had suffered during her early childhood were firmly locked away. Life had to move forward. She kept her mind set to the future hoping now that she could drive the vehicle of her own destiny as much as fate would allow.

During her time in Manchester she had met Tom who was reading law at university. They had begun their friendship as just that. There were no romantic interludes between them but they were close and were always there for each other.

'Are you coming out tonight?' Tom would say. 'The others will be there. We could go to the pub or to the flicks.'

'All right,' Carenza would say. She was determined to enjoy her student days without attachments. Her reaction was to giggle at Tom when he said 'flicks' in his received pronunciation English. There were times when he wanted to be one of the gang rather than one of the chaps.

'What's up?' he would say but his innate good humour made him laugh at himself.

Although Carenza did not deny her roots it was impossible now to detect that she had begun life in the East End. Her world in academia had become her greatest influence. As her studies were beginning to come to an end the axis of her relationship with Tom had turned full circle. He felt that their separation in the future as the outside world beckoned was not what he wanted. Their relationship which had begun life as a good friendship had deepened into something else, certainly on his own part. But Carenza remained true to her ideals of not rushing into anything too soon as they had all the time in the world.

Chapter 16

Tom Heston had wanted to become a solicitor for as long as he could remember. It had become a tradition since his great grandfather's time that the male members of his family followed the path which had been set out for them, joining the family firm when they had finished their law degrees. This law firm had been established well before the end of the previous century and its reputation was well known through the local area attracting clients from all walks of life but mostly the affluent frequented the offices of J. B. Heston and Associates. The wealth of the family had grown steadily over the years and they no longer acknowledged their once humble origins. In fact the menfolk had married well into other wealthy families. Tom's mother, Lorna, came from a titled family and although she did not bear a title she socialized amongst the elite of society. She had experienced the coming out ball at the palace in front of King George and Queen Mary. She had hoped to find a husband that year but had not met the man of her dreams until a few years later when her path crossed that of Tom's father, Spencer Heston.

Tom was snobbish in many ways having been brought up to live a life amongst the upper middle class but his time at university and the aftermath of war had made him more realistic than the generations that preceded him. He wanted to bring the solicitor's firm into the twentieth century. He knew that his grandfather ran it as his family had always run it. Although old Jeremiah only now worked two days a week his finger was still firmly on the pulse of all the happenings within the offices. Spencer Heston was waiting for the day he could take the reins to make the business truly his own. Tom was aware of all these problems but it had not deterred him from believing that he was the man to continue the way forward. He possessed a young man's vision and idealism believing that his father would continue much in the same vein as Jeremiah.

Tom had graduated from university with a first class degree in law. His father believed that Tom needed time to enjoy life before he settled down into the world of work. His mother was not so sure.

'Darling, you know that Tom needs direction. He will spend his time loafing about with old friends with no direction. He will be away for weekends anywhere in the country.' Lorna Heston wanted her only son where she could keep an eye on him.

'My dear you know I have made up my mind. It will be good for Tom to have a break from his studies. You know he has met a girl during his time at university. It will be good for him to get her out of his mind and then settle down to the next phase of his life before he marries.'

'He has not mentioned anyone to me Spencer. Who is she?' Lorna whined at her husband.

Spencer knew the signs after many years of marriage. He also knew that Tom would not confide in his mother about his personal life because she would interrogate him beyond endurance. Tom was their only son, which placed him under enormous pressure academically and emotionally. Spencer was too involved with the family firm to live and breathe his son's life. It was not that he was disinterested but his wife still lived the life of a pre-war lady of a certain age. She expected her menfolk to pay her attention and spoil her as had been the custom during her privileged childhood. Spencer did not feel able to accommodate this side of his wife's life. Their marriage had been under great strain for a number of years.

'She is nobody of consequence my dear; just a passing acquaintance of Tom's. She is going to be a teacher. He met her in Manchester: Carenza somebody or other.'

'Oh,' was all that she could utter, totally flabbergasted that Spencer had received so much news from their son and convinced that this girl would not be good enough for her precious son.

It had been decreed that Tom would enter the firm after Christmas with a stipulation that work was then his top priority. In the intervening months he was allowed to do what he liked within reason. He had his allowance, which he had to agree had been settled upon him very generously by his father and grandfather, but when he started work he had to earn his own living which was the benchmark by which he had to learn life skills. His father was adamant that Tom would become a sensible member of society as well as the person who in future years would run the firm of solicitors wisely in readiness for future generations. If it was left to his wife, Lorna, Tom would be ruined by money and snobbery.

Tom knew that he was fortunate to have this time for self indulgence. He also knew that he wanted to make Carenza a more established part of his life. These thoughts had come very late in his friendship with her. Tom had met Carenza through mutual friends. Carenza's friend Jennifer had been her best friend through their two years of teacher training. Tom's friends, Joe and Hugh, had met the girls at a dance in Manchester and over time the five of them had become inseparable but were not romantically linked. Now Tom wanted to put this relationship on a more permanent footing. He wanted Carenza to be his girl. This would be more difficult to achieve if the friends continued to spend so much time together. Carenza had realized that Tom wanted more from their friendship than she was ready to give emotionally. She cared for Tom but not enough to put their relationship on a more permanent basis. She knew that she had to be true to herself and to May before anything else. Her teaching meant financial freedom and more responsibility for herself. May had been her anchor over the years taking on an emotionally disturbed child late in life. Now Carenza wanted to lessen the burden on May who deserved so much at this time. It was the moment for relaxation and fun.

'Tom, let's keep it light shall we. You know that we are going to stay in touch.'

'All right,' he had agreed not wanting to lose her by being too heavy into the relationship which might mean losing her. He also knew that neither of them was mature enough for marriage but it was what he wanted once he had established himself in the law firm.

Chapter 17

It was turning out to be an Indian summer. The days were shortening and the evenings growing cooler but the warmth of the autumn days was a joy. May spent her days in the garden tidying up in preparation for winter. She shuddered at the mere thought but laughed at her silliness. Her watch stated that it was lunchtime. She hoped that Carenza might come home for lunch today but she suspected not. Her new job at the school had taken over her life. She was enjoying it so much that she spent longer time than she needed making her classroom bright for her pupils and giving extra help to the children who were hoping to pass on to grammar school. Carenza remembered the extra tuition she had received which resulted in her success. It never hurt to give a little back.

On this late September day it was too hot to stay working indoors. The noise in the playground reminded Carenza that she still had some of her lunchtime left. She exited the school building crossing the minefield of a playground. It took her two minutes to stride purposely home to find May munching her sandwich under the trees sitting on the old bench trying to keep cool. They smiled contentedly at each other. Carenza reached out to take an apple that May had placed in the basket. She had collected up the windfalls as one of her morning chores. Carenza rubbed the apple against the skirt of her dress and with a crunch bit into it.

'There was a telephone call for you,' May said.

Carenza looked surprised.

'Who,' she replied.

'Tom somebody, I didn't catch his last name.'

'Tom Heston. You know, my friend from college days.'

'No. I don't know, only a friend?'

May raised her eyebrow in question. Carenza giggled.

'I may have mentioned him to you in passing. There is nothing else to say really. We might have walked out a few times before we left.'

'Well he seemed very keen to get hold of you.' May kept her face straight but was secretly pleased that there might be another part to Carenza's life other than work. Carenza had the good grace to blush before she giggled to break the intensity of the moment.

'What did he want?'

'He wanted to see you as soon as possible. He said that it had been weeks since he had spoken to you. I told him to visit on Saturday but to bring some nightwear if he wanted to stay.' Her lips twitched with amusement.

'Oh May you didn't did you.' Carenza was helpless with mirth but tried to look stern at the same time. Her face became distorted until she had pulled herself together.

'You know I always tell you the truth. That was one of my rules before you came to live with me.'

Carenza's face had sobered. She knew this to be true.

'What time is he coming then?'

'He will be here for lunch on Saturday. Have you seen the time?'

Carenza looked at her watch. 'Oh my word I'm going to be late,' she squealed.

'I expect that they'll sack you.' May shouted after her with a gleam of mischief in her eyes.

The last comment was lost on her daughter as she ran down the path without looking back. May smiled. She had no intention of interfering in Carenza's affairs but a romantic interlude did not hurt anybody. She sighed loudly remembering the loss of her own young man during the First World War. What might have been, she mused to herself, but pulled herself together. Her path might have taken a different direction but she had no regrets as life was too short. Carenza had always been the greatest gift that the Almighty had placed in her path.

*

Tom had missed Carenza. How long had it been since he had seen her? He was struggling to remember but he could not let her go. His mother's reaction to Tom's romance had convinced him that their relationship was worth fighting for. Lorna Heston was of the opinion that her only son should make a marriage that would be suitable for his class. He had several girl cousins who would all fill this void if necessary. Love did not always enter into marriage in their class but Tom was a romantic at heart. But Lorna did not want some girl who had grown up in a rural backwater to feel that they could take Tom away from her. She knew that Spencer thought that she was being ridiculous.

Lorna had managed to fill Tom's free time by endless rounds of parties and tennis matches where the young offspring of family friends were paraded in front of him but he was not interested. It had taken him some time to work out his mother's motives but now he had decided to take his life in his own hands before his treasured free time ran out. He had lied to his parents on several occasions by telling them that he was going to stay with various friends, some of whom did not exist.

'I'm going to stay with Hugh down in London. I haven't seen him in ages,' he blustered. He did not want his mother ruling his life.

'But you can't darling,' Lorna purred at him.' Your cousin Sadie is coming to stay. She hasn't seen you for ages.'

'She was here three weeks ago.' His voice had taken on an acidic tone. 'I have no wish to see the Honourable Sadie for quite some time.'

'But Tom, be reasonable she will be so disappointed if you are not here. Spencer, reason with him please.'

'Mother you are only trying to match make and I'm not yet ready for marriage,' he lied.

Spencer Heston looked at his wife with annoyance. She had seen the withering look on his face. It had been there quite a lot lately. It had the effect of silencing her immediately. She did not want to push her husband beyond the limits of endurance. She had been worried lately because the rumour monger had been at work. A friend of a friend had commented that Spencer had been seen coming out of a restaurant in Manchester only two weeks before with a fashionably dressed woman on his arm. They had seemed very cosy together. Lorna had known it had happened before but she had chosen to turn a blind eye for the moment. However, she knew that she was not going to do this indefinitely. She was not prepared to be the laughing stock of local society. She would have to remind Spencer that her inheritance had helped the Hestons when the law firm had gone through a rough patch and it had bought the imposing Edwardian house where they now resided.

Spencer did not wish to be reminded that during certain times of his marriage his wife's wealth had made a difference to various facets of their lives. He had felt humbled by such an event, rather unmanly in fact. It had enabled them to keep up the pretence of the prosperity that they enjoyed even when business was at a low ebb. But the house was the crème de la crème of the ostentation that fronted their life together. It was a large house built in a huge acreage of land. It offered all the trappings of the era in which it was built. There were stables and servants' quarters which were rarely used since the war years, which had changed most people's lives forever. This had been one of the greatest regrets of the Heston family. This was one area in their joint lives where they agreed unanimously. Lorna was not prepared to lift a finger in her home. They had staff, who came daily, but they paid well for the services they received and managed to keep their servants longer than their more impoverished friends.

Spencer read Lorna's facial expressions well. Even now he knew that it was his turn to backtrack. He was not sure that Lorna knew about his most recent indiscretion but it was a lady of whom he felt very fond. By keeping the peace in their marriage he felt that he could continue his dalliances without losing face.

'Son, would it be a good idea if you met your friend this weekend but placated your mother soon?'

Lorna had noticed that she had scored in this round and was magnanimous to concede to the idea. Tom smiled his handsome smile. He had won too.

'Of course Ma,' he replied.

'Don't call me that dear. It is a little too common for my liking.'

Tom ignored the comment. 'Is it all right if I have the car this weekend?'

Spencer nodded.

'Go easy on the petrol though old thing.'

'Will do.'

*

Carenza was excited about Tom's impending visit. She was fond of him but would not go as far as saying that she loved him. Marriage was out of the question. Her immediate focus was her career and her independence. May had insisted that she still keep her allowance that she had received once she had gone to college to do her training. It was the one thing that they had argued about

135

since Carenza had returned home. But May was determined that Carenza would have the life that had been denied her in her early years in the East End. May was far from snobbish but she was practical and Carenza was the daughter that she had always wanted if her fiancé had lived. Carenza was May's heir and she could not have been prouder of her. Her full knowledge of Carenza's early years in the East End had not been divulged fully at the beginning of their relationship but over time the pieces of the jigsaw had begun to fit together. Elsie and Nancy, the two young teachers had given her information, as much as they knew, and Carenza's pieces, offered after her mental well- being was on the mend, filled in the gaps until finally May had the full picture. She was full of admiration for Doris and the way that she had kept the family together under the most difficult of circumstances. Poverty was a killer but pride had to be kept intact if there was any left to hang on to. Her assessment of her daughter's natural parents was enough to make her blood boil but these thoughts she kept to herself. The fact that Carenza had turned into the well balanced young woman that she was, was credit only to herself and nobody else. May's ego was not huge and brushed aside any thought that she might have made some contribution to the process.

May was also anxious for Carenza to marry well. She was not pushing her into marriage yet because Carenza was not ready for such a gigantic step. Her independence was legendary and May was ready to support her all the way but she had to make provision and protection for this child who had come to her so late in life. It had been on her mind lately that time was marching forward at high speed and she might not be around for Carenza when she required the wisdom of an older person. May had approached Edgar with these morbid thoughts wanting to seek advice on such matters. Edgar had laughed at her.

'You have many years left in you yet May. You are as fit as a fiddle.'

May smiled feeling foolish, 'May be Edgar but it is a niggling worry when you get to my age.'

'But you know that Jeannette and I will be here for her. She might have been our daughter if circumstances had been different,' he smiled sheepishly remembering back over the years. 'And just think how old I was when we had Helen. Even Jeannette was regarded as an older mother.'

'You have been a good friend to us Edgar and I know how fond Carenza is of your family,' she replied, 'I'm just being a foolish old woman and Carenza will marry one day. I often forget that she has nearly reached the legal age.'

The subject had never been mentioned again but May in her observations knew that she seemed to be having more visits from Jeannette and Helen than she had had in months. She blessed Edgar's kindness and thoughtfulness. They were the best and their friendship was treasured above anything.

Chapter 18

Tom had never visited Nether Heydon before. But he had consulted his map and realized that the journey was only thirty miles away. He could take his time meandering along, taking in the scenery as he drove or he could even stop for a pint before he arrived. It might be difficult to get one during the rest of the weekend. He knew that his mother disapproved of him drinking while he was driving but she was not here now. There was nothing like severing the umbilical cord he mused. Would life have been easier if he had had siblings? He didn't know but his mother might have been less possessive if he had. But he knew that Carenza was an only child and she never complained about any such problems but then again she divulged very little about herself.

He drove into the village of Nether Heydon. The Indian summer was still holding making everything golden hued in the autumn sunshine. He knew that Carenza had said that he had to look out for a black and white cottage near the centre of the village so he slowed his speed to a crawl. The only black and white cottage he observed was quite a substantial dwelling. Carenza was adamant that it was a cottage but he was quite amazed at the size of the building. Was his Carenza from an affluent background after all? He was not in any way interested in the fact that Carenza might come into money one day because he knew that he would inherit well in the fullness of time but this knowledge would somehow placate his snobbish mother.

The door opened revealing a pink cheeked Carenza, suddenly feeling a buzz of happiness that she had not expected to happen because she had sternly lectured herself on her independence and her reluctance to commit to any permanent relationship until she was ready.

Tom had parked the car on the side of the road. He stepped out with a jaunty air which made Carenza giggle and opened his arms wide allowing her to walk straight into his embrace.

'Hello stranger,' he said. 'What a prize for sore eyes you are. Missed me?'

'Actually I have,' she said surprising herself. 'Come on in and meet my mother.'

Tom sobered up at the thought. 'Will I pass muster?'

'Oh Tom, don't be ridiculous. May is not like that. She is the most down to earth person I know. She never passes judgement on anyone.'

Tom visibly relaxed and picked up his small, brown leather suitcase.

The front curtains of the other houses in the direct vicinity twitched as the young couple hugged again. Among the people who had observed this event was May. She smiled to herself but a tear travelled down her downy cheek as emotion overwhelmed her. She wiped it away in irritation scolding herself for having spied on her daughter. Carenza would not forgive her if she knew that she had emulated the actions of her neighbours.

May opened the French windows into the garden. A sweet smell of autumn flooded the room. Carenza was showing Tom the garden, allowing themselves a little more privacy before she brought her sweetheart indoors to meet her mother. If May was honest she was nervous too. The old structure of their world was changing. It was difficult for her to fully accept that Carenza was an adult now. At her next birthday she would be twenty one and able to make her own decisions. There had been too many changes since the War but they had all to be dealt with as stoically as possible. Carenza brought Tom indoors. They were both animated by their togetherness once more but it was now time for May and Tom to meet.

If Tom was honest with himself he was quite taken aback by the age of May. He had expected someone no older than fifty like his own mother. But here there was a matriarch who could have passed as Carenza's grandmother. Carenza put her arm round May, hugging her reassuringly. Tom did his best to cover his confusion.

'May, I want you to meet Tom Heston.'

May offered her hand to be shaken. 'Hello, Tom. It is good to meet you at last. I have heard all about you and welcome.'

He had the grace to blush slightly.

'I hope that it was good stuff, Mrs. Faithful.'

'Miss Faithful,' May corrected him straight away. Get it right from the start, she mused to herself.

Tom looked embarrassed by this statement feeling that May was being rather bold in her forwardness. He felt that he was a modern young man but perhaps this was taking things a step too far.

Carenza had witnessed this conversation in a state of amusement. It did not hurt Tom to get something so wrong. He was quite a snob in many ways but she intervened to put him out of his misery.

'Tom, May is Miss Faithful. She adopted me when I was fifteen. She is the best mother in the world.' Her arm still encircling May hugged her tighter to endorse her words. Tom smiled sheepishly.

'Sorry my mistake.'

'There is no problem Tom. I never married as simple as that. Now shall we have a cup of tea before you two decide what you are going to for the rest of the day?'

Carenza had found the whole business very amusing and knew that May would comment on the situation at another time. Her mother's sense of humour was legendary.

May was relieved that their first meeting was over. She would be more relaxed when they returned from their walk but they would not be long for the days were rapidly shortening and it looked as if the Indian summer was coming to an end. The sky was overcast and stormy.

Tom had enjoyed his visit to Nether Heydon. His reunion with Carenza had gone better than he could have anticipated. He was certain that he loved her but was unsure about her true feelings towards himself. He had tried not to be too forward in his advances but knew that their blossoming relationship would have to be nurtured like a delicate flower. On Sunday they attended morning service at church. Edgar had stood by the door of the old and rather beautiful church after the service speaking to his flock like he did every Sunday. He was aware of the new presence at his service and wondered where the romance would lead. Would he be marrying Carenza and Tom in the fullness of time? He reached for May's hand squeezing it harder than normal.

'Lovely to meet Carenza's young man at last May. Perhaps I might be marrying them one day,' His eyes twinkled in merriment.

'Hush now. Don't let Carenza hear you say that or you will be in terrible trouble,' came the retort.

'What are you two plotting.' Carenza had caught the hushed whispers.

'Why ever would we be plotting my girl? Hello Tom. Good to meet you. We have all heard a lot about you,' Edgar offered his hand.

'Good to meet you, Sir.'

'Right, best foot forward if Tom has to go back after lunch.' May gave Edgar one last glance but now his attention had moved to the rest of his parishioners.

'Glad to see you,' he could be heard saying repeatedly until they were too far away to hear any more.

Chapter 19

Autumn had passed into the crispness of shorter winter days. Carenza had never felt so happy. She loved her job more than she had ever imagined. Life was full of excitement. Her contentment was mirrored by May who understood the fulfilment of the career that they had both shared. But May was aware of Tom's encroachment into their lives. He had still not started his career and was free to come and go whenever he liked. He did not out- stay his welcome but the two women who shared a close bond found that they had little time to enjoy each other's company.

His appearance every weekend was as if it was his right to be there. Tom was enjoying the relaxed atmosphere of Carenza's home and he could not but compare it to the strain and tension that raged between his own parents. It was when he visited other people's homes that he realized that he lived in a potential minefield and had to tread on eggshells to retain any harmony. May wanted to know his intentions but was reluctant to intrude into their private world. There were times when she wanted solitude but she did not want to upset Carenza who was so happy. Carenza had had a lot of heartache during her life and now all of that was changing. May was protective of her daughter at all costs. She wanted to see her well established in her life before Carenza was able to leave her home and set up on her own.

Christmas loomed. It was now only three weeks away. The Christmas Carol concert was the highlight of the end of term. There was hustle and bustle in the school and excitement all around. The classrooms had been decorated by the children themselves. Sticky gummed paper had been transformed into paper chains and hung at jaunty angles. Carenza had caught the infectious excitement of the children. But the more experienced members of staff were bad tempered. They had been through all of this before.

'What are you doing Billy?' Carenza asked one member of her class.

'Nothing Miss,' he said but the colour of his cheeks told rather a different story.

'Why are your pockets bulging.' She wanted to laugh at the villain she had caught. 'Empty them please.'

'Don't want to Miss,' Billy continued.

'Well if you don't then I shall have to take you to see Mrs Carter and I know how good she is at using the cane.' Her voice had become grave and her look was one of severity.

Billy hung his head.

'I didn't mean to do it Miss.' His pockets were emptied onto the nearest table where fruit and some sweets rolled about. The staff had done their best to collect small luxuries for the children as a Christmas treat. It had taken all their efforts to achieve this with rationing still a major problem. Carenza looked at the child knowing that he came from a very poor home and he had several siblings who had to fight for anything they had.

'Billy you are being greedy and selfish. You have taken your share and other people's. You must never do this again.'

'No Miss,' he said as the tears began to fall. Carenza put her arm around him and remembered how little she had had as a child but she had never stolen. She could smell the stale odour of unwashed clothes. Her heart went out to him for the neglect that he suffered.

'You must promise me that this will never happen again.'

'I promise that this will never happen again Miss.'

Billy was not a naughty boy but an unfortunate one. It made her count her own blessings all over again.

'Well on this occasion we will leave it there.'

'Yes Miss. Thank you Miss.' Billy grateful that he was not to receive the cane, disappeared as quickly as he could, leaving Carenza with a lot to think about.

On her return home that night, Carenza recounted the tale as it had happened.

'Who is the child?' asked May.

'It's Billy Pearson,' Carenza told her wondering if her mother could throw any light on the family with her great knowledge of the locality.

'The Pearsons are very dysfunctional. They have a small-holding not far from where the Dunwoodys used to live.' She glanced at Carenza to see if this knowledge would cause a flicker of response but her daughter had kept her equilibrium.

'The children have always brought themselves up. There have been generations of neglect,' she continued, 'and they steal because they have no love or attention.'

Carenza exhaled loudly

'How terrible. What can be done about it?'

'Not a lot,' said May. 'People have to rise above adversity and wish to help themselves.'

May looked at her daughter thinking that although Carenza had had much help in her short life, it had been her own tenacity, her inner strength that had ultimately set her on the road to success.

Behaviour had nosedived into rudeness and back biting. Even the most amenable of children had changed within days of the mention of Christmas. May laughed when Carenza told her tales. Memories came flooding back to her of her own experiences at school. But she knew that she would not want to return to such events now. The village church had been decorated. The large models of the nativity had been carefully removed from their tissue paper and set the scene for the festivities. The crib was placed in front of the rood screen where it could be observed by the congregation when they came up to the altar during their turn for communion. The school children were led to the church to view the proceedings and to practise their carols. Some children would never set foot in the church if it was left to their parents. Edgar and Jeannette did whatever it took to make the children as welcome as they could. The whole village was busy and amidst this melee Tom had made a decision to invite Carenza to his own home for the festivities.

He did have the courtesy to ask if it was a possibility, but he approached his father first.

'I don't see why not old boy,' Spencer replied, 'but you must ask your mother first. She always has these plans for the festive season.'

Spencer was not a great lover of the festive period. It conflicted with his own activities which he had to curtail for appearance sake. He still had his mistress but he knew that he would not see her for days. He knew that Lorna had her suspicions but by being malleable and agreeing to whatever had been arranged he was keeping his wife sweet tempered. She would also believe that she had misjudged him.

Tom approached his mother one evening when her best friend Lady Margaret Sands had dined with the family. Lorna could hardly make a fuss in front of her guest. Appearance and etiquette were everything to her.

Tom lingered in the drawing room until there was a break in the conversation.

'Darling, what can I do for you?' Lorna looked at her son with adoration. Lady Margaret looked in anticipation. She had no children of her own and felt a great affection for this good looking young man.

'Well,' he stuttered not finding it easy to approach the topic of Carenza. His mother never wanted to know. 'Dad thinks that it would be fine to invite Carenza for Christmas. But he did say to ask you out of politeness of course.' He looked straight at his mother and smiled the smile that she could never resist. Lady Margaret looked on indulgently waiting for Lorna to acquiesce.

Lorna's eyes narrowed into almost cat like slits but her voice retained the same calm tone. Tom was fully aware that his mother was angry inside and possibly jealous of his blossoming romance. Lorna liked to have her finger on the pulse of every event within the family but she was gradually losing control. Lady Margaret looked on with interest. She had not known that Tom had a young lady in tow. She wondered who had bewitched him sufficiently to enable Lorna to react so badly. Lady Margaret knew her friend and her faults well enough.

'Darling, can we discuss this at a later time? Margaret and I have a lot to talk about,' Lorna looked steely-eyed at her son. Lady Margaret was enjoying this brief exchange of words. Obviously things were not right here. She wished to know more so that she could pass on titbits to her more exclusive circle of friends. She admonished herself for her lack of loyalty to her friend.

'Don't mind me Lorna dear,' she oozed charm. Lorna had no choice but to listen to her son.

'It will only be for a couple of nights, Ma. I have spent so much time in Nether Heydon that I thought that it might be only fair to reciprocate with our hospitality. You have brought me up to be respectful and well mannered to others.' Tom knew that his mother could not disagree with that, particularly in such prestigious company.

'Oh very well,' Lorna smiled icily at her son. The conversation was at an end as she turned once more to Lady Margaret. 'Where were we my dear?'

Tom beamed. He had got what he wanted without all the hassle that he had expected. He telephoned Nether Heydon before his mother had the opportunity to cancel the whole proceedings.

*

May answered the telephone on the third ring. It was Tom. He was rather taken aback to hear May because it was usually Carenza who answered but he was not about to inform her why he was ringing. He did feel some semblance of guilt that he might be taking Carenza away from May at such a special time of year. He was not usually prone to feelings of guilt but he was concerned that Carenza would decline his invitation.

'Is Carenza there May? It is rather important.'

May grimaced. Carenza stood in the doorway to the sitting room waiting to be handed the telephone. May smiled and handed over the receiver. She returned to the sitting room and closed the door. Her curiosity was aroused but she would never be accused of eavesdropping on her daughter. That was not her style. She was sure that Carenza would tell her in time.

A few minutes later May's curiosity was rewarded.

Carenza was caught in a dilemma that she was not sure how to handle. She did not want to leave May by herself over Christmas but she also wanted to meet Tom's family. He had talked so much about them that she felt that she almost knew them.

'Bad news?' May asked observing Carenza's expression.

'Not bad news, just unexpected.'

'Out with it.' May cajoled her daughter to tell her the problem.

'Tom wants me to spend Christmas with his family. I couldn't give him an answer so he was annoyed with me.'

May nodded in sympathy.

'Don't mind about me Carenza. I shall be fine. I have plenty of friends I can see. Go and ring him back and tell him that you can make it.'

Carenza was not sure. She did not want to leave May on her own but her mother was insistent. Carenza returned Tom's call. She felt disloyal about leaving May to her own devices over the festive period. When she had finished her conversation with Tom she had an idea which would salve her conscience. Carenza had always possessed too much of a conscience and was constantly guilt ridden. Quietly she took her coat from the chair in the hall and put it on. May was too engrossed in her book to hear the front door open and close.

Jeannette opened the front door of the vicarage to Carenza. It had turned very cold over the previous few days and it seemed strange to be making social calls at this time of day when the temperature was at its lowest. Carenza slipped through the half open front door into the ever draughty hallway of the old vicarage. They entered the high ceilinged sitting room where the log fire roared in the huge fireplace. Edgar and Helen were playing chess and the wireless was turned low but a classical pianist played her piece of music sweetly to contribute to the homely atmosphere of the room.

'Welcome,' Edgar boomed from his corner. Helen turned and smiled at Carenza. Their game had reached its conclusion with Helen looking smug from her triumph. Jeannette kept her face straight knowing that her husband had allowed her daughter to win again.

Carenza recounted her problem. Like May she found it easy to confide problems to Edgar and Jeannette. There always seemed to be a simple solution when she had off loaded them onto the shoulders of this wonderful couple. Their patience was endless but they had so much time for everyone.

'I don't know what to do about it. Tom is very persuasive. But May should not be left on her own, especially on Christmas Day. She has done so much for me over time that I feel so guilty if I leave her,' she had said.

'This isn't a problem Carenza, May must spend Christmas with us.' Jeannette had found the solution so simple. 'You often spend part of Christmas here, so this year will be no exception. May knows that at some point that your lives will change, so you do not need to feel guilty.'

'I don't know how to thank you,' Carenza was overcome with gratitude and now her conscience felt clear.

'You don't need to thank us Carenza. We are like family.' Jeannette put her arms around Carenza's shoulders and hugged her.

After Carenza had departed Edgar looked at Jeannette. 'Carenza is the most wonderful daughter to May.'

'And don't you ever doubt it Edgar that May knows that. They care for each other very much. It has been so wonderful to see their lives work out so well. It makes me feel inadequate to think that we failed Carenza all those years ago.'

'You did not fail her, my dear. I made the final decision on the matter.' Edgar was always prepared to take the feeling of guilt on his own shoulders. 'I wish more of my flock were like that.'

'Edgar, it was both our faults that we could not cope with Carenza and her problems. May has been a tower of strength throughout Carenza's childhood.'

He smiled.

'I know,' was his reply. 'And it will be good to have her for Christmas. Carenza is now an adult so there could be more of these occasions in the future.'

Chapter 20

Carenza's first term of teaching had finished five days before Christmas. She was jubilant about her survival and about what she had achieved. As the last of the children left to begin their holiday she looked around her domain where, as recently as the day before Christmas, friezes had lined the walls showing the nativity and wintry scenes depicted by the most talented of artists and the least. The battered paper chains were spilling over the sides of the classroom bin. Any decorations that had survived the festive period had been claimed by children who had very little at home and they treated these treasured possessions like gold dust. Littered on the teacher's desk was a detritus of presents. There was a mixture of the expensive to the home made offerings. It was the home made cards that brought a lump to Carenza's throat. These she valued above all else for they showed the genuine affection of her children but it brought back memories of her own impoverished childhood when she had made her own cards for her teachers and her family. These emotions had lain dormant for so long. They had been buried deep inside her but had surfaced so easily after all this time. A tear trickled down her cheek as she remembered Doris, Hannah, Frank and her father Ray.

What would they think of her now? Her life bore no resemblance to her early years in the East End. She had a career, money in her pocket and a home life that was very middle class. Guilty emotions overcame her. Her whole life had been transformed the day that she had stepped off the bus in Nether Heydon. She would always love her birth family, always be grateful for Doris's love and care but she knew without doubt that she loved May as much as she could love anyone.

She could not believe where this well of emotion could have erupted from so suddenly. She heard the creak of the classroom door as it was opened. The back of her hand rubbed the remnants of her tears as she turned to see who was there. May, heavy-footed entered the room and surveyed the chaotic scene before her. She remembered many days such as this at the end of term.

'Come on home Carenza,' she said. 'Let's collect up all your things and celebrate the end of your first term.'

If she had noticed Carenza's tears she did not comment but placed the higgledy piggledy mass of gifts in her shopping bag as they turned out the lights allowing the gloom of dusk to embrace them as they left the old building.

May was happy to visit the vicarage for Christmas. The solution had freed Carenza from guilt and had enabled her to visit the Hestons on Christmas Eve, but before she left she had many things to do. She had visited Worcester to do her shopping. This year there were more presents to buy. Her visit to the Hestons meant that she had to buy for people she did not know, and that in itself was a great dilemma. Alcohol was a safe present for Tom's father. Tom had implied that he enjoyed his whisky but his mother was proving to be particularly difficult. In the end she bought a silk scarf in subdued, muted tones. It was better to be subtle in her choice rather than too flamboyant. Her gift for Tom proved to be far easier. He was starting work in January and she had chosen a pair of cufflinks which he had pointed out to her on a previous visit to the city.

Loaded down with her purchases she stepped off the bus which dropped her on the main road before it wound its way through the narrow lanes to the other villages on its route. There was still daylight left but she could feel the temperature dropping. Carenza shivered, only too pleased that she had such a short distance to walk before she was home. She knew that May would have the huge fire lit in the drawing room and she could not wait to be inside in the warm. As she drew level with her home she recognized the car that was parked outside. She was puzzled by Tom's presence two days before he was due to pick her up on Christmas Eve. She was not pleased by the intrusion his presence would bring. Both women were due to enjoy a festive time together before her departure. It was part of their ritual that they would do so even though they often spent time with Edgar, Jeannette and Helen.

Tom and May were in deep conversation as she entered the drawing room.

'Hello,' she said waiting for an explanation for his unexpected appearance.

This intrusion into their plans annoyed Carenza. She had wanted to make the evening special for the two of them. It was their opportunity to exchange presents and to enjoy each other's company. That was part of their relationship. They enjoyed their time together. It was precious.

'Carenza, hello, I've come early. I will stay until Christmas Eve. May doesn't mind, do you May?'

May smiled thinly at them and Carenza knew that she did mind but Tom had invited himself without any thought or feeling for anybody else.

'Dinner won't be long then,' May rose stiffly from her chair to attend to the meal which was exuding a delicious aroma from the kitchen.

Carenza was becoming intolerant of Tom. He was beginning to take over their lives and that had not been part of her plan, to be possessed by anyone. She was not engaged to him and had no intention of that happening for quite some time if at all. Her independence was sacred. If she married him she would have no life of her own.

'Tom. Why are you here?' She could not afford to be too subtle in her attitude towards him. Tom looked bemused. He was not used to such straight talking.

'I thought you would want me with you Carenza. It is Christmas after all,' he managed to look hurt. He had used these tactics when he was a child, allowing his mother to melt inside. On many issues Lorna Heston had a hard heart but Tom had always melted the iceberg. These days he was not as malleable as he had been as a child and they were often in conflict.

'Tonight is my special night with May. This will be the first Christmas I have spent apart from her in years. You could have waited as we had arranged.'

'Well I'll go then if I am not wanted.' He sounded petulant.

'Of course you'll stay but be more thoughtful in future.' She reprimanded him sternly but she was unable to be angry with him for long and had to admit that she cared for him more than she had let on. May had observed this conversation from the kitchen doorway. Although she had not been experienced in the art of love it was not difficult to see the bond that had developed between the two young people.

Tom beamed at Carenza. He knew that she was vulnerable and soft hearted under her steely exterior. Leaning back in his chair he sat comfortably listening to the homely noises that emanated from all around him. There was much clattering from the kitchen where

May was in full control of all procedures. His mother was never one to cook. It was far beneath her to visit the kitchen where someone else produced their meals which were eaten in the formality of the dining room. Here May and Carenza ate their meals in the informality of the homely kitchen. Their dining room was rarely used. On the rare occasion when Tom had seen the dining room, the long refectory table was often cluttered with school books or May's detritus of untidiness.

'It's ready,' May shouted from the depths of the kitchen. The two young people smiled at each other as they followed the delicious aroma of the food that awaited them.

Tom enjoyed his visits to Carenza's home. It was full of love and togetherness, which was not found in his home environment. His mother wanted to control and manipulate himself and his father. Now that he was an adult he could understand why his father spent as much time away from home as he could. He often suspected Spencer of having an affair but now that he was older he was past caring. He would leave home before too long and produce his own safe world which he hoped would include Carenza and children. But he had not believed that Carenza's independence meant so much to her. He had grown up in an environment where women wanted to be married and cared for. It was May who had set the precedent of being independent and in charge of her own life. He knew nothing about Carenza's early life and the poverty of the hand to mouth existence that had been all consuming. Wanting security was her top priority but it did not have to be in a married way. She did not want other people to keep her, for marriages did not always work out as expected. She wanted to be at the helm of her own ship without being reliant on others. There was no way that she wanted a man who might turn out to be a wastrel like her father nor did she want to turn out to be like her mother whose dreams had been ground into the dust because she was too weak to keep on top of events.

Carenza knew that she had inherited Doris' wisdom and determination to set her life on the right course but her greatest educator had been May who had always been in control of her own destiny.

Chapter 21

It was just after lunch that May waved Carenza and Tom off on their journey to spend Christmas with Tom's parents. May was more upset about these events than she had realized but her pride prevented her from showing Carenza her true emotions. She knew that she was being ridiculous because Carenza was due to return home in two days. There was a busy schedule ahead of her which, once she embarked on the forthcoming activities would keep her entertained and her mind occupied.

Carenza had been perfectly aware of May's feelings but had disguised her knowledge by her flurry of activity to load her case and bag into Tom's father's car. Tom was anxious to be off so that he and Carenza had time together before they reached his parents' home.

'You take care now,' May put her arms around Carenza to hug her tightly.

'I won't be away long,' Carenza reassured her mother. 'Make sure you enjoy your time with Jeannette and Edgar. They are looking forward to having you.'

'Everything will be fine,' May smiled. 'Off you go.'

As the car drew away May waved and watched it turn out of sight. 'You're a silly old woman,' she admonished herself as she rubbed a handkerchief across her teary eyes. There were no curtains twitching to witness her moment of weakness and for that she was very grateful.

It did not take Tom and Carenza long to drive to his parents' home but en route they had stopped to finish their Christmas shopping in Axley, a small market town a few miles from Tom's home village of Abford. It was a pretty town even in the gloom of a winter's day. In the distance they heard the festive rendition of early Christmas carols and the late shoppers buying the last of their presents. Carenza was pleased that she had completed her shopping in time. Tom was the last minute shopper scurrying to buy what he could for his family. His mother had always scolded him about his lack of thought in this direction. It was not good manners to treat people like that but she knew that the younger generation was different from her own. She blamed the war for many things.

People did not know their place like they once had. The old order had shifted in the wrong direction as far as she was concerned.

'Tom, you are useless,' Carenza admonished him.

He laughed easily with her.

'I am always like this. I'll never change unless in the future you will do it for me.'

'I don't know who you buy for or what they want,' came the quick retort. She had an idea where this conversation might lead.

'But you will Carenza as soon as we are married.' It had not meant to come out like that but it was what he had been thinking for weeks now. Tom had hoped to propose to her over the Christmas period before she returned to Nether Heydon.

Carenza turned to Tom in a huff.

'Married, Tom. Where on earth did you get such an idea from? Don't be foolish. Neither of us is ready for marriage. We hardly know each other and we are far too young.'

Tom looked taken aback.

'But I thought we were heading that way very quickly. I start my career in a month and it would be lovely to come home to my wife in the evenings. Anyway all women want to be married.'

Carenza took a puzzled look at Tom. Had he not listened to anything she had said over all the time she had known him? He looked hurt by what she had said but Carenza was beginning to believe that Tom was a manipulator at heart. He did like to have his own way about most things. A smile crossed her face and the term 'male of the species' entered her mind. Tom took this smile as complicit that at some time she would marry him and was now relenting.

'Let's leave it for now and enjoy Christmas.' A quarrel was not the best way to start the festive season.

As it began to grow dark they had finished all the shopping. The air was cold and a frost was beginning to glisten on the pavements. They loaded the car with all Tom's presents. The store in the High Street had wrapped the gifts at a little extra cost. Carenza had shaken her head in despair but she knew that money was no object to his family. She would never have done that but she knew that she was squirrelling all her spare money away to give herself independence. It was ridiculous really because she knew that May had made her financially secure. Her early years had left her with feelings of insecurity which she could not eradicate even after all this time.

'Look there it is,' Tom pointed to the Heston residence as he began to slow the car. Carenza was dumbstruck. She knew that Tom was from a wealthy background but the house was palatial, covering three floors. His mother had heard the crunch of the car wheels on the gravel as it pulled off the road. She had been waiting in anticipation of their arrival desperate to meet the girl who had stolen her son's heart. Few girls would have been right for her son except the ones who bore a title or brought wealth into the family. She was certain that Carenza had no such credentials.

Lorna opened the porticoed front door. This was not usually a custom that she practiced but on this occasion she wanted to show a display of family spirit in front of Carenza.

'Tom. Glad you are home.' She stretched her arms out to hug her son.

'Hello Ma.' He allowed himself to be hugged. 'Meet Carenza.'

Lorna stretched her hand towards the girl noting the way she dressed and spoke.

She retained a civil air but there was no warmth in her demeanour.

'Welcome for Christmas,' she said.

'Thank you,' Carenza did not know what else to say. She had detected the coldness in Lorna's manner and the fixed smile on her face held no warmth. Carenza could not help but wonder what the next two days would bring. Part of her wished that she had remained at home with May. But Tom, aware of his mother's frostiness, hugged Carenza tightly to himself, hoping to give his mother a warning that nothing was going to spoil the few days that lay ahead of them.

Christmas Eve dinner was always formal in the Heston household. It was held promptly at eight o'clock and any tardiness was heavily frowned upon. Tom usually arrived on time but tonight he knocked on Carenza's bedroom door waiting to escort her to the dining room. He was playing the role that his mother had taught him.

'Tom, you are being silly.'

'Not silly at all Carenza. You look ravishing. Red suits you darling.'

Carenza had the grace to blush. He had never called her darling before but she supposed that it was an endearment that was used in his circle of family and friends. She had to admit too that she had taken her time to choose her dress for this very purpose and had spent a little too much despite the fact that there was still rationing. It had given her a feeling of poise and confidence to undertake meeting Tom's family for the first time. The way he had talked about his mother and her upper class connections had left Carenza feeling self conscious and gauche and she did not want to let Tom down. Taking her by the hand Tom led her down the stairs into the drawing room for pre-dinner drinks.

The room was pleasantly full of members of the family who were introduced to her. She could not remember all the names but found a rapport with Tom's father and grandfather. They were warm and inviting. Lorna was ingratiating herself with the titled cousins and their adult children. She managed to ignore Carenza for the rest of the evening but she could not side step the questions and interest that Carenza's presence engendered. Carenza was able to relax and enjoy the evening knowing that she was not under Lorna's close scrutiny. Tom had maintained a presence at her side for the duration of the evening not allowing Carenza to be eaten alive by the gossips and busybodies who frequented such social events.

Christmas Day passed in a haze of meals, presents and more family members who arrived for drinks. Carenza had enjoyed the day despite the fact that she had not felt too well. The business with Lorna had left her feeling ill at ease. She had had to make small talk to people that she did not know. She thought about May but she knew that she would be happy with Edgar and Jeannette.

During the night she woke feeling unwell. A great, heaviness hung over her chest, her head ached and her throat was sore and she could not sleep. She was meant to be returning home during the afternoon but as breakfast time approached she could not lift her head from the pillow. Tom knocked on her bedroom door to escort her downstairs.

'Are you up yet sleepy head?' he shouted to her.

Carenza's throat hurt too much for her to make any response and she lay still wondering what she was going to do about her return home. She was not sure that she would cope with the journey. Not receiving a reply Tom turned the handle of the door.

He expected Carenza to be asleep but instead he found her on fire. Her head felt hot to the touch and a temperature raged.

'Poor you,' he soothed her. 'I think that it is the doctor for you young lady.' Tom knew that she could not travel and was not fazed by the fact that her visit was extended. His mother was not pleased. She had not wanted the girl under her roof in the first place but the doctor had been adamant that Carenza could not be moved.

'I am afraid Mrs Heston it would be unwise to move Carenza. She needs to rest and must stay in bed for a few days,' the young doctor was adamant.

'But for how long?' Lorna blustered. 'Christmas is a busy time for us socially.'

Doctor Pembroke looked at the woman who stood before him and it was difficult for him to conceal his distaste.

'I will return to see my patient tomorrow,' he emphasized as he shrugged on his overcoat and picked up his Gladstone type bag to continue on his rounds. He could not understand the selfishness of some of these aristocratic women who did little to help the rest of society. These thoughts he knew were not quite accurate for many patronized charitable causes but he had met many such women who were remarkably like Lorna Heston.

Carenza had a severe case of influenza which had concerned Tom. His reaction was unlike his mother's attitude but he had not heard what she had said to the doctor. He was more than willing to be Carenza's nurse for however long it took for her to return to full fitness. For the first two days of her illness, she slept for most of the time waking just occasionally to consume fluids. When she was beginning to feel more human they would talk and he would read to her some of his favourite poems from Byron and Keats. They had found a common denominator in their interests and aspirations. It was this togetherness which had encouraged Tom to feel that he had a future with Carenza. He had not revisited his suggestions of marriage to her but he was in no doubt that he would raise the topic again in the near future.

Tom had informed May about her daughter's illness.

'How is she?' May had asked in a rather concerned way.

'She is feeling a little better,' Tom tried to reassure her. 'The doctor says she can get up in a day or two and when she is feeling better I will bring her home.'

'Should I come?'

'No May. She is getting better all the time, so stop worrying.' Tom had a feeling that his mother would not approve.

It was nearly New Year's Eve when Spencer Heston had approached his son about visiting the office to sort out some of the details of Tom's initiation into work. Tom was becoming quite excited about starting his new life. His interlude in between leaving university and the onslaught of work had given him a breathing space to enjoy himself, a little too much his father feared, and a time to clear his head before the hard graft of the real world beckoned. He was anxious to please his father and grandfather but he now wanted to earn real money. Part of this lay in the fact that his independence would allow him to marry Carenza against a tide of criticism from his mother. Although his mother had said very little he knew that she was not happy about the relationship between them but he knew that his father would be on his side but his mother's financial independence from his father made it a more difficult proposition to convince her that what he wanted to do was the right thing.

It was on one of these sorties into the office when the house was quiet that Lorna Sefton decided to strike. Carenza was now allowed out of bed for a few hours but returned as soon as her strength waned. The doctor was not convinced that she would be able to return to school for the start of the new term because she had had a most virulent strain of influenza. Carenza was not happy about that but she knew she was far from fit. She was grateful to the Hestons' kindness but she was now feeling homesick. In particular she wanted to return to May and her own life.

It was mid-morning during one of Tom's absences that Carenza was paid a visit by Lorna. There was no knock on the door but the handle turned heralding Lorna's presence. Carenza looked up from reading a book to encounter the sight of Tom's mother standing in the doorway. There was an icy glare on her face as she regarded her. Striding into the room without an invitation she sat in the Lloyd Loom chair under the windowsill directly in Carenza's line of vision.

'How long are you staying?' she enquired bluntly. 'Tom must have no distractions when he starts work in a few days. Anyway tell me about yourself, your origins.'

Carenza was dumbfounded by the inhospitality of her hostess and the directness of the question she had asked. Her incredulity made her gawp stupidly at the woman in front of her.

'Well?' Lorna was relentless.

Carenza stammered.

'What do you mean?' She was not feeling up to an inquisition.

'It is quite obvious what I mean. Tom is one day going to be a wealthy young man. I will protect him from any gold diggers that I can. So what is your background? Do not spare me the details.'

Carenza was consumed with rage at the audacity of Lorna Heston's probing. She was intimidated by her air of authority which was part of her inheritance as a member of the junior aristocracy. Somewhere she recalled Tom mentioning that his mother was the Honourable Lorna Heston but this did not give her the right to treat others badly. Carenza's anger gave her an inner strength. There was no way that she was a gold-digger and his mother had no right to delve into her past as if she was a common criminal.

'I am not after Tom's inheritance,' her calmness surprised Lorna. She had expected a lack of dignity which would betray Carenza's roots. Carenza continued, 'my past is mine and mine alone. It is of no consequence to anybody else. I have nothing to hide but I will not divulge what is private. I have no intention of marrying Tom, although he has asked me.'

Her reply had struck its bull's-eye. Lorna was taken aback with the forthright reply. Although Carenza had not been rude, Lorna was not used to people who did not react to her authority and capitulate.

'I shall make arrangements to go home as soon as possible. I am grateful for your kindness but I cannot outstay my welcome.'

Lorna's attitude softened slightly, 'well, we must get you home safely in one piece. I am glad you have seen sense. Tom is not for you. He needs to marry someone from his own class. He is infatuated with you at the moment, but it will die a natural death.'

'And if it doesn't?' Carenza was playing her own game.

'There is no choice. Of course it will end. I will see to that.' The older woman was emphatic.

Lorna rose from her chair feeling placated that the matter was at an end. There was to be no further discussion. Her victory was sweet. Now she had to work on Tom to make him realize that he had responsibilities to his family and the law firm which he would one day inherit.

*

May had been concerned by Carenza's illness. She had missed Carenza at Christmas but not as much as she had thought. The festive season had been busy passing in a whirl of activity but when Carenza had not returned home it struck May how empty the old house was. Carenza had filled her latter years with so much joy that she could not imagine what it would feel like when her daughter moved out permanently to marry and have her own family. May had rung her daughter on a daily basis to obtain a bulletin on her health. Tom had kept her up to date with all the news but eventually Carenza had gained in strength to speak to her mother and convince her that she was really on the mend.

On New Year's Eve after the conversation with Lorna, Carenza telephoned May with the sweet words.

'I am coming home.'

'Are you well enough to travel?' May was full of maternal concern.

Carenza heard the question and smiled.

'Oh yes May. I cannot wait to come home to you. I would crawl home if I could. Tom has agreed to drive me back the day after New Year's Day. He starts his new job any day and I should be well enough to return to school.'

'You will only return to school if Doctor Fulbrook says so.' The joy in May's voice was apparent.

Carenza smiled to herself, welling up inside with love and gratitude for everything that this wonderful woman had done for her.

'We will see,' she replied, a note of rebellion rising from her lips.

'Indeed we will,' May's voice disguised its amusement. 'See you soon. All my love,' she said sentimentally and put the telephone back into its cradle.

Carenza had not told Tom of his mother's visit to her room. She knew that he would have been hurt and angry, so angry that he would have confronted her which would have caused so much upset in the Heston household. The situation was better left as it was with Lorna believing that she had won. But deep down Carenza knew that this was not the case. It was not the right time for her to marry Tom even if she did consider it in the future. Her career meant so much to her. Now that Tom was about to start work he would have less opportunity to visit Nether Heydon and their courtship might end as a consequence. The old adage that time would tell was at the forefront of her mind.

Tom was intuitive enough to realize that Carenza was not herself. He knew that she had not completely recovered from her severe bout of influenza but he suspected that it might have had something to do with his proposal but he was not sure. There was remoteness about her but nothing substantial that he could pinpoint pertaining to her mood. She remained kind and considerate as well as being grateful for the care she had received. Tom knew that his mother had not been overly thoughtful but that was the way she was. A comparison to an iceberg was the best example he could think of and one that rarely melted at that. Generally there was a thaw in her demeanour when she could manipulate everything and everybody around her. As her stay reached its conclusion Carenza did not want to seek out Lorna but on the morning of her departure she found Spencer in the hallway shrugging himself into his great overcoat in readiness for his return to the office after the festive break. There was considerable affection between them which had not gone unnoticed by his wife.

'I just want to say goodbye and thank you for looking after me so well,' she said. Spencer turned to look at her and a smile creased his rather serious face. Carenza could not help but notice how handsome he looked, rather like an older version of Tom.

'It's been our pleasure. Come as often as you like. Keep well,' he looked at her earnestly to see if she still looked ill but then his face relaxed as he held out his arms and gave her a bear hug. 'You are good for Tom.'

Carenza smiled and hugged him back. She could not help but compare the generosity of spirit of husband and wife.

'Thank you,' was all she could say.

On their journey to Nether Heyford Tom asked her again if she had given any more thought to his proposal. Carenza remained grimfaced and determined to make no commitment until she was sure of her own emotions but she would not allow Lorna and her bullying to influence any decisions that she made for her future although she did not wish to return to Tom's home to suffer Lorna's abuse again.

'Have I done anything wrong?' Tom probed. He was like a dog with a bone. He would not let go until he had found the underlying cause of her problem. 'I do love you, very much in fact. Is that wrong?'

She smiled at him now aware at how earnest he was being. A lot of Tom's confidence had been knocked by her reluctance to commit to a more permanent relationship.

'Nothing is wrong Tom but I am not ready to marry. Give me time.' And he had to be satisfied with that answer.

Carenza wanted to confide in May and use her wisdom as a benchmark by which to judge her own very confused emotions. May would not be able to answer her questions but she knew that her advice would be sound.

She suspected May would say, 'follow your instincts but if you are not sure wait for a while.' But even Carenza was not sure about confiding in anybody right now. Lorna's nastiness had left her world as a very insecure place to inhabit just at the moment. It would help her to return to work to think about school rather than problems.

Tom left Carenza in Nether Heydon with mixed emotions. He had promised to ring and visit soon but could not make further commitments until he knew the demands of his job and its expectations. It was on his way home when his mind had the freedom to dwell on the Christmas period that there came a new clarity to his thoughts. He realized that Carenza had been left alone for long stretches when he had made visits to the office with his father to establish his new career. He knew that Sylvie, the maid, tended to Carenza's needs during his absence. His mother had made it clear quite vociferously that she was out of her depth in a sick room but the question lay heavily in his mind whether Lorna had made a secret visit to the invalid during his absence. He made a mental note to question Sylvie and perhaps there lay the answer to the mystery. He knew that if there was a choice between Carenza or his mother there would be no contest.

Chapter 22

'Mother, did you speak to Carenza about personal matters?' Tom asked the question very directly. There was hardly any point in doing anything else. His mother looked vague but inside she wondered what Carenza might have said. Her only defence was to plead ignorance.

'What do you mean, spoken to Carenza? I hardly saw anything of her during her illness.'

'I know but did you talk to her about anything specific. You had plenty of opportunity when I was in the office. I have never known her so upset but she refuses to tell me anything.'

'I cannot remember anything untoward. Are you seeing her again?' Lorna Heston was a good liar. Her son watched her acting skills with an acute interest and his dislike of her had never been so intense. Sylvie had revealed that Lorna had visited her guest where at one point she had heard raised voices but could not make out the nature of the conversation. Tom knew by instinct that Sylvie had overheard the conversation for she had been found listening at doors before but he was not prepared to force her hand into revealing all.

'Of course I am seeing her again. Why shouldn't I?' His voice adopted an aggressive tone.

Lorna scrutinized her son more closely but her defences remained firmly in place.

'Oh, no reason except that you have to get down to work now that the festive season is over. I expect that you won't be able to see her too often.' Lorna blustered hoping that the relationship would cool between them. Tom could now totally see through his mother's manipulation, knowing that he would never trust her again. She had lost him as she had his father.

'You do like her, Mother?' Tom was blunt. His mother had to learn her lesson the hard way.

'She is charming, Tom darling but not quite your background I would say. Do you know anything about her?'

'Mother you are such a snob. I don't know a lot about her but I do know that she was adopted by her mother, May, who is a wonderful woman. They live in quite a large house in Nether Heydon. There does that satisfy you?'

Lorna's lips stretched into a tight line but her silence spoke volumes to Tom. He rose from his chair to leave the room. He could not bear to be in the same place as his mother. Lorna watched his disappearing back and knew she would discover all she could about the girl who had stolen her son. She wanted him back at any price.

Doctor Fulbrook assessed Carenza's condition critically. It was true that she had improved over days but he was not prepared to send her back to school until her strength had returned. From attending many teachers over his long medical career he knew that teaching was a hard profession where physical fitness was important. School was also a hotbed of germs ever ready to catch the least suspecting of victims. January was a time when coughs and colds were at their height. The hygiene of the children would be poor among some families. Washing hands would be a non event and dribbly noses were often wiped on sleeves leaving the evidence behind for the foreseeable future. Were clothes ever washed he wondered? All this was apparent just by looking at the children who were less than happy with their lot in life. The teachers did their best to maintain standards of hygiene but it could often be a lost cause.

May had agreed with the doctor.

'You have got to be sensible Carenza. You have had a bad bout of influenza and Doctor Fulbrook knows what he is talking about.'

Carenza raged at her enforced idleness.

'Oh May you are a good one to talk. What about last year you had that migraine and you were told to rest. Would you stay in bed? No. Did Doctor Fulbrook know what he was talking about then?'

May had the good grace to blush but she would not succumb to Carenza's bamboozlement.

But eventually Carenza gave way to the pampering that she received. Staying in bed until late morning allowed her energy levels to rise. Food was made tempting within the constraints of food rationing but country living made food supplies easier. Everybody helped each other out. May was well regarded in the village and well loved. Often an offering of eggs or a chicken could be found as a donation on her front doorstep. A brace of pheasants had been left occasionally hanging from a wall nail near the front door. There would be no message with the gift and usually she was unable to express her gratitude.

May's standing in the community was legendry. Her status as a former head teacher and a designated pillar of society opened her world to many confidences from local people who felt that she held the answer to most questions in the palm of her hand. Now when her front door was opened the offerings were for Carenza. Homemade get well cards were delivered by children on the way to school. They were missing her. Carenza was touched by the concern of her pupils which made her restless to return to the real world. Her enforced idleness did not distract her from mulling over her conversation with Lorna Heston. Her brooding was noticed by May who never forced her daughter to divulge problems but knew that over time Carenza would confide in her when she was ready.

Tom, who was full of his own new world, still rang regularly but was too busy to make an appearance in Nether Heydon. Carenza had not realized that she would miss him quite so much but she chided herself that once she had returned to work she too would be well and truly occupied and forgave Tom his lack of attention.

Lorna, too, had noticed Tom's world revolved around his job and his happiness seemed complete now that he was fully occupied. Were her prayers being answered that his involvement with Carenza was over?

*

By the middle of February, Carenza's world had returned to normal. Her brooding on events had ceased much to May's relief. Her pupils had welcomed her back with open arms and Carenza no longer thought about Lorna Heston who occupied another world but not the one she frequented. Tom appeared occasionally to spend a weekend in Nether Heydon but he no longer mentioned marriage. Both young people were too engrossed in their own lives to worry about the other but what was strange was the fact that their mutual feelings for each other without them realizing had become strengthened. Tom did not force Carenza to stay with his parents allowing her the time to recover from his mother's indiscretions. He was always happy to visit Nether Heydon where he could bask in the warmth of May's generous hospitality.

*

Lorna had been watchful and furtive in her attempts to keep Tom away from Carenza. As the winter progressed she had noticed that Tom was disappearing at weekends more often without commenting on his whereabouts but she knew all the same. Carenza's wizardry was ensnaring him once more. It had become a game to keep ahead of events by both mother and son. Family events were planned regularly by Lorna, filling weekends with visiting cousins and daughters of friends, hoping fervently that the right woman would catch his eye. Tom played his part but knew exactly what his mother was trying to do. He made excuses to disappear whenever he could. Fictitious friends were invented and special outings were created while he slipped away to Nether Heydon. Both mother and son knew what the other was doing, allowing their relationship to suffer immeasurably. Lorna had made up her mind that something must be done but that decision could only be made if she found out about the girl's mysterious past.

Lorna had lost both her men folk through manipulation and interference. Spencer was no ally. He had a deep affection for Carenza whom he knew would be a special addition to his family but by refusing to comment on such matters he could carry on his own life free in the knowledge that Lorna was too immersed in Tom's affairs. He knew it was a cowardly approach to events but his home life was made intolerable by Lorna's actions.

Chapter 23

Lorna looked at the piece of paper in her hand containing a name and telephone number. Her hand hovered over the telephone receiver waiting for her to make up her mind to dial the number. Normally she was not so indecisive but what she was about to do could have repercussions which would reverberate through the family like a tornado. But any indecision was cast aside as she dialed the number and waited for the receiver to be picked up at the other end.

'Masons private detective Agency, how may I help you?' A mature female voice oozing confidence travelled down the line.

'Hello. This is Mrs Heston here. I would like to see someone about an extremely delicate matter. It is confidential of course.'

'Everything is treated in confidence madam. Shall I make you an appointment?'

'Yes, of course but it will have to be here. I cannot come to you. I might be recognized by somebody.'

Liza, the secretary raised her eyes to the ceiling. 'Not another one,' she thought maliciously. How many such requests had she received over time? She knew the type, too much money and so much time on their hands that they did not know what to do with themselves. This kind of behaviour filled the long hours of the day until husbands returned. Some charity work would do them good. Liza pulled herself together after she noticed her boss giving her odd looks across the office. Knowing that it was not her concern the professional voice went into business mode as she gleaned the address of their new client.

'Mr. Mason will be with you at 10.30 a.m. tomorrow. Good morning and thank you.' The telephone receiver was replaced before Lorna could utter another word.

'Trouble?' Joseph Mason enquired.

'The usual,' Liza replied setting her lips in a tight smile. 'You'll cope though.'

Joseph nodded wondering what he was in for this time.

*

May had never discovered what had troubled Carenza while she had been ill but observing her return to a full life she was sure that whatever it was had been resolved. Carenza's silence had hurt May more than she had realized. Their relationship was based on openness and the sharing of problems. After Doris and Hannah had died during that dreadful time in London, May and Carenza had discussed the subject at length until Carenza had reached an acceptance of the situation allowing her to find coping strategies of her own. It was during that traumatic time that the bond of complete trust had been forged.

Over the years Carenza had recovered to the extent that she could discuss her family without too much emotional turmoil but they were never far from her thoughts. May had never tried to replace Hannah as a mother substitute but had become a guide and mentor to the child who had stolen her heart.

*

Lorna had often looked through lists of private investigators in the past. Some she had been tempted to use when she had suspected Spencer of having secret trysts with other women but had stopped herself in time not wanting to know every nuance of her husband's infidelity. But this occasion was different. It concerned Tom her beloved son. There would be no gold-diggers to touch her money which would be inherited by Tom, and a suitable spouse would be inspected by herself. Her estate was left to Tom in its entirety. But she could still change her will if he was not compliant with her wishes. There was no reference to Spencer. He would know that she had watched his antics over the years of their long marriage and suffered humiliation as a result. It would be his turn to suffer. There was nothing like the vengeance of a woman scorned. She believed that she could control and manipulate Tom by using threats of disinheriting him should the occasion arise. But she had no doubt that she would never have to use such tactics.

Lorna had found the telephone number of the Mason Detective Agency from her friend Lady Margaret who had been forced to use it on numerous occasions. A father and son provided the service and they were renowned for their discretion.

On the morning of her meeting with Joseph Mason, Lorna had sent her maid out on numerous errands. There were so many of them that she could almost guarantee that the girl would not return until early afternoon. It suited her purpose that nobody knew of her business but herself. Sylvie had been discovered eavesdropping on more than one occasion. Lorna would have dismissed her on the spot but she knew that maids were not so easily come by since the war. She had given the girl a good telling off instead and threatened her with dismissal, as well as no reference. Her flood of tears and the threat of losing her job were enough to convince Lorna that it would never happen again.

Promptly at 10.30 a.m. Joseph Mason rang the doorbell of the Heston residence. While he waited he regarded the property before him noting its grandeur. It screamed wealth. Many places he visited these days were quite run down after the war but he noted that the outside of the building was well painted and the garden was neatly attended. The front door was opened by a well dressed woman. This surprised him. She spoke with a refined accent, 'received pronunciation' it was called, if he was not mistaken. Lorna held out her hand in greeting.

'Mr Mason?' she enquired looking at the well dressed man in front of her. She was mildly surprised because she had been expecting a seedy looking character. He was dressed for the elements in a charcoal grey overcoat which reached below his knees. Her gaze travelled to his feet where black highly polished shoes gleamed at her. She was suitably impressed which was a novel experience for Lorna Heston. His large hand clasped hers in a firm grip.

'Come in please. It is cold today.' She had left unsaid that they were not to be observed by watchful eyes.

Lorna led her visitor into the sitting room where a welcoming fire flickered in the grate keeping the depression of a winter's day at bay. Her eyes still feasted on her guest. The pin striped suit looked expensive. His manners were impeccable and there was a certain *je ne sais crois* about him. Business must be good she reflected as she allowed herself to smile at the man before her.

'Please do sit down,' she indicated the seat opposite her own on the other side of the fire. Perching on the edge of his seat he waited expectantly for her to speak. It was not his style to rush his client. She would be paying handsomely for his time as it was. A slightly embarrassed cough emanated from Lorna as she cleared her throat to begin. Joseph was not fazed by any requests or revelations from his clients. His ten years of working for the family firm had left him unshockable. His assumption was that Lorna wanted her husband followed. Ladies like Lorna Heston with money and time on their hands were often convinced that husbands were unfaithful. It was as the story unfolded about Tom and Carenza that Joseph Mason was taken aback. This job was quite different from anything he had undertaken for quite some time.

'There you have the whole business Mr Mason. I want every morsel, scandal, anything that you can find out about this young woman.' Her voice now sounded hostile as she spoke of Carenza. It had quite unnerved the private detective. He was not expecting her to be so venomous in her attitude.

'I will do my best for you Mrs Heston.'

'You will do more than your best young man. I am paying your company more than the going rate. Leave no stone unturned.' She rose ending the meeting abruptly.

Rising from his chair, Joseph was relieved that the meeting had reached its conclusion. Perspiration glistened on his brow. He thought to rub it away but changed his mind. His hand went to shake his client's but she walked quickly to the sitting room door wanting him gone now. He followed her into the hall and out into the cold of the late winter's morning. Before putting his hat on his head he doffed it in farewell before turning to the road and his car parked discreetly a short walking distance away. Her body language had dismissed him making him feel like something nasty under his shoe. Joseph Mason did not like this aspect of his job when he was treated as someone inferior. It had happened before but not often. Instinct told him to forget about this assignment but he knew that the money was good and he was a man in a hurry to improve his lot. Their next meeting would be interesting he mused as he opened the door to his car.

*

Nearly six weeks had passed since Lorna's interview with Joseph Mason. The days had been endless while she awaited the report concerning Carenza. During that time Tom had visited Nether Heydon on a regular basis even if it was only for one night over a weekend. She hardly ever saw him now with the visits away and the hours he put in at the office. It never occurred to her to invite Carenza to stay so that they could pretend to play happy families. Even Spencer spent more and more time avoiding her with work and his affairs. Loneliness was engulfing her and she was allowing it to happen on account of her bitterness and snobbishness. There seemed no way out of the depression that had overtaken her.

A few days later Sylvie brought the post to her as she ate a late breakfast. Tom and Spencer had long gone to work. There were the customary bills as well as a long brown envelope which appeared to be very thick. It was the long awaited report from Joseph Mason. Her feeling of expectancy was high. The paper knife slit the sealed envelope and Lorna pulled out the wad of paper. Just at that moment Sylvie appeared to remove the breakfast dishes from the table. Lorna automatically hid the envelope and papers beneath the pile of correspondence. That furtive movement was enough to attract Sylvie's curiosity. She stared at the pile but could not see anything untoward.

'Hurry up girl. Stop your dawdling,' Lorna snapped nastily at the girl. Sylvie's movements became clumsy as she spilled tea onto the white starched cloth. Lorna had had enough of the girl's behaviour so she pushed her chair sharply backwards and snatched her post away. Her retreat to her own private domain was hurried. Sylvie watched her employer with the utmost astonishment, wondering what had got into her. She made a face as the door closed on her mistress. What a tartar of an employer she had proved to be.

The lengthy, very professional report was perused thoroughly. Lorna absorbed every detail of Carenza's early years. She was touched by the tragedy that had followed her but in her latter adolescence she had found happiness with a spinster teacher who had adopted her. There was no evidence that Carenza was a gold-digger and she was not needy. When the time came the girl would inherit a substantial property and possibly a healthy amount of money. She recalled that Tom had already provided her with this piece of intelligence.

These facts placated Lorna to a certain extent but Carenza's humble origins were a huge humiliation. How could she condone Tom marrying the girl? What would all her friends say behind her back? She could not bear the thought that she might be laughed at leaving her feeling humiliated by something which was not of her own making.

Lorna had not come to terms with the fact that the war years had gone a long way to liberating the working classes and women in particular. Time had moved on but Lorna had not. Considering that she had married beneath her she did not want Tom to make the same mistake. Although she now considered herself upper middle class she had been born the granddaughter of an earl but her own mother had married into the middle classes.

Although Lorna had had a comparatively happy childhood she had rushed into a marriage with the first man who had shown her any genuine affection. Her grandparents had not wanted her to marry Spencer. They had wanted her to wait until she was sure of what she really wanted or until somebody more suitable came along. But they had to admit that Spencer had a good professional career ahead of him and Lorna married him at twenty two. Their relationship deteriorated after the birth of Tom seven years into their marriage. Tom became the apple of his mother's eye and Spencer became neglected. This caused the onslaught of numerous affairs. It was at this time that Lorna wholeheartedly wished that she had listened to the advice of her grandparents. She found Spencer slightly vulgar these days and her snobbishness had increased tenfold during Tom's childhood allowing him to grow up fully aware of his illustrious relations and where this might lead him socially in the future. Both warring parents loved Tom unconditionally. He was the glue that held the marriage together. Spencer hoped that middle class values were now part of his son's ethos. Hard work allowed people to hold their heads high and could be passed on to the next generation as a shining example of how to live a satisfying and successful life.

Chapter 24

Lorna was unsure as to how to use the information concerning Carenza. She knew with certainty that both Spencer and Tom would be appalled at her subterfuge in approaching a private investigator to unravel Carenza's history. It would alienate her and there would be two opposing camps. But after suffering much inner turmoil she believed that Carenza was the only person she could approach on the matter. If she explained that her early origins might be unhelpful for Tom's future career Carenza might just understand. But Carenza might also love Tom enough to fight for a future with him. The dilemma reared its head once more. Her thoughts turned to May. May was of mature years with life experience enough to understand Lorna's inner dispute. Her assumption that May had not experienced love as a young woman was based on the fact that she had never married. An old maid had certain values but romance was not part of their credence. It was this certainty that led Lorna to seek out May in the April of 1949.

May heard the telephone ringing in the hallway. She had been sorting through old clothes in her bedroom for the pending jumble sale which was being held in the school hall the following week. She cursed inwardly at the interruption of her task. The thought to let it ring travelled through her mind but she admonished herself. It could be something important. Her journey down the stairs was protracted and painful. Her knee was playing up again and Doctor Fulbrook had told her to keep it bandaged for additional support. Perhaps the telephone would stop before she reached it she mused but its ringing continued relentlessly.

'Hello,' she said putting the receiver to her ear.

'Is that Miss May Faithful,' a posh breathy voice replied.

'Who is this?'

'Are you Carenza's mother?'

'Who is this? What do you want?' May was in pain having put pressure on her knee and her abruptness made her sound rude.

Lorna had taken the telephone from her ear and shook her head in dismay. She wondered if Tom had to put up with this woman's attitude all the time.

'I am Tom's mother. I would like to come and see you. It is rather urgent.'

'Urgent,' May repeated rather stupidly. The other woman tutted in exasperation feeling that she was quite justified in her original thoughts. May heard her and thought she should pull herself together. Tom's mother would think that she was a simpleton. 'Why do you need to see me?'

'I would rather speak to you in person. The subject is a little delicate for over the telephone. Would tomorrow be all right? About eleven o'clock?'

There was silence for a moment while May considered this request. There was nothing planned for the next day.

'Yes, that would be fine,' she heard herself saying.

'Oh and by the way don't mention this conversation to Carenza.' Before she could answer the line had gone dead. May had been totally shocked to receive a telephone call from Lorna Heston. Nothing sprang to mind that could possibly account for the visit except that Carenza was involved somehow. The subterfuge that was tangled in all of this had set May on edge. One of her headaches had returned. Occasionally she suffered from them in times of stress but had been free of them for a while.

'Always when there is a trauma,' she mused.

While her daughter was at school May cogitated on as many possibilities as she could concerning the pending visitation. She told herself off mentally for reacting as she had done. She remembered many occasions when she had to take life in both hands and deal with problems and the unexpected.

The next morning May was up earlier than usual. Carenza was amazed to see her mother boiling the kettle and preparing breakfast for both of them. The quiet of the early morning was the time of day that Carenza liked best. She could think clearly about the day ahead and what she needed to do in school.

'What are you doing up?' she asked her mother. 'Didn't Doctor Fulbrook say that you had to rest your leg?'

'What an old woman he has turned out to be.'

'May really, that is unlike you to be so rude about him.'

May looked contrite as there was no other explanation she could give. The real one would have alarmed Carenza too much, and would have resulted in her taking a day off school purely to hear what it was all about.

'Look at the time.' May deflected any more questions. The clock registered 8.15 a.m. Carenza was usually passing through the school gate at this time.

'I must fly.' She picked up her coat and bag full of yesterday's marking and fled shouting her goodbyes as the front door slammed behind her. May sighed with relief.

*

Lorna Heston arrived in Nether Heydon in plenty of time for her appointment. Travis, her chauffeur drove steadily around the village allowing his employer to see for herself the place where Tom visited so regularly. She had to acknowledge the village was pretty enough. Travis found the property that they had been searching for. Lorna's reaction was the same as her son's. This was a substantially sized building, not a cottage in the real meaning of the word. It did not compare with the Heston residence but the ambiance of the building was quite different. Lorna wondered what would await her inside but she had to admit that she had brought this entirely on her own head. Travis parked the car at a discreet distance from the house allowing his mistress time to gather her thoughts before her meeting. Lorna walked along the path of the large front garden which was awash with daffodils and tulips until she reached the front door where she raised her hand to ring the doorbell. The door opened instantaneously. May had been waiting with a feeling of expectation for her visitor. The two women faced each other for the first time. Both were surprised to feel such a reaction. Lorna was confronted by an ageing matron who keenly was not a follower of fashionable trends. May was dismayed to see a woman who clearly looked down her nose at those she deemed inferior.

'Do come in Lorna. Welcome.' May hid her emotions under a cloud of effusive charm disarming Tom's mother with her good nature and cheerfulness as well as the informality of using her Christian name.

'Thank you,' she replied stepping over the threshold into the inner sanctum of the hallway. Lorna cast her eyes about her appreciating the lovely interior of the old Elizabethan property.

She followed May into the sitting room where an occasional table had been laid ready for a cup of tea and other delicacies.

'You have a lovely home Miss Faithful.' Lorna was quite amazed at what she saw.

'Call me May,' came the reply.

In spite of the early spring day outside a fire blazed cheerfully in the hearth. Lorna looked and felt uncomfortable. She noticed how homely the room felt and there was a faded grandeur about it. Obviously May's origins were rooted in old money. There were no titles here but instead she saw an understated elegance from the past. Observing May's white hair, her shapeless figure and baggy clothes Lorna felt she was meeting someone comfortable in her own shoes who had no need of pretence to live her life the way she wanted. For once she felt dismayed that her son was comfortable within these four walls on his frequent visits and had felt more at home here than living with his own parents.

It was obvious that few concessions had been made for this visit. In return May had the measure of Lorna who was fashionable in style. Her hair was coiffed regularly and her face bore the latest colours from the cosmetic industry. Their outlook on the world could not have been more different. Their values might touch in certain areas but May was not one to stand on ceremony when receiving visitors.

'Sit down Lorna. Make yourself comfortable while I go and boil the kettle for tea.'

'Thank you,' Lorna replied watching her hostess hobble away on her painful leg. She noticed that there was no maid to perform such rudimentary tasks.

May's escape to the kitchen allowed Lorna the opportunity to regard her surroundings more closely. The long case clock in the corner of the room ticked sonorously breaking the silence. There were several armchairs placed at random here and there. Their arms were frayed from years of use but their decline did not detract from the ambiance of the room. May returned carrying a blue and white teapot which was partially covered by an old cosy.

'Here we are then,' she smiled observing the woman before her who perched tensely on the edge of her seat. Her body language could not hide the fact that there was something extremely wrong. May wondered what the trouble could be but suspected that it was something to do with the relationship between Carenza and Tom.

'How do you like your tea dear?'

'Oh, very weak please.' Rather like you May reasoned but mentally chided herself for such uncharitable thoughts.

'I will go and replenish the pot before we chat.'

Lorna sniffed loudly. She opened her handbag to find her handkerchief and dabbed at her eyes but a deluge of tears gushed in tracks down her ravaged face allowing her makeup to run. May had returned with the refilled pot of tea. Her facial expression showed compassion as well as total amazement at what confronted her.

'What is it?' she asked the other woman. The hot teapot was placed safely on the table. May's attention returned to her guest. The tide was turning as the storm was beginning to run itself out.

'I'm sorry,' Lorna snuffled into her handkerchief which was wet and knotted from it's over use.

'Tell me what is the matter? Is it the children?'

Lorna nodded, telling her tale of woe about hiring the private investigator. Feeling ashamed and contrite she unburdened her guilty conscience. May looked suitably shocked, not knowing what to say. Eventually she found her voice.

'But Lorna if you had needed to know anything you could have come to me like you have done now.'

'But I had so wanted Tom to marry well and into money. The firm of solicitors has not done well in recent years and my money has had to prop up the business.'

'My father was a solicitor. In fact there is still a family business. Everything has highs and lows,' May replied totally puzzled by this woman's rationale. 'The war has not helped but everything begins to level out over time. It did after the Great War. Carenza is an intelligent young woman who can earn her own living just as I did. She has not mentioned to me about marrying Tom. Has Tom said anything?'

Lorna shook her head.

'Only that Tom is very fond of her. And I am so frightened of losing Tom'

'Why don't we let events take their course instead of jumping to conclusions,' May said wisely. But she was still shocked by what Lorna had done. She was not about to announce how comfortably off Carenza would be in her own right one day. That was their business. She was also adamant that Carenza's money would not be used to help the Hestons. This dreadful woman had to learn some lessons even if it was through difficult means.

'You won't tell Carenza or Tom will you?' Lorna's voice had turned to a whine.

'I don't know why you wanted to see me if Carenza isn't to know. Nobody would have suspected anything if you had kept quiet.' May was not about to mince her words. Her patience was beginning to run out.

'I just felt that I had to tell somebody. I couldn't tell my husband. He would have been ashamed that I had done such a thing. Tom would disown me. I just thought that another woman would understand.'

'But my loyalty is to Carenza. I cannot condone a private detective snooping into her life. She had a most difficult start but she has overcome it. Life is just wonderful now. I am so proud of her.' May was in full flow now endorsing Carenza's qualities. This snobbish woman was not going to castigate Carenza as a person any more than she had done.

Now Lorna had composed herself and was back in character playing the persona that had become second nature to her. It was so rare for her to display such human qualities. Even as a child she had created the person she had wanted to become.

'Well thank you for your kindness,' Lorna condescended, rising from her chair and picking up her gloves and handbag. She considered the whole visit to be a complete waste of time as well as the fact that she had lost face over her lack of tenure over her own emotions.

'My advice is to allow the young people to find their own way forward without any assistance from ourselves. But I believe that nothing should be said about this detective business. You could find yourself losing a son and he a potential wife if they ever found out about it,' May had made her point forcefully.

Lorna looked suitably chastened. She nodded her head at the older woman's words of wisdom and hastened her step through the front door towards her car. May closed the front door forcefully behind her guest full of rage at the audacity of the younger woman. Feeling like telling Carenza about the events of the morning was high on May's agenda but she knew that she had to follow the advice that she had handed out so readily to Tom's mother.

Part 3: 1952

Chapter 25

May had spent the morning in the kitchen baking and catching up with various chores. It was not her favourite place to spend her day but as she looked out of the window on this grey February morning the rain lashed against the glass and the wind was beginning to send stray leaves scurrying across the lawn. It had hardly been light since she had come downstairs to make her first cup of tea. Her longing for spring was so acute that it almost left a pain inside her. But she reflected that it was only weeks until she would be attending to her beloved garden. 'What a lot to do,' she reflected. She knew it would take her weeks to clear up the ravages of winter.

Glancing at the clock on the kitchen wall she noted the time, 'Carenza will be home within the hour. Must get on,' she thought out loud.

Turning the knob on the wireless to listen to the latest news she began to prepare lunch for herself and Carenza. It was Carenza's midweek treat to spend a lunchtime away from school. It helped her to regain some sanity after the demands of her job. She loved teaching but it did become necessary to escape from the children as well as giving May company. The aches and pains of old age sometimes depressed her in the dark winter days particularly when she was more confined to the house. Carenza's effervescence over the years had remained a tonic to light up May's life.

Stopping midway between the sink and the stove with the kettle dripping excess water onto the lino May stood still listening to the wireless. Her face had taken on a grey tinge as she heard the depressing news.

'He was too young to die,' she commented to herself.

The sound of the front door opening and closing brought May to her senses. The dripping kettle was placed on a low heat on the stove in readiness for the lunchtime cup of tea. The kitchen door opened allowing Carenza to burst in bringing youthful exuberance into the room. Her nose was a bright red beacon from the excessive cold. Rubbing her hands together she walked towards the stove to warm her chilled bones.

'Gosh it is so warm in here. School is freezing today. The children have been sitting in their coats all morning and the boys' lavatory is frozen again. They have had to use the girls' under supervision.' She giggled as she recounted these anecdotes but her eyes caught sight of May's grave face which was still ashen.

'What is it?' her voice was a whisper beside the droning of the wireless.

May looked at her.

'It's the King. He has passed away in his sleep at Sandringham.'

'Oh, how awful,' Carenza did not know what to say.

'What about the Princess or Queen as she must be now. She's abroad at the moment. She will be coming back then I suppose.'

May nodded not having taken in the full extent of the news. It was a new age beginning. She had taught enough history in her own time to pinpoint some of the important events of a new age. This would be a new Elizabethan Age.

This day would be etched on Carenza's memory for ever. The news about the death of the king had been discussed as people passed each other in the street. They had not lingered long on account of the inclement weather but they had had to make a remark as a sign of respect for their late sovereign. It was a momentous event for the nation. After the abdication of Edward VIII at the end of 1936 King George had gained in popularity with his wife steadfastly beside him. They had shown that family life was important and gave a good example to the country. The king and queen had been well respected during the war years for their courage to remain in London during the air raids over the capital. Had her Majesty the Queen not said that they could now look the East End in the face after Buckingham Palace had been bombed .

It was on that night of the King's death that Tom rang Carenza as he did every week. Their relationship had gathered momentum over the intervening years. They were close but Carenza had remained true to herself and her plans not to marry until she was ready. Tom had accepted her decision too but had a feeling that it would not be long before Carenza capitulated to his constant pestering. Lorna had accepted Carenza to a certain degree but they met rarely to the relief of both women. The young people were none the wiser of Lorna's visit to May since both the older women had kept their word although May often wondered what would happen when Carenza eventually agreed to marry Tom. She knew it would happen at some point. It was the natural way of things and she did not want Carenza to be alone in the world when her own time came to pass over. May was not maudlin by nature but she felt her age at times. Since Tom had started working for the family firm his life had been a roller coaster. His training as a solicitor had started well but before long he had been called up to do the compulsory National Service. The eighteen months that he had served in the army had seen him in Germany.

The army had made Tom grow up more than he could have imagined. He had been used to living away from home during his three years at university but he knew that he could nip off home if life became intolerable but in the army he became more self-reliant. His friends came from all walks of life and friendship bridged the class structure especially when they depended on each other sometimes in the most difficult of situations both emotionally and militarily. The friendships he had made continued long after he had left the army. In previous years he would have kept these people sometimes from less prosperous backgrounds hidden away from his mother and her world but now he brought them home hoping that she would see the good in all levels of society. It became an ongoing struggle and a hard lesson for Lorna to learn.

During the time of Tom's long absences Carenza had also grown as an individual. Teaching had taken over her life but she missed Tom passionately and the short leaves he was allowed became precious for both of them. But as it became time to return to a civilian role once more Tom returned to his life as a solicitor and made the decision to move out of the parental home into one of his own. He and Carenza had had fun doing it up. While this was going on he hoped that it was preparing Carenza for their future and her involvement in the process of home making would make her feel that it was theirs together.

The telephone rang in the hall. May looked at the clock and smiled at Carenza. Eight o'clock on the dot she reflected. It would be Tom. Carenza rose from her comfortable armchair by the fire where she had been marking her class's books and opened the door into the hallway. The draught of cold air that rushed into the room hit her like a wave from a tsunami. She shivered.

'I won't be long if it is this cold,' she said to May who was once more involved with her knitting.

'Answer the telephone and I will bring the old blanket from the cupboard to wrap you in,' May answered rising from her chair. The blanket was kept in the under-the-stairs cupboard. It had been used during times of illness when the invalid was allowed downstairs for the first time. May had often called it the comfort blanket. She found it where it had been placed but could not quite remember the last occasion when it had been used. That must be good. Good health was a blessing she mused.

She wrapped it around Carenza's shoulders as she heard her say.

'Hello Tom.'

May returned to the sitting room and closed the door quietly behind her. Both women respected the other's privacy but also shared so much.

'Have you heard the momentous news today?' he asked.

'I heard it at lunchtime when I came home. A new queen on the throne. She is not much older than me. What a responsibility.'

'Yes, we all have to face up to responsibility at some time,' he replied mysteriously.

'Is there anything wrong Tom,' Carenza had picked up on the strange comment.

'Nothing is wrong. I will see you as usual on Friday if that is all right with you and May.'

'You know that it is fine,' Carenza smiled down the phone. Tom could hear the smile in her voice and it lifted his spirits to hear it. There was a silence for a few seconds and then Carenza heard his voice again.

'Well I had better go. I have some documents to deal with before morning. By the way Carenza,' his voice broke off again.

'Yes,' she replied.

'I haven't asked you for weeks but will you marry me.' the line went quiet. Tom was awaiting the usual reply.

'Yes,' came the reply and a giggle erupted from Carenza.

'What did you say?' Tom felt stupefied.

'I said "Yes"!' she shouted down the phone. Even May heard her from the sitting room.

'You said "yes",' Tom reiterated stupidly. 'You mean it?'

'Yes!' she shouted again. May shifted uneasily in her chair wondering what on earth was going on.

'But why now Carenza? I am speechless.'

184

Carenza was speechless too. She had not thought that she would agree just yet.

'I don't know Tom. It just came out.'

Tom was consumed with doubt.

'You do mean it,' he faltered hoping that she would not backtrack now on the progress that had been made having waited so long.

'I must do,' she giggled again down the telephone. 'Goodnight Tom. 'See you at the weekend.'

'I love you,' was all he could say at this moment in time as he replaced the receiver into its cradle.

Carenza returned to the warmth of the sitting room. Her face matched the colour of the flames dancing in the hearth. May looked up from her knitting which she had had to unravel having dropped some stitches. The noise from the hall had caused her to lose concentration. Her daughter's flushed cheeks and excited face had not passed unnoticed.

'Are you all right Carenza? Is Tom all right?'

'Oh he's fine. He'll be over at the weekend as normal.'

May nodded her affirmation. Tom had a special place in her heart. He had not pestered Carenza into marriage but had been prepared to wait until the time was right. No comparison could be drawn between Lorna and her son, for which May was grateful. Deep down May had an inkling of what had taken place over the telephone but she was not going to ask. A lot of discussion would take place over the following weekend and she would be the first to know when the time was right. Of that she had no doubt.

*

Tom had not known what to feel after his conversation with Carenza. He was puzzled by her sudden capitulation but at the same time was euphoric that she had consented to become his wife. There were many issues that had to be resolved and the weekend was the ideal time to do it. At the same time he was frightened that Carenza might have second thoughts. Now he was not prepared to allow that to happen and to deflect any such reaction he was taking the reins of responsibility. There were so many issues to discuss but he was determined to take control to prevent Carenza reneging on the promises that she had made.

On the Thursday afternoon after his telephone call to Carenza Tom had made the decision to leave work early. Any work that was urgent could be taken home to be read later. Spencer was tied up in meetings all afternoon while Tom's grandfather had finished for the day. Tom drove his car into town and parked near to where he banked. His first port of call was to see his bank manager. He had made his appointment in the morning. The Hestons had been good customers over the years and Arnold Goodwin was never too busy to accommodate any member of the family, especially young Tom whom he had known since childhood when he had come to bank small amounts of money, encouraged by his grandfather's generosity.

He wanted to know that his finances were in order if he was to have added responsibility. Carenza would not be working and there was the fact that before long that they would have a family of their own. The visit to the bank had reassured him that his finances were fine. His second call was to the jewellers to look for an engagement ring. Only the best would do for Carenza. The main jewellers shop on the High Street was still open when he approached it. It was now quite late in the afternoon and it was getting dark. It had been one of those grey winter days which had hardly been light since daybreak. He had pulled his hat well down and the collar of his coat shielded the back of his neck from the biting wind which blew icily around him and any shopper who was around.

Tom opened the shop door while the bell tinkled heralding his approach. An elderly man shuffled into the shop from the depths of the back room where he had been mending jewellery. He peered at Tom questioningly as his guise made him look suspicious.

'Can I help you?' the old man enquired. His shaggy white eyebrows knitted together as one as he made his request.

'Could I see the tray of engagement rings that you have in the window please?'

The old man regarded Tom's demeanour. He believed that the young man standing before him appeared overexcited. There was always the worry that there might be a raid on the jewellery at this time of day.

'Which tray would that be?' the old man asked. Tom pointed to the one that he required. He had already decided on the ring that he wanted. It was quite a large sapphire surrounded by diamonds. His mother would approve of the quality but would balk at the fact that it was to be given to Carenza. He knew that the fit could be altered at another time. Carenza's fingers were only small so he was not too worried about choosing the wrong size. He just wanted to make sure that he had something concrete to place on her finger before she could change her mind.

The elderly shopkeeper shuffled to the back of the window and produced a set of keys from his pocket. Giving Tom a surreptitious glance as he turned the key in the lock, he withdrew the tray from the window and locked it again. By this time Tom had removed his hat allowing the old man to take a good look at him. It was quite unusual for a young man to come in to buy a ring on his own but the feeling of pessimism that had lain at the back of his mind was beginning to dissipate. Nothing sinister had occurred. He bought the tray of rings to the counter and placed it in front of Tom who lifted the one that he required out of its rest.

'Will it fit?' the old man asked.

Tom smiled, 'I don't know but she is only small fingered.'

'We can alter it if necessary. Bring it back if you need to,' the old man smiled his toothy smile. He felt happy and relieved now that he knew Tom was a credible customer.

'Thank you,' Tom replied putting the small box safely into his coat pocket having spent a considerable sum for the ring.

'Well goodbye then.' He shook the man's outstretched hand.

As he walked out of the shop he knew that he was entering the most exciting phase of his life so far. It had also occurred to him that he should ask May's permission to marry Carenza. It was the normal custom in his family's social circles to do such a thing. As Carenza had no father May was the one to ask but he knew that his new fiancée was of an age to make her own decisions. His thoughts turned to his own family. His father and Carenza were close. They had forged a friendship over the years sharing a similar sense of humour and ideology but Lorna was a different proposition. His face clouded as he considered his mother. In recent years she had remained aloof from family gatherings. He knew that there was a void between Lorna and Carenza which neither of them could quite bridge. There was also a yawning gap between himself and his mother. He felt that the closeness of his relationship with her during his childhood had disappeared into the ether. Perhaps Lorna was suffering from a form of depression. Mothers sometimes did when their young flew the nest. His parents' marriage was another issue. They had never been close but Tom was convinced that his father saw other women. Perhaps this was an issue they could not resolve. He felt sorry for his mother, believing that he would never treat Carenza in such a way. He truly loved her, of that he was certain.

He considered Carenza's refusal of an early marriage when they had little experience of the adult world and now bowed to her wisdom. They had both matured beyond recognition. His thoughts turned to his leaving university. Now he knew what a prig he had been, expecting the world to jump to his tune. His mother had spoilt him and his father had hardly been there. His knowledge of Carenza's past was scant but he knew that she had suffered hardships and it had given her an inner strength knowing that she only had herself to rely on until May came along and changed her life beyond recognition. Tom could not thank May enough for what she had done for Carenza. She was a wonderful woman.

Chapter 26

Carenza had shocked herself by her acceptance of Tom's marriage proposal. She had not told her mother but she had guessed that May had a certain intuition about what was happening. The best time to tell May would be when Tom came at the weekend. It was during the long nights before Tom's arrival that Carenza lay awake analysing her relationship with him. She knew that she loved him but her acceptance of marriage had to be on her own terms. Equality was the key to its foundation as well as security within its safe harbour. Her memories of her parents' marriage were as vivid today as they had ever been. Ray had treated Hannah badly for as long as she could remember. Her mother had loved Ray once but in the latter years she had been frightened of him and what he could do to her.

Her grandparents' partnership had been a shining beacon showing the world how two people loved each other without reservation. But Doris's indomitable spirit had nearly been broken by abject poverty and hard work. Carenza wondered what would have happened to Hannah and Doris if they had not died in the Blitz. But she too would have had a very different path in life. Her emotions were more in check now that she was older when she considered the tragic events of her past. How lucky she had been, the way her life had changed course only for the better. May's strength of character and philosophy on life had filled Carenza with optimism as well as planting her feet firmly on terra firma. May had been a woman on her own, but had succeeded where many married women remained doormats for their husbands. Carenza wore her independence as a badge and hoped to continue working for as long as possible. One's personal history she mused shaped the future if you did not take the world in your hands to control as much of your own destiny as you could.

*

Tom arrived as expected on Friday but he had left work early on the pretext of an out of town appointment. Spencer had wished him a pleasant weekend presuming that he was going to visit Carenza as normal. Very little passed Spencer's eagle eye.

He had noticed that Tom was in a happy mood. He corrected his first impression. He would have to say that he was behaving in a most excitable fashion. Spencer's intuition was often correct and he believed that it must be something to do with Carenza. But his train of thought was interrupted by his secretary announcing his next appointment.

Tom arrived at Nether Heydon at three o'clock on a cold but bright afternoon. The winter days were beginning to lengthen and there was a hint that spring might not be too far away. The good weather had buoyed up his feelings even more. He had chosen this time to arrive to be able to approach May before Carenza returned home from school. His car was parked around the corner from the house in its usual place. Curtains no longer twitched for it was no longer a novelty to see Carenza and Tom together. The short walk to the cottage began to calm his nerves. He had never felt that May would refuse him permission to marry Carenza but there was always that chance. He lifted the large brass knocker but the door swung open before he could knock. May was standing before him beaming.

'I saw you coming,' she enthused.

His surprise was apparent. Later when he thought back to that moment he wondered if May might have had a premonition that he would arrive early and what would eventually transpire that afternoon.

'Come in, come in,' she fussed taking his coat, scarf and hat and placed them on the hall chair. She had hardly given him an opportunity to cross the threshold.

'You are early today.' Tom had remained mute during May's monologue but he found his voice.

'Hello May. Sorry for being so early but I needed to speak to you urgently before Carenza came home.'

'I thought you might,' she replied enigmatically, leading the way into the drawing room. Would you like a cup of tea or do you want that little chat first?'

Tom had the grace to blush. So she knew already. Nothing passed May's radar. 'Wily old bird,' he thought but there was no rancour in his feelings.

'Let's talk first shall we?' It was a rhetorical question.

Tom felt that he had to take the bull by the horns so to speak. He ploughed straight into the speech that he had been practising.

'Well May you know that I have loved Carenza for many years ...' He paused to see the affect that his words had upon his impending mother-in- law. She looked him straight in the eye hardly blinking and did not utter a word. There were times when she did this. It had been a useful tool during her teaching days when she had to handle people who could be difficult.

Tom blundered on, 'I wanted to ask your permission to marry her.' Relief emanated from him now that he had said it. May continued to look him straight in the eye for a moment.

'You should know that you have my permission to marry her. I know that you love her but,' May lifted her finger to emphasize her point, 'all I ask Tom is that you continue to love her and to treat her as well as you do now. Keep her happy. She has had difficult times in her life which she will tell you about if she wants to. I know that she cares about you but she must never be hurt. If anyone ever hurt her they would have me to deal with as long as I am still on this earth.'

Tom was taken aback by May's forthright delivery. He knew that the bond between mother and daughter was strong but it was also unbreakable.

'You know that I will do everything within my power to make her happy. You have my word on that.'

May had not finished yet.

'So be it Tom. You both have my blessing. You know that Carenza will be a wealthy young woman one day but her inheritance is her independence. That clause is written into my will.'

'Of course; we will be financially well off in time but we don't need to talk of that now, surely.' Tom was blustering rather taken aback by May's direct approach.

'Carenza has no idea how wealthy she will be,' May was in full flow and was not prepared to be diverted by the young man in front of her. 'She knows that she will be well provided for but as yet has no knowledge of all the facts. She loves her work which is of extreme importance to her. If she wishes to continue to work after marriage then that should be her decision alone. Her independence is a fundamental right to her sense of wellbeing. I would rather tell you now before she comes. And … we never need to mention this again.'

'That is all right by me,' Tom was exhausted by the conversation but he knew that May only had Carenza's interests at heart.

May rose to her feet.

'Well what about that tea then?'

Tom stared after her departing figure quite dismayed by the conversation they had just had. It could hardly be called a conversation because the advantage had mostly been in May's court. But it had all been said and he knew that May would be true to her word not to mention it again.

*

Carenza had been late returning home. A child had misplaced an item of clothing and his mother had grumbled vociferously as if the fault lay with Carenza. The whole of the lost property box had been turned out and rifled through before the errant article was discovered in the cloakroom behind the shoe rack. Both parent and child left the school building in a state of despondency. Having cuffed the child around the head the mother ranted as if the world was at an end. The feckless child sobbed under the blows which rained down on him and put his arms above his head to fend them off.

Carenza watched this departing spectacle. She could not help but suppress a smile, wondering if she and Tom might feel the same way about any future children they might have.

*

After their early evening supper, May had made the excuse to visit Edgar and Jeannette at the vicarage. Her objective was to leave the two young people alone to discuss their future. She knew that Carenza had accepted Tom's proposal. The fuss over Tom's telephone conversation earlier in the week had made that self evident. Her welcome at the vicarage would be the same as ever, warm and inviting.

Chapter 27

The engagement was now official. Most of the people who had to know had been informed. Carenza had not had second thoughts much to Tom's relief. The engagement ring glittered on her finger and she wore it proudly. There had been no need to return it because it fitted snugly, looking exquisite, as she told Tom. May also thought that Tom had made a good choice in the matter. Her acceptance of him as a future son-in-law was complete but her only reservation was that Carenza should have security for life without having to rely on Tom. She was only repeating what her father had done for herself. Times had changed she acknowledged from before the war years when women had been liberated from drudgery but it would be her final gift to Carenza and what she made of it was her gift to herself. May knew that her daughter had a wise head, and was almost certain that she would use the impending gift sagely if there was a moment of crisis. Although she trusted Tom, there was something May needed to do which was for Carenza's information only. There was one stipulation that she would make to Carenza and that lay in the fact that neither Tom nor anyone else for that matter would need to know what she was about to divulge in a few days' time. This secret was to exist between the two of them. Keeping secrets from a spouse was not always the ideal policy but May was determined that it had to be the case on this occasion. The thought of discussing this business with Jeannette and Edgar had entered her mind but it was obliterated before it could take hold. She had a feeling what Edgar's view would be.

No date had been arranged for the wedding. As usual Carenza was not in a hurry to sacrifice her freedom. That would come soon enough. Tom was just overjoyed that she had accepted his proposal. His next task lay in the fact that he had to tell his parents. That was not quite accurate. It was his mother who would present the difficulties. The age old problems of Carenza's suitability would arise but this time his mother would have to live with a fait accompli. He was now in control of his destiny with a career and home of his own. His mother's influence over recent years had lessoned its hold on him. He believed that if she threatened him he could easily cut her out of his life completely. It would be a different story with his father whom he saw daily at the office. His relationship with his father was solid although he did not agree with his extra marital dalliances. Tom knew that he was not made that way and Carenza would never be treated that brutally. When he made his vows they were for life. The immature Tom was long gone. Looking forward to a new life and a family was an exciting prospect. Life had to be very different from the dysfunctional one he had experienced as a child. His frown revealed his thoughts on Carenza's childhood, one which he knew that she would never disclose. Could he bear such secrets? He knew that he had no choice but to acknowledge and accept her feelings otherwise he might lose her. That was not an option that he was prepared to risk.

*

Two months had elapsed since the announcement of the engagement. Life had resumed its normal routine. Tom continued to visit most weekends but he never offered Carenza a return visit to his parents' home. May had made a mental note of this but had failed to pass comment to Carenza or Tom. She suspected that Lorna lay at the root of the problem. Her intuition told her that it was a problem that would not go away even after Lorna's confession all those years ago.

However, Tom and Carenza had begun to make tentative plans to marry in the late summer which meant that she would leave her teaching job in Nether Heydon. This thought had saddened her. She loved the school and the children but she hoped to find a job again. The idea of losing her independence was beyond imagination. This she had confided in May who had not commented but in her own head had been mulling over the problem at length. It was time to act upon what had lain at the back of her mind for weeks now. The time was right for Carenza to share the secret but there were conditions that her daughter had to adhere to. The early April sunshine streamed through the hall window as May picked up the telephone. This call would set in motion what she had been planning. If the call was not made today, Carenza would be finishing school for the Easter holidays which would enable her to overhear the gist of the conversation. May needed Carenza to make a journey into town with her once the holidays had begun. It was like making an appointment to see her daughter she mused.

May did not know the telephone number and dialed the operator.

'Could you put me through to the Midland Bank in Worcester,' she asked.

'Hold the line caller,' the operator intoned.

A nasal voiced spoke down the line.

'How may I help you?' The sound of the girl's evident problems grated on May's already unsteady nerves.

'May I speak to Mr Fairweather please?'

'I'm afraid that Mr Fairweather is busy today,' came the standard reply. May was not about to take 'no' for an answer.

'If you tell Mr Fairweather that it is Miss May Faithful on the telephone he will speak to me.' Her voice had assumed the role of a person in authority. It had been used so often in the past in her capacity as headmistress. Smiling, May knew that 'the voice', as she deemed to call it, could be conjured from the depth of nowhere. Once a teacher, always a teacher she thought.

'Ah but as I have said ...' the girl stuttered trying to maintain a semblance of control.

'Just go and do it. He will speak to me,' May was becoming annoyed and rude for she did not suffer fools gladly.

'Oh,' was all the girl could say as she dropped the telephone.

Minutes later Russell Fairweather breathed heavily down the line as if he had been rushing.

'Hello May. What can I do for you?' May smiled into the telephone. Having known Russell Fairweather for many years, she knew that he would speak to her. The Faithfuls had been customers of the bank going further back before Russell's time. He had inherited them from the previous bank manager.

'Hello, Russell how are you? I would like to request a favour and make an appointment for next week?'

'What kind of favour?' he was puzzled by the request.

'The safety deposit box you have stored for me. Could you change the name on it to Carenza?'

'Are you sure May? It is quite a big step you are taking you know.'

'I am sure Russell. I expect that I will have to sign something. Could you draw up the necessary paperwork? The other issue is that I would like to bring Carenza along to view the contents and to know that they belong to her.'

Russell scratched his head, perplexed by the nature of the request

'Very well May. You don't need an appointment because you know that I will see you any time. Make it Tuesday afternoon. We will find you somewhere quiet and secure to view the box.'

'Russell you are a dear man. Thank you for your consideration. Goodbye.'

Placing the telephone back in its cradle, huge feelings of relief overwhelmed May. What she was about to do, should have been done before now and her next task was to persuade Carenza to journey into the city with her. Tom would be at work for most of Carenza's holiday, so there should be less of a problem.

*

The term had finished in the usual way. The behaviour of the children had been wild. But it was normal for the term to close in a wave of excitement and a feeling of relief by the teaching staff when they closed the door thankfully on the last of the miscreants knowing that they had two full weeks to recover their equilibrium.

Having spent another weekend at Nether Heydon, Carenza was relieved to see Tom return home on Sunday afternoon so that she could begin her recovery. May's suggestion of a sortie into the city on Tuesday had not filled Carenza with much enthusiasm. Surprised at her mother's insistence, Carenza had reluctantly agreed. They had decided that it was going to be a shopping trip to look for ideas for the forthcoming wedding dress. Lunch would be the icing on the cake for mother and daughter who needed to spend quality time together. Those times would become rarer once Carenza was married. It was unusual for May to initiate a shopping trip. Her wardrobe did not contain pretty clothes for she rarely had reason to dress up for special events. The wedding would give her a good excuse to buy a new outfit and a hat. May's normal attire had not changed in years. It was practical and unfussy.

The morning of the visit was glorious. Spring had really sprung. Blossom flowered and daffodils still grew in clumps along the roadside and in gardens. The queue at the bus stop was a higgledy piggledy mix of adults of all ages as well as children ready for a rare day out in the city.

'Hello Miss,' the children called out to Carenza.

She smiled and waved at them. Although she loved them one and all including the rogues who incessantly plagued her working life, it was not always a good thing to see too much of them out of school but this was what happened in village life. The bus arrived and mothers staggered up the steps with infants of all ages. There were a variety of reasons why mothers were prepared to take their offspring into town May observed. Some of the boys looked as if they were growing untidy mops on their heads which heralded a visit to the barber before school began again. Their shoes were in a sad state of repair. Toes poked through the tips of their already scuffed shoes. Carenza followed her mother onto the bus, having noticed May's lack of athleticism ascending the steps. This was a health warning as far as Carenza was concerned. She made a mental note that she should keep a closer eye on her mother. These days she lived in a selfish bubble she admonished herself. Her time was taken up by her career and her weekends with Tom. Making a mental note that eventually she would move away, she made a conscious decision that she must visit May regularly. The thought of buying a little car passed through her mind. She had driven Tom's car on occasions so that would be a possibility. May could come and stay with them sometimes.

The two women found a seat at the back of the bus. The back seat was already full of children kneeling to see through the dirt smudged window. It was a rare treat to go somewhere for the day. Many of the boys played in the fields in the holidays, wielding sticks as weapons and playing fantasy games. They were rarely supervised. It was no wonder that it took a few days at the beginning of term to restore discipline in the classroom.

The bus took about forty minutes to reach the outskirts of the city. It had picked up its full capacity of passengers along the route. Observing the majestic rise of the cathedral before them, May and Carenza disembarked at the nearest stop. The town was already busy.

'Shall we go for lunch first?' May suggested.

'That's fine by me,' Carenza replied.

They would have all afternoon to shop. There was nothing pressing for them to return home to. They were here to enjoy themselves. Having found their usual restaurant nearly empty they found their seats and ordered their usual dish of fish and chips. Carenza was now pleased that she had consented to the day out. It was relaxing to chat over a leisurely lunch as well as enjoying precious time together.

'Well, where shall we start?' Carenza asked.

'Well,' began May,' I must go to the Midland Bank first. I have a little business to attend to first.'

'We could arrange a time to meet after your business.'

'No Carenza. I want you to come with me. What I am doing today concerns you.'

'Me! Whatever for?' Her expression was incredulous.

'You will see.' May was not prepared to divulge any more at this moment. The mystery deepened. Having paid for their lunch the two women returned to the balmy spring day.

Chapter 28

The bank was located on the High Street. May strode out in a hurry hoping to accomplish her task as quickly as possible. Once she had completed her business she and Carenza could enjoy the rest of the day. Carenza followed her mother into the dark interior of the bank. Having visited the bank on numerous occasions she found that this visit was shrouded in mystery. Russell Fairweather appeared from behind a desk. He was a great bear of a man but his demeanour was gentle and his eyes twinkled. His hand stretched to meet May's. The warmth between them was genuine.

'You remember Carenza,' May introduced them.

'Of course I do. How are you Carenza?' he asked politely smiling benignly at her.

'Very well thank you,' she dimpled at him.

'This way then,' he indicated a door which led into the heart of the building. Along the passage, he opened another door into a dark room which boasted a single light bulb hanging from the ceiling. The only other light came from a small barred window high up in the wall. Carenza shivered slightly. The sheer coldness of the room struck her forcefully as a deep contrast to the warm sunshine that they had left outside. The stark interior of the room reminded her of a prison cell.

'What was May up to?' she asked herself, glancing at her mother.

'The box is there. I will go and get the key.' Russell Fairweather's voice interrupted Carenza's reverie. For the first time she noticed a rectangular box in the centre of the table. As Russell disappeared, May pulled the box towards her. It was such a long time since she had seen the contents. It must be years, she mused. Her mind floated back to another time when her father had been alive. She had stood in this same room viewing the contents for the first time.

The door opened and closed quickly heralding Russell's return. He handed a small key to May. Now Carenza was more than intrigued. Wondering what she was about to witness her eyes were riveted to the metal box. She had to stifle a giggle as the words 'Pandora's box' drifted through her mind. This behaviour had to stop she reprimanded herself. A few days before the end of term Carenza had nearly been caught out for not listening during school assembly. Mrs Brookes, her head mistress had fired a question at her in front of the entire school. She had to use her wits to remove herself from a difficult situation.

'Well, I shall leave you now. Make sure that you return the key to me before you leave. Oh, and there will be the papers to sign.'

'I will Russell and thank you,' May was forever grateful for his discretion. The door closed quietly behind him.

'Well now Carenza, the contents of this box belong to you. They are an early wedding present to you. But there is one stipulation you must agree to before you receive them.'

The puzzled expression on Carenza's beautiful face told a story of its own.

'What must I agree to May?'

May looked at the daughter she thought she would never have. Her heart filled with love for her as it had done so many times over the years.

'You must agree to not telling anyone about the contents of this box. Not even Tom.'

'But why May?'

'The contents of the box are valuable. You will see that when I open it. This is your nest egg, your security if times in the future are tough. I will not be around forever my girl.'

'Don't say that please May.' Carenza's eyes watered at the mere thought. She could not envisage a world without May.

'Don't be maudlin Carenza,' May's voice had a sharpness to it which disguised her own emotions. She turned to open the box.

As the lid opened Carenza gave a gasp. There were boxes stacked inside the main box. Business like, May removed every one and laid them out on the table. Once she had done that she opened each individual box revealing an article of jewellery inside.

'These are yours now Carenza.'

Carenza was staggered.

'But where have they come from?'

'They were my father's gift to me for the same reason that I am giving them to you. I had brothers who inherited a law firm and made a fortune in their work. Although I had my independence, through teaching, these items were to ensure my security and my future. I have no need of them now. I have never had need of them for my requirements are modest as you know.'

Carenza viewed each piece in their magnificence. 'What is this beautiful egg May?' She held it reverently.

'That is a Fabergé egg which is very valuable. It is from Russia. These necklaces are from Asprey Garrard which my father bought for my mother from New Bond Street in London. They were presents over the years. This one was a wedding present for her and she received one on the birth of each of her children.'

'Oh May, Whatever would I do with these? I could never wear them. They are too valuable,' Carenza placed her arm round May in a gesture of affection.

'Perhaps you won't wear them but they are yours from now on. They are your legacy and nest egg if times become financially difficult. That will probably never happen but there is always the chance in a difficult world. But if it ever came about you must have them individually valued.'

May picked up a plique-a-jour enamel brooch from its box. 'This was my twenty first birthday present from my parents,' she said wistfully. Her hand reached into another box. 'This was my mother's 14 ct gold Cartier wrist watch. And this was my father's gold Hunter pocket watch and Albert chain. I can remember him wearing that to go to the office at his law firm.'

The jewellery contained many fine pieces, some more valuable than others.

'Carenza you will always have something to fall back on. If you don't need these pieces they can be passed on to your own children. And remember that you will inherit many other things that Tom can enjoy with you but not these. They are yours alone.'

'May I don't know what to say to you. Thank you is not enough.' She hugged her mother tightly.

'You, being my daughter has been enough over these last years. You have brightened my life beyond all recognition. For that I cannot thank you enough.' She turned from Carenza and replaced the items back into their boxes before turning the key.

Russell Fairweather tapped on the door before peering into the gloom.

'Everyone all right?' he asked. He had watched the hands of the bank clock go round without hearing a sound emanate from the room.

'Everything is fine Russell thank you,' May said lightly. The two women followed him back into the bank and then into his office. He indicated chairs where they could sit.

'The paperwork is in order if you would care to sign May. And then Carenza could you sign in the other box underneath.'

May picked up the document to peruse before she signed it. It was her father's legacy to his family that every document should be scrutinized thoroughly before any signature was added to it.

'That seems to be in order Russell.' She signed her name with a flourish before passing the document to Carenza.

The key was returned to Russell's safe keeping.

'Thank you Russell. You have been so kind and considerate today.' Her hand shook his.

'My pleasure May, any time. You are a very valued customer.'

Returning to the afternoon sunshine was a considerable shock. The light was too bright after the gloom of the bank's interior.

'Well what's stopping us going to view wedding dresses then,' May smiled at Carenza as she began striding off towards the Foregate.

Carenza shook her head.

'What a woman,' she thought. 'If I have a fraction of her drive and stamina I will be lucky.'

*

Tom was due to arrive on Friday evening as usual. Carenza had had a lot to think about since the visit to the bank in Worcester. There were still questions that she wanted to ask May but it would not be possible in Tom's presence. That evening when her mother had reluctantly finished her chores in the garden where she had begun her spring tidy up, Carenza had decided to ask her as they sat down to their supper.

'May,' she asked, 'how did your father have a Fabergé egg and trinket box in his possession? Had he travelled to Russia?'

May beamed. 'I have been waiting for you to ask that.'

'Come on then. Tell me. I know that they must be worth a fortune.'

'My father did some legal work for a Russian count and his wife. They had escaped from Russia during the time of the Revolution. They had little money so they paid my father with the egg and the trinket box. He did not want to take it but they were insistent.'

'But surely the legal work did not mirror the value of the egg?'

'No, but you must understand that was all they had. These Russians who escaped the 1917 Revolution left the country in a hurry. Practically with only what they were wearing. It is said that some women sewed jewellery into the hems and linings of their clothes to smuggle it out. They could then use it as collateral.'

'What would they be worth?'

'I don't know the full value of the jewellery but it will be a lot. But what I can tell you now is that many years ago the egg was valued at £1000 and the trinket box at £500. If you ever needed to sell these items, my advice to you is to have them valued by a creditable dealer before you decided to sell them. Prices do not remain the same over time.'

May knew that she had said all these things before, but she wanted her daughter to be fully aware of these conditions so that somebody unscrupulous would not take advantage of her should the case arise.

Carenza nodded her head thoughtfully. Having known that she would be comfortably off after May's demise, the events of the previous few days had put a different perspective on everything. She did not like the thought that she could not tell Tom but she knew that her mother meant well. Not all marriages were made in Heaven.

Chapter 29

It was time Tom thought that he should tell his parents about the engagement. He had felt this for weeks but his courage was at a low ebb. Carenza had admonished him for not telling his parents.

'You've just got to get on with it Tom. Your mother might not agree but you are an adult and there is nothing she can do about it.'

She felt guilty that her mother and their close friends had known for weeks but she did understand his reluctance in telling his mother and father. During the past few days Tom had been short tempered. It had been noticed in the office. Most especially his father, Spencer, knew that something was the matter and had decided to have a quiet word with his son. Knocking on Tom's door, Spencer put his head round to see if he was there. Tom looked up from the document that he had been reading to observe his father watching him.

'Have you got a minute old boy?' Spencer asked.

'Yes, sure come in and sit down.'

'Thanks. Is everything all right Tom? It's just office gossip says that you're a bit edgy.'

Tom grimaced

'You've noticed.'

'Not too difficult. You've been like a bear with a sore head. What's the matter? Tell me.'

'Oh, I might as well. I'm engaged to Carenza, two months ago precisely.'

Spencer's face brightened like the sun coming out from behind a cloud. But a puzzled expression replaced the joy.

'Why the bad temper then. Did Carenza push you into it?'

'No, of course not,' Tom laughed for the first time in days. 'It was finding the right time to tell mother. You know what she can be like.'

'Ah! Your mother,' Spencer pulled a rueful face. 'I indeed know what she is like but she must be told today old boy. I am out for the evening. Why don't you go round for dinner and tell her then. You can't avoid it much longer you know and by the way I think it's wonderful. I love Carenza like a daughter.'

Tom could not help but smile at his father's response. He knew that fundamentally he was a good man. What a pity that his mother never witnessed this side of him. The two men hugged affectionately.

'Thanks Dad, you are the best.' They both laughed. Feeling somewhat better, Tom then contemplated the evening ahead of him with some reluctance but it had to be done.

*

Arriving promptly at his parents' home at seven o'clock having agreed all the details on the telephone, Tom sat for a few minutes in the car thinking about how his mother might react to the news. Under normal circumstances the engaged couple would have come together to share their good fortune he mused. The delight in his mother's voice when he had suggested dinner *à deux* was evident. Guilt engulfed him, knowing how much he neglected her these days. Noticing differences since his last visit which must have been weeks before, he saw that the front door had been painted and the front lawn had been crisply cut after the long winter. After he knocked the front door was opened by Esther, the new maid. Taking off his hat and coat, he handed them to the girl before walking into the sitting room. He could feel the doom entrenched in his heart. His mother rose to greet him with a smile of pure pleasure etched on her face which transformed her usual sour expression into a radiance that he had not witnessed for a very long time. In fact he was taken aback by her beauty. He had never thought of her as that before but this must have been what his father had seen in her all those years ago.

'Hello Mother,' he smiled back. Would what he was about to divulge be as bad as he expected?

'Lovely to see you, Tom,' she enthused. A thaw had set in after a general frostiness that had existed between them for months. 'Would you like a drink?' she purred. Tom went to the crystal decanter where he poured himself a good measure of whisky. He knew that would calm the nerves and soften the bombshell that he was about to drop which would shake his mother to her very core.

'Would you like a drink Mother?' he asked before noticing that she had an empty sherry glass on the occasional table next to her chair. He had never known her drink alcohol when she was on her own before.

'I'll have a sweet sherry, darling, please.'

Tom placed the new glass of sherry by the first. Wondering if he should comment, he then decided against it. It would not be wise to cross her before he had delivered his news. They chatted amicably for a while discussing family news. Some of Tom's cousins were about to marry soon.

'You need to put those dates in your diary Tom. Keep those dates clear and perhaps you can accompany me. I can never quite rely on your father these days.'

Tom made no comment. He was not prepared to discuss his father with his mother realizing that he knew where his loyalties lay these days. There was a leisurely dinner and conversation was easy. After Esther delivered the dessert, Tom knew that the time had arrived to deliver the fait accompli. There was no other way to say it but to come straight out with it.

'Mother, Carenza and I are to be married soon.'

Lorna's cutlery landed with a crash onto the plate in front of her.

'You are going to marry her.' The well of tears flowed from his mother's eyes. 'Tom you cannot. You don't know anything about her.'

'I don't need to,' he blustered. 'I know what is important. I love her. That is all that matters. Dad has given his blessing. I would like to have yours too, Mother. That is not too much to ask surely?'

'So you told your father before you told me. Thanks very much.' Her voice was full of bitterness and the beautiful face was contorted in fury.

Tom had been right all along that his mother would not accept Carenza.

'Why do you dislike her so much? What has she done to deserve your bitterness?'

'It's her background,' spat Lorna.

'You know nothing of her background. Not even I know.'

'I know all about it,' Lorna knew that she had made the biggest mistake of her life passing that comment. It had slipped out in the shock of digesting what her son had revealed. Only May knew what she had done in the past.

Tom was perplexed by what his mother had just said. How would she know about Carenza's past?

'What do you mean Mother, that you know?'

'I just do. Leave it there.' Lorna was not going to divulge the details about the hiring of a private detective. She was not proud of stooping so low. But Tom was not satisfied by what he was hearing.

'Did Carenza tell you when she stayed here? Surely you did not stoop so low as to drag it out of her. I know that she never wants to come here.'

Lorna was rendered speechless. If she said any more, she would give everything away.

'Go on tell me. Who told you?'

'It was May who told me,' she lied.

'How do you know May? She has never been here.'

'She telephoned me once. She did not want you and Carenza to be involved either.' The lies were growing by the minute.

'I don't believe you mother. May is not like that. I have known her for several years and she would never do such a thing. She is thrilled by the engagement.' Tom stood up abruptly in his anger and knocked his chair abruptly in the process.

'I am going Mother. Don't contact me for the time being. I need to think before we meet again.' He could not wait to leave the room or the house and he wanted to speak to May to find out more. Why would his mother say such a thing?

'Don't go Tom,' she screamed as he fled into the hall. The tears poured in a torrent down her face gauging great rivulets in her makeup. This was a moment of true pathos for her face was ravaged, looking like a clown's, but her tears were the most genuine that she had ever shed. As the front door shut behind her son, Lorna reached for the sherry bottle. It gave her more comfort than anything or anybody.

*

There was no sympathy left in Tom for his mother. She had manipulated so much over the years, interfering in his life where it was his right to make decisions for himself. He did not know whether he ever wanted to see her again. Having left the house in such a hurry, he had forgotten his hat and coat but he was not prepared to return to collect them. His car keys jingled in his pocket as he searched for them. By now he was so furious that he did not know whether to drive home or to drive to Nether Heydon to confront May. The car seemed to make up its own mind. He was lost in deep, resentful thoughts when he realized that he was nearing Nether Heydon. The lights were still switched on in May's cottage. Glancing at his watch he noted that it was 10.30 p.m. and he knew that the two women would be preparing for bed. By this time he had worked himself into such a state of anger that he hammered on the front door.

'Who's that?' Carenza shouted down the stairs.

'Go to bed Carenza. I'll deal with it.'

Carenza sat on the top step to listen. She could not abandon May to a possible stranger. The lights were immediately switched on in the hall and May peered through the window but could only see the outline of a male form. She was rarely afraid living in the village but the force of the knocking had unnerved her. The front door was opened a little before she recognized Tom standing there, whereby she flung it wide. Tom pushed his way rudely passed the two women. Carenza had by this time crept downstairs to give her mother support.

'What are you doing here Tom?' May could not hide her surprise for they rarely saw him during the week.

'What is it Tom? What has caused you to be in such a bad mood?' Carenza had sensed his agitation before he even spoke.

'Everybody knows but me. I'm the person that you are marrying but I'm not told,' he shouted at them, his emotions etched firmly on his face.

'You don't know about what, Tom?' But Carenza had her suspicions.

May took control and steered Tom into the sitting room where he was made to sit in the chair next to the dying embers of the fire. He was shaking but neither of the two women knew whether it was from shock or anger. Lifting the stopper from the cut glass brandy decanter she poured a generous measure into a brandy balloon and handed it to her future son-in-law.

'Here you are Tom. Drink this and do try and calm down.'

Tom gratefully took the brandy and nearly swallowed it in one go. Both women watched him visibly relax as the anger began to dissipate. Gradually he began to unburden himself as he related the events that had unfolded during the course of the evening. May sank into the chair opposite Tom. So Lorna was still embittered even after all these years. Who would have thought that she would harbour a grievance for so long? But to claim that it was herself who had divulged the details of Carenza's history was unforgiveable.

'Did you tell her May?' Carenza did not know what to believe.

'It is time to tell you both the truth, and Carenza you must tell Tom about your childhood.'

As May's story unfolded about Lorna's visit to the cottage all those years ago, both young people could not believe what they were hearing.

'She hired a private detective to find out about me. Does she dislike me so much?'

'I think you have to feel sorry for Lorna. She is not a happy woman. We both vowed we would not tell you about it. However, under such circumstances I had to tell the truth. I am not prepared to listen to the lies that she is telling. Tell Tom now Carenza.' May rose from her chair and kissed them both on the cheek. 'Good night.' Opening the sitting room door she then closed it softly behind her allowing the two young people time alone.

*

Dawn was beginning to glow in the April sky as Tom and Carenza finally went to bed. The tale of her early childhood had been told. Tom had not interrupted her during her monologue but on completion he took her in his arms knowing that she was one in a million. He could not have been more proud of her or loved her any more than he did at this moment. But there was one decision that Tom had made that night concerning his mother. He would never see her again. There would be no invitation to the wedding. His father could come on his own or take sides with his wife. It was his choice.

Chapter 30

After recounting her early history, Carenza was exhausted. But she was reassured by Tom that her early years had no bearing on their relationship. He was quite perplexed as to why there had been so much secrecy in the first place. These thoughts had been quite a revelation to him too. Of course he had memories of being as big a snob as his mother during his formative years but life had been the greatest educator that it always was. His time doing military service and his occupation as a solicitor where he saw every rank and file of humanity had made him what he was today. Snobbery no longer played a part in his world. Compassion had become a main force in his life as well as gratitude for the privileges and the education he had received.

Carenza had made Tom promise one thing

'You have to apologise to May. You doubted her and she doesn't deserve that.'

Tom hung his head in shame, sending Carenza into a fit of giggles.

'I will,' he promised, 'I'm sorry that I ever doubted her.'

'So you should be,' Carenza wagged her index finger at him. 'And don't cold shoulder your mother. Life is too short to have regrets. She is to be pitied more than anything else.'

'I know but at the moment I can't forgive her for what she has done to you.'

'Speak to your father. He will help you sort out your problems.'

Tom looked doubtful

'Perhaps but I don't want to dwell on it now. Probably in a few weeks I might feel better.'

*

Tom and Carenza's relationship had matured and deepened after recent events. May saw this and nothing thrilled her more. An apology had been forthcoming but it was not in May's nature to bear grudges but what had saddened her was that Lorna could do such awful things. It was the lies that bore the fruit of her wickedness. Wondering if she should visit the other woman to clear the air, she took some time contemplating this thought but eventually decided that it was another occasion of someone going behind the backs of the two young people. Perhaps Lorna would change her ways if there were grandchildren and she could see what she was missing. But could any of these bridges which Lorna had constructed ever be crossed?

'Only time will tell,' she muttered sagely.

May's relationship with Tom was back on track but Carenza was still unhappy about the secrecy of the jewellery. Time and again she had been tempted to divulge the news of her nest egg but each time had wavered remembering her mother's warning.

'Do you think that I should tell Tom?' She asked for the third time in as many days.

May was adamant.

'No. If times become difficult you could cash it all in and use the money but the way I see it is that Tom has a good income. You have an income from teaching and eventually you will have all of this and more.' She wafted her arms about theatrically indicating the house and its antique contents. 'Let's not hear any more about it. One more secret won't hurt.'

Carenza was still not sure. She had never regarded the house and its contents in that light. It had always been home, warm, loving and comfortable. The antiques had always been there. Her new insight into a wealthy future made her think about May growing up in this house and her father before her. The antiques were family heirlooms which had been passed down through the generations. In the drawing room where she was now standing, she listened to the sonorous tick of the long case clock and the hourly striking of the Vienna wall clock. The fender, surrounding the coal fire, which always blazed in the grate, summer or winter alike, was elaborate in its decoration. There were also the andirons majestically sitting erect, either side of it. The dark oak dresser stood against the wall next to the French doors leading into the garden. Old blue and white pottery, no doubt a Faithful inheritance, stood mellow in colour against the backdrop of the dark hue of the piece of furniture. She touched a plate tracing the willow pattern with her finger. Her finger withdrew almost as quickly as if she had been burnt. But now she was afraid that it might break under any pressure that she put there. Wondering why she had not seen her home more clearly before, she now knew how much she had taken it all for granted. But this puzzled her knowing how little she had had in her early life.

Continuing her journey into the hall, there in front of her hung the hunting watercolours which she gazed at as if seeing them for the first time. Near the occasional table where the telephone resided, a stick barometer hung on the wall revealing the high pressure that they were enjoying now that spring had come. Along the hall was the study which had been used by May's father all those days ago. She could imagine him sitting at the large oak desk which stood in front of the window overlooking the garden at the side of the house. He was almost alive before her eyes having listened to May recounting stories about him. She knew his face by heart having regarded the photographs of him scattered round the house. This room remained almost untouched from the time he had lived there.

The dining room boasted the long Pembroke table which was surrounded by a set of Victorian ladder back chairs, again in the dark wood which complemented the cottage. A sideboard lined another wall where more china was displayed. Again the blue and white pottery jumped out at her.

'What are you doing Carenza?' asked May.

'Just looking,' she said as she turned towards her mother. 'I think I have taken this for granted over the years. I am sorry.'

May's wise old face twisted into a smile.

'We always take our home for granted. It is where we close the door against the problems of the world and hope we are safe for at least part of our lives. Stop thinking so deeply Carenza. There is no need.'

'You know that I will never sell any of this, when it all becomes mine, a long way into the future I hope.'

She did not know how prophetic that comment would be.

Chapter 31

Tom had made an appointment with his father at the office. The very idea of doing so had made him chuckle. But at the same time it was a serious issue that he had to discuss with him. There was no way that he would return to his parents' home where he would encounter his mother but on the other hand his father was always out on the pretext of a business meeting . And there was no guarantee as to when he would return home.

Spencer Heston sat behind his large, imposing mahogany desk. Curiosity had taken hold of him when Tom had asked for this audience but he made the assumption that the matter must be quite serious because he was not taking his problems to the house. Therefore, they must involve Lorna. Spencer frowned when he thought of his wife. There was no love lost between them these days and no common denominator to connect them except for Tom. He supposed that he had loved her once long before Tom was born. When Tom was born he became the focal point of her life which left little time for Spencer's needs. In more recent years she had developed into the selfish and snobbish woman she now was. Once Tom had reached adulthood and was out of her jurisdiction Lorna returned to her inner circle of well to do friends. It had taken Spencer years to realize how much his wife despised him for his lack of fortune and middle class roots. She had never left her aristocratic up bringing however minor the titles were.

Spencer had experienced a crisis of confidence while in his middle forties. This he now attributed to Lorna's goading of him to make more of his life. Lorna had taunted him with the fact that it was her inheritance alone that gave them the quality of life that they enjoyed. Spencer had been so belittled over time that he decided to seek solace elsewhere. His eyes had begun to wander beyond the confines of his home. Through his occupation, he had made new friends and had attended dinner parties on his own. He had made excuses that he was making new contacts for business and the prospective clients could only meet him outside of office hours. At the dinner parties he became the single male who was seated next to the unmarried or widowed lady of an uncertain age. But marital status had not mattered. His affairs had become numerous and legendary amongst his peers. Over time one woman had stood out from the crowd. His eyes softened at the mere thought of Camilla Wagstaffe who eventually had become his mistress. Their affair had moved from passion into genuine love. Spencer would be prepared to divorce Lorna if the circumstances were right. He did not want anything from her and she would not need anything financially from him. But he knew that Lorna would not want a divorce. Although their marriage had been over for years, gossip and stigma were the two advocates that she was not prepared to fight. Losing face before her social climbing friends was something she would not do. So the sham of a marriage continued. There had been a time when Spencer had asked for a divorce declaring that he was prepared to take the blame, allowing his wife to remain above reproach in such matters.

Lorna had refused carte blanche. Again she had goaded him with the loss of the house and friends. His life style would disintegrate before his eyes if he behaved in such a way. Spencer did not care about any of those things but he knew that Lorna would take revenge. She would be a woman scorned and as such she would become malicious and as a result would bring him down. But Spencer's trump card was Tom. She would not be prepared to damage him. The family business which was Tom's inheritance would have to flourish at all costs.

Spencer thought about Camilla who had brought a joy into his life that he had not known for so long. They had first met at a dinner party where her husband had been present. Bruno was a dominating force on many levels. His conversation at table was heard many decibels above other guests. His opinions on many varied subjects were the only ones which counted. He could be obnoxious and overbearing but he was still invited to social functions. It was his status as a well known barrister and possible Queen's Counsel which many people courted. He was useful to know. Under his domination Camilla became subdued. His constant intimation that she was just the mother of his children without any purpose of her own had allowed her self esteem to plummet into depression and lassitude .

Spencer had often been placed next to her at dinner. They had talked at length about their lives and interests, allowing them to become better acquainted. Secretly they began seeing each other. At first it was snatched meetings in town over cups of tea and coffee in cafes where they would not be known and gossiped about. When Bruno had to go further afield for business, perhaps to London, their life became less restricted. They could take in a show with dinner afterwards but they always made their own way home. It was into the third year of these clandestine meetings that their situation changed. Bruno Wagstaffe had a major heart attack while staying at his London Club. His body was brought home and buried with great pomp and circumstance. Dignitaries from the local area attended the funeral of the great man but nobody witnessed the relief of his widow who played her part accordingly. Camilla was free now to lead her own life. Her two sons had left home years before to pursue their own careers and she was left to live in a mausoleum of a house. This she had sold for a considerable amount of money bringing her an independence of which she would never have dreamed. Having bought a smaller property on the edge of town in the leafy suburbs, she could welcome Spencer now without the world knowing what went on behind her front door.

Spencer thought about Camilla. She was everything that Lorna had never been or would ever be. Her compassion and her love for him flowed from her and since Bruno's demise she had flourished under Spencer's care and attention. She became animated and her innate intelligence shone through. Camilla was no great beauty as Lorna had been in her time but Spencer did not care. He had married the beautiful socialite but it had not worked. Instead Camilla possessed an inner loveliness which he would not swap for anything. He was passed his passionate youth. All he desired was peace and tranquility with the woman he loved. His desire was to do the right thing by Camilla but there were still many hurdles to overcome before that could be achieved.

It was during this jumbled array of thoughts that Tom's knock came, followed by his head peering around the door as he observed his father.

'Is it the right time? You're not too busy?'

'Come on in Tom. What can I do for you?' Spencer rose from his desk to greet his son.

'I don't quite know where to start, Father,' Tom replied.

'Is it about your mother?' Spencer had hit the nail on the head.

'Why, yes. How did you guess?'

'Just my intuitive mind,' Spencer grimaced. 'What has she done now?'

At the end of the hour Tom had divulged all of Lorna's misdemeanours and had related Carenza's life history. Spencer was speechless at Lorna's audacity. But Carenza's history did not faze him. He was remarkably fond of the girl and was certain that she would make Tom a good wife.

'I don't want Mother to be at the wedding but I want you to be there.' He had dropped his bombshell.

'This is going to be a difficult one to contend with, Tom. I will certainly be there for you but this problem with your mother has to be sorted out once and for all otherwise she will plague your lives forever. I can have a word with her but you know that I am like a red rag to a bull these days. I will get back to you as soon as I can.'

'Thanks Dad.' Tom was grateful for any support against his mother's veiled threats.

He loved his father and had realized in his adult years that Lorna gave him a hard time. Nothing had been revealed about his father's extra marital affair but Spencer had felt that was to be divulged at another time. The suggestion of divorce was an unsavoury business at the best of times. Patting his son heartily on the back he returned to the business at hand. His pride in his son's handling of his career and his relationship with Carenza knew no bounds. They were a fine young couple but he was full of trepidation of the impending conversation he was to have with his wife. But a thought struck him which might be the answer to all his prayers.

Chapter 32

The summer term had begun. The weather was warm and balmy for a late April day. Carenza could not believe how quickly the holidays had passed. It had been exciting discovering the jewellery but it had definitely been a difficult time when they had discovered Lorna's deceit. Taking May's advice she knew that it all had to be put behind her. It had been the last weekend of the holidays when May had sat the couple down to discuss the impending nuptials. They had nothing finite planned and were aghast at how quickly the time was approaching.

'You must get on with the planning you know,' May had grumbled at them. 'Weddings don't just happen themselves.'

'Have you planned many weddings May?' Tom asked innocently.

May had the grace to blush.

'Of course I haven't,' she blustered, 'but I have plenty of common sense.'

'She does,' Carenza agreed, keeping her face straight.

May regarded the young couple in front of her but could not quite work out if they were poking fun at her. If they were she was not happy about it but she battled on regardless.

'You need to make lists of guests you want to invite and so on,' she continued and then left the young couple alone to do just that. As she left the room she heard Carenza giggle. She stuck her nose in the air trying to keep her dignity intact.

'That was mean Tom.'

'You were no better,' he retorted, 'but she is right we must get on with it.'

They had both made lists of what needed doing and the people who should be invited to the wedding and then all they had to do was to put the planning in motion. During the week before Tom's return Carenza had begun to think about practical solutions to some of the problems she foresaw once she and Tom were married.

May, in her eyes, was one of these problems. Although, she was not frail and could live quite happily on her own at the moment Carenza did not want to live too far away because she felt that it was her duty to look after her mother in her encroaching old age.

Her gratitude to her for all that she had done over the years knew no bounds. May had never made her feel this way but she just did. Carenza had always been a person who thought of others before herself.

May was beginning to lack mobility which had made Carenza send her to the doctor. Doctor Fulbrook could do little to alleviate the arthritis but he had been adamant that a stick was a necessity to provide support for the condition. Vanity played no part in daily health matters. Carenza had made the visit with her mother and had guaranteed that May, despite her protestations, would do as she was told. The stick had been purchased on Carenza's next visit into Worcester and May had to suffer the ignominy of using it in public. It had also been Carenza's threat that if the stick was not used people would tell her and then she would have to punish her. May had had the good grace to laugh at the threat knowing that her daughter only had her best interests at heart.

Another problem was the losing of her job after the wedding. She was happy at the village school and to start again was going to be a huge wrench. The fact that Tom would not have to move jobs made her annoyed. Why did women have to sacrifice so much? The old upsurge of independence ruffled her feathers once more. Her legacy was there secreted away in the bank vault and she was forbidden to tell Tom. She could not wear her independence like a badge on her sleeve to show the whole world that she was a person in her own right. There was a lot of work still to be done before women were fully liberated she thought.

There was also the issue of Tom's house. Carenza did not want to live there because of its close proximity to Lorna's home. She did not want to be a sitting duck for her future mother-in-law to be able to take pot shots at her whenever she felt like it. The wounds that Lorna's treachery had inflicted on them were still too raw. After much inner angst Carenza began to see the light of day. Answers to the problems began to appear but she had to persuade Tom to agree.

There was also something Carenza had to do for herself and that meant learning to drive. She could afford a small car which would increase her independence. On many an occasion she had driven Tom's car with learner plates fastened to the front and back of the vehicle. They had driven mostly along the leafy country lanes but it had not been the ideal situation for it had led to arguments. Tom was notorious for his impatience. Carenza knew that she could not be like that. A teacher had to have the patience of Job.

*

When Tom returned to Nether Heydon the following weekend May was waiting for him. As he turned from locking the car door and carried his holdall along the path towards the cottage she noticed how tired he looked.

'Has the week been that bad Tom?' she asked noting the dark circles under his eyes.

He pulled a wry smile, 'It has sort of. I spoke to my father about all this fuss my mother has created. He is going to speak to her soon. But their relationship is not too good at the moment either.'

'Ah! I see,' May grimaced but said diplomatically, 'I'm sure that it will work itself out.'

Tom's body language suggested something else.

'Is Carenza around?' he asked.

'No, but she won't be long. She has just gone to Edgar about wedding dates. She is quite anxious to start making arrangements. Time is marching on she feels.'

'Too true,' he said placing his weekend bag down where nobody could trip over it. 'I can't wait for the day to come.'

*

During Tom's visit many issues had been rectified but there was the dilemma of the house which they had bought as a potential future home. They could not find common ground to find a lasting solution to the problem. The house was in close proximity to the Heston family home. Carenza was not prepared to live anywhere near Lorna where she could easily become prey to her vicious tongue and devious behaviour. Tom agreed with these sentiments entirely but it was the house which he was reluctant to let go of. He had grown to love the place and had spent a lot of money in having it renovated. There was no easy solution to this problem. He did not want to be stretched too far financially and he was not in a position to ask his mother for a loan. His copy book had been blotted too heavily on that score already and he was not prepared to be beholden to anyone. But he wanted Carenza to be happy. From now on she would be his family and perhaps with children one day they would be complete.

'I doubt that we could afford a second mortgage until the house was sold,' he said,' even if you continue to work Carenza. But it is a good idea to keep your job at the school. That would be sensible to begin with.'

'Tom, May says that we can live here until we have sorted out a home. There are two bedrooms upstairs at the back of the house which can be used as a bedroom and a sitting room. They join in the way that you have to walk through one to reach the other room. You know what these old houses are like.'

Tom's face visibly brightened.

'That would be a short term solution but I do want a home of our own soon. I suppose that we will have to sell our house if you want to live nearer May.'

'Of course we want a home of our own but not near your mother Tom.'

'Well we have a short term solution and I will set the ball rolling to sell the house. Now we just have to concentrate on the wedding.'

'Edgar says he has a spare Saturday at the end of August, the last but one Saturday to be exact.'

'Well, how about the honeymoon?' he smiled as excitement began to take over. It felt that all their plans might reach fruition.

'What about London? That is my home town.'

'I know,' he said looking at her intently. 'You told me recently.'

'Of course I did,' she replied sheepishly.

*

Spencer had been highly concerned about tackling Lorna. He had always tried to avoid confrontations but he had promised Tom that he would speak to her and he wanted to play his own trump card. The day he chose was a Saturday when Camilla had family commitments and Lorna was at home. Spencer had consulted the calendar in the bespoke kitchen of the family home and noticed that Lorna had no prior engagements. This was an unusual occurrence.

She had been sitting in the dining room writing letters, her regular glass of sherry within reach. If she was honest she was lonely. Tom had deserted her, but she felt no rancour towards him because she knew only too well that she deserved everything he was measuring out to her. She knew that she had made a mess of her life lately and her control over events and people had vanished. Even Spencer was lost to her. She suspected that there was another woman. She had reached a part of her life where she knew that she no longer loved him but it left her socially inadequate. It limited her evenings out when other women went to dinner parties or the theatre on the arm of their husbands. She was becoming a social pariah. A single woman was always a threat to other women. In Lorna's case it was especially so. Having retained her looks and figure, she dressed well for the more mature woman. There were times when she could still turn heads and there was also the attraction of her personal wealth which she wore like a badge on her sleeve. Her choice of jewellery was ostentatious. There were pieces that she had accumulated over time as well as the inheritance that she had received on her grandmother's death. She knew that she could have almost any man who courted her attention but she was only too aware of gold diggers. That was the one benefit of being married to Spencer who had not married her for her money.

The door to the dining room was ajar. Spencer stood observing his wife who was completely unaware of his presence. He had to confess that he had not looked at her properly for quite some time. Her beauty could still affect him and a wave of sadness engulfed him. This was the woman whom he had once loved. He knew that love had been returned all those years ago but now their world was empty except for the bitterness which filled the void. Tom also was a shared interest but there was a chasm which they failed to bridge. Spencer steeled himself for the approaching onslaught. The pain that he knew he was about to inflict on his wife would be raw and deep-seated. He just wished that it was otherwise.

Spencer pushed the dining room door fully open. Looking up at the intrusion Lorna was startled to see her husband standing there. She thought that he had left the house hours ago.

'Lorna I need to talk to you and what I am about to say, you are not going to like.' There was no point in being diplomatic.

Lorna narrowed her eyes as was her custom when there was going to be a confrontation.

'What is it now Spencer?' she spat at him. 'Do you want me to lend you some money?'

Spencer visibly flinched at the tone of her voice. Lorna observed this and smiled maliciously. She had not lost her hold over him. The fact that she controlled the purse strings affected his manly pride. He had never provided enough income to keep Lorna to her accustomed life style. But he ignored her jibe. This was not a time to be defeated.

'I may as well come to the point Lorna. I don't want your money and never have but I do want a divorce.'

'Never,' she replied, 'married for better or worse. Have you forgotten?'

'I want a divorce because I want to remarry. I have wanted to do this for years but you are adamant. I promise to take the blame. Your name will go unscathed.'

'It is still no Spencer. Now leave me in peace. You can have your mistress on the side but no divorce.'

Lorna bent her head to continue her letter writing. Spencer moved to stand closer to her and his shadow fell over the written word. Looking up again her eyes expressed surprise but she noticed the hatred locked into her husband's expression. She had usually been the one to instil unease into a situation in order to achieve her own ends.

'I will have my divorce Lorna and it won't be too long in coming,' he reiterated.

Lorna mocked him with a gale of laughter.

'Don't be so ridiculous Spencer. You would never cope without me in your life.'

For an instant Spencer realized how easy it would be to put his hands around her throat and she would never mock him again or put him down in order to have control over him. Oh how easy it would be but he knew that was not his way. He had never been one to advocate violence.

'Well let's see.' He began finding his courage. 'Tom does not want you at his wedding to Carenza. He has asked me to speak to you. By your own actions you have lost your only son. He knows what you did behind Carenza's back. And let's just say that if you don't give me a divorce I will tell the world why Tom has disowned you.'

Lorna visibly paled under his close scrutiny. 'That's blackmail and you know nothing,' she bluffed.

'Oh but I do Lorna. Is it not a question of private detectives hired to find out some grisly deed in Carenza's past but there was no dirt to kick about.'

'Oh,' she shrank back into her chair completely taken aback that at last everything had come to light.

'I have wanted the best for Tom like any mother.'

'Stop being so foolish, it was your snobbery and your reputation which was ruling your world as usual.'

The fight had gone out of her. For the first time in years Spencer Heston held the trump card. The experience was liberating.

'As I have said I will have my divorce or your circle of friends will know about it and you will be the biggest laughing stock in the county.'

'You wouldn't do it. You don't have the courage. You never have,' she bluffed.

'I would definitely do it my dear,' he sneered. 'I want my divorce but not until Tom has married Carenza. I would not spoil their day for anything. Shall I pour you another drink? And that is another thing. Are you becoming an alcoholic? Do you want the world to know about that too?' Lorna looked at the empty glass on the table and shook her head. She would refill it when he had gone.

'I think that you need to get a grip on life my dear,' he felt triumphant at obtaining the upper hand.

Spencer turned his back on his wife and left the room feeling particularly pleased with himself. He did not say anything to Esther who was cleaning the entrance hall although he suspected that she had overheard the entire conversation. After the front door closed behind him with a resounding bang, Esther looked into the dining room and observed her mistress who had slumped in the chair, visibly stunned by what had happened.

Chapter 33

The summer term was beginning to advance at a rapid pace. Coupled with the fact that the wedding was not far away, Carenza and May felt that their feet had not touched the ground for weeks with so much to organize. It was now the middle of June. The weather had been a little dismal of late but it had not dampened the enthusiasm of the happy couple. The church was now booked for late August and Jeannette and Edgar had been more than happy for Helen to be Carenza's flower girl. It was decided that Helen should wear a pretty summer dress now that rationing was beginning to ease. Carenza did not want any fuss for she had opted to marry in a lacy cream suit that a friend's mother was making for her. The pattern was still reminiscent of the war years but she was happy because it was stylish and suited her slim figure. The whole ensemble was to be finished off by a spray of flowers in her hair.

The printers in Worcester had sent the invitations for their inspection earlier in the week. This just left enough time to send them out to the small number of guests who were being invited. As for the wedding breakfast May had made the suggestion of having it at home. The cottage was large enough to entertain guests to a buffet even allowing for inclement weather. The caterers had been organized and a small staff had been employed to wait on the guests which allowed freedom for the family to enjoy themselves. The emphasis had been placed on simplicity. Only close family and friends were to be invited.

'Are you sure about not inviting Lorna?' May had asked in her concern for Tom's mother.

'Tom is adamant that he does not want her at the wedding. He says that he can't trust her not to cause mischief.'

'And how do you feel?'

'I'm sorry that it has to be this way,' Carenza sighed at all the anxiety that Lorna had caused over time. 'But it is Tom's decision.'

'I suppose it is. The woman needs to sort herself out. Only she can do that,' May mused, quite mystified that events could have come to this.

*

Spencer had found a moment at the office to relate to Tom the tale about his meeting with Lorna. He wanted his son to be fully informed of the facts in case Lorna exercised her charm on Tom to inveigle him back into the fold. Blackmail was not something to be proud of but Spencer confessed his tactics explaining that he had used it to turn the whole unhappy affair to his own advantage.

'That was very unlike you, father.'

'I know. But sometimes one has to be cruel to be kind. I can't live with her any more Tom. At least you are old enough to be able to deal with the break up. Your life with Carenza will move on. The only one to suffer will be your mother but this situation cannot go on.' Spencer had found profound relief that his own life could move on too.

Tom was now aware that once the wedding was over, his father would start divorce proceedings. It was difficult for Tom not to feel slightly sorry for Lorna but he knew that it was of her own making and nothing would make him go back on his word about not inviting her to the wedding. Spencer confirmed that he and Camilla would be marrying once the divorce came through. It was difficult for Tom to imagine the breakup of his own family. As old as he was, he still longed for his parents to stay together. That was a natural thought for children of a marriage he thought wistfully but then his thoughts turned towards Carenza who had experienced so much insecurity in her early years that he felt ridiculous even contemplating the failure of his parents' union. He turned to his father.

'Where will you live?' He asked.

'I will live with Camilla. And before you ask your mother has all the house and contents. I will make sure that everything is done properly for her. I will not resort to bitterness. If she has problems I will help to sort them out. I have only asked for my freedom after all these years.'

'I don't blame you Dad. It has been hard on you. I feel guilty myself for deserting her but I could not put up with her dreadful treatment of Carenza which could all happen again.'

'I know but I do believe that she might learn her lesson one day. Just think about it Tom, perhaps you could invite her to the church for her to see you marry but not to the reception. I also have a selfish reason for asking. I would like to bring Camilla to the wedding. It would do your mother good to see that I really mean what I say about the divorce. Then she could get on with her own life.'

Tom could not look his father in the eye for he was quite taken aback by this latest revelation. It was one thing his father having a relationship with another woman but to flaunt it in public was too much for him to handle so near to the eve of his own wedding. Knowing Edgar he also felt that the clergyman would have some opinion on the matter which would be quite forceful. May could also be quite vociferous about morals too. She still retained her maidenly values, even though she had become the mother of a young girl. He wanted nothing to prejudice the wedding and his relationship with Carenza. It had taken him such a long time to reach this safe haven in their relationship for anything to jeopardize it now.

'I don't think so Dad. It is not right to flaunt your new lady friend at our wedding. Wait until you are married then we can celebrate as we should.'

'I thought that it would be all right. You are a modern young man.'

'I am but not everyone feels that way. You have to respect Carenza's wishes because it is her day too.'

Spencer did not say any more. On reflection he had to agree that his son was probably correct on the matter but it would be rather strange to attend the function on his own. For most of his adult life he had been part of a couple whether legally or illicitly. It was going to be a strange experience he was sure. Then his thoughts flew to May who had no husband and he smiled. As they left the church he could feature May on his arm. There was usually a solution to most problems.

Part 4: The Wedding

Chapter 34

'You look particularly lovely tonight, Mrs Heston. Tom smiled at his wife across the candlelit table. His hand reached out to take Carenza's much smaller, more delicate one in his own. Carenza giggled as she gazed into his soft brown eyes which reflected a tenderness that she felt too.

'Three years. Where has all that time gone?' he added.

Carenza giggled again, this time patting her stomach which was heavily enlarged by her six months of pregnancy.

'By the way, how is Mr Heston junior?' Tom asked in a more serious tone of voice. He was immensely proud that he was to become a father for the first time and was convinced that his first offspring was to be a son. Taking his glass of champagne, he raised it to his wife. How he loved her. It had been the best three years of his life but perhaps that was a slight exaggeration for there had been many problems too, but none of their own making. Somehow they had entered stormy waters on several occasions, but had reached a safe harbour in recent months. Their love had remained strong and endurable despite everything.

'To us,' he said taking a sip from his champagne flute.

'To the three of us.' Carenza raised her glass allowing the bubbles to float up her nose and make her sneeze. She took a sip from her glass and then put it on the table in front of her husband for him to finish. Her consumption of alcohol had been non-existent since she had first learned of her pregnancy.

The candle danced and flickered in front of them coating their faces in a rosy hue. They were sitting in the dining room of L'Esplanade, a small French bistro in Atthorpe where they had celebrated their anniversary every year since their marriage. They reminisced about the good times and the people they loved but they rarely discussed their wedding day which had not gone according to plan. The service had been beautiful. Edgar had seen to that. The church was full of flowers and the sun blazed through the stained glass windows sending a myriad of colours dancing across the church.

Spencer had kept his promise of not bringing Camilla to the service while Lorna had not been invited. There were rumours of her heavy drinking now. Spencer was not prepared for his only son's important day to be spoilt by his soon to be ex-wife. As a result they had decided not to have 'his' and 'her' sides. Instead Spencer had sat next to May who was quite overcome by the whole proceedings. Never in her life had she experienced such emotion. She had sniffed loudly into her handkerchief through much of the service, causing Carenza to look around on several occasions in a state of anxiety only to see her mother beam through her tears. Carenza smiled too now knowing that May was happy for her. It was that she just had an odd way of showing it. May, later, could not believe her own behaviour, but everyone looked upon the event benignly knowing that she had had very little experience of such highly charged emotional moments in her spinster years.

Carenza had looked resplendent in her cream lace suit. The colour had complemented her raven black hair which she had twisted into a high chignon on top of her head. Helen had followed Carenza down the aisle dressed in her burgundy red dress with a cream lace collar to match the bride's outfit.

The service had been a dream for both of the young couple. The weather had smiled on them. It was one of the best days of the summer. The wedding had been wonderful but it had all fallen apart when Tom and Carenza had returned from the vestry to begin their walk down the aisle as husband and wife. They walked steadily acknowledging their friends and family with happy smiles when suddenly a wail, followed by others echoed through the squat arches of the Norman church, which had witnessed many such occasions before, but not quite like this one.

'Tom what have you done?' the voice screeched. 'You will live to regret it my son.'

Lorna had arrived at the church unbidden and had missed the service which she hoped had not taken place. The whole congregation turned in unison to witness the intrusion. Smiling faces had turned to spectres of astonishment. Spencer, who had been following the bride and groom with May on his arm, had been quick witted enough to take control of the whole of the proceedings. Edgar came to May's rescue while Spencer moved swiftly to his errant wife and steered her through the heavy portals of the church into the sunlight. Lorna swooned in his arms and that was the moment that he realized that she was drunk.

He blamed himself for not having seen this event occurring for the signs had been there staring him in the face for months now.

'Help him,' May mouthed at Edgar who nodded, discreetly following Tom's parents around the side of the old church away from public view.

'I'll take her home,' Spencer told Edgar. 'We cannot have another scene to spoil the day.'

Edgar was in agreement but felt a twinge of regret that Spencer could not enjoy the rest of his son's wedding.

'I will explain to Tom and ask him to telephone you later to see what has happened.'

'Thanks Edgar.' Spencer did not know what else to say. He saw Lorna's chauffeur standing next to the car smoking the butt of his cigarette. The man witnessed what was happening and immediately strode to help his employer. 'Take us home Parks that's a good fellow.'

Parks opened the back door of the vehicle to enable Spencer to guide the unstable Lorna onto the seat. Sitting next to her, he could keep her under control but she had already slumped into the corner. He noticed a half consumed bottle of vodka lying on its side on the car floor. That verified what he had imagined over previous weeks. He wondered why Parks had not said anything to him but he had to admit to himself that he was hardly at home these days. Spencer looked at his inebriated wife. Her hair was a chaotic mess, not resembling the well groomed woman in her prime. Her clothes had not been chosen with the usual care of a woman of her standing. It certainly did not look as if she had been planning to attend a wedding for she was always well groomed for even the simplest of visits.

'Parks, when did Mrs Heston ask for the car?' he asked.

The chauffeur part turned his good ear to his employer.

'Not long before we left, sir,' he chose his words carefully.

'What kind of mood was Mrs Heston in this morning?'

Parks did not like the line of questioning which was putting him on the spot. He was not responsible for his employer. He just did as he was told but he answered politely.

'A bit anxious sir, as she was not sure about the time of the wedding.'

Spencer did not reply but mused on this new piece of intelligence. This action of Lorna's was not premeditated as she would have arrived at the church in plenty of time to prevent the wedding, but she had obviously been in an agitated state of mind. It was most difficult to know what to do for the best. The first thing to do was to wait for her to wake up and talk to her while she was in a more lucid state of mind.

'Has Mrs Heston been like this before, Parks?'

Parks felt annoyed. Shouldn't his employer know what state his wife was in? Perhaps if he came home at a respectable time, he would know what happened and could take some of the responsibility.

'Perhaps once or twice, sir,' he tried to answer diplomatically.

Spencer lapsed into his own thoughts, not asking any more questions for he knew that he had the answers.

*

At the church the guests had followed the wedding party along the aisle and out into the afternoon sunshine. They milled about in a confused state not knowing quite what to think. Eventually they broke up into small groups chatting and waiting for instructions about what would happen next. May had regained her equilibrium, and began moving between the wedding guests chatting as if nothing untoward had happened. Her lead had been followed by Jeannette and Edgar but the young couple were caught up in the melee of their thoughts after the strange events of the afternoon. Tom was consumed with guilt at his treatment of his mother but also furious at how she had once more treated Carenza and her gate-crashing of the wedding itself. Carenza knew that the afternoon had to be rescued and it looked as if it was going to be her decision to take control.

'Shall we move onto the reception?' she called. May seconded her proposal. As it was the photographs were to be taken in May's garden which at this time of year was particularly lovely. Much effort had been made over the summer for this reason alone. Carenza slipped her arm through her husband's.

'Come on Mr Heston, let's get on with married life,' she whispered to him.

His face wrinkled into a smile knowing that they had to make an effort to reclaim the day as their own. The beginning of their married life was too important to be spoilt but a cloud still remained for they knew that Lorna had to be dealt with before they could move forward.

The cottage had been festooned with decorations to mark the important occasion. May had spared no expense in honour of her daughter's marriage. On the large lawn at the back of the house a marquee had been erected in case of inclement weather but that now seemed unlikely as the sun shone from a cloudless sky. May had wined and dined the guests extravagantly and the outburst in the church had been a temporary blip but as the evening began to wind down, Edgar took the young couple aside,

'Don't let what has happened today upset you too much,' he said sagely. 'It is the start of your new life together. Your parents, Tom, must sort out their own differences for I honestly believe that this is more about them. Lorna is crying out for attention and is making it worse by focusing on your relationship.'

Tom shook his head.

'I don't know what to believe. She has not been happy about Carenza from the start.'

'I would go and see your mother but not yet. Give your parents time to find their own way. Enjoy your own time together for the moment. You are now a couple in the sight of God.'

Turning to look at Tom, Carenza saw the sadness etched on his face. Her hand reached for his, all she wanted was to be a source of comfort to him. How grateful she was to May who had only filled her life with happiness, but she knew that if she dug deeper into her own past, maybe her life might have reflected Tom's.

*

During the journey home Spencer had done much thinking. He was far from happy with the entire circumstances. He laid much blame at Lorna's door but he knew that some fault lay with himself. Much of the misery that had been caused, he should have foreseen and put a stop to it. If he was entirely honest he was a little afraid of Lorna when she was in full flow and he was scornful of his own cowardice in not tackling her head on. But what he had not foreseen was her slide into alcoholism. He looked at her as she slept on the seat beside him, a mere shadow of her former self. He knew that he had to rectify some of the problems immediately, others would take longer. His mind was made up as to what he had to do but it meant hurting the woman that he loved. Camilla did not deserve the course of action that he knew he had to take. He loved her still but Lorna was his wife.

Parks pulled up outside the Heston residence. He viewed the scene behind him thoughtfully.

'I will go and call Esther,' he said. But he heard the front door open and Esther appeared on the step. She had heard the car arrive but had not expected the scene before her eyes.

'Help me get her upstairs Esther,' Spencer said.

'Yes sir,' was all the maid could manage as she helped him with the dead weight which lay in his arms.

'Go and prepare her bedroom and then I want to see you in the drawing room,' Spencer instructed.

'Yes sir,' she replied again. Spencer carried his wife up the wide staircase into the bedroom they had once shared. His face momentarily twisted in pain as he knew that he would never sleep with her again. If he resumed his life of pretence, it would have to on his terms. She would never taunt him with her vitriol again. He did not want anything from her and he would continue to live his own life. It was his duty though to see Lorna fit and well. That was his goal.

As Esther cared for her mistress and saw to her comfort Spencer opened cupboards and sideboards in the dining room looking for alcohol which he found in abundance. He gathered it altogether on the dining room table. Esther had heard him and she stood before him now wondering what he was about to say.

'Can you throw all this alcohol away down the sink and get rid of the bottles. Mrs Heston must not have alcohol at any price. If you find her drinking you must tell me.' Spencer was pained at asking the maid to spy on his wife.

'Yes sir, whatever you say sir,' the maid's face was expressionless as she looked at her employer.

Spencer frowned, a thought had occurred to him that he could not let go.

'I don't want anything that happens within these walls to become gossip. If it does I will know where it has come from. I will appoint another maid to help you but you must be vigilant at all times.'

Esther's face was still expressionless. She did not want to lose her job because it had taken her long enough to find this one. When Spencer had dismissed her he knew that he had to telephone the doctor to seek advice. It was a hard rocky road that lay ahead. There was also the thought of Camilla on whom he had to turn his back. He had promised marriage once his divorce had been finalized but that was no longer possible. He desperately wanted Camilla to be part of his life but he could not force her to wait for him. She was a free woman with a choice to make and possibly it could be one he would not like.

*

Tom looked at Carenza with such tenderness that she almost had to look away. Their feelings for each other were so intense that it almost hurt inside. She had brought a different dimension to his life that he had not felt before. There was a feeling of security that he had not even experienced as a child living with parents who argued all the time. Carenza demanded little but gave much. The candle on the table flickered as it grew smaller and the restaurant began to empty but they were content to remain, totally lost in their own world. Suddenly Tom dug deep into his pockets searching for something. Carenza watched, puzzled by what he was doing. From his pocket he withdrew a small, square shaped box which he placed on the table in front of her.

'This is with my love,' he grinned at her.

'Oh Tom you don't have to,' Carenza groaned but opened the box anyway. Observing the contents she gasped at the diamond eternity ring in front of her.

'Put it on,' he instructed her.

Pulling it from its rest she placed it on her finger. She looked closely at the diamonds which twinkled in the candlelight. Turning the ring she could see that the diamonds did not stop but went on forever.

'It's like our love. It goes on forever,' her voice trembled.

'It's you, me and our children,' he said taking her hand. 'We are the most important people in our universe.'

Carenza knew that he could not have said a truer word.

'I love you Carenza, now and always.' He brought her hand to his lips and kissed it.

Chapter 35

The first year of marriage had flown for Tom and Carenza. They had lived with May for all of that time, enjoying a great deal of privacy and the arrangement had worked well. But during the start of the next year they both felt that it was time to spread their wings. May had used her time profitably after the wedding by joining more village activities. She was filling her days knowing that the inevitable would happen. She no longer wanted to rely on Carenza who now had a life of her own. When their lives touched through visits, she knew that would be wonderful but there were to be no long days where she had nothing to do. It was inevitable that children moved on and flew the nest.

Her friendship with Edgar and Jeannette became her saving grace as she now became involved in church activities and charitable causes. Jeannette was grateful for the extra assistance, freeing her to give more time to Helen. Helen was an academic like her father. She now attended the grammar school in Worcester and was doing well and even better than many of her peers. Her ambition lay in gaining a place at Cambridge, her father's old university where he had read divinity. She was a quiet, studious girl with university at this moment some distance away but Jeannette wanted to give her daughter time to accomplish her ambition. Even Jeannette was beginning to realize that she was becoming an ambitious and pushy mother. May's involvement in the church released Jeannette from some of her duties as the wife of a clergyman.

It was during this time that Tom's house had sold releasing capital to spend on a new property. Carenza had been in her element planning a new home. They had found a house in Dalton which was a village nearer to Tom's office. His commuting time had lessened enabling him to spend more time at home. Carenza no longer had the luxury of walking to school. Her greatest self indulgence had been the acquisition of a car, a small Ford which propelled her along the country lanes to Nether Heydon. During the week she tried to spend part of every day with May when work allowed. It was usually a cup of tea together at the end of the school day or a precious lunch time when she could tear herself away from the classroom. Carenza loved her own home which was situated on a quiet lane with a large garden to the rear. The large garden had been Tom's idea for he was already imagining a house full of children who would play safely away from the road. Tom was becoming desperate to become a father, in sharp contrast to Carenza's lack of maternal longing. She was still not ready to give up her financial independence. Tom knew that he would have to take things slowly but he was confident that he would make headway in the end. He had promised Carenza an allowance but she had other concerns. At the moment she did not want to be at home with a small child so Tom had to wait until she was ready; after all it was going to be her sacrifice in the end to give up all that she had achieved. Marriage had been a happy realization for the pair of them as time had progressed and it was not going to be a huge sacrifice for them to enjoy more time together before the inevitability of children happened.

It was six months after Tom and Carenza's move to Dalton that she received a telephone call at school one lunchtime. It was Jeannette telephoning from the vicarage to explain that on one of May's visits, she had been taken unwell. Doctor Fulbrook had been called and he had diagnosed a mild heart attack. Although, she was shocked Jeannette could not believe that May could be ill. She was an indomitable rock and a mainstay of the local community. But Jeannette had taken charge immediately, not listening to any of May's protests that she was going to be fine. It had not taken her long to make up the spare bedroom for May was not going home to an empty house, and it was not safe for her to travel to Carenza's home as she required quiet and rest. Edgar was in full agreement with his wife that the correct decision had been made. Although the heart attack was not severe it was enough to serve as a warning to May that she had to think more carefully about her lifestyle and be prepared to take better care of herself.

Jeannette had assured Carenza that May was not in imminent danger and she could visit her mother at the end of the working day. For the rest of the afternoon Carenza was in a heightened state of anxiety. The children seemed more difficult than usual but she knew that it was her own stress which had caused her impatience. As the bell heralded the end of the school day, Carenza was impatient to leave but the usual malingerers were taking an age to find lost shoes and coats. The classroom was left with a pile of detritus to be cleared but for once Carenza shut the door on it knowing that it would have to be tidied the following day. Hurrying from the building she managed to dodge the caretaker and his army of cleaners before they discovered the mess that had been left behind.

The vicarage was only a five minute walk from school but the walk seemed to take longer today. Jeannette opened the front door as Carenza walked up the drive. She put a finger to her lips.

'She's asleep,' she mouthed and gestured with her finger to the upper storey. Carenza nodded and followed her friend into the sitting room where Jeannette had prepared a light tea for them.

'I've felt so guilty about leaving her on her own,' Carenza began.

'Don't start that,' Jeannette said fiercely. 'You have done nothing wrong and we have a right to our own lives as well, particularly after getting married. There are always too many demands on women's emotions.'

Carenza smiled through her tears, clasping her friend's hands.

'You are wonderful.'

'Nonsense,' Jeannette replied in a matter of fact manner. 'Anyway I have made some decisions but pardon me for interfering. You only have to agree.'

'Decisions?' Carenza repeated stupidly.

'Yes decisions. Hear me out first. May will stay here until she has recovered. We have more than enough room. We owe it to her anyway. You can carry on as normal and come and see her every day. Edgar is quite in agreement. Then, when she is ready to return home we wondered if she could have a live-in house keeper. It would relieve both of you of a lot of worry. In fact we know somebody who would be quite the right person.'

Carenza reflected on Jeannette's words and then smiled.

'You have been busy with your thoughts and I think you have about covered everything, but would May agree to someone living in the house permanently. You know what she is like.'

'You are going to have to bully her Carenza. Threaten her.' Carenza had not seen this part of Jeannette's character before. 'She cannot live on her own now and you cannot be with her all the time. She knows that you are a good daughter but her fierce independence can also be a catalyst too.'

Carenza smiled at the words 'fierce independence' which were so redolent of her own nature even though she had not inherited those genes from May.

'I will sort it. By the way who is this person and would she want to be with May all the time?'

'It is Avril Jones and she would need time off but I think that we can help May out at the weekends.'

May had enjoyed her enforced rest in the company of Jeannette and her family but she would never admit it or if she did it would only be grudgingly. But she was profuse in her gratitude. Carenza had not tackled her on the forthcoming housekeeper until her time to return home was imminent. May refused straight away. She did not want strangers living in her house and she could cope on her own. Carenza knew this would be the case and had already sorted out her blackmailing strategies.

'What do I want a stranger living in my house for?' she had said truculently.

'Well May in that case I shall have to leave Tom and school to come home and look after you. There is nothing else to be done.' Carenza held her face straight waiting for her mother's bluster which did not arrive. Within only a few minutes she had made a volte-face.

'Well so be it. I must agree to someone living in. I would never interfere in your life Carenza.'

Carenza was dumbfounded for she had won before a battle could erupt.

'Well, so be it,' she said giving her mother a kiss before leaving her to read her book.

Downstairs Carenza repeated the story to Jeannette.

'May has finally acknowledged that she needs help. I am so pleased.'

*

Avril Jones had accepted the position of housekeeper gratefully when Carenza had interviewed her. In fact she knew May well from years gone by when she had been a pupil at the village school. Avril's life had not been easy from the outset. She was the only child of elderly parents and much of her youth had been spent looking after them in their dotage. After they had died she was left with very little for herself. She had no money or work experience. In the end she had become a housekeeper to an elderly widower who had never had children. She was doing the drudgery which had plagued her from childhood but after several years Morgan Jones had asked her to become his wife, not a wife in the true sense of the word but as his unpaid nursemaid. Avril had accepted, not for love but security. She felt that life had passed her by and opportunities for marriage would be scarce. After only seven years of marriage Morgan died of a heart attack. Avril was not devastated because she had never greatly cared for him as a husband. However, her care for him was rewarded when he left her the cottage and a small annuity. It was more than she had received in the whole of her life and for that she was grateful to him. The offer to become May's housekeeper had come at the right time. If she was careful with her money, she felt that she would have security for life. Her plan was to rent out her cottage as she would be living with May and then when she no longer needed to work she could return to an independent life.

On a cold Saturday in February Carenza had made the journey from Dalton to visit her mother. It was not going to be long before she could move back to her own home. Avril had done an early spring clean as a welcome home present for her new employer and everything was in readiness for May's return.

Carenza found her mother sitting up in bed with a crimson bed jacket around her shoulders. Her cheeks reflected the colour of her clothes as a coal fire roared in the fireplace making the room unbearably hot and stuffy. She was knitting a jumper for the church fair timed for later in the summer. These activities had kept her occupied during the time that she had been an invalid. Gradually she was allowed to come downstairs for longer periods of the day but at present she had been suffering from a bad cold and had been forced to remain in bed again. Now, she believed that Jeannette was a tyrant to rule the roost. Carenza's visit was a welcome relief from the monotony of her days. Carenza appeared with a high colour in her cheeks brought about by the cold February winds. She knocked on the bedroom door and poked her head round.

'Can I come in?' she asked chirpily.

May looked up and smiled.

'Of course; are you on your own?'

'Yes. Tom has gone to see Spencer for an hour at the office. They had business to discuss.'

Suddenly May broke into a deluge of tears. Carenza had not seen this side of her mother before.

'What is it?' she asked taking her mother's hand and stroking it sympathetically.

May sniffed as a tear ran down her downy cheek.

'I feel like a prisoner here and I don't want to be a prisoner in my own home with Avril as my jailer'

Carenza burst out laughing

'May, you are not a prisoner here. This has been for your own good otherwise you might have had to go into hospital. Edgar and Jeannette have been wonderful to you.'

'I know. I'm just a crotchety old woman who doesn't deserve such wonderful friends.'

'Well what is the matter then?'

Another tear emerged and dropped.

'I don't want to be old and infirm. I am not used to being ill. I like doing what I want to do. It is usually me who takes care of others.'

Carenza passed her handkerchief to the older woman.

'You will have your freedom back soon,' she reassured her. 'You know Avril well and you like her. She will do the chores and you can relax and have the freedom you deserve. Just accept changes have to be made. You deserve to be looked after. I will be around too and we will still be able to do things together like we have always done. Very little will change providing you look after yourself.'

'I know,' May sniffed her agreement, 'but people see the old as a nuisance.'

'May, you are not a nuisance. And I am not people. I'm your daughter who loves you and wants the best for you.'

'I know,' May patted her hand, 'I know.'

Carenza felt that their roles had been reversed after all these years. She knew that May would be happy to go home again but the problem would be to make her slow her pace to suit her advancing years.

*

Spencer had made the decision to stay with Lorna, at least until she was well again. He felt some guilt that their relationship had deteriorated over the years but he was fully aware that most of the problems lay with Lorna and her innate snobbery. She just refused to move with the times and to realize that there was a new world opening up. There was a new youth culture mirrored by the teddy boys with their DA hairstyles, drainpipe trousers and their winklepicker shoes with the dance craze called the jive. He had even witnessed Tom and Carenza dancing to the music of the new pop phenomenon from America, Bill Hayley and the Comets. Even he watched these events on television sometimes just so that he could understand what the young people were talking about.

For the first few months of their reconciliation Lorna had been quite contrite about her treatment of other people. Her doctor had managed to find counselling for her over her drinking problems which had now come under control. Spencer had wanted her to give up alcohol altogether but her doctor had exercised caution in many ways. He felt that if she had less stress in her life it might be controlled naturally and she would no longer need to use alcohol as a crutch. Spencer had totally disagreed with the doctor whom he thought was giving in to his wife but they had agreed that they would see how it all went and would change course if it did not work.

There had to be compromises in the marriage but Spencer was definite that he would not share Lorna's bed. That part of the marriage was over but for appearances sake they occasionally attended dinners and social events as a couple. Lorna had played her part well even theatrically. Her snobbishness had not diminished but it was more under control now that she could keep up appearances. The world did not see that once they had returned home the pretence faded and they lived separate lives. They remained polite and civil to each other, but that was where it all ended.

Lorna had expressed a wish to be reconciled with Tom. There was no mention of Carenza in these thoughts which made Tom doubtful that his mother could be civil to his wife and accept her as an important part of the family. After persuasion from Spencer, Tom had agreed to go and see her but he went alone. Carenza had no wish to see her mother-in-law or to inflame a situation. She knew that she had to give a little too, particularly for Tom's sake.

The visit had gone well. Mother and son were reconciled as far as appearances were concerned but Tom felt that he could not trust her to treat Carenza properly. Future visits would be short and sharp to prevent further confrontation. Tom had even asked his father to be present at these visits particularly if Carenza came too. Spencer was in full agreement for he knew that the situation needed monitoring. Lorna must never be allowed to be alone with Carenza. Parks, the chauffeur, had been instructed not to drive Lorna to Dalton at any price and Spencer had made it clear to his wife that her visits were by special invitation only and if she reneged on that he would leave her again. Lorna's boundaries were clear.

Spencer had been saddened to sacrifice his relationship with Camilla. As soon as he had known that Lorna had problems he had visited Camilla for the last time so that she was in full knowledge of the facts and where his loyalties lay at the moment. Camilla had been undemanding in her relationship with Spencer. She knew he was not free, as well as knowing that Lorna was difficult. If he had been free to marry her she would have been happy to do so because Spencer was nothing like her own demanding husband had been, but she did not want to be drawn into other people's personal problems having experienced so many of her own. Their separation had been amicable and open -ended. They had agreed that if the gods were to smile favourably on them they might have a future together. But life was full of unexpected twists and turns and their paths might never cross in the same way again. Spencer had to make a supreme effort not to feel embittered towards Lorna whom he knew would not be his wife indefinitely.

Chapter 36

Carenza yawned loudly and stretched her body cat-like in the early morning light. She had risen early because she had woken with lower back pain and had not been able to sleep. However much she had tried Tom had been sound asleep in the tumble of sheets and blankets and she envied him this ability to sleep through anything. Sleep had eluded her in recent weeks. The baby was large she had been told by the midwife and comfort in bed was not a luxury she would enjoy until this offspring made its appearance. 'A woman's lot,' she thought wryly as her hands cradled the arc of her stomach protectively. It would not be long now until her world would change forever. On the pine kitchen table stood her first cup of tea of the day. She picked it up and moved to the window observing the large garden where future Heston children would play safely. Her thoughts turned to her own childhood where there had not been the luxury of a garden, but in its place were drab streets and back yards with washing hanging limply to dry. Children had played games, kicking stones as footballs or the older, more responsible ones had run errands down to the corner shop for harassed mothers. How her life had changed over the years. All these twists and turns, many of which had been out of her control altered life's path for better or worse.

Outside the autumn morning was misty, while the grass glistened with heavy dew. It seemed strange to not have to rush out at an unearthly hour to go to work. In many ways she still missed school. It had been her life line over the years and the day of her leaving had left her bereft for quite some time afterwards. But she had acclimatized over the past few weeks. In fact she was beginning to enjoy the tranquility of her days but she knew that it would not last once the baby had arrived.

Occasionally she would spend her free time with May who had made a complete recovery from her illness. Her energy levels had risen dramatically but she had followed the doctor's advice in taking care of herself. Avril Jones had blended into May's life unobtrusively. She ran the house efficiently and was discreet in all matters. Her self contained unit was the suite of rooms where Tom and Carenza had started married life. Here she was happy to have her privacy and had made the space her own. With Avril's presence in the house, May had regained her confidence while Carenza had peace of mind that her mother was well taken care of.

Tom's arms slid around Carenza's thickened waist while he nuzzled her neck.

Carenza laughed.

'You'll be late again Tom.'

'I know,' he said not appearing to care too much. 'Anyway why are you up so early when you don't need to be?'

'I had backache. I felt it yesterday too. I couldn't get back to sleep so I thought that I would get up.'

'Why do you want to do housework when Mrs. Carmichael comes in three times a week?'

'I think they call it nesting instinct,' she laughed.

'The baby is not due for another couple of weeks. Do you think that you will have it early?'

'Of course not but I am not going to panic anyway. My case is packed and I only have to call you to take me into the cottage hospital,' she replied calmly.

'Well I had better be off. You know that I won't be out of the office today and the rest of the time Stella has the telephone number of where I shall be.'

'Tom, stop fussing. Off you go.'

He kissed her on the cheek after he had picked up his briefcase and car keys.

'See you tonight Mrs Heston.'

'Of course Mr Heston,' she laughed.

She followed him to the front door and blew him a kiss. Not feeling as calm as she appeared Carenza's back was aching like toothache. Her niggle of doubt made her feel that she was not going to last much longer. It looked as if the baby would be born early. Wondering why she had sent Tom on his way without telling him she really knew that it would be Tom who would be agitated not herself. She wanted a calm atmosphere for her child to enter the world. Glancing at the clock she noted the time. 8.35 a.m. She would wait a little longer and then she would ring the cottage hospital to ask for advice. As the hands of the clock turned to 10.00 a.m. Carenza knew that something momentous was happening. She rang the midwife, Sally Merryweather, who had not yet started out on her rounds.

'Carenza, you are naughty. You should have called me sooner. From what you describe this could be it. Be ready. I'll take you to the hospital; won't be a tick.' She worked quickly to gather all she required for her day's work. Knowing how large Carenza had been in this first pregnancy she thought that there was no time to waste but had not wanted to convey her anxiety to her patient.

The telephone went dead. Carenza collected her case. Her back was aching so badly by now that she could not move. But her greatest fear was if she gave birth on her own. She need not have worried because Sally had reacted very quickly to the call out. After several years of being a midwife she remained unfazed by such emergencies although in this case she harboured suspicions which she had not voiced to the prospective parents. Sally found Carenza in a state of agony. Her efficiency was legendary. The front door of the passenger seat was opened before she ran up the path to help her.

'Have you got everything?' she asked breathily, as she picked up the small case. Sally helped Carenza into the front seat. The cottage hospital was only ten minutes away by car but even that could be too long sometimes. 'Have you rung Tom?' Sally drove the car steadily down the lane until it joined the High Street.

'No, he fusses over me like a mother hen. He's worse than May sometimes.'

Sally's lips were set in a tight line. Her professional journey with Carenza's pregnancy told her that this young woman could be tough and headstrong which made their nurse-patient relationship quite difficult at times. But she knew that the birth looked imminent and Carenza would have to do as she was told. As the car pulled up outside the double front doors of the cottage hospital a nurse appeared pushing a wheel chair. A porter opened the car door to help Carenza out and into the chair. She was wheeled down the wide corridor leading to the delivery room where she was subjected to an examination.

*

An hour and a half later Tom stood in complete shock outside the delivery room. Sally had telephoned him as soon she could after the birth which had happened so quickly that nobody had had time to think. Their training clicked in as they moved on auto pilot.

'Hello. You can go in now Tom,' Sally beamed at him, patting him on the arm in a gesture of comfort and congratulations. He nodded but his sense of shock rooted him to the spot. 'Go on then. She's waiting for you.'

Tom walked into the room where Carenza looked tired but also exultant.

'Are you all right?' he asked taking her hand and kissing her cheek. But her unusually pale complexion had not gone unnoticed.

'I'm fine but feel as shocked as you look,' she smiled at him.

'Where are they?' he asked.

'They have been taken down to the nursery to allow me to rest. I will be placed in a ward soon. Why don't you have a look at them. They won't bite.' Her head fell to the side as she struggled to keep awake.

'I'll see you later.' He bent and kissed her cheek. 'Thank you, you are so clever,' he whispered in total awe of her achievement as if this was the first birth on the planet but Carenza had not heard him for she was already asleep.

Excitement at being a father had not quite registered with Tom but there was something beginning to buzz inside him and as he walked towards the nursery he was already beginning to develop a swagger. The window of the nursery revealed a neat line of plastic see through cots where the new arrivals slept. Tiny fists sometimes moved while their owners slept, revealing pink or blue plastic bracelets as a reminder of the identification of the infants. The nurse in charge of the nursery glanced up from what she was doing and observed Tom trying to work out the identity of his children.

She put her head around the door.

'Are you our latest dad?' she asked jovially.

Tom nodded.

'The twins,' he said.

'Well these are your daughters, Mr Heston. Aren't they beautiful? You must be very proud.'

'Rather,' Tom replied. 'We were never told about having twins. It has been a bit of a shock!'

The young nurse laughed at him.

'They all say that,' she said.

*

Tom drove home. The shock was beginning to wear off but he was wondering how they would cope with two babies - an instant family. He had been told that one baby could be exhausting but two was beyond contemplation. Now he had to telephone the family to give them the news.

May had been very confused by the state of affairs. She had rarely heard of twins in her limited experience of very young children. However, she had never been a person who did not think of solutions to problems. Quickly, she had moved into practical mode.

'Don't worry Tom. I know what we can do to help events along. Just leave it with me. Will you go along with what I suggest? I don't want to interfere but I feel that at least the early weeks can be made easier,' she said mysteriously.

'Whatever you suggest May. I will be at home for a while.'

'Very well leave it with me and I will get back to you.'

Once their conversation had concluded, May stood deep in thought for a few minutes. As much as May loved Tom she was not sure how he would suddenly cope with so much responsibility. As a boy he had obviously been very spoilt and did not cope well with additional pressure. She had witnessed this over the time that he and Carenza had been married. It was always Carenza who was truly the responsible one if she was honest. Carenza had had to grow up quickly during her early childhood but May had tried to give her back her youth after she had come to live in Nether Heydon. Childhood was precious and could not easily be replaced once lost. But the early years in London could not be eradicated. May was confident that once Carenza became less tired she would manage her two babies but a third in the guise of Tom might be too much. She had made her decision and she knew that it would make all their lives much easier. What was money for she mused if it was not to make life easier? What she was about to do was going to be her gift to the young couple.

*

Tom had rung his parents in the early evening, knowing that they would be at home together. There had been little point in speaking to them separately. The news could give them a common ground in their otherwise fragile relationship. It had been Lorna who had answered the telephone. He delivered his news and for once detected a note of pleasure in her voice. Carenza had not been mentioned during the course of the conversation so he knew that rancour still lurked at the back of her mind. But they had moved forward which was an improvement and then she delivered her bombshell.

'I was one of identical twins,' she revealed.

'Really?' Tom said in utter astonishment. 'You never said. What happened to your twin?'

'She died at birth. My parents, your grandparents, were devastated and would never talk about it.'

'Well it obviously must run in the family. We never suspected twins but Carenza was rather large throughout her pregnancy.'

At the mention of Carenza Lorna passed the receiver to Spencer who had been loitering in the background.

'Fantastic news old boy,' he drooled contentedly. It was the first piece of good news that he had received since he had returned home. He felt that this could be a common denominator between himself and his wife, something to talk about that was uplifting. A new generation brought hope.

When Tom had time to himself, he experienced a mixture of emotions, mostly highs, but he did wonder how they would cope with two babies. He was fairly sure that May would think of some rational solution to the immediate problem. Carenza would be spending some time in hospital before she would be allowed home. He pulled the stopper from a crystal decanter set on the long sideboard in the dining room before pouring a generous measure of whisky. It was medicinal he thought. What a day it had been.

May also knew that she had a few days' grace to put in place the plan that had been formulating in her mind. Her consultation with Avril had been positive. What a wonderful addition to her life her housekeeper had proved to be. She often wondered how she had managed without help after Carenza had left home. Her life had become invigorated by not having to run the house alone.

It took May several days before she returned Tom's call. She had imagined that he might be rather desperate about what was going to happen on Carenza's discharge from hospital. Now all her plans had come to fruition. Carenza was to return to Nether Heydon with the twins for a few weeks until she was strong enough to return home. Tom could join her at weekends rather like he had done in their courting days. Avril had not minded the extra workload which the intrusion involved but she was less happy about the live-in nanny who had been appointed to enable Carenza to jump the first hurdle of early motherhood. The new housekeeper felt that there could be sharp words if nanny overstepped the mark. She had become very territorial about her own area of the house, which happened to be the kitchen. Even May was rebuked occasionally but in a jocular fashion. Avril had developed a way of dealing with such things without causing offence. The additional workload which Carenza's arrival would bring was of no consequence to her. In fact she welcomed the diversion from routine and the fact that she was needed even more was important to boost her own confidence. It was a way of being loved. She knew that May treasured her presence because she constantly told her so. The two women lived in harmony for most of the time. Even Avril's own time was rarely spent away from the house. She had felt fulfilled for the first time in her life.

Carenza had left hospital feeling weepy and unable to cope with the responsibility which lay ahead of her. This was very unlike Carenza who had always felt in control of whatever destiny threw at her. But there was little structure to her life. The babies fed on demand and chaos reigned around her. The nursing staff in hospital had been kind but firm, that baby knew best, but Carenza felt that her life was out of control. Maternal instinct had kicked in soon after the birth but something within her which she could not quite define made her look back quite nostalgically to her teaching days where she had been at the helm of her ship. Guilt- ridden at such thoughts, she tried to push them away. If she was honest she felt depressed partly because it was taking longer to recover after the birth.

May's decision to employ a nanny had emanated from her knowledge of Carenza as a person. She knew that her daughter had wanted a child but the adjustment was going to be harsh for her. To be a stay-at-home mother meant surrendering her independence. As much as she loved Tom and a baby it was not her ideal to subjugate all that she held dear. Her higher aspirations were difficult to quell. May wondered what the future held for Carenza in this direction but her feelings that a nanny might take up permanent residence in the Heston household were very strong. She was aware that Tom earned a good living but was not in the higher echelons of earners.

The nanny was going to be her gift to her daughter, or both of them, she corrected herself. It would be no sacrifice as she could afford it and her own requirements were simple.

Carenza had been so grateful to her mother for employing a nanny and had left the cottage hospital in a more positive frame of mind. Tom had collected her with Dorothy Yates, who was now in full command of proceedings. Dorothy was a buxom, no nonsense woman of thirty five, who had never wanted to marry. The children she nannied became her surrogate family and she could become very possessive of her charges. May had been fortunate to find Dorothy because she had just relinquished her position as nanny for a well-to-do family whose children had just flown the nest. She had been looking for a more permanent situation but was prepared to take on short term work until the relevant job came along. May had hinted that this new position might lead to a more lengthy employment but it depended how Carenza took to parenthood. If she coped well with motherhood a nanny might not be necessary but May had suspicions that Carenza might not adapt so easily. She knew that the babies were loved but Carenza's independence lay at the root of everything.

Tom had been perfectly happy with May's decisions for the immediate future. His amazement at her strategies, considering she had remained a spinster all her life, knew no bounds and his gratitude was immense. His main concern was the expense of the nanny and the possibility that Carenza might demand that luxury long term when she had become used to the idea. He reflected on his own childhood knowing that he had had a nanny. His mother had not been a hands-on parent because that had been the way he had been brought up. Apart from the fact that the world was changing, his parents or his mother to be precise could afford to employ someone to look after him. Tom knew that he had not attained such financial security yet to allow this to be so in their case. His own mother had not been forthcoming to help them financially. He had never expected it nor did he want to be indebted to her because of recent circumstances. But his incredulity lay in the fact that May could afford such luxuries but did not wear her wealth as a badge like his own mother did,

Carenza was enjoying her time in Nether Heydon with May. The babies were no problem but their destiny lay in the hands of the professional who knew what she was doing. Perhaps when

Carenza was in control chaos would reign supreme but the present tranquility was to be enjoyed while it lasted. Dorothy Yates had taken over the other rooms at the back of May's cottage. One room was hers and the other had been converted into a nursery. It had been the nursery when May had been a child and she and her two brothers had used it all those years ago. May had never revealed these facts to her daughter.

Carenza was making an excellent recovery from the birth and was bonding with her babies but in some ways she felt that they were not her own. Nanny was a strict disciplinarian and would not allow the twins' routine to be disrupted. She was allowed her special time with them but in between she had to be patient. Tom was treated in the same way but during the week he was away at work but he had grown up with this type of regime in his own childhood.

'You would think they were nanny's children,' Carenza complained to Tom one weekend.

He smiled at her.

'Are you feeling better than you did when you came out of hospital?' he asked her.

'Of course; you know I am,' was her puzzled reply.

'Good and that is down to having Dorothy here. Just be patient and accept what a privilege you have. Not many mothers are so lucky.'

Carenza looked at him, giving him a knowing smile.

'I suppose I shouldn't complain. I should be grateful.'

Tom cuddled her and gave her a kiss on her cheek.

'So you should Mrs Heston.'

Carenza had been contemplating the naming of the babies.

'Tom have you any ideas about names for the twins?' She asked him on his first weekend visit to Nether Heydon.

'I have no idea Carenza, but we could name them after their grandmothers.' His imagination in this department was limited. Carenza laughed. She certainly did not want another Lorna in the family but was not prepared to voice her opinion for Lorna was still a sensitive, almost taboo subject between them.

'Tom, they must be people in their own right. Perhaps they could have their grandmothers' names as second names.'

'That old thing again,' Tom said with a trace of sarcasm which was not like him at all.

Carenza looked at him sharply. It was rare that cross words were spoken.

'What do you mean, 'that old thing'?'

Tom looked at her sheepishly. 'It doesn't matter.'

'Oh but it does Tom. I want to know what you meant by that remark.'

Tom knew that unless he owned up Carenza would keep on about this until she had wormed the truth from him.

'The independence thing. It never goes away. Now it is focused on my children.'

'Our children,' she corrected. 'As for all this I have never hidden my feelings about what I want out of life. You have known since the day we met. Why have you brought it up now?'

Tom did not know how to answer her. Life was just not the same since the twins were born. His hesitation made Carenza smile.

'Tom Heston I do believe that you are jealous,' she teased. 'Come on confess.'

Tom made a rueful expression.

'Well maybe a little'

Carenza could not contain her mirth and jumped up to hug him.

'Oh you silly man. I will be home soon but babies do take up so much time. May says that she will pay for Nanny to stay for as long as she is needed. How do you feel about that?'

'Guilty at the expense of it all and rather unmanly not being able to afford it myself, though extremely grateful too.' He smiled a lopsided smile which set Carenza's heart aflutter.

She hugged him tightly.

'Everything will be fine; now about those names. How about Georgia May Heston and Lilian Lorna Heston, known as Lily?' She had acquiesced about Lorna. She had learned that there were times to be subtle and manipulative. It had been Jeannette who had given her lessons about subtlety during the early days of her marriage. Carenza had been a little taken aback by this attitude for she had always assumed that Jeannette's marriage had been made in Heaven. But this piece of advice had been so useful to Carenza in order to gain her own way. Jeannette had been regarded in a different light after such revelations.

Tom had capitulated about the names to be given to his children. Now he felt a sense of completeness. His sense of insecurity about the condition of his parents' marriage had been wafted away by the security that his marriage to Carenza had given him and then the subsequent birth of his daughters. They were a stable family unit which was something he had always aspired to in his adult years. After much soul searching he knew that he could not clip Carenza's wings or he might lose her too. She was too precious for that to happen and without telling her personally he had given his blessing to her independent spirit which could fly whenever it wanted providing that it came home to roost in his safe harbour.

Chapter 37

Carenza and her children had stayed at Nether Heydon longer than had been anticipated. Her pleasure at living once more in her childhood home was euphoric. May was also guilty of encouraging Carenza for she had enjoyed the company of her daughter. As time went by Tom wanted his family to return home where they belonged. He had remembered his own promises to himself not to hem Carenza in but he felt enough was enough. It was not unusual for a man to want to return home to his family at the end of a working day instead of only seeing them at weekends.

'Time to go home next weekend Carenza,' he said on the Sunday afternoon as he was about to leave to return to Dalton.

'Just another week or two,' she wheedled but Tom was not going to move on the subject. They were going home with Nanny and the twins.

*

The return home to Dalton had not been nearly as traumatic as Carenza had thought. In fact, she felt a rush of new found independence. Nanny Yates had proved to be indispensable, allowing Carenza to come and go as she wished. The children were thriving and well taken care of. Even school seemed a distant memory these days and Carenza surprised herself when she admitted to herself that she did not wish to return now or in the future. Often she made return visits to see May without the children. She had made new friends and acquaintances but it was not really her way to indulge in afternoon tea visits or in charitable causes. They bored her. There were more interesting challenges to be met. Guilt made her contribute generously to these causes enabling her conscience to remain clear. A greater stimulus was required but she had not decided what that could be. She did not want to return to an ordinary job and she had to acknowledge that her role as a mother could not be neglected even though she was fortunate to have Nanny Yates. Whole heartedly she wished that she could discuss this with somebody. May had not had to think about working after she had adopted Carenza and Lorna had never worked in her life and even if they had been on speaking terms it was not something they had in common.

For a while time was spent in self indulgence. Shopping became a favourite hobby but there was little point hanging clothes in the wardrobe which would never be worn. As Carenza trailed the back streets of the local towns she had discovered small antique shops hidden away. Many of the shop keepers had bargain articles which gathered dust and lacked care in their maintenance but excitedly Carenza began to see through the detritus of dirt at what lay potentially below the surface. She bought small antiques which she cleaned but did not display at home but found nooks and crannies where she hid them away for another time. She learned about jewellery and used her own money to buy cheaply. A germ of an idea was beginning to grow. It was during these happy days that Carenza discovered that she was pregnant again. The twins were only nine months old but there was no problem because nanny was still there to look after them. Tom was thrilled. He wanted a son to balance up the odds in the family. His imagination ran wild sometimes when he thought about a family of daughters. Every man wanted a son. It was only natural.

In due course Carenza produced the long awaited heir. Joshua Spencer Heston entered the world as a sturdy, lusty baby. Tom could have cried with happiness. Their family was now complete.

The new baby had arrived as quickly as his sisters but this time Carenza did not return to Nether Heydon. She recovered at home while baby was initiated into Nanny's rigid routine. Carenza was so grateful for Nanny Yates' presence, but not half as happy as Nanny who loved working for the Hestons whose young family kept her gainfully employed.

As her recovery became complete Carenza returned to her shopping trips and had forged a plan which she greatly hoped would come to fruition.

Part 5: Four Years Later

Chapter 38

The twins were now five years old with very different personalities but they were so close that they could not bear to be apart. They were the apple of Tom's eye but there was something about Josh, now a rumbustious three year old, who made Tom so proud. He could not actually say what made him feel this way but during his free time the two of them did much together. The twins were now attending a private day school which was situated at the edge of Dalton. This had been at Lorna's insistence. Over time she had learned how May funded the nanny to her own amazement. It had been a considerable shock to her to learn that May was a woman of substantial means. Her prejudice towards Carenza melted just a little. These events had led to her opening her own purse to pay for the education of her grandchildren, which included Josh when his time came. But of course there were strings attached to her generosity. She wanted to see more of her grandchildren. Carenza had been annoyed by the interference in their lives but on a rare occasion Tom sided with his mother.

'If she is prepared to be so generous it is the least we can do. May sees the children a lot.'

'I know,' Carenza agreed. 'I know that I must be fair but you know what your mother is like.'

This caused a stalemate between them but Carenza had to capitulate and allow Lorna access to her grandchildren, but she would not allow them to stay with her mother-in-law. Tom had to agree with her on that issue. There was no knowing what Lorna would do if she was given free rein over her grandchildren She could even poison the children's feelings towards their mother.

Since the onslaught of parenthood Tom had matured. He took the responsibility seriously. Other areas of his life also demanded a more mature attitude. He had been made a partner in the law firm alongside his father. Although Carenza had always had a sensible side to her nature, she felt that Tom was becoming stuffy and old before his time. He would want pipe and slippers at the ready she mused. There were times when she felt stifled by family life. She was a good mother, loved her children with a passion but there was still something else that was lacking. Tom was adamant that there was no need for her to work and did not listen to her protests of boredom. There had been those times when he had agreed that she needed her freedom but it looked as if he had reneged on those promises over the years. She felt that she was dancing to his tune and not rowing her own boat. The children were happy and well cared for but it was her time to branch out and regain her independence.

One weekend she arranged to go and see May without the family. Dorothy was happy to look after the children while Tom played at his new hobby of golf. Having informed Tom that she would not return until Sunday afternoon, she had the distinct impression that her husband was not too happy at her decision but she was not prepared for his feelings to blight her freedom. As she drove away she felt euphoric. It was like being let out of prison. She mused on these thoughts and then admonished herself for being overdramatic.

It was a lovely, warm autumn day as she drove into Nether Heydon. She looked around at the familiar scenery and felt a stab of homesickness. The front door was opened by Avril who greeted her warmly with an affectionate kiss on the cheek.

'Come in. Let me carry your holdall.'

Carenza handed over her overnight bag knowing that Avril would take it straight to her childhood bedroom.

'May's in the sitting room. She has a touch of cold today.'

'Thanks Avril. I will go straight to her.'

When Carenza entered the sitting room she found her mother huddled over the fire wrapped in a blanket, her nose a bright red and her eyes saying that she was feeling sorry for herself.

'How long have you been poorly?' she asked in a concerned voice.

'There is no need to fuss. I have enough of that from Avril.' Carenza smiled knowing that May was intolerant of any illness.

'Well, never mind. I can keep you company now.'

'Don't you think that you should go home? The last thing you want to do is catch a cold and give it to the children. Heaven only knows where I caught it.'

Carenza drew her chair a little nearer to the fire opposite her mother.

'May I need your advice,' she said.

May raised her eyebrows quizzically.

'Why, what's the matter?' her tone of voice changed from self pity to concern. 'Is it the children?'

'No. It's Tom. I cannot do what I want any more. I'm bored with being at home. Nanny looks after the children most of the time and Tom won't let me think about working.'

'Have you talked to him properly? He knows how you feel about having your wings clipped. He learned that right at the beginning of your relationship.'

'I know but he refuses to listen. I don't know what to do about it. He is being so pompous. He says that we don't need the money.' Carenza started to become agitated all of a sudden.

'Do you want to return to teaching?' May asked knowing how much her daughter had loved her career.

'I have been mulling over new ideas and I would like to open a shop.'

May's jaw dropped over the mere thought.

'What kind of a shop?' she asked, her eyes beginning to twinkle for the first time since Carenza's arrival.

'I was thinking in terms of antiques and jewellery.'

'But you know nothing of any of that.'

'But that's where you are wrong,' she replied guardedly. 'I have been thinking about it for a few years, just after the twins were born in fact. I have also done my homework. I have used the public library to study and improve my knowledge. I have nearly enough stock to fill a shop already.'

May raised her eyebrows again at this piece of intelligence.

'Where have you got that from?' she asked.

'Well I have been buying it for years and have been storing it at home until the time was right.'

'Does Tom know?'

'Of course not. He would have had a fit if he had. I intend doing it with or without his consent. Why am I talking about consent? I am a free person in my own right.'

May observed Carenza's flash of defiance and independence resurface. She had to admit that Carenza had been under Tom's thumb for far too long. It was high time that she should rise above it to become herself once more.

'Well, I agree with you. As much as I love Tom, it is time for you to rejoin the human race and not be dictated to.'

'Oh May, you are wonderful.' Carenza had jumped up in readiness to hug her mother.

'Don't hug me. You might catch this.' May instructed. 'You must tackle this issue with Tom.'

'I will,' Carenza promised.

'And where might you want to open this shop?' May continued.

'In Worcester.'

'And what if it does not work out, this enterprise?'

'Oh but it will. I am sure about that.'

And May just knew that she was.

*

Carenza's confrontation with Tom occurred when she returned to Dalton on Sunday afternoon. His mood was dark and brooding. He had missed Carenza more than he would care to admit to anybody, even himself. His body language spoke volumes and the children had kept their distance in the safety of the nursery at the top of the house. They were unsure of this side of their father which had not manifested itself to them before. He usually played with them at weekends or they ventured out as a family. They had also missed their mother. Tom had taken refuge in the sitting room with a glass of beer lodged in his hand and a boring old film playing on the television. Pathetically he had not known what to do with himself and it had not occurred to him to take the children out helped by Dorothy.

The front door opened and closed noisily.

'I'm back,' shouted Carenza cheerfully. Two identical pairs of eyes appeared at the top of the stairs followed by the thunder of feet. The twins fell into their mother's arms much to her amusement. She hugged and kissed them as she shrugged off her coat to hang in the downstairs cupboard.

'Hello you two,' Carenza snuggled up to them. 'Have you been good for Daddy and Nanny?'

Both heads nodded in unison, 'Yes,' they lisped together.

'Where's Daddy?' she asked gently unpinning herself from their pincer style embrace.

'In there.' They pointed towards the sitting room. 'He's in a grumpy mood.'

'Is he now,' Carenza said more to herself than to anybody else. 'Off you go to Nanny and I will be with you shortly. I need to talk to Daddy about something important.'

The twins ran back upstairs while Carenza poked her head around the sitting room door observing how correct the twins' perception appeared to be.

'Is my favourite husband in here?' she asked to lighten the heavy atmosphere.

Tom had the good grace to blush and then smile which lit his face like a beacon.

'Hello. I have missed you,' he had the good grace to confess.

'Good,' Carenza returned the smile and bent to kiss him before she delivered her fait accompli.

Tom was a captive audience. It was not a conversation which ensued but Carenza in full flow delivering her proposals while Tom listened slightly dumbstruck at what she had decided. This new business venture had been meticulously planned without even consultation. His amazement knew no bounds when he discovered that the stock had been bought over time and secreted away until the time was right to display it in the appropriate way. His demeanour told Carenza that he was not a happy man.

'What about the children and my career?' he whined at her.

'The children are well taken care of. The twins are at school and Josh will join them next year. As for my husband I think that he is a grown up now.' She put her head on one side and grinned at him, knowing that he had been thoroughly spoilt with all the attention she had lavished on him. She would have had less time for him if Nanny had not been there to help. Carenza had always tried to temper her relationship with Tom with humour but this time she was determined that at all costs she would have what she wanted. Her time was beginning but she knew that it was not going to be easy to juggle family life and a business venture.

'This is the right time to do it Tom. I do not want to wait until the children are grown up and then I won't know what to do with my time. I have a brain and it needs indulging now and then. It is fine for you because you go to the office.'

Tom frowned.

'But ...'

'No buts, Tom. I have decided. Next week I am going to look for the right property to rent in Worcester.'

265

'Don't I get a say in the matter?'

'None at all but I will need your help and support to be able to do it.'

Tom had suffered a crushing defeat. Carenza was at her assertive best. He had not seen her this way in such a long time and had thought that parenthood had mellowed her. But he was wrong. He brooded on what she had said and felt that if he objected vociferously he would lose her. That was not something he wanted to happen. Her hunger for independence had won again but he supposed that it always would.

'All right, let's see what happens,' he consented.

'Oh Tom,' Carenza squealed. 'It will really work.'

*

The following day Carenza telephoned May to tell her the outcome of their discussion.

'I am pleased. Good for Tom.'

'I was rather pleased myself. By the way he missed me this weekend. Perhaps I should go away more often.'

May chuckled. She knew how deeply they loved each other and was gladdened that Tom had given Carenza the freedom to do what she wanted. If he had not, there could possibly have been a rift in their marriage.

Carenza had made it her business to make a collection of local newspapers to search for adverts of shops to let. At the moment she was looking for somewhere small. She was ambitious but was prepared to start slowly so that she could learn as much as she could about a retail business. There was an advertisement for a small shop for let in the black and white shambles area of Worcester. The location seemed ideal if she was going to sell antiques but it required her perusal first. An appointment had been made to view it that afternoon around three.

Carenza parked her car near the magnificent cathedral which she had always loved and made her way along the High Street slowly before turning off the main road towards the Shambles. It took her a while to locate the property but she was in no hurry because she had set out in plenty of time. But there it was. She stood and regarded it for a few minutes before she looked through the window at the interior.

It appeared to be exactly what she wanted at the moment. It occurred to her that it also needed to be an area to attract shoppers. The street was not crowded but there were shoppers around as well as some ideal shops to attract potential customers. There were other thoughts about advertising her business. It would be very important to draw people into the shop to buy before word of mouth would prove to be another recommendation. Her imagination was in full flow visualizing the grand opening with a champagne party inviting all the people they knew when a voice interrupted her train of thought.

'Mrs Heston?' the voice said. She turned to view a stocky man regarding her patiently. He produced a key which he placed in the lock and turned allowing the front door of this building to open before them.

'Hello,' she said placing her hand into his open palm. 'Yes, I am Mrs Heston. We spoke this morning.'

'Of course, how do you do?' He spoke formally. 'Well come in and see what you think.'

He stood back allowing Carenza to enter. Walking inside she knew immediately that the shop was the right size and the atmosphere of the beamed interior presented the right ambiance that she had hoped for. There was even a glass counter in situ, left by the previous business personnel. This could be used for displaying the jewellery or locking away more expensive artefacts. At the rear of the shop was a small store room which could be useful for keeping extra stock that could not be displayed immediately. There was even a sink which she could block off to make a small kitchen if she bought some electrical appliances. Suddenly she was overcome by sheer excitement.

'I'll take it,' she said.

'Well, that was a quick decision. Let us go back to the office where we can do all the paper work. It is only a few minutes' walk from here.'

*

Tom took a few days leave from the office to help Carenza set up the business venture. Carenza's buzz of excitement was beginning to pass to Tom. He had not seen her so animated for a long time and realized that she had been right when she said that being at home with little stimulus shrivelled her like prune. This was the Carenza from the early days of their marriage. She was vibrant once more and full of expectancy that she could make a success of this new scheme. Shame engulfed him when he felt that it was her place to stay at home. Several times over the years he had fallen back into old ways of expecting her to be what he wanted but he was aware that the war had changed attitudes and women were entitled to follow their own dreams. He had to leave the door open in their marriage for Carenza to fly freely like a butterfly backwards and forwards for the rest of their lives.

The shop had been creatively designed to encompass what was being sold as well as attract prospective customers. Several adverts had been placed in the local press and invitations had been sent out to numerous friends and acquaintances to launch Carenza's special project. The grand opening was to be held at the beginning of April with a champagne reception. Carenza's feet had not touched the ground for weeks.

Days had been spent buying more stock in case much sold and she was required to restock shelves quickly. May had been carried away on the tide of Carenza's euphoria. Unbeknown to her daughter she had spent an entire afternoon locked away in her bedroom. The key had been turned in the lock against any intrusion. Avril occasionally had a habit of entering May's bedroom on some pretext or other. A drawer had been unlocked in her dressing table. Within lay a jewellery box which had remained untouched for some time. May had never been known for her vanity and had made little use of this legacy left to her by her mother.

May's mother had been a beautiful Edwardian lady who had enjoyed her baubles. Much of the jewellery had been costume and paste which her mother had worn with aplomb. The seriously valuable jewellery was still lodged in the bank vault and had not been touched since the day that May had legally transferred it all to Carenza but here in the locked casket were the remnants of her mother's collection. Even Carenza had not seen the pieces which were now laid out on May's comfortable bed. Memories were triggered when she handled them but she was not unduly sentimental. The memories that had been conjured up were so long ago that they belonged to another life. May was bound up with the present and the joy Carenza and her children brought to her at this moment in time. She felt that these objects might as well be used for a purpose. If Carenza wanted any pieces for herself or her daughters that would be her choice but the rest could be sold as part of her daughter's business. After a few moments she replaced the jewellery and locked the cabinet deciding that it was important to speak to her daughter soon before she became embroiled in her business empire.

May rang Carenza the weekend before the shop was due to open. Everything was in place for the grand opening which had made Carenza decide that she would have some time to herself and her family.

'Can you come over,' May asked. Carenza felt her stomach tumble. This was the last thing that she wanted. 'I have something to show you. Come on your own if you can.'

May had been so insistent that Carenza felt that she could not refuse. These secret visits at her mother's insistence had become more regular over time.

'I'll be there tomorrow afternoon but I won't be able to stay long because I have promised Tom and the children that we will have the weekend together.'

'I won't keep you long. Bye.'

Carenza wondered occasionally if she was doing the right thing in taking on the shop for there were already so many demands on her time but she pushed the thought away as soon as it entered her mind. It was going to work, she told herself seriously, knowing how confident she had felt in the beginning.

She was still intrigued by her mother's subterfuge. The next afternoon she left the children with Nanny while Tom was indulging his current favourite pastime of listening to the newest rock and roll songs on his Dansette record player. Elvis Presley had become his favourite singer and he used anything at hand as a microphone as he crooned to his idol's voice which blared as loudly as he dared from the record player. Carenza kissed him and hugged the children before slipping out of the house to her car. She wondered why she had bothered organizing a family weekend for nobody appeared to be too bothered by her departure.

On the journey she thought about May. Her voice had not given anything away. There was nothing wrong or Avril would have telephoned her but she could not fathom what the problem was. As Carenza pulled the car to a standstill outside the cottage, the front door was flung open by Avril.

'Welcome,' she shouted down the path. 'Would you like a cup of tea?'

'Oh Avril, I would love one.'

May suddenly appeared alongside Avril, almost pushing her aside.

'She has no time for that,' she said almost rudely. 'Come with me Carenza.' Carenza and the housekeeper made eye contact and smiled at each other knowing exactly what May could be like at times.

'Follow me.' May directed as she ascended the quite grand staircase rather laboriously. Her arthritis was playing up again. At the top she turned to the right towards her own bedroom. Carenza followed full of amusement. This was May at her best.

The bedroom door was locked. This was stranger still. May never locked her bedroom door from the outside. It crossed Carenza's mind that May might be losing the plot as she grew older but she dismissed that thought as quickly as it had entered her head. On entering the room May locked the door once more but Carenza's attention had been diverted to the glittering array laid out on the counterpane of the bed. They gleamed in the light from the window and the bedroom lamps which had all been switched on.

'May, where have all these come from?' Carenza asked in astonishment.

'These were my mother's.'

'But what about the ones in the bank vault?'

'Some of those were hers too. These are not worth a lot. I want you to choose something for yourself and the twins. The rest can be sold in your shop.'

'May, you cannot give everything away. You might want to wear some of these pieces.'

'When have you ever seen me wear anything like this,' she scoffed.

'Well, never,' Carenza had to admit. 'I've never seen them before.'

'Quite,' May's chin was set at a stubborn angle. Carenza knew that she had to capitulate.

'Well this will go with my new evening dress, as will this and that one. I will allow the twins to have these. Thanks May.'

'Right, let's box up the rest and then you can take them with you.'

Carenza was amazed that her mother was clearing out so many personal belongings and could not understand the reasoning behind it. But looking at the stern set of her mother's face she decided that at this moment it was not worth challenging her on the subject.

'Off you go then. That's all I wanted to show. Get back to your family weekend, what is left of it.'

'What family weekend? Nobody seemed to notice that I had left. What about that cup of tea that Avril offered me? I think that I could do with it now!'

Chapter 39

The opening of the antique shop had been hailed as a success. Carenza was like the cat which had the cream and took her time to come earthwards from her cloud. But the following few months taught her many things about the type of business she had become involved in. Business could boom but if there were highs there were also lows and there was no logical pattern to any of it. Generally it was doing well. After six months Carenza renewed the lease on the shop. The one downside was the fact that she could not be in two places at once. If she was working in the shop she could not be out buying new stock or making contacts who would bring in items to her. The closing of the business meant that she could possibly lose sales. A swift decision had to be made to engage someone to work with her.

Coincidentally at this precise time Patricia Conran walked into her life. She was a woman of forty who was desperate to find a job. The type of job was immaterial to her because she had to earn money. The divorce from her husband of ten years had now been finalized. The separation had been acrimonious and Patricia had walked away with very little to show for the years of abuse she had suffered at his hands. The fact that there were no children was a blessing as well as a huge disappointment.

Carenza and Patricia became firm friends from the beginning of their association. Although there were several years between them in age, that had not mattered to either woman and they worked as a team. After several weeks, Carenza felt that she could trust the older woman in most ways.

After nearly two years of working in this fashion, Carenza thought that she could move the business into a new dimension. She was excited by what she had achieved, but it was the future which engrossed her knowing that she was able to expand her business and accept the challenges which lay ahead. She was ambitious but she had not neglected her family for every area of their lives was covered by the help that she had hired. Carenza always made sure that she was home to spend time with the children at the end of the working day and it was a rare occurrence which saw her work at the weekends when family life was too precious to give up.

The new shop premises were located not too far from the cathedral and the Royal Worcester porcelain factory. Carenza felt that there would be many visitors to the city and the location of the new shop would be another attraction in the area. For the previous two years she had sold mainly silver and jewellery but now wanted to extend into small antique furniture with a view to expanding again sometime in the future. The plans had been made to leave Patricia in charge of the small shop while Carenza and Tom set about preparing the new premises. This time trades- people were brought in to create the desired affect for a vastly superior shop. Luxurious shop fittings were created to display everything to its best advantage. It became a truly glamourous business venture oozing charm and elegance and wealth.

The opening of the new shop was more prestigious than the previous occasion. People of note within the community were invited to a champagne reception. It was widely advertised to take full advantage of tourism and during the first few weeks after its inception the business was doing well.

'Carenza, I am so proud of you,' Tom said to her one evening, when he had taken her out to dinner to celebrate their wedding anniversary.

Carenza basked in the praise that he bestowed upon her.

'I couldn't have done it without your support Tom. You have been wonderful, taking on more responsibility than other men would have done.'

They looked at each other with love illuminating their faces. It was the love of two people who were at ease with each other and the life that they shared. He took her hand and kissed it.

'I love you and always will. You are the best thing that has ever happened to me. There is one thing that I want you to do. Please listen to what I have to say before saying anything. It is now time that this war with my mother came to an end. Could we invite her to lunch and show her the new shop? I shall ask my father as well.'

'I know it is time that there was peace between us all. You can try but ...'

'Ssh, I know. But we can try and see what happens.'

Several days later Tom rang Lorna and offered the olive branch in the hope that his mother would accept it for what it was - a peace offering. The line at the other end went quiet.

'Mother, are you still there?' Tom asked.

'Yes Tom, I'm still here but I don't think that I am ready to accept the invitation at the moment.' Tom detected the strain in his mother's voice. It did not take him long to finish the conversation but he was furious with her. Would she never learn?

When Carenza heard the outcome of the conversation, it was all she could do not to laugh out loud. She was past caring about her mother-in-law but at the same time she felt sorry for Tom and Spencer. Lorna was the loser in the game of happy families and Carenza was not prepared for the children to remain for any length of time in their grandmother's company in case the venom that could pour from her lips affected her children in any way now that they were growing older.

It was Spencer who became a frequent visitor to the family home in Dalton. He loved the harmony of family life which existed within its walls. Tom's childhood had not been idyllic. Lorna had not wanted to play the part of the warm, loving mother although there was little doubt that she loved her son. Her own childhood had been far from loving. Lorna Heston had come from the higher echelons of society. It had been her upbringing to be snobbish and high handed. Her birth in the late Victorian Age into a titled family meant that she had an air of authority and was regarded highly. Her own mother was a lady by right but she had fallen in love with Lorna's father who was a down-at-heel artist without prospects. Lorna had been the product of that union. In fact there had been twin girls but one was still born. Lady Sofia Hurst had married, much to the extreme disappointment of her parents, and proceeded to live a Bohemian life style. There was no place for a child. Lorna had been left with her grandmother, who brought her up as her own child, passing on the standards and snobbery of the upper classes which Sofia had shunned. It was this inheritance that Lorna had brought with her to her marriage to Spencer Heston. Her choice of husband had been limited as England emerged from The Great War. A new world was opening up and the order of change was apparent. But Lorna Heston was not about to change and brought to her marriage the standards that she had learned at her grandmother's knee. Spencer had never felt Lorna's equal and that was the key to the downward spiral of their marriage.

Spencer was still living with Lorna but it was a sham of a marriage. There were times when he resented the fact that he had forsaken Camilla's love all those years ago. He knew that she had not remarried but had lived quietly, occasionally seeing other men but none of these relationships had lasted very long. In all that time Spencer had never looked at another woman but the temptation had always been there. Work had become a substitute for love and he had found immense pleasure in the time he spent with his grandchildren. These days Lorna had a tolerant relationship with Tom and occasionally her grandchildren. Spencer hoped that she had learned some lessons along the way otherwise she would enter an embittered old age.

The new business had been open a few months when Carenza discovered that she was once more pregnant. Her reaction was one of devastation. The children were beginning to grow up and become more independent and she saw less demands on her time as this happened. Her reaction was to delay telling Tom the news. She knew that he would be thrilled for family life was important to him and he made up for the deficiencies that he felt he had endured during his own childhood. He had always been a good father. Carenza drove to Nether Heydon to see May. She wished to discuss her latest predicament with her mother. There was still a little feeling of guilt in not confiding in Tom first.

May opened the front door smiling happily to see her daughter. Carenza regarded her critically for a moment before shock overtook her. May looked as if she had aged since she had last seen her only a few weeks ago. May never changed. She had always remained the same since Carenza had first seen her.

'Are you all right May?' She asked

'Yes. Why?' came the abrupt reply.

Carenza backtracked, not desiring to enlarge on her feelings. She felt that she should have a quiet word with Avril before she went home. Even though the day was pleasant outside a fire gave a homely glow to the sitting room. The small windows sometimes gave a chill to the room but the presence of the fire made all the difference.

'How is the shop?' May asked.

'Couldn't be better but that is not why I came.'

May regarded her quizzically.

'Problems? Tom and the children?'

'Everybody is fine but I may as well tell you. I'm pregnant again and I don't want to be.'

'Is that all? I thought it was something dreadful. What does Tom say?'

'May, I haven't told him yet. He will be thrilled. You know what he is like.'

'But you're not; why not?'

'Well four children is rather a big responsibility.'

'Carenza, do you remember what you used to say all those years ago? Let me remind you'

'You don't need to May. I remember. I always wanted a large family to replace my blood family. But I have three children already.'

'This baby is a gift to you and Tom. Don't throw away such an opportunity. Tom has rights too. This could prove to be such a special child. You have nanny and the business can be run by someone else until you are ready to be in charge again.'

Carenza looked at the wise old face in front of her and felt a rush of pure love for May who had never had the opportunity to have a natural child of her own but had lavished so much affection on her adopted daughter. She smiled at her mother.

'I am being selfish, aren't I?'

May smiled back.

'Yes, very.'

'Don't mince your words will you,' Carenza laughed. 'Straight talking was always your way.'

'It still is, my dear. Have you decided when you will tell Tom?'

'It will have to be soon. I just needed to tell somebody.' With that comment she hugged her mother. 'You always manage to put life in perspective for me. This will be the last baby though.'

It was not until her fourth month that she told Tom the news. His reaction had been as expected. The expression on his face had been one of pure delight. He had pulled her into his arms and just held her. He knew that she would be back at work just as soon as she could and the new baby would be with Nanny in the nursery. He did not know how they would have coped without Dorothy. Dorothy had been in her element looking after the Heston children and the news of the new baby heralded the need the Hestons had for her. She could not imagine her luck that her employment would continue way into the future.

Carenza found a new manager for the shop. Even though she was pregnant it did not hinder her ambition to expand her business further. She had set her sights on other large towns such as Gloucester and Hereford but the new pregnancy had slowed her and tired her more than she would like to admit. May felt that Carenza was flying too fast in her ambition but the new baby was the catalyst to slow her down. This pregnancy had laid Carenza low in terms of health. The doctor had instructed her to take bedrest or he had threatened her with an enforced rest in hospital. Carenza had capitulated knowing that hospital would make her life unbearable and she would be under close scrutiny but at home she had a little more freedom to be herself. Once more she had grown large and cumbersome very quickly which rang alarm bells in her head. She had not voiced her opinion to Tom who as it was fussed over her unbearably. The least fuss the better for Carenza. May came to stay for short sessions which relieved the boredom threshold. Her presence had a soothing affect for May discussed other issues beside babies. Carenza felt that this was probably because she had never produced any of her own although May loved the Heston children as if they were of her own blood.

When Carenza had reached nearly the end of her eighth month, the midwife on a routine visit, confirmed that she had heard two heartbeats.

'Well Mrs Heston; two heart beats. Isn't that wonderful? Twins again.'

Carenza did not know how to comment. She twisted her lips into a smile and pretended that she was radiant with happiness.

Nothing shocked her any more but Carenza knew that this was going to be her last birth. Something was going to have to be done to enable her life to be more normal. She could not be producing children at this rate. Decisions were to be made. Tom had been visibly shocked to hear that his family was about to nearly double after the imminent arrival. Carenza had spent the next two weeks in the cottage hospital awaiting the birth. She was tired and nothing soothed her ill humour but before her time the pains started in the middle of the night. Nobody was allowed to call Tom. She was going to do this on her own as she had the first time. As dawn broke Alexa entered the world followed by Meredith only minutes later. The Heston family was now complete.

Chapter 40

Life never appeared normal in the Heston residence. Tom often complained that the house was no longer large enough for its inhabitants but with all the busyness of the family there was too little time to search for a larger property. Tom had more responsibility within the family law firm now that Spencer had reduced his hours of work enabling Tom to become a senior partner. Carenza's own business empire had increased with new antique shops in Hereford, Gloucester and Cheltenham, which caused her regular absence from home, much to her husband's irritation. Then there was the concern of the children who over time had taken control of the house. There was child paraphernalia everywhere despite Tom's ill humour at the chaos and noise that ensued. He felt that he had finally lost control of his own home. Carenza's absence caused him increased anxiety for he felt that it was her duty to restore a calm and order to all these troubled waters. Carenza would not capitulate to Tom's grievances. She felt that he had known when he married her that she was her own person first and foremost. She knew that she was being selfish but when did men relinquish their freedom and ambitions. The answer to that question went undisputed in many households. Even in this more liberated age women still bore the full mantle of responsibility.

The Hestons were now affluent in their own right. After many arguments with Tom over domestic problems, Carenza made a decision without even consulting him to put to right the problems within the house hold. Order was to be restored in the form of a live-in house keeper and a household help. After interviewing several women Carenza found the delightful Emma Sharp, a widow of mature years who loved living within a family atmosphere. The chaos that existed within the walls of Heston House, as the residence became known, was smoothed away into a calmer atmosphere. Tom, who had hated the intrusion at first of another body added to his home, became transformed once more into a man of peace and enjoyed the tranquility of a well ordered home life. The older children now attended a weekly boarding school and it was only weekends and holidays which became more hectic but by then Carenza was home focusing on family life. The twins, her babies as she called them, were now nearly two and remained in the capable hands of Nanny. Carenza often thought ahead to the days when her family would not need Dorothy Yates as much. A need to maintain a mother figure at home was to be all important in future years if she was to continue her business. It worried her that Dorothy might seek employment elsewhere once the twins were old enough to go to school. She had been such a treasure to the family over the years that the thought that they might lose her one day left Carenza feeling bereft. There was no way that she wanted to discuss the matter with Tom because he often grumbled, as it was, about the house groaning under the weight of so many occupants.

An opportunity arose one day when Carenza had stayed at home to do some of the paperwork which every so often consumed her time. The twins were having their afternoon sleep when Nanny appeared at the bottom of the stairs en route to the kitchen to make a cup of tea. The two women almost collided, both thinking along the same lines.

'Sorry Carenza,' Dorothy said. Since the first time that Dorothy had been employed by the Hestons the use of first names had been used to make the relationship start on a more informal footing. Tom had not been so sure. He had not heard his own nanny call his mother by her first name. But times had changed so much since before the war. He had never remarked about this to Carenza, but as time had moved on, it had all fallen into place as the expected way.

'Are the twins asleep?' Carenza asked.

Dorothy smiled.

'Like two little cherubs, tucked up with their thumbs in their mouths.'

Carenza could not help but smile. The thought of another baby had shocked her but now there was no way that she could envisage a life without the twins. They were loving and put their arms around her when she returned home at the end of each day full of love and happiness. The time she spent with them was precious as it was with all her children. By now they had reached the basement kitchen. Carenza placed the kettle on the Aga before taking two cups and saucers from the top cupboard.

'I'll do that,' Dorothy said reaching up to take the crockery from her.

'No. You sit down Dorothy. You are run ragged all day long by those scamps up there. Anyway while I have you to myself I want to ask you something. It has been on my mind for a while.'

'Anything wrong?' Dorothy asked, feeling a sensation of disquiet overtake her.

'Nothing is wrong,' she reassured her. 'I just wondered what plans you had for the future after the twins are less needy.'

This turn of conversation had taken Dorothy unawares. She often pushed away thoughts of the future. She had worked out from pieces of conversations that she had overheard that there would be no more Heston babies but had not liked to dwell on the matter. Her life with the Hestons had made her the happiest she had ever been in her entire life. The thought of finding another position within a new family filled her with dread.

'I cannot say that I have given it a lot of thought. Moving concerns me.'

Carenza nodded in sympathy. She realized that she had her answer.

'Dorothy, would you ever consider being a general factotum within the family after the twins are less needy? Let me explain. All the children will need someone to refer to for a long time to come but I will also need someone who can reduce my workload. Perhaps be a help with the business, be someone that I can totally rely on. You can still live in but I will continue to have someone here to take some of the workload from me. You don't have to give me your answer now. Think about it.'

'I don't need to think about it. It sounds wonderful. Once the twins are old enough I don't want to return to looking after babies.'

'Well, that's settled then.' The two women smiled at each other and an enduring friendship had been born.

'I had better go and wake the twins or they won't sleep tonight.'

Outside the darkness of a winter's night was gathering. As Dorothy disappeared up the stairs the telephone shrilled on the kitchen extension. Carenza put her hand out to answer it.

Chapter 41

Carenza sat at the kitchen table drinking a cup of very sweet tea as her eyes were drawn to the circled date on the calendar. Tears filled her eyes and dripped down her cheeks making huge rivulets in her makeup. With the back of her hand she wiped them away but in defiance more deluged and suddenly her body was engulfed in racking sobs. Her whole body shook with emotion and it felt that life would never be the same again even after all this time. It was exactly a year since she had received the telephone call telling her that Tom had been fatally injured in a car crash on his way home from work. He had reached the outskirts of Dalton but the weather had changed over the previous few hours and the temperature had dropped to below freezing. The weather forecast had warned of bad conditions on the road. This had made Spencer close the office earlier than usual. It had not mattered for it was a Friday night and everything was winding down for the weekend. Tom had been anxious to go home because Friday night was always a special night with everybody at home for the weekend and it was the time to catch up with the whole family's news. This had started as a special night when he and Carenza had first married and after the children had come along the pattern continued. He had left the office very aware that he had to drive carefully but his car had skidded on an icy stretch of road and hit a wall. The car had been unrecognizable when the police reached the scene and his body had had to be cut out of the wreckage. Tom had been taken to the cottage hospital being the nearest in the area but he was pronounced dead on arrival. Carenza thought of the hospital as the place of tragedy after she had had to identify Tom's body as his next of kin but only years earlier it had witnessed the times of so much joy when the children had been born.

Two little bodies had crept into the warm kitchen and cuddled up to their mother vying for attention. Meredith, the more dominant twin succeeded in climbing onto Carenza's lap.

'Why you cwying mummy?' she lisped.

Carenza looked down at her youngest children and smiled through teary eyes. These two were the culmination of hers and Tom's love for each other. They were the last children they would ever have together. She remembered back to the time of their birth and remembered feeling relief that she would not have to give birth again. How fickle was human nature. If Tom was here now she would gladly give him another child as long as he was alive and well.

Dorothy put her head around the door.

'There you are you scamps. Come on up to the nursery and give Mummy some peace.'

'No,' they replied mutinously. 'Mummy cwying.'

Dorothy knew exactly what day it was. She recollected the telephone call on that night of the accident after Tom had been identified from the contents of his wallet and the conversation she had had with her employer just prior to it. Looking back everything appeared to be so ironic and her time as a surrogate parent since had been surely put to the test. Carenza had needed her more than anything in the time since Tom's death. Dorothy did not know how Carenza had coped. There was many a time she felt that Carenza carried too much on her shoulders. She was a parent, ran a home and a huge business which was growing steadily bigger. Dorothy thought that she would make herself ill with all that she was doing, but being busy filled the void that was left by Tom not being there. It was days like this when an anniversary occurred that Carenza reached rock bottom emotionally and nobody could console her. It had proved better to leave her alone to burn away her grief until she bounced back and took the helm once more.

Dorothy remembered the day of the funeral. It was a cold frosty day with a clear blue sky. There could have been no better send off for Tom. The parish church in Dalton was packed to capacity with friends and relatives and sunlight poured through the stained glass windows, the colours seeming to lend a festive air to the proceedings. The three elder Heston children encircled their mother clinging to each other not fully comprehending what was happening to tear their happiness apart. Carenza sat dry eyed looking at Tom's coffin which had been placed in front of the rood screen. Shock had rendered her emotionless. She had walked behind it to the graveside with tremendous dignity but she was aware of nobody except her children who kept pace with her, clinging to her hands. A step behind followed Lorna and Spencer both united for once in their grief. Lorna looked like a character from a Greek tragedy and grief was etched on Spencer's face for the passing of his only son. May limped badly on her arthritic knee. She had been determined to come despite Carenza forbidding her to in her state of health but May had loved and respected Tom and deemed it only fitting to mark his passing by her presence. It was the least she could do but she also wanted to be strong for her daughter and her family. There was a great worry about Carenza who had not broken down since the accident. May was concerned that the healing process would not begin until that had happened. After sods of earth were thrown onto the coffin and the prayer was finished, Carenza turned to make her way back to the awaiting car. It was then that her eyes made contact with Lorna's whose witch-like face was contorted with grief.

'You killed him,' her mother-in- law spat at her. 'If he had never married you Tom would be alive now.'

May heard the allegation and placed herself between the two younger women.

'Enough,' she said. 'Say no more. Let any rancour rest before more harm is done.'

Spencer pulled his wife away.

'Sorry,' he mouthed at May and they walked towards their own vehicle and home to their own private grief. Nothing had been real for them since the news of Tom's death. Carenza had been in such an emotional state that the police had taken it upon themselves to break the news.

After the day of the funeral, Carenza had to face the world alone. Responsibility sat heavily on her shoulders. She knew that the family was secure financially for she had seen to that over the years. Tomorrow would be the reading of Tom's will but she was not sure what that would contain. Her husband had not revealed his own financial affairs to her for he felt strongly that Carenza had enough to dwell on with the weight of her own business.

Early the next morning Carenza made her way to the solicitors to hear the reading of Tom's will. Tom had not used his own firm for he felt that privacy was important but since his marriage he had used the firm that had served his mother faithfully. This business was situated in Gerrard Street in Dalton. Manning and Jones, the elderly partners had worked as a team since their fathers had been partners in the 1920s. Now a younger generation was finally emerging in the role of their sons who were looking forward to making a mark within the firm but the older partners wanted them to earn their spurs before they were promoted.

Carenza entered the dark interior of the building. The inside looked as if it had not been touched to bring it into the twentieth century. At the reception desk a woman of mature years with iron grey hair read papers set before her as if her life depended on it. After a while she looked up.

'Yes. Can I help you?' Her intonation was flat and monotonous bordering on being rude.

'I have an appointment with Mr. Jones at ten,' she replied.

'Name?' Came the curt retort.

'Mrs Heston.'

'Let me see if he is available.'

Before she could move from her seat an office door opened and Walter Jones came to the reception desk. He knew that his secretary could be abrupt at times. His awareness of Carenza's predicament made him pre-empt any more difficulties and as he looked at her ravaged face his heart went out to her.

'Mrs Heston?' He enquired.

Carenza nodded. She felt suddenly quite choked by the whole business and wished that Tom could be with her before realizing how bizarre the thought was. She would never have had to face this situation if he had been alive. The kindly Walter Jones looked at his secretary.

'I think that a nice cup of very sweet tea might be in order don't you Miss Moss'

The receptionist sniffed her indifference at the request and disappeared into what was obviously a kitchen, banging the door behind her.

'Come into my office Carenza and have a seat.' They wandered into the cluttered office where Walter indicated a black leather upholstered chair which sagged slightly in the centre. Carenza perched on the edge of it and placed her handbag at her feet.

'Such terrible news about Tom; the shock is just too much. How are you bearing up my dear?'

'It is not easy Mr. Jones.' The tears welled once more. Walter discreetly waited until the floodtide had passed.

'Quite so, I don't know what to say to make you feel any better,' he said looking at her kindly over the top of his glasses as was his habit.

'There is nothing that you can say, Mr. Jones but thank you all the same,' Carenza attempted to smile through the remnants of her tears.

'No quite,' he said. 'And now to business, I am afraid that it is not particularly good news. Tom was not too well organized with his affairs though I gather he did rather better with other people's.' He tried to make light of the situation but he now had gained Carenza's full attention as she wondered what he meant.

'If we begin with the house where you reside now, I'm afraid it is a property belonging to Mrs Lorna Heston. She purchased it at the time you decided to leave Nether Heydon. Young Mr Tom did not have the financial resources to buy a house so his mother offered to do it for him. The house belonged to Tom for his life only. Mrs Heston stipulated that in the unlikelyhood that her son predeceased her it would revert back into her own hands. She has since issued the statement that she would like to put it on the market as soon as possible and for it to be vacated likewise. I am so sorry my dear. It has come as a shock to you.'

Carenza sat silently for a few moments weighing up what she had been told.

'I thought that Tom used the money from the first house to help fund Heston house.'

'I'm sorry. That is not the case. Lorna lent Tom the money for the deposit and the rest was paid for by a mortgage. When Heston House was purchased Lorna paid for it and it became a private matter between himself and his mother.'

'Did Spencer know anything about this?' Carenza asked.

'I believe not,' Walter confirmed.

'Well, why would Tom not tell me? We kept few secrets from each other.' Carenza felt her cheeks grow hot as she remembered the jewellery locked away in a bank vault.

'It was the wish of Mrs Lorna Heston that that information was not to be divulged. Mr Tom had to agree in order to put a roof over the head of his family.' Walter sat quietly contemplating the young woman in front of him wondering what she would do after his revelations. It was times like this that he hated his job witnessing the distress that vindictive people meted out to their victims.

The feeling of shock was enormous, weighing heavily upon her after Tom's sudden demise. Then her thoughts turned to Lorna realizing how she was having the last laugh by her treachery towards herself. It was her revenge on Carenza for having married Tom despite Lorna's wishes. Had Lorna thought what she was doing to her own grandchildren? Carenza thought not but had made up her mind that Lorna was not to have any access to the children from this time on.

'So that then makes us homeless. How long have we got before we have to move out?' She said looking at the elderly solicitor.

Walter Jones looked at the young woman before him. He was full of admiration for her courage and fortitude.

'A month,' he uttered, silently cursing Lorna Heston for her unkindness to her son's young wife and children. He had never liked the woman since he had first met her more than thirty years before. He was aware that there was a vendetta in the family but could not understand that her own grandchildren could be treated so badly or the young widow.

'I see Mr Jones. Was there anything else for me to know?'

'Well Tom was not a wealthy young man. He depended quite a lot on his mother's generosity but he did make provision for the children's education. As well as that he has bequeathed all the furnishings to you but that is all.'

Carenza rose to her feet and shook the hand of the elderly solicitor.

'Thank you. You have been most thoughtful.'

She picked up her bag and with all the dignity she could muster she opened the office door and walked into the street. As she walked to her car she could not fully understand the cruelty of the other woman. She did not care for herself but what was she to do for her family They had a month to find a home and she did not want the children's lives to be upset more than they were already. What was she going to do? She found her car and drove it back to Lorna Heston's house that was no longer her home. When she opened the front door she heard children's voices and the hum of the television in the background. Josh ran to meet her. She looked at him and for the first time in ages she was struck how like his father he was. Her arms opened wide to hug her son knowing how much his father's death had affected him too.

'Hello, Darling. Do you know where Nanny is?'

'She is up in the nursery with the babies,' he said referring to the younger twins.

'Could you go and ask her to come and see me. By the way could you stay with your sisters until she returns to them?'

'Of course,' he said in a very matter of fact way. Carenza realized how much her ten year old son had grown up. The fact that he and the rest of them would have to grow up very quickly was more than she could bear.

Dorothy Yates put her head around the door of the sitting room.

'Josh said that you wanted me Carenza.'

'Yes Dorothy. Do come in'.

Dorothy entered the room and took the chair next to Carenza. She looked at her employer and noted how pale she was. It was not surprising considering the shock she had received recently but she could tell that there was also something else bothering her. She knew that Carenza had been to the reading of the will but did not know what had transpired. All that she could think was that the news had not been good.

'Dorothy, do you think that you could hold the fort over-night? I need to go and see my mother. It is quite important but I don't want the children to feel that I am abandoning them so soon after Tom's accident.'

'It is no problem Carenza. Do what you have to do. We shall be fine.'

'Thank you Dorothy. What would I do without you?' The question hung heavily in the air unanswered. Carenza was more than grateful to the nanny who had been with her family for years, but at this time she was like a second parent to the Heston children since Tom's death.

Chapter 42

Carenza took very little time in organizing her departure. She had spoken to the children to tell them that she was only going to be away overnight at Grandma May's and she would return as soon as she had completed all that she had to do. Josh was feeling insecure now that his father had disappeared from their lives. Their relationship had been particularly close as he was the only boy in the family. At times they had done things together which Josh now felt would be lacking from this time forward. But after much reassurance that all the children would be happy during her short absence, Carenza had placed her overnight holdall in the car and had driven away at a steady pace very conscious that it was the driving conditions on the roads which had caused Tom's untimely death.

She had not informed May of her impending arrival as she believed that she would worry. But when she arrived in Nether Heydon she found her mother sitting knitting by the fire in the sitting room. May was as usual attired in her baggy waistcoat and thick stockings to keep the cold out. It could be said that May was definitely not a follower of fashion like her daughter who wore her hemlines fairly short and her hair geometrically cut Mary Quant style. It made Carenza happy that this part of her life remained unchanged. May was an endless source of stability but for how long. Although Carenza was renowned for her independence, everybody needed someone to rely on. The shoulder of responsibility was a heavy mantle to carry.

Avril had opened the front door to Carenza's knock.

'How lovely to see you,' She had exclaimed. 'This will perk up May no end.'

'Why, has she been down in the dumps?' Carenza asked hoping that there were no more problems to deal with but straight away chastised herself for bringing her own problems to her mother.

'No she is fine but she has been worried for you because …' Her voice trailed off because she did not have to say any more.

'Quite. I'll just go and tell her that I'm here.'

Carenza entered the room unannounced to May's enormous surprise. They kissed and hugged. May waited patiently for Carenza to explain this sudden unexpected visit. Eventually it came out in a torrent and a rush of tears about the reading of the will and its contents. They sat in companionable silence for a few moments. May gazed into the fire watching its flames dance and flicker while she mulled over what her daughter had revealed. Eventually she raised her head and looked Carenza straight in the eye.

'There is only one thing to do. You and the children must come home. This will always be your home and now it will be the children's home. I would also love you to come home. I have missed you more than I can say.' She volunteered this last piece of intelligence as she observed the response forming on Carenza's lips. It came anyway.

'May, we cannot do that to you. For one thing there are too many of us and I need Dorothy to help with the children more than ever now. Plus Avril will not take kindly to an extra workload. There is also my furniture to sort. It is all a nightmare. I cannot believe that Tom would do all this to me.' The tears brimmed as she contemplated all that she had to do. May rose slowly and stiffly from her chair and stood beside Carenza. Her hand reached down and took her daughter's which she patted in consolation.

'Tom did not do this on purpose. It would be only natural to believe that he would outlive his mother. That is the natural way of things. Mother Nature can upset the apple cart or freak occurrences may happen which change the order of events but he had not been in debt which would have given you a far greater headache than the one you have already, but nor has he been totally honest about his general lack of finance. The question is how are you going to cope financially yourself. You do of course have the jewellery. That is why I gave it to you.'

'Oh I won't have to use that. My business affairs are on a very sound footing May. I have made sure of that from the beginning. If this had not happened I would be looking to expand the business further but at the moment my priority is to see to the happiness of the children. As it is Josh is very clingy. Georgia and Lily are coping and the little ones don't fully understand.'

May nodded.

'Did Tom know how well your business was doing?'

'Not exactly,' Carenza had the good grace to blush.

'That makes you as bad as Tom in one way, although you are on top of your own affairs as I expect a daughter of mine to be.'

'Say it as it is May,' Carenza had laughed lightheartedly for the first time since Tom's death.

May smiled in spite of herself feeling very proud at the way that her daughter was coping.

'You must move home. I also miss you Carenza. It would be lovely to have you here. You could put all your furniture in storage until it is required again. I will speak to Avril and we can hire more help if necessary. The house is too big just for me. The next question is to see about Lorna. She cannot keep doing these spiteful things to you. It has been going on since you married Tom. Now it must end legally, if necessary, so that you can move forward with your life. Tom would want that for you. You no longer need a thorn in your side. There is no Tom to upset by any course of action you might take to sort out this most unpleasant situation.'

'Legally? What do you mean? How can I do that?'

'Quite simply by making sure that Lorna has no contact with you or the children at least until they reach their majority at twenty one.'

Carenza stared at her mother as she contemplated this statement.

'Would it be legally binding? Haven't grandparents got a right to see their grandchildren?'

'I suspect not if the parents won't agree to it. You are now their only legal guardian and it would be up to you to decide this for them.'

'It would be worth a try in order to keep the family protected now that Tom can no longer do it.' Carenza sat quietly for a few minutes contemplating all that they had discussed. 'What about Spencer? I could not prevent him from seeing the children. He has been so good to us over the years.'

'Spencer is a good man but a little weak in my opinion. He should have sorted Lorna out a long time ago before it all reached this situation. But he has every right to see his grandchildren. This is purely Lorna's doing and should only affect her. You need to see a solicitor very quickly.'

'Could you make me an appointment with your solicitor May? I cannot use any solicitors used by the Hestons.'

'I will as soon as I can.'

A week later May had made the appointment and a legal document had been drawn up after Carenza's interview with Ray Marchant of Marchant and Marchant-Solicitors. Carenza was recalled to sign the document before it was sent to Lorna Heston. It stated that there was to be no contact between Lorna and any member of the family in the written form or personal contact. If there was to be any contact at all it had to be made through their solicitors. All her life Carenza had never been a vengeful person but for once she felt personally free of the abuse that had been meted out to her by her mother-in-law. The sensation was totally liberating to feel free of any connection with Lorna although she suspected that there might be a protest made through her lawyers.

It was now almost a month since Tom's death. There had been so many problems to deal with but Carenza had coped remarkably well while she was thus occupied. It was during the quiet, dark hours of the night that she missed him most of all. An outstretched hand would touch the empty space where he would have lain beside her and it was then that her heart would ache for the personal side of her marriage. There was nobody to share the anecdotes of the day, nor the humourous events which happened in their lives. In fact she was lost and lonely for the one man that she had ever loved but there were times when she remembered her days as a single person. She had been self reliant and resourceful and some inner strength told her that she would be again. During those darker days and nights there would be another occupant or two who would climb into the bed beside her and snuggle into the security of her warmth not fully understanding the devastation that the family still felt by Tom's absence. For Lily and Georgia, although they missed their father, Carenza had sent them back to school as quickly as she could to continue some form of normality. Their lives were busy with schoolwork and the friendships that they had formed but they had a unique closeness only possible with identical twins. Normality had helped their healing process to begin.

Josh had not been as fortunate as his elder siblings. He grieved for his dead father and felt that he had nobody that he could relate to. His mother seemed to him remote at the moment tied up with the practicalities of the aftermath of Tom's death and all that ensued. But Carenza was not insensitive to Josh's predicament and had mentioned the problem to May. Her own well of emotion was running dry as she shared herself with her children and all that she had had to do. As usual May rallied to the call for help but her physical frailties these days were a frequent source of irritation to her.

'Send him here to live with me until you all move,' she had said. 'I will give him my undivided attention. He can start at the village school and then I shall keep him so busy that he won't have time to dwell on anything.' May had a solution for everything.

For only the second time in weeks Carenza laughed heartily.

'Like you did with me.'

She remembered back to the time she had first come to live with May after her mother and grandmother had died in the Blitz. May had regimented her life then. There was so much to do that she had had little time to dwell on that old tragedy. Even now those days seemed so far away in time. How easy it was to forget. Time was the healer that it was said to be. For some reason she felt less worried about the impact Tom's death had had on his children. She would not allow them to forget their father but over time all their grief would become less raw and life would go on as it had always done. But Tom would not be forgotten and would be talked about with love and affection and living on in their hearts.

While Josh was under May's jurisdiction he was subjected to the life his mother had experienced. At the end of the day he was so tired that all he wanted to do was to go to sleep. Never had he been so grateful to welcome bedtime. May could only smile at this reaction. She knew that Josh would grieve for his father but he would survive to move forward with his life. The regret that May had was the lack of a father figure for young Josh but then she remembered Spencer and felt that relationship might be a journey of healing for both of them.

May had had much to organize on her own home front. She had appraised the situation critically wondering how she was going to accommodate the family and she had reached the conclusion that Avril might have to move back to the cottage she owned in the village. It seemed the obvious solution particularly as it was no longer rented out to local tenants. Avril had indicated that she would prefer to live in her own home but would still work for May for as long as she could. That solution meant that there was room for Nanny to remain with the family. The dining room was to be dismantled to serve as an extra sitting room and doubling as a study for Carenza. This meant that May could keep her own sitting room so that her peace would be safeguarded. Carenza knew how noisy her household could be particularly when the older twins were home at the weekends.

The furniture at the Dalton house had been registered for storage until further decisions could be made about the family's future. Carenza wanted to find a house in Nether Heydon but knew it had to be a house of a certain size to accommodate her large family. She realized that May was happy to have them all with her but the reality of everyone living together was going to be another story. May had been used to peace and quiet in her latter years but all they could do was see how it worked out over the next weeks and months. It had solved the immediate problem.

A month after Tom's death the house in Dalton was empty. A removal van took away the large items of furniture while a second smaller van transported the rest of the Hestons' possessions to May in Nether Heydon where the task of storing everything became the nightmare that Carenza had suspected that it might be. The large attic rooms were explored by the children. It was during this time that Carenza climbed into this unknown territory and had a good look for herself. Her reaction was one of amazement. This part of the house could have been a nursery in former times when families were larger. This thought made her smile. It could have been a family the size of her own or even larger. It could also have been the maids' quarters. She had lived in this house for years before her marriage to Tom but in all that time she had never climbed the stairs to this upper level of the house and could not understand why she had never been curious to find out more about it. After some reflection she realised that she and May had had so much space that they had no need to use any other areas of the house and the attic had been closed off. At first it had been her idea to store many of their possessions here but as she explored further she saw the potential for the space to be used as bedrooms. There were three attic rooms with small windows overlooking the front and back of the house. The place was covered in dust and cobwebs but after a good clean and some renovation she saw that her three eldest children could use the area as their own and the noise they made would be contained away from the rest of the family. For the first time since Tom's death she felt some excitement. She loved this old house and was happy to be back but had always felt that the upheaval would have an adverse effect upon her mother.

It did not take Carenza long to put her new ideas to May hoping that she would agree.

'It sounds wonderful,' May had enthused. 'We will draft in extra help to clean the entire top floor and do all the necessary jobs to make it habitable. It shouldn't take too long to do it.'

'Oh May. That's wonderful,' Carenza enthused and the well of tears which at this time was never far away surfaced as she realized that one major problem had been sorted.

Chapter 43

The post had been delivered to Lorna at breakfast time. Spencer had long gone to the office. He could not bear to be around his wife more than he needed. His workload had also increased since his son's death. He had hoped to retire in the next few years and hand the business over to Tom and the junior partners. Since Tom's death there was much to organize and his workload had to be sorted before being passed on to some of the younger solicitors. There was also the need to appoint another senior partner to help with the running of the establishment. It was not just the business to organize but Spencer did not know how to cope with his own grief. He felt that he had little in his own life to compensate for his loss. He and his wife could not console each other in their joint grief because there was not a common denominator that could bring them together. It had become a wedge that had driven them even further apart than they were before.

The office became his refuge and he worked late into the evening to keep his mind occupied. He was also considering leaving Lorna for good now that there would be little contact between the two warring women. He hoped that he could continue to see his family for they were the only family he had left. Spencer had no reason to believe that Carenza would be cruel in that way. It was with feelings of deep rancour that he received the news of Lorna's dealings over the house. Carenza had telephoned him at the office with the news that they were leaving Dalton and returning to Nether Heydon.

'I am so sorry Carenza. I cannot believe that she could do this to you and the children,' His voice had sounded choked as he spoke. 'You know that it is not of my doing. Lorna holds the purse strings tightly I'm afraid.'

'I know that Spencer. She has always hated me. I can accept for myself but why does she have to be so spiteful to the children. They have done nothing wrong.'

'You did nothing wrong my dear. It is Lorna's way. There is something badly wrong with her. In the head I mean. I shall be leaving her as soon as I have all our affairs sorted out. I cannot go on living this way.'

'Oh Spencer, what can I say. I have seen a solicitor and have legally severed all contact with her for myself and the children. I cannot put up with this sort of behaviour any longer. It does not affect you. You must come and see us often and you know that Josh will need you as a male figure in his life. He misses Tom so much. Remember you are welcome any time. We love you.'

'Thank you,' he said but Carenza could hear the tears brimming in his voice.

The conversation ended. Both Carenza and Spencer were too full of the loss that they felt over Tom's death.

Spencer was shocked on many levels after he had spoken to Carenza. The fact that she had taken legal action to preclude Lorna from their lives was more than he could cope with. He wondered what repercussions there would be once Lorna had found out. His feelings were such that he would be used as the whipping post if he stayed much longer. As for his gratitude to Carenza for allowing him access to his grandchildren, this could not be measured in words.

Lorna had not fared much better than Spencer but her problems became magnified by the fact that she had too much time on her hands. Her friends who came to express their condolences soon turned against her. She was embittered by Tom's death and blamed Carenza for so much. Other people could not quite understand what such a successful daughter-in-law had done to be on the receiving end of such derision and scorn. They kept their distance feigning other prior engagements. So after a few weeks Lorna became ostracized by her so called friends. Her venom was once more directed towards Spencer but he was not prepared to have his life ruined any more.

The letters had been delivered that morning, containing bills and an envelope from a firm of solicitors whom Lorna did not recognize. She slit the envelope with the paperknife which was placed on the breakfast table every morning and then perused its contents. Her face frowned, puzzled by what she was reading. Without any more thought she rose from the table and walked into the hall and picked up the receiver and dialed.

*

'Oh, my word May, it is fantastic.'

Carenza stood on the topmost landing with her mother. The entire upper floor had been transformed over recent weeks into a habitable space. May had banned Carenza or the children from entering this part of the house until the project had been completed. The effect was to be a huge surprise for everybody. May had used her time to plan this remarkable area and had found all the handymen and furnishers through word of mouth amongst her network of friends in the village. Everyone had come thoroughly recommended. This was also May's first time at viewing her achievements because she found it now a momentous effort to climb the stairs and two sets had become an almost impossibility. Now the two women stood viewing the weeks of work that had been put into making this pipedream a reality. The three bedrooms had been designed around the characters of Carenza's eldest children. There were sunny colours complementing the natural light which managed to enter the rooms through the small windows. The furniture was new and was designed to suit teenage girls. Even an extra bed was placed in each room allowing for the children to have friends to stay if they so wished.

May was full of her own achievements. Carenza laughed uproariously at her mother knowing how this project had given her a new lease of life, having allowed her to plan all the details, but the greatest pleasure was seeing the house return to its full potential after so many years. It was now a house for a family not just for a spinster who only occupied a small part of it. The older twins were returning for the holidays and were due to move into their new rooms. Carenza knew how excited they were when she had last spoken to them.

'They will all love it May. Thank you so much.' Carenza kissed the downy cheek.

'I hope so. It is lovely to see the house come back to life with a family to enjoy it,' she enthused. 'This will probably be the last time I shall come up here. My knees are not that good nowadays.'

'Oh, I expect that the children will want you to come upstairs to see what they have done to make it their own.'

'Well, just once more then,' May laughed.

Carenza descended the stairs in front of her mother but turned every so often to check on the slow progress. Not for the first time she wondered if there was anything that could be done to alleviate May's suffering. It had even occurred to her that it might be a possibility for May to sleep downstairs but she knew that that suggestion would be disregarded for as long as possible. May had her pride after all.

*

Lorna had telephoned Walter Jones in a moment of panic and anger. 'How dare the woman prevent me from seeing my grandchildren?' These thoughts had raced through her brain. There must be something that could be done to prevent this from happening. She of course never cared whether she saw that woman again but Tom's children were her own flesh and blood. Tom would turn in his grave if he knew what that woman was doing. It had never occurred to her that under similar circumstances he might feel the same as his wife.

Walter Jones had taken the call. Usually he recommended that clients should make an appointment to see him but Lorna was another matter. If he was honest with himself he was rather in awe of her. He was not honest enough to admit that he was afraid of her but her upper class manner, demands and arrogance he found rather daunting. He always gave way to her demands.

'Hello Mrs Heston. How may I help you?' He started to bluff for he had a good idea about the reason for the call. He had received a copy of the letter that had been sent to his client and if he was honest he admired Carenza's courage to make a stand against her mother-in-law.

'You know very well why I am ringing. You have received a copy of the letter that has been sent to me by that woman.' Walter could hear the vitriol in Lorna's voice and the soft side of his nature made him recoil. He did not need this aggravation at the moment. 'This cannot be legal to prevent a grandmother from seeing her grandchildren. Write her a letter telling her not to be so stupid,' Lorna snapped in a vicious way down the receiver.

Walter knew that he should wear his professional hat and give his client the appropriate legal advice. 'Courage, mon brave,' he said to himself but he flinched at his own cowardice.

'My dear Mrs Heston.' He began in the best authoritative voice that he could muster, 'I am afraid there is little you can do to challenge the legality of this document.'

'Well, what am I paying you for then if there is no solution to the problem. What about her being a bad parent?'

'Now Lorna.' He had found his courage as he used her Christian name. 'It would be impossible to prove this. Carenza was still living with Tom when he sadly died. It is evident that they had a happy marriage. Carenza provides for the children and they are not neglected. There is plenty of help on hand to see that they are properly cared for. She is and will remain their legal guardian.'

Lorna demonstrated her frustration down the telephone. She blustered;

'She cannot do this to me. Anyway they have no permanent home. That should count against her.'

'But Lorna have you not heard that the little family have returned to Nether Heydon to live with Miss Faithful. They will always have a permanent home with her.'

The telephone went quiet. Lorna felt as if someone had struck her in the face.

'I would suggest Mrs Heston that the only way forward for you in this tragic affair is to find a way back through your husband for I realize from the document that he remains on good terms with his daughter-in-law and her family.'

The telephone went dead. Walter held the receiver stupidly in his hand for several seconds before realizing the implications of Lorna's action. A smile graced his countenance. For once there was nothing that Lorna could do about the whole state of affairs.

Chapter 44

Spencer turned his house key in the lock. Everywhere was quiet but a light shone under the door of the sitting room. He felt tired. That was not a strong enough word to describe how he felt. He was exhausted emotionally and physically and tonight he did not want a fight with Lorna. It had happened a lot in recent days. Just as these thoughts passed through his beleaguered mind the sitting room door opened and Lorna stood silhouetted against the light.

'What time do you call this coming home?' She asked icily obviously preparing for a fight. Her speech was slurred and she waved a rather large glass of whisky precariously in the air.

Spencer turned his back to her as he prepared to walk up stairs away from her.

'That's right. Walk away from me why don't you?' She sneered at him.

Spencer continued walking.

'I hear that you are friends with that so called daughter-in-law of ours. She doesn't want to see me, only you.' She hiccupped.

Spencer turned around and appraised his wife with a look of disdain.

'And why am I on good terms with her may I ask? Do you never think of anybody but yourself? You have been unkind to her from the first day that she walked into our lives. Just take a look at yourself Lorna. You just sicken me to my very core. You have become a drunk and your friends don't want you and most of all I don't want you.' He had even surprised himself at his outburst but the knowledge that every word he uttered was true gave him the courage he needed. He had no need to protect Tom and Carenza had taken legal steps to protect her children but this woman he still called his wife could not see what was happening under her very nose.

However, Lorna blanched at the accusation and the general way that Spencer had spoken to her. She was the one who held the moral high ground in this relationship she thought but on this occasion she had the common sense to say nothing.

'Did you know that she has made it legal?'

Spencer looked down on his wife from his position of halfway up the stairs.

'Yes,' he said. 'She told me herself a few days ago. She could not take the aggravation that you mete out now that Tom can no longer protect her and the children. And to take things a stage further Lorna nor can I. I am here to pack a few things and I am leaving you.' He turned once more to continue his climb up the stairs. A demented cackle stabbed him like a knife in the back.

'You will never leave. You do not have the guts Spencer Heston. You have never had them. What makes you think that it will all change now?'

But Spencer never turned round to be goaded by his wife. He was looking for a suitcase to fill. He had decided to take enough clothes for a few days until he had found a place to live. It was not an ideal situation but he knew he would never return to live with Lorna. Her mockery still resounded in his ears but now he had made the final decision. As he descended the stairs she stood in the hall.

'Bye, Spencer. See you on your return,' she sneered and turned her back on him as she walked into the sitting room and slammed the door behind her.

Spencer felt nothing. There was no regret that his marriage was over. It had been over years ago. Before he closed the front door he glanced around him feeling that his next visit to collect the remainder of possessions would be his last. The memories held within those walls were bitter except for the years when Tom had been a child but even now that happiness eluded him.

*

Carenza had welcomed the twins home for the holidays. It gave her a feeling of completion to their family unit to hear the noise that emanated from the upper floors of the old house. Tom's presence would be the icing on the cake she felt but now to some extent she was beginning to find an inner peace of acceptance that he would never be part of their lives again. The family was beginning to settle into their new lives and home. Josh saw his grandfather regularly which had established a tight bond between them and this partly compensated for Tom's absence. May had encouraged Spencer to join the family for weekends. They had room now to accommodate guests after the completion of the upper floor. Spencer had learned to feel part of a happy family unit and drove regularly down to Nether Heydon at weekends to join in the fun. As much as she had loved her son, Lorna had never encouraged family life like the way Carenza had. The sound of laughter was never far away in this home with so many children and several generations living in harmony under the same roof. He was full of admiration for May and how she and Carenza had so much love for each other and the children. It saddened him to think how much he and Tom had missed out on over the years. But there was no time to look back with regret. He wanted to move forward with his life.

On one occasion he had had a long conversation with May who had much insight into the human character despite the fact she had been a spinster.

'I really appreciate my time here with you all. I just want to say thank you for all the kindness you have shown me.'

May looked at him for a moment and then smiled.

'You know Spencer, you are only here because the whole family loves you and long may it continue.' She rose to her feet on unsteady legs and took his hands firmly between her own wrinkled ones and squeezed them hard to show that she meant every word. When she eventually looked up into his face tears filled his eyes. What a good man he is she thought and what a dreadful life he had had to endure. As on many occasions in the past she was filled with gratitude that she had been lucky to live a life of happiness.

'Do you know Spencer I should never say this, but I am going to anyway. I think that it is high time you brought this dreadful marriage to an end and sought happiness for yourself. But there we are, I am just an old busybody who knows nothing,'

'No May, I believe you to be the wisest woman I know.' With that comment he hugged her tightly knowing that Carenza was well blessed to have a mother like this woman but he also knew that his daughter-in-law knew it too.

A divorce from Lorna would enable him to be free to lead a happier life and perhaps to marry again if he wished. There was nothing to glue him to Lorna except for the grandchildren but that had been dealt a death by Carenza's decision to remove them from Lorna's orbit. He had never blamed Carenza for this and Lorna hardly knew the children. She had been interested in them when it suited her and felt that money was a way to buy their love but had never offered affection instead. The children suffered the few visits that had been arranged over time but as they grew older they had questioned why they had to go and see someone they did not know or love.

After one of these weekends in Nether Heydon, Spencer was returning to the flat he had rented in Dalton. The place felt sterile after the fun of May's household. He felt starved of affection and lonely by his solitary existence but there had been no other choice open to him unless he had remained with his wife. These depressing thoughts had been the deciding factor for him to make a visit to Lorna to collect more of his possessions. He wanted to make a better home for himself and when he had straightened out his thoughts he was going to start divorce proceedings. He was quite happy to take the blame for the failure of the marriage if it speeded up the process and then there would be no need to see her again. It was the only way he could cope with his situation if he was to move his life forwards.

He decided that if he had more of his possessions he could entertain himself during the course of the evenings by making his new flat into more of a home. Once he had done this he would have somewhere to entertain his friends. It would give more credence to his life for he wanted to move on from the crossroads and the void that his son's death had left behind. Spencer had become sensitive and demoralized since his bereavement but he knew that he had to fight this state of depression. He realized that over time life would be better but at the moment it had taken its toll. He dreaded meeting Lorna. These days she always seemed to be at home and he was not in a frame of mind to be attacked by her ill humour which was fueled by alcohol addiction but this was something he had to do. Some inner strength had to be found to make this his last visit. There was nothing else he wanted from her now or ever.

As he pulled into the avenue where he had lived for so long, he was aware of a flurry of activity in the road. A police car with its revolving blue light was parked outside his house. In the distance a siren could be heard, becoming louder by the minute. He pulled the car over to the kerb and parked. For a few moments he watched the comings and goings of police personnel, wondering what was happening. Eventually he opened the door of his vehicle but did not lock it. A young policeman stood at front door barring his entrance.

'Sorry sir, you cannot come in here,' the police constable said officiously.

'What's the matter,' Spencer felt a stab of fear inside himself.

'Fraid I can't tell you that Sir.'

A pair of legs appeared down the stairs and evolved into another burly man in a suit.

'Good evening Sir,' the man said. 'Can I help you?'

'Can you tell me what's going on,' he said.

'Can you tell me your name Sir?'

'Spencer Heston. I live here or I did. My wife and I have parted.' Spencer corrected himself.

'Let the gentleman pass, Burrows.' The constable moved to the side allowing Spencer to enter the hallway.

'Can you come this way, Sir?' The police detective sergeant led Spencer into the sitting room. 'Have you any form of identification on you to confirm that Sir?'

Spencer was growing impatient by the minute. He wanted to know what was going on. Inside his wallet he found his driving licence which he handed over.

'All that seems in order Sir. Please sit down. I am afraid that I have some difficult news for you concerning your wife, Sir. Your maid Sandra …' He consulted his notebook.

'Yes, Sandra.' Spencer was nearly beside himself with impatience and trepidation.

'Yes, well she called us saying that she had found your wife dead in bed, I'm sorry to say, Sir.'

Spencer exhaled, having been unaware that he had been holding his breath.

'Dead!'

'I'm afraid so Sir. It looks like a straight case of suicide. There was a note addressed to you.'

The sergeant showed Spencer a piece of writing paper. It was a pretty sheet from a writing set that Tom had given her a few Christmases ago. Spencer felt strange remembering such frippery at a time like this.

'Spencer,' it began.

My life is at an end with the death of my beloved son. How can I live without him? By doing what I am about to do means that I can meet him again in a far happier place. My life of misery will be over. I regret our problems Spencer and hope that you will reach a happy place within yourself in time. Lorna'

Spencer reread the note but felt no emotion. He wondered if the whole thing was a joke. This was so unlike his wife who had felt very little for others during her life.

'Where is she? Can I see her?' he asked.

'If that is what you want Sir, but let me caution you not to touch the body.'

The sergeant accompanied Spencer up the stairs into Lorna's bedroom. She lay peacefully in the bed almost as if she was asleep. He had not seen her for years without strain on her face. Death had left her almost how he had remembered her in the early years of their union. She was older but her basic beauty remained unflawed now that the lines that had etched her face had fallen away. He could not cry. They had not known each other in the latter years and had never truly loved each other in the beginning.

'What happens now?' he asked still starring unemotionally at his dead wife. The ambulance had arrived and there was activity down stairs in the hallway.

'There will be an autopsy to ascertain the cause of death and you will be informed. Can you give my constable a telephone number and an address, Sir? I seem to understand that you don't reside here.'

Spencer nodded.

The sergeant had never once said how sorry he was about Lorna's death. Spencer wondered if this was all in a day's work to the police. He took one last look at his wife. She had never looked more beautiful. As he turned to go his eye noticed a set of pill bottles and a whisky decanter, all empty, standing on the bedside cabinet. There was nothing to say. It all seemed self evident with or without an autopsy. Nodding his head at the officer, he left the house stunned by what had happened. He returned to his car feeling quite numb. There was nowhere to go and nobody to see and for the next hour he just drove aimlessly around while he collected his thoughts on what he should do next.

*

The telephone rang. Carenza glanced at the clock on her desk and frowned. It was midnight. She had been working on her books for the business and knew that she was behind with them. If she did not catch up soon she would have a backlog which would keep her here for days. Carenza felt that it was time to do her tour of her business empire for it had been neglected after the turmoil of her private life. It was good fortune that the people who worked for her were hand-picked for the qualities that they possessed.

The telephone continued to ring. It was late to be ringing at this hour. May would wake if she was not careful and would want to know what was the matter. Carenza dashed along the downstairs passageway to where the telephone sat on the hall table.

'Hello.' Her voice was barely above a whisper.

'It's Spencer,' came the unrecognizable voice. He had left Nether Heydon just a few hours before.

'What is it?' she asked.

'It's Lorna.' There was a choking sound in his voice.

'Lorna. Is she ill?'

'No. She's dead.'

There was silence for a moment, then her voice repeated,

'Dead!' Carenza was aware that she was repeating every word that was being uttered. 'How can she be dead?'

'Suicide. There was a note. The police were there.'

Carenza was silent for a moment trying to absorb all that she had been told.

'How did the police know about it?' she asked.

'The maid found her when she went into the bedroom. She was just lying there as if she was asleep.'

'And what did the note say?' she asked, but all this was becoming too much after the trauma of Tom.

'It said that she could not live without Tom.'

There was silence. This was not credible. Had they misjudged her after all this time?

'Spencer, do you want me to come? I can come now or first thing in the morning but I will need to speak to May or Dorothy.'

'There's nobody else I can ask. I have no one.' His voice was raw with emotion and then he broke down into heart rendering sobs.

'Stop right there Spencer Heston. Don't you dare think like that.' Her voice had risen in anger and with it came a new strength.' You are a major part of this family and don't you forget it. I'll come to the flat in the morning. Get some sleep. There will be a lot to sort out. And Spencer, it will be all right.' The telephone went dead.

Carenza had put the telephone back in its cradle. Waiting for a few moments to see if anyone had been woken by the call, she then walked back along the corridor to the sitting room where she sat at her desk trying to think about what she was going to do. The shock of the news had stunned her beyond belief. This was Lorna at her best. If the news had not been so shocking she could have laughed out loud at the woman's audacity. Had she been so affected by Tom's death? Carenza remembered the day of the funeral and the accusation that Lorna had levelled at her. Tears filled her eyes as she remembered but there was no way that she could believe that the woman would take her own life. Slowly the shock began to wear off and she tidied the papers that had been spread across her desk. She groaned knowing that the business was to be put on hold once more. There was nothing else that she could do but her thoughts turned to Lorna. There was something wrong. It was unlike Lorna to love anyone unconditionally. She knew that she had loved Tom but there were always strings attached. Hers had always been a manipulative love. There were no answers to the questions that leapt into her head.

Sleep had been elusive for much of the night but when the alarm clock rang at about six, Carenza felt drugged by sleep. It took a supreme effort to wake up and to make her sluggish body move from the warmth of her bed into the darkness of a winter morning. Knowing that May would be awake as she did not sleep well these days Carenza draped her fleecy dressing gown around her and crossed the landing to her mother's bedroom. She did not knock but put her head around the door and waited to see what response there would be. May was propped up in bed with a bed jacket around her shoulders. A book and a pair of spectacles were placed to her side. As ever Carenza had interrupted an early morning reading session.

'I'm sorry to interrupt you but ...'

'The telephone last night,' May interjected. 'I thought that it couldn't have been much because you went straight to bed, but was it?'

'I didn't think that you had heard it.'

'And?' May waited, noting that there was urgency in Carenza's voice and manner.

'It was Spencer. He had called at the house to collect more of his possessions to take to the flat. When he arrived he found the police there. Lorna had committed suicide. There was a note.'

May hitched herself to sit up straighter in bed.

'Oh my God!' her hand flew to her mouth in horror. 'What did it say? The poor, stupid woman,' she said.

'That she could not live without Tom,' Carenza sniffed and tears rolled down her cheeks. This was all hitting a raw nerve just as she was starting to find a way forward with her life. 'Spencer feels that he has nobody in his life he can turn to.'

'Stuff and nonsense,' May replied in her usual pragmatic way. As usual she was looking to find a way forward in the emotional turmoil. 'The man knows that he has us. That will never change.'

'I told him that May, but I fear that was shock talking. Like us he has been through a lot in recent months.'

'Are you going to him?'

'Yes, I must. He can't cope with this on his own. Could you tell Dorothy? I will be back later on today.'

'Yes of course. What on earth did the stupid woman want to go and do that for? She was always dramatic. Does she want to make everyone feel guilty?'

'I expect so but Spencer is in a very bad way. I know he did not love her but feelings are feelings after all.'

'Off you go. Everything will be sorted here.'

Carenza bent and kissed May's cheek. She knew like always she could depend on her.

'Keep me informed, my girl.'

'I will,' Carenza blew her mother a kiss and left to start an emotionally charged day.

Later that morning Carenza parked her car outside the building where Spencer's apartment was situated. The house was part of a terraced row which had been transformed into flats in recent years. She rang the doorbell and waited. Spencer appeared at the front door looking dishevelled while a six o'clock shadow was visible on his jaw line. The state of his appearance shocked Carenza who had only ever seen him smartly attired even on the most casual of occasions.

'Come in. I am sorry for the state of me but I have only just got up. I couldn't sleep properly just thinking about …' His voice trailed off.

Carenza understood. Following him inside and up the stairway, she looked around her. Depression descended on her. It was appalling to think of Spencer living in a place like this after the luxury of his life with Lorna. He never pleaded poverty but she had the feeling that he was struggling financially. Tom had always said that his mother held the purse strings.

Inside the apartment, Carenza entered a high ceilinged living room. She sat in an overstuffed armchair while Spencer disappeared to make a pot of tea. She appraised the small room which appeared clean and orderly to her eyes but there was little space to keep personal items. A few family photographs were scattered here and there on the mantelpiece. There was one of Tom graduating from university and next to it was one of her entire family smiling broadly into the camera. Tom stood with his arm around her waist. It was what he had always done when they were photographed together. At this moment she would have given anything to have had them comfortingly around her and she could nuzzle into his strength. It took its toll on her to be strong all the time. Pushing such thoughts away, her eyes wandered further round the room. On the floor in the corner a pile of law books were stacked haphazardly, great tomes which were well thumbed after all these long years of Spencer's career. The room remained austere except for these few items.

Spencer returned with a tray which was laden with biscuits and tea. Carenza had not the heart to tell him that she could not eat anything.

'Are you all right Spencer?' she asked.

'Yes. I am just rather shocked that she could do such a thing. To see her lying there was a great shock. Do you think that I could have driven her to do it?' he asked, guilt etched on his weary face.

'Stop right there. No Spencer,' Carenza's voice was stern. 'Never. You must not think that way. Lorna made her own bed years ago. You know that. You also know that she manipulated all our lives in one way or another. She played us off one against the other. She made all our lives a misery. That was why I took legal advice. I also have a feeling that there may be more to this than meets the eye.'

'What do you mean?'

'I can't explain,' Carenza continued, her face perplexed by the whole situation, 'and I haven't anything to base it on. It is just the way my mind has been working since you first told me.'

'I had a telephone call from the police this morning. They said that the autopsy should be tomorrow and we would have the results in a few days. But they think that it was a cocktail of alcohol and pills due to the debris on her bedside.'

Carenza nodded.

'Have you thought about the funeral?'

'The police said that I could arrange it as her body will be released soon.'

'And where do you want her to be buried?' The question had to be asked.

'I thought next to Tom after what she wrote in the note.'

Carenza remained quiet for a few minutes mulling over Spencer's words.

'Well that is a consideration,' she said non-commitally.

Deep down she had a feeling that Tom would not have wanted this. He only tolerated her in life but to remain with her for eternity was a step too far but she could not think of an alternative. Perhaps she should acquiesce. To flaunt her disapproval at this stage would not do Spencer any good. She only had to gaze into Spencer's ravaged face which had aged dramatically in the past twenty four hours, to know that he could not take much more. Guilt had eaten into his soul but none of this was of his own making. She felt that she should place the guilt purely on Lorna's shoulders so that Spencer had a sense of perspective about the whole affair. Depression seemed to be setting in and she did not want to leave him alone for long to brood on the events which had turned all their lives upside down.

'I think that Lorna should be buried with Tom,' she lied but what else was there for her to do.

A sign of relief flickered in Spencer's eyes.

'Thank you for that. It is a relief to know that you agree. I had felt under the circumstances that you might object to her being laid to rest beside Tom. It is no wonder that Tom loved you the way he did. I will make an appointment with the vicar as soon as I can.'

Carenza turned her face away to hide the expression which she knew must have masked her face. An element of guilt engulfed her but her father-in-law had suffered quite enough without any more aggravation thrust upon him.

'Do you want me to come with you?' she said wanting to help alleviate the tensions which cloaked all the proceedings.

For the first time Spencer smiled uncertainly.

'No. I can manage. I shall go back to work to keep myself busy. I can see that you are concerned about me but don't be.'

It was Carenza's turn to feel relief.

'You only have to ask if you want me with you.'

'I know and I'm sorry about last night. It was all too much. Shock I suppose. But I appreciate everything you have done Carenza. You have been a beacon of light in these past months considering you have had your own problems and suffering too.'

Chapter 45

The results of the autopsy had not been revealed but Lorna's body had been released for burial. Spencer had made an appointment to see the vicar of St. Clements, the church in Dalton, where Tom had been buried. George Samson was appalled at the level of bereavement that Spencer and Carenza had had to suffer in the past few months. He listened with mounting sympathy to all that Spencer had to tell him.

'I can't begin to conceive the amount of pain that you are going through,' the vicar had said.

'Thank you,' Spencer had acknowledged the vicar's kindness. 'You do know that my wife and I were separated at the time of her death but I don't think that had any bearing on what happened.'

'I am sorry to hear that Mr. Heston but I am not here to sit in judgement on people's personal lives. If there is anything else that I can do to offer comfort please let me know.'

'I will and thank you,' he reiterated.

The vicar had asked the appropriate questions about the family which he could use in his eulogy and discussed the details of the funeral. As he left Spencer felt quite drained by the whole proceedings but there was still much to do before Lorna could be laid to rest.

An appointment had also been made to see Lorna's private doctor, Ian Jarvis. Spencer believed this to be just a formality and felt irritated at the amount of time this would take when he had so much to do. The whole business of Lorna's death, which could have been avoided so he felt, was becoming more irksome as time went on. She was as irritating in death as she had been in life. He was desperate to start living his own life in earnest because Lorna had dominated the whole of his marriage but now that he was free he wanted to start living in the real sense of the word. His depressed state of the previous week had been replaced by a full blown anger aimed at his wife and the way she had treated the family over the years. Even in death she had everybody dancing to her tune.

His appointment, at Doctor Jarvis's surgery, was at eleven o'clock. It had been made outside surgery hours for a reason that remained undisclosed. Doctor Jarvis sat behind a large Victorian mahogany desk looking through a set of papers. Glancing up as Spencer was shepherded into the room by his receptionist; he rose from his chair and outstretched his hand in welcome.

'It is a sorry business Spencer, though hardly inevitable under the circumstances.'

Ian Jarvis had known Spencer personally for many years. He had not been his medical practitioner but had used the Heston law firm on several occasions for personal and professional reasons.

'Sit down my friend, please.' He indicated the chair opposite his own before gathering together the papers of the report in front of him into a semblance of order.

Spencer had picked up on the words 'under the circumstances.' His silence spoke volumes.

Ian Jarvis looked up at Spencer.

'My dear fellow let me fill you in. The autopsy was straight forward. Lorna had taken a mixture of sleeping pills and alcohol to a level that would have killed her very quickly. The rest I can now reveal whereas previously patient confidentiality prevented me.'

Spencer leaned forward in his chair wondering what was to come. He fiddled nervously with the buttons of his jacket and waited impatiently.

'Lorna came to see me a few months ago having found a lump in her breast. I referred her to a top consultant in Birmingham. To put this very concisely she had left it too long before coming to see me. The cancer had taken hold very aggressively and she had been given only a few months to live. She was offered treatment but declined. Personally, I think that was for vanity's sake but she was determined to take her own path. She was prescribed pain killers and sleeping pills. She never came to see me again. Each time she required a repeat prescription she would telephone and then it was delivered to her door. The knowledge of her illness had to remain within these walls. She was adamant about that and we had to respect her wishes.'

Spencer sat back in his chair and exhaled loudly. This was another piece of shocking news which was totally unexpected. Should he feel guilt at not having given her more attention and then he would have known. Ian Jarvis seemed to read his thoughts.

'There was nothing you could have done to persuade her otherwise Spencer. I have known Lorna a long time and she knew what she was about. She was a strong and forceful character.' The fact that he omitted to say, 'and difficult' was by chance.

'So she took her own life because she could not cope with the inevitable.'

'I would say so. She was a very proud woman but sometimes the balance of the mind is affected by the trauma and there was the distress of Tom's untimely death.'

'Well thank you Ian. I find this all a little too much to take in at the moment. I appreciate your honesty in this.' There was nothing more to be said.

'It will come as a great shock to you Spencer, so go easy on yourself. I know Lorna could be difficult at times and I am aware that you were separated at the time of her death but don't allow yourself to feel guilty. She must have decided her course of action some time ago.'

They shook hands once more.

'If there is anything else we can do …' The doctor uttered the inevitable.

'I don't think so.' Spencer turned and left the surgery needing to be on his own to digest all the facts. He decided to walk for a while to give himself thinking time. It now occurred to him that the message in the suicide note did not ring true. It had not been Tom she was thinking about but herself. She was still manipulating even after death.

*

'The funeral is on Thursday, May,' Carenza said.

'Are you going?' May asked.

'I don't want to,' Carenza admitted. 'The woman was a demon but I can't let Spencer go on his own. That would be like deserting him at the last minute.'

'I'll come too,' May replied. 'Perhaps I can give some support to the pair of you.'

'No you won't.' Carenza's retort was swift. 'You're not fit enough. You already have your leg up on a stool so how can you walk.'

'I can try. I want to be there for you.'

'Don't be so ridiculous.' Carenza was annoyed at her mother but she had to smile at May's belligerent manner. Her mind was strong but her body was weak. May would fight a war every time.

'Why are you smiling?' she asked crossly.

'Oh, what can I do with you?'

This time it was May's turn to smile at her own foolishness. She did not want to go but as always she felt that she had to support her daughter.

'And what about the children? Are they going?'

Carenza shook her head.

'No. I don't want them so upset again so soon after Tom. They did not know Lorna very well. I just want normality for them. I will just tell them that she has passed away and keep it low key.'

'I think that is a very sensible decision Carenza. Do you think that there will be many there?'

'I don't know. Perhaps some of her snooty friends might turn up. There won't be many family members as there were so few of them at our wedding.

'Quite so, it is such a sad affair altogether.'

*

Carenza arrived in Dalton early on the morning of the funeral. She and Spencer had decided to have a cup of tea before they carried on to the church together. The door was answered by a very different Spencer from the one that she had encountered only days previously. This time he was immaculately attired and clean shaven. There was an air of the inevitable about him.

'Come in,' he beckoned in an almost jovial fashion. Carenza's face reflected all that she was thinking.

'I have something to tell you,' he said.' I haven't wanted to tell you over the telephone. It didn't seem quite right but I do believe that you will be amazed.'

Carenza could not understand what he was talking about. There was time to recount the tale of Spencer's visit to Ian Jarvis. Carenza sat and listened to every word without interrupting. By the end of the monologue she felt totally incredulous.

'She made you believe …'she began.

Spencer nodded.

'She made me feel guilty for all that had gone on over the years. She didn't even kill herself over Tom. Her note left me to believe ...' There was no time for him to complete his sentence before Carenza interrupted him.

'I don't wish to speak ill of the dead but she was evil and manipulative, Spencer.' Her voice had risen in her state of anger and disbelief.

'I know. I now wish that she was not going to be buried with Tom but it is too late for that now.'

Carenza could not reply to this comment as that had been her innermost wish all along. She just hoped that if Tom was looking down on her now, that he would have the heart to forgive her for what she had agreed to do.

The journey to the church took only ten minutes by car. Both Carenza and Spencer had found an inner calm after their conversation but neither wanted to attend the funeral to pay their respects but it was their consciences that drove them forward. The date and time of the funeral had been placed in local newspapers. When they arrived at the church the hearse bearing the coffin was stationary, parked outside the old lych gate waiting for the vicar and the chief mourners. Carenza and Spencer followed in its wake. There had been no cars parked near the church which they had found very surprising and as they entered the dark interiors of the old building it became obvious that there were no other mourners present. The sad, little procession wended its lonely way up the aisle and when the pall bearers had settled the coffin on the trestle in front of the rood screen they sat one side of the aisle and Spencer and Carenza took the pews opposite them. Just as George Samson was to begin the service, the church door opened and the click of it shutting could just be heard. The sound of the clacking of high heels on the stone flags was short as the service continued. The eulogy was delivered and the rendition of the funeral music reached out to them again making the few present feel oddly desolate at the lack of friends and family to mourn this woman who had not completed her three score years and ten on earth. It was little to show for a lifetime. As the funeral procession returned on its journey once more there was no evidence of the third mourner.

The brief service at the graveside was a moment of raw emotion. Neither of them felt able to remain long as the coffin was lowered into its last resting place and the dull thud of earth hit its target .Tears were shed but they were only for Tom whose last resting place was perilously close to that of his mother. The vicar shook hands with them as he felt deep sorrow for the woman he had buried whose life had had little impact on the world around her.

'Thank you for what you have done,' Spencer said.

'Peace be with you,' the vicar said and inclined his head as he turned to walk back to his church.

Neither Spencer nor Carenza turned towards the grave to give it another glance or thought. They would have missed the grave diggers standing at a discreet distance ready to complete their task. As they made their way down the gravel path towards their car Carenza noticed a solitary figure standing by the lych gate staring into oblivion.

'Who can that be?' Carenza asked.

Spencer looked up but could not recognize the woman who stood there.

'I don't know,' he said. He was feeling numb inside, a kind of emptiness that he was unable to explain. There was now no one left from the early part of his life and it felt as if it had all been to no avail. The woman must have heard them coming for she looked up at their approach. Both of them recognized her but it had been many years since they had set eyes on her.

'Hello,' she said. 'I only wanted to give my condolences.'

Carenza half smiled at the older woman. 'I'll meet you at the car,' she told Spencer.

He nodded and turned to the other woman he had once loved. The years seemed to have left her untouched. She still possessed a luminous beauty which had drawn him to her all those years before.

'I only wanted to pay my respects, Spencer. I read it in the paper but I had to come.'

'Thank you. That was really good of you Camilla. Not everyone has treated Lorna so kindly.'

'Well, I had noticed the lack of friends but well you know …' Her voice trailed off and she shrugged her shoulders.

They felt shy and restrained in each other's presence after all this time.

'Well, I had better be going,' she said. 'It was nice to see you again.' She stood on tip toe giving him a chaste kiss on the cheek. 'If you need something.' Her voice trailed off as she regarded him properly for the first time after all these years.

'Thank you. It is very kind of you after the way I left you.' She smiled at him not knowing how to reply and turned to go.

'Camilla ... could we have lunch when all this is over?' Spencer said even surprising himself.

'Yes, I would like that. I am still living at the same address.'

Both smiled at each other but did not touch this time.

'I'll be in contact.' She nodded and passed through the lych gate without turning back.

Carenza sat in the passenger seat of the car observing the older woman walk away to her own vehicle which had been parked discreetly at some distance. Camilla had appeared warm in manner, obviously concerned about Spencer even after all this time. It took a while for her father-in-law to return to the car. He had made his way back to the graves of his wife and son wanting a moment to reflect on all that had happened. He shed a tear for them both in private wondering how it might have been had everything been different and offered up a prayer to whoever was listening. His faith had been badly knocked in recent times. He was not sure if his tears were also tears for himself. Never in all of his adulthood had he experienced such turbulence in his private life. But maybe there was a hope that he could rekindle a flame that had gone out all those years ago. Life was strange he reflected as he rubbed the remnants of the tears from his eyes to return to face Carenza who had suffered as much as he had in her young life. Her joy would be her children and her youth as she still had so much time ahead of her. He had to rebuild his life on crumbling foundations but Camilla's appearance had given him a semblance of hope.

As he opened the driver's door of the car, Carenza looked intently at him and observed the ravages of pain carved deeply into his face.

'Are you all right?' she asked reaching out to take his hand.

'I will be. Give me time.'

She nodded and knew from her own experiences that time put everything into perspective but it did not take away the hurt. That took much longer but eventually it would grow less but much assistance was required to reach calmer seas. May had shown her the way all those years ago and more recently with Tom. She knew that she must be there for Spencer too.

May was waiting patiently for Carenza's return. When she heard the car draw up outside the house she hobbled on her painful legs to the window. She wished to judge Carenza's demeanour. This would give her some indication as to how the day had developed. Carenza strode up the path to the house not failing to see her mother at the window. Raising her hand in acknowledgement, she smiled thinly. The day had drained the vitality from her.

She and Spencer had parted, agreeing that they both needed some space from each other to grieve in their own way. There had only been deep affection between them but the sadness had been too much to bear. It had only happened within a short time, both funerals a few months apart. It was time to return to the needs of the living for they were the ones who needed them most of all now. Too much grief could become a selfish indulgence but they both knew that they were only a telephone call away from each other if they needed to talk.

Carenza walked through the front door, shrugging her black coat off as she did so. On entering the sitting room she threw it casually over an armchair and walked straight into her mother's open arms, her body shaking violently in racking sobs. May in her wisdom had felt that this would happen at some point. She held Carenza for a while gently rocking her backwards and forwards as she would a distraught child. The children had been placed in Dorothy's care as far away from the adults as possible. Jeannette had rung to invite everybody to tea knowing that it would a tumultuous day, full of emotion and drama. What a dear friend and an intuitive person Jeannette had proved to be over the years.

The storm had broken at last. All the months of Carenza's stoicism, carrying the full burden of business and single parenthood, had taken its toll, but now she could move forward with her life. Mother and daughter sat for a while side by side in quiet contemplation of the chain of events that had led to this moment in time. May was sensitive enough not to question her about the traumas of the day knowing her daughter so well that at some point she would reveal all.

Carenza had made the decision to return to work full time. The children were as happy as they could be; even Josh had survived his initial upset. The events of the previous year had dominated her own life but the business still flourished owing to Carenza's prowess at selecting the best team possible to run it in her absence. It ran like a well oiled machine. There were buyers who knew what each shop required. They had their sources and contacts who even brought antiques to the showrooms, and there were customers that they would buy specifically for. There was no reason to feel anxious but Carenza wanted to move forward with her life and take the helm once more. May had interfered in her daughter's decision feeling that it was right for her to take time to heal after the emotional upheavals of the recent past. Carenza took time to reflect on May's words and had agreed that a slow build up might be the best solution after all. The healing process after so much emotional turmoil took its own time to reach the end of its journey and of course her children needed her most of all.

Carenza had heeded May's advice. She allowed the business to follow its normal course. At times she made it her policy to visit each branch and to peruse sale records and the books. Visits to her accountants made sure that there were no great financial problems to be sorted and the taxman remained happy. Much cherished family time had been spent in taking walks, shopping and just general togetherness.

Georgia and Lily had celebrated their thirteenth birthday. This event had coincided with an exeat weekend from school. This allowed Carenza to indulge her elder daughters with a shopping trip to town followed by a very adult dinner where they dined on several courses with much attention lavished on them by the maître d'. The bond between them had never been closer. There was humour and banter as there had never been before. It made Carenza remember her own thirteenth birthday. It had been a sober time. The war years had brought so much austerity into everybody's lives but it was Carenza's own insecurities at that time which had caused so much sadness. Her own natural mother and grandmother had died leaving her bereft until May came into her life.

Sitting back in her chair Carenza observed the chatter and the close bond that connected her own daughters and she smiled believing that she and Tom had done the right style of parenting. Parenthood could be such a lottery she mused. Here were two well adjusted young adults living the life of the well-to-do. They had lost their father but the old adage that children were more resilient than adults she realized was true in this case. They spoke of their father almost all the time but with much happiness rather than in a melancholy way. They were secure in their world and lived in an affluent era which was forever changing its attitudes and values.

All Carenza could feel was a rush of love for her family and for Tom who had helped create them.

Chapter 46

Ten days after May had imposed a forced idleness on Carenza, a letter from Walter Jones, Lorna's solicitor, dropped through the letter box. The contents included a request for her to visit his law practice the following week along with Spencer. The word inheritance came to mind but she did not dwell on the matter. She knew for certain that it was nothing to do with her unless … but she waved any specific thought away, deciding not to speculate on events. As they had promised both Carenza and Spencer had not made contact since the funeral, respecting each other's time and space to grieve and move forward with their lives. This summons to the solicitors was to be their next meeting. Carenza had told May about the impending visit. Neither of them tried to put much thought into the forthcoming events but each of them had their own flicker of interest in what might be about to happen.

'Could this be another of Lorna's games?' she asked her mother one day as they were enjoying a quiet time together over a cup of tea.

'I am not sure what to think. There was always an agenda with Lorna and a deviousness that upset everybody. There again it might be quite straight forward.'

'Mmmm, I can't get my head round it. I'm not going to inherit anything.'

'No I don't think you will my dear,' May said ruefully as she placed the tea cozy back on her favourite blue and white teapot.

The following week Spencer and Carenza arrived separately but within minutes of each other in the outer offices of Walter Jones and his partners. They both hugged affectionately and Carenza detected a new sprightliness in her father-in-law's demeanour. She wondered mischievously whether anything had come of his renewed acquaintance with Camilla but this was not the time or place to pursue a certain line of questioning within the sanctuary of the solicitor's outer office. The begrudging Miss. Moss shepherded them into the inner sanctum to be welcomed by the kind Walter Jones.

'Sit down, sit down,' he enthused indicating the same saggy leather chair where Carenza had sat previously. Another chair had been placed alongside for the extra visitor.

'This is about the last will and testament of Lorna Heston made only days before her sad and untimely death.' He peered over his half moon glasses at his client's relatives.

Both nodded but Spencer asked.

'Why just before her death?'

Walter Jones remained silent for a moment.

'Well,' he began, 'the previous will left everything to young Mr. Tom but unfortunately …' The rest of the sentence remained unsaid.

'And now?' Spencer said with a flair of impatience.

'I am coming to that but firstly I have to say that it was Lorna's wish for you both to be executors of her will along with this law firm.

Carenza spluttered and then proceeded to cough to cover her incredulity.

'Me?' she said, but Spencer's look in her direction stifled any other comment that she may have had.

'Yes, you are both named as executors,' Walter smiled over his glasses fully understanding Carenza's incredulity. 'She felt that Spencer as her husband should be given the opportunity to redeem himself because of past misdemeanours. I'm sorry Spencer. I am only quoting what she decided.'

'Don't worry Walter. Lorna and I knew each other well enough,' he tried to soften the older man's embarrassment at Lorna's duplicity.

Walter smiled in spite of himself.

'Quite so. The children are the sole beneficiaries under the terms of the will. They will inherit the money when each of them attains his or her majority at twenty one. This is all to be tied up in a trust fund which has been set up for them. Now there are two houses which may be disposed of as you please with relevance to the children's interests. The possibilities are as follows. The properties could be sold and the money placed in a trust fund or they could be rented out and the money reinvested in the original trust funds obviously boosting the profits. As for Lorna's personal items, such as jewellery, it is left to all the granddaughters. It is highly valuable and will be kept in a bank vault until the younger girls have reached their majority'

Walter took a breath and scrutinized the two people sitting before him, observing their body language very carefully. However, he could not detect a great reaction from either of them.

'The contents of the house are to go to you Spencer to deal with as you wish. You may keep them or sell them but the money will be yours to keep. Lorna said that was the only thanks you would receive as it was you who gave her her beloved son, Tom.'

Spencer's facial expression showed incredulity for he had never expected a mention in his estranged wife's will.

Continuing Walter turned to Carenza.

'Lorna wishes you to be an executor of her will for her beloved grandchildren. This is in case Spencer predeceased them before they reached their majority. There is no legacy left to you as the pair of you had never seen eye to eye but she believes that you would act in the safe interests of the children.'

Walter went silent, looking embarrassed by what he had had to deliver.

'I'm sorry,' he said, 'those were her express wishes.'

Sitting back in his chair, Spencer remained thoughtful while his daughter-in-law was finding it difficult to contain her mirth. Never had Carenza expected to inherit from Lorna's estate, neither did she want to do so. The fortune that she had accumulated and her inheritance from May at some time in the future saw her secure for life. The amusement that she had felt came from the fact that Lorna could not do without her assistance even in death.

Spencer leaned forward again.

'You said that it was our decision to deal with the two properties at our discretion.'

'That is what the will states.' Walter endorsed everything. 'You are both trustees along with the solicitors' practice until the children reach adulthood.'

'I think that Carenza and I will need to discuss this at length and then we will return to you with our decisions.'

'Was there anything for my son Josh as the girls have been left the jewellery?' asked Carenza.

'Nothing was specified by the deceased but I rather imagine that she thought Spencer would take care of that for her.'

Carenza was bemused by this thought and looked at her father-in-law.

'Do not worry on that score Carenza. I know Lorna had a strange way of doing things but she was all too aware that I was playing a fatherly role in Josh's life so that will be well taken care of.'

Carenza visibly relaxed knowing that Spencer would be true to his word.

'Thank you,' she mouthed.

'Well is that everything Walter?'

Walter nodded.

'We'll be off then,' Spencer said.

Standing up, they shook hands with Walter Jones leaving him to his embarrassment and discomfort which only Lorna could do from the grave. Relief that he had almost carried out her wishes was obvious.

The two silent figures left the office, sidestepped the miserable Miss Moss and opened the door into the street where they were hit by a deluge of rain. Spencer opened his umbrella to shield Carenza from the downpour and then tucked her hand under his arm. As if by mutual consent they started walking down Dalton's High Street towards a small restaurant which Carenza and Tom had frequented during the early years of their marriage before the children had come along.

The memories that were generated made Carenza blink back tears. It could have been yesterday that they had been sitting at a corner table discussing their future which had seemed so bright and full of hope at the time. Spencer, noting the signs of her still raw grief, patted her hand in a gesture of understanding. He could have felt a twinge of jealousy because he had never experienced that kind of love with Lorna. At least Carenza could hold that love that she had experienced with Tom in her heart forever. Spencer only had rancour to embitter his feelings towards his late wife but he hoped that he could turn the future around to erase these emotional scars from his heart.

'I'm sorry,' he said,' I should have thought. Shall we go somewhere else?'

'No. It's all right. I was just not ready to be in one of our old haunts,' she admitted.

'Let's sit by the window. It's lighter here. Would you like lunch or a coffee?' he said. Spencer, forever courteous, reached out to take the menu.

'I think a pot of tea is all I can manage at the moment,' she smiled at his kindness.

'I think that will suit me just fine as well.' The menu was replaced in its holder.

'Well that was Lorna at her best,' he commented ruefully. 'She chews you up and then spits you out.'

Carenza half smiled at the droll comment. 'You knew her better than anyone. We don't seem to be able to shake her off even after the funeral. We shall have to live with her decisions for years to come.'

'I know, but we can make some decisions. You can return to live at the house in Dalton as before. The children will let you stay on as long as you wanted after they have inherited.'

'I don't want to come back to Dalton …ever. I could never be happy in that house without Tom. Besides it is not fair to uproot the children again. They are happy and settled in Nether Heydon. That house will be mine one day and it has always felt like home. I couldn't leave May again. She is such a dear, and over the last months couldn't have been kinder.'

'I know, so what do we do?'

The tea arrived at that moment, making them lapse into silence. A tray of cakes was placed in front of them. Delicious as they were they remained untouched.

'You could go back to your old home. That old flat of yours is gloomy and draughty.'

'You leave my old flat out of this,' Spencer chuckled. 'I have it as I want it these days.'

Carenza gave him a look of amusement before smiling.

'So we have to come to some decisions. It is not a good idea to leave houses empty for too long.'

'True,' he said, 'shall we sell them and invest the money in the trust fund.'

'I believe that is the only answer. What will you do with the contents though?' she asked.

Spencer went silent for a moment, then looked back into her face seeing the genuine concern that she felt for him.

'A thought has occurred to me that that I might keep one or two pieces that mean something to me, sentimental old fool that I am. You could choose some pieces too if you would like.'

'I wouldn't do that. There is nothing there that I would want but the thought was wonderful. Thank you.' She placed her hand over Spencer's and squeezed it with affection.

Looking up into her eyes, Spencer could see what Tom had loved about her. The string of epithets was endless. There was her beguiling beauty, intelligence and her integrity.

'I have a proposition to put to you Carenza. Would you sell the antique contents of the house? Your business would profit from it and I would be financially rewarded as well.'

'That is a good idea.' Her face brightened at the thought. 'Would Lorna approve of me being rewarded for such an endeavour if she is watching us?' Her finger pointed upwards in mischief.

Spencer took her hand in his and laughed at the thought.

'There is nothing that she can now do about it or anything else for that matter.'

'What would you want to sell through my business?' she asked.

'There are a few items of value which I would not want to keep. There is a lot of silver which belonged to her grandmother. In fact it has come down several generations. I don't think that I would be very good at cleaning it in my little flat,' he joked. 'There are also some valuable clocks, which I wondered if I sold them they could be a little nest egg for Josh. That would replace what the girls had.'

Carenza looked at him for a few moments. Spencer found it difficult to read her mind. Taking his hand again she looked straight at him.

'I don't deserve you as a father-in-law. You're too kind. But I shall say no on behalf of Josh. Thank you, but no. Josh is not to have it yet. In time maybe but first of all Spencer you must promise me that you will sort out your finances so that you do not have to work for much longer. You should have retired by now.'

Spencer looked hurt by her refusal but she continued unabashed.

'It is like this Spencer Heston. I have become a wealthy woman over the years and May keeps reminding me regularly that I will inherit from her very handsomely in the future, a long time in the future I hope. My life would be very empty without May.

'But as for you, what have you received in all this turbulence? You must not think of Josh just yet for I will compensate him in full when the girls inherit the jewellery and in the future when you have sorted your finances, you may think about it then. Now is the time for you to sort a nest egg for yourself after all these years. You cannot have worked a lifetime without something to show for it. You can sell whatever you want through my connections and I don't want anything for it. It will be all yours.'

Spencer looked taken aback by Carenza's rhetoric.

'I don't know what to say.'

'You don't have to say anything. I just want you to feel secure and happy for once in your life. Take it as my gift to you.'

'Thank you,' was all Spencer could say. His heart was full of love for Carenza. He felt that she was one in a million.

Their tea had gone cold and untouched in their cups.

'By the way, you were looking too happy going to the reading of a will this morning,' Carenza teased, trying to lighten the atmosphere between them.

Spencer had the good grace to blush.

'I have seen Camilla twice for lunch. It has been as if life has stood still. It could have been yesterday when I had last seen her and the aggravation of living with Lorna has just melted away.'

'I am so pleased for you. Could anything come of it?'

'I hope so. Time will be the judge but we still have feelings for each other.'

'Spencer Heston I'm so pleased,' she reiterated. 'Keep in touch and come and see us as often as you want. We will also be in touch about all this business.'

Spencer kissed Carenza's cheeks and they hugged with true warmth and affection before turning in different directions to continue their lives.

Six months after the reading of Lorna's will the two houses had been sold and the capital that had been released was transferred into the Trust fund as promised. This was the end of an era for Carenza. She had felt nothing over the sale of her former home. There were many memories of happy times there with Tom and the children but there was a bitter sweet taste left after what Lorna had done. The house sale had released her to move forward with her life.

There was a genuine happiness about her life in Nether Heydon that could not be replaced by moving elsewhere. May wanted the family there and now they had plenty of room to accommodate them all.

Spencer continued to visit occasionally to see the children but he did not appear as needy as he had done only months earlier. His life was changing for the better as was her own. She still mourned for Tom but it was becoming easier to deal with after all this time. There was no problem talking about him to her children as she frequently did but she found difficulty visiting his grave. The only explanation she gave herself was that Lorna had taken him back as her own. This thought was revealed to no one in particular, but May would say that she was being ridiculous.

Then one October day, the postman delivered news of a very different kind. May was in bed suffering from a severe bout of influenza. Between coughing and sneezing she did nothing but complain about her enforced idleness. The doctor had ordered her to bed to rest as well as keeping her away from the family. Carenza had refused the children visiting rights as they did not want the whole household to fall victim to the germs. Dorothy had acted as nurse but refused to cave in to May's threats of firing her if she did not let her rise from her sick bed. Carenza had acted as mediator between the warring factions and May had had to capitulate.

'You will stay there whether you like it or not May and you will treat Dorothy properly. I can't afford to lose her because you are not behaving,' Carenza had said.

May now knew what her daughter had been like as a teacher. In order not to lose face she often feigned sleep when either women came to see her. It was not her way to lose face in front of others.

But on this particular morning Carenza had crept up to May's bedroom and put her head around the door. May was looking brighter and her attitude of anger and frustration had been replaced by her more sanguine nature. Carenza waved the envelope in the air as she entered the sickroom.

'Are you waving a white flag?' May asked showing an attempt at humour after the trauma of previous days.

'It might look like that May but you have been bad,' she scolded. 'Poor Dorothy did not deserve such treatment.

May had the good grace to blush. Even she knew that she could have made a good thespian over time.

'Anyway we have an invitation to a wedding. And if you don't do as you are told you won't be able to go.'

The threat had hit its target.

'What wedding?'

'Spencer's and Camilla's of course. You knew that they were going to get married but now it is official.'

May's face brightened visibly.

'How lovely,' she said hitching herself higher in the bed to take a look at the card Carenza offered her.

The wedding was to take place in a month's time. There was to be little fuss or formality for the two love birds wanted a registry office wedding. They had been through the large wedding in their younger days and now wanted simplicity. Afterwards there was to be an informal meal for a few friends and family.

Spencer had basked in the sunshine of Camilla's love. There was now nobody who could threaten their union. They were both free of spouses who had used blackmail to keep them chained to their sides. As a result their love had been rekindled and had flourished. All that anybody had wanted was their happiness. Giving up his draughty flat without reluctance, Spencer had moved into Camilla's comfortable home without having a second thought. Although he still had to work, Camilla had persuaded him to keep regular office hours because he no longer had to fill the lonely time which had flowed like a blank canvas in front of him.

The sale over time of Lorna's antiques had left him better off than he had expected. His gratitude towards Carenza was endless. Her staff had collected the furniture and antiques from the house in Dalton and they were placed in the many showrooms Carenza had around the Midland towns. Over the following months they had sold steadily. The upsurge in the antique market had come at the right time for them all. What she had done for Spencer was a gift to thank him for his steadfastness in her life over the years during her marriage to Tom and the subsequent time after his death which had been so filled with heartache. His lack of financial security so late in life had caused her concern but now he had the nest egg to take forward into his new life with Camilla. It felt wonderful to be able to do something for him after the neglect that he had received at Lorna's hands. Her own experience had left her feeling particularly strong to now move forward into unchartered waters.

May had made a remarkable recovery from her illness and was convinced that she was fit enough to attend the wedding. There was generally an air of excitement within the household during the weeks leading up to the nuptials. Carenza, Dorothy and the four girls had indulged in several shopping expeditions into Worcester to attire themselves in readiness for the important day. Carenza had bought a jade coloured suit which offset her hair that she had grown again after flirting with various fashionable styles over the years. Lily and Georgia had opted for red mini dresses which were to be complimented by sprays of flowers woven into their dark hair, so reminiscent of their mother's. Carenza had laughed at their choices but had felt pride in her teenage daughters. They were becoming very like herself. She pitied their future husbands if they gave them as hard a time as she had given Tom. She could think of Tom now in a more rational way and knew that she would always love him but slowly he was letting her go and life was moving on as it should.

'Flowers are the in thing, Mother,' said Lily interrupting her train of thought. With complete authority on the matter she continued, 'Remember this is meant to be the summer of lurve. Remember, "Are you going to San Francisco ..."' She sang the song tunelessly. Georgia joined the rendition restoring the melody which had captured the hearts of many people over the summer months.

'Summer is over silly. It is October now,' Georgia said as the song had finished owing to the fact that they had forgotten some of the words. She aimed a playful punch at her sibling's arm.

Dorothy and Carenza exchanged secret smiles. The girls were becoming children of the time, true teenagers. In other words they were growing up. Both women who had helped in the process of bringing them up felt rather choked at the thought that it would not be long before they were adults in the true sense. Neither woman could articulate their true feelings on the issue without feelings of anguish.

Alexa and Meredith, the younger twins had chosen sailor type dresses. They were five now and had started at the village school just as their brother had done.

Carenza had not wanted to send them away to boarding school like their older siblings who had been well established at school long before Tom's death. It had been Carenza's thought to keep the younger children at home closer to her. Over time Josh had lost his insecurities and this term had started at The Boys' Grammar school in Worcester where he was doing well academically and on the sports field. Carenza knew how proud Tom would have been of him. This made her thoughts turn once to Spencer who had forged the special bond with her son just as he had promised. Carenza had felt so grateful that he had kept his word. He saw all the children regularly but Josh had replaced Tom if that was ever possible.

'I hardly ever saw Tom when he was growing up. He was always away at school and when he was at home he became Lorna's son,' Spencer had confided in Carenza in one of his depressed moods during the early days after Tom's death. 'This bond with Josh has given me a new lease of life.'

'I'm glad.' Carenza had meant it sincerely.

Now, they were facing Spencer's wedding day to a wonderful woman. Camilla had brought out the best in Spencer. He had lost the haunted air that had become so apparent in recent years. He was free again to pursue the life that he wanted. There was no doubt that Camilla had made him happy. Carenza had taken to this woman who possessed an inner calm which had an effect on the people around her. Even May had come under her spell in the last few months. This was an accolade, as few people could claim such a thing.

'She's the best thing to have happened to Spencer except for you and the children,' she had said in her no nonsense way. 'It's time that he had a life of his own.' There was a dramatic pause and then, 'and you.'

This last comment had left Carenza reeling.

'What do you mean? I have a life,' she said defensively.

'Well,' she grumbled. 'It's either work or the children. What do you do for yourself?'

This comment had struck its target. May was correct in many ways. The trouble was that she nearly always was right. Her incapacity had rendered her an observer in life's game and had made her think deeply, too deeply at times. Carenza had felt such responsibility for her family since Tom's death. She was playing the role of mother and father to her children. What else could she do? Life had become exacting with little time for frivolity. Without Dorothy and the constant help that she bestowed on the family, which was given freely because she loved the family so much, it would have been difficult to cope. Carenza rarely saw friends except for Edgar and Jeannette but those moments were fleeting. The friends she had shared with Tom in Dalton had faded away. It was not because they were uncaring but there was little time to nurture these relationships. They had to be indulged and worked at. May was right as usual. It was time that she took time for herself again. Single women were not always welcome in mixed groups. They became like predators at dinner parties trying to steal husbands. The mere thought amused her but all this became food for thought.

Chapter 47

The wedding was to be held at the registry office in Worcester. It was to be a low key affair with mostly family and a few friends present to celebrate the love of these two people. Some of Spencer's friends from the time of his marriage to Lorna had drifted away. Some had been appalled at the swiftness of his new marriage but they had never known the true facts behind his relationship with Lorna. It had been rare for them to do anything together in the latter years but on an occasion where they had stepped out together as a couple to a social function they managed to put on a united front only for it to dissipate when they returned home to their separate lives.

However, today Spencer stood waiting for his new bride in a state of pure optimism that the future looked bright. It was a feeling of euphoria. The guests on both sides were seated in anticipation awaiting Camilla's arrival. Carenza sat in silence appraising her father-in-law. It was a momentous occasion on many levels but she had never seen Spencer look so happy. He was dressed smartly in a well tailored suit which showed off his lean frame to perfection and his hair, now grey, lent him a distinguished air. Tom would have been proud of his father on this special day. She looked across the short aisle towards Camilla's family and then suddenly someone waved at her. It was a youngish man sitting near one of Camilla's sons. The face was familiar but she could not quite place where she had seen him before. She smiled and then turned away, distracted by Alexa and Meredith wriggling with boredom from the long wait.

'Sit still,' she whispered to them, 'it won't be long now.'

They looked at her through lowered lashes; the picture of innocence but their mother knew better and wondered what they would be up to later.

The wedding march began and Camilla appeared on the arm of her elder son. Her eyes were only for Spencer. At the start of the music he had half turned to look at the woman with whom he would spend the rest of his life. He beamed in response. Carenza could not contain herself for she had not witnessed such happiness mirrored in his eyes during his marriage to Lorna. Even May, who had managed the journey and the walk with the aid of her stick, was enjoying the sentimentality of this occasion. Spencer and Camilla were counted among her truest friends.

The service was short. It was a formality to legalize the union between the couple. As they signed the register the guests began to file out into the more public areas chatting as they went. Carenza had remained behind with Camilla's son Jonathan to sign the register as witnesses. Dorothy had gathered all the children together and had found a place where May could sit down. Her knees and ankles were no better these days but she rarely complained. There was no point. It was just something with which she had to live.

Carenza had made her way from the wedding venue, out to join her family. As she passed through the door she felt a tap on her arm. Glancing up she gazed into the smiling face of the stranger who had waved at her across the aisle.

'Hello Carenza,' he said. 'It's lovely to see you again.'

She smiled at him feeling ridiculous and embarrassed that she could not put a name to his face.

'You don't remember me,' he said.

'I'm sorry but I don't. Your face is very familiar though.'

'It's Hugh Groves,' he enlightened her, holding out his hand to shake hers.

A light dawned as recognition of his name triggered something inside her from long ago. He had been a friend of Tom's from his university days but she had not seen him for years. During those heady student days, now long forgotten, Tom and Carenza had made a foursome with Hugh and his girlfriend Pippa.

'I'm so sorry not to remember you but there is so much happening in our lives just at the moment,' she apologized feeling genuine guilt at what she thought mounted to rudeness on her part.

'I know. I'm sorry about Tom too. It was a bad business, such terrible luck. He was a good friend to me at university, particularly when I was going through a bad patch.'

Carenza had a vague recollection of some family problems that had upset Hugh's equilibrium. Tom had always been good at supporting his friends if they were in trouble. He had always cared for people. A lump rose in her throat as she thought about him. With all the numerous events happening since his death her mind had suppressed many thoughts of him but on occasions like now small reminders would surface and cause her to well up with tears. She had hoped it was all behind her.

Hugh put out his hand and touched her arm quite concerned by the fact that a careless comment could cause such anguish.

'Are you all right?' he asked.

'Yes, of course,' she replied without conviction. 'Most of the time I'm all right but today has allowed many memories to surface. Tom would have been pleased for his father today.'

The wedding party began to gather together to walk the few yards to the restaurant where the wedding breakfast was to be held. It was a small place but intimate enough to have the right ambiance for such an occasion. Hugh followed Carenza into the street where a watery sun was making an appearance through the clouds. Carenza was aware of Hugh's closeness and wondered if there was any significance to this. A vague memory stirred and she felt that he had married Pippa.

'Is Pippa with you still?' The question hung heavily in the air.

'We parted three years ago and then divorced.'

'I'm sorry. It can't have been easy. Have you children?'

'No. It was never the right time.'

Silence enveloped them like a shroud. Carenza was distracted by the behaviour of her youngest children who were pushing each other near the road. Dorothy's hand reached them before hers. Each offender was sternly reprimanded and reminded that their behaviour was to be of the best. Carenza had been right when she thought that the twins would cause trouble after their time sitting still during the ceremony.

The dining experience had been special befitting the occasion. Camilla and Spencer were the first to leave amid cheers and laughter. The speeches had been kept short but they were poignant reflecting the absence of people who should have been there if circumstances would have allowed. Carenza slipped out of her seat to speak to Spencer and his radiant bride.

'Be happy,' she whispered into his ear, aware of Camilla's distraction with another guest. 'These are new times, better in some ways.'

Her arms spun round him as she hugged him tightly.

'We all love you and Camilla.'

She could not help the welling of tears for the second time that afternoon.

He hugged her back.

'Your turn will come again. You are still young.' His eyes glazed at the thought of Carenza in the arms of someone else. Tom should have been here to witness this occasion. Camilla's attention returned to her new husband.

'What are you two plotting?' she laughed at them.

'Only your happiness,' came Carenza's quick retort and her arms encircled the new bride. 'We'll see you soon. Much love.'

With that the happy couple waved their goodbyes. There was to be no honeymoon. Spencer had insisted romantically that the whole of their life from now on was to be such an event. Hugh appeared at Carenza's side waving too.

She looked up at him and said:

'You never told me how you came to be at the wedding.'

'Ah. I had been working abroad for a while; banking in Hong Kong. I returned about six weeks ago and I contacted Spencer because I had lost Tom's address. I hadn't seen him for years. And he told me. Rather a shock I should say; poor you.' His hand stroked her arm in a very familiar gesture. 'Spencer asked me to the wedding.'

'Well, it has been lovely seeing you again Hugh. Perhaps I should take my rascals home. They look as if they are going to cause mayhem any minute.'

He laughed heartily as he watched the antics of her children. They had been teasing and tormenting each other, now bored by the lack of activity while waiting for the adults to finish conversations. Carenza was surprised by his good humour. Not all adults who had not had children of their own would have been so patient at the behaviour of other people's offspring. She had enjoyed seeing him again even though she had struggled to place him at first. It had also been wonderful to go to a grown up event. Her world at home revolved around her children and little sophistication entered her sphere these days.

Hugh turned his attention once more to Carenza. He looked pensive. Suddenly he said.

'Can I see you again Carenza?'

Carenza looked awkward. She had not been expecting such an invitation. Hugh had seen the surprise in her eyes.

'Just as an old friend of course.' He was swift to suppress any other thoughts that might be milling in her head.

'Yes. That would be lovely,' she said but inside her emotions were in turmoil. A date after so long was a sortie into foreign territory. The mere thought terrified her.

'Spencer has my number. I live at Nether Heydon.'

'I'll be in touch soon,' he shouted after them.

May looked at her daughter but said nothing.

'Trust her radar to be working well,' Carenza mused and smiled secretly to herself without catching the eye of her mother.

Having given this snippet of information Carenza gathered her overactive brood together, including May, who now looked as if she was ready for a rest. She steered them through the restaurant doorway into the quiet of an early October night.

Chapter 48

Carenza heard from Hugh Groves sooner than expected. In fact she had not been convinced that she would hear from him again once real life took over once more. However, ten days after the wedding Hugh rang her at Nether Heydon early one Wednesday evening when she had just returned from work.

Her day had been quite difficult as it had been peppered by a series of business meetings in three of the stores. This had meant a lot of travelling through the day and a missed lunch. The business had taken over her life once more and the excitement that it generated within her had set her on fire with renewed ambition. The thought of opening another shop in a small town, Upton on Severn, which was only a few miles from Nether Heydon had appealed to her. It was a busy, thriving little haven and it might be just the right location for extending her business further. This time she did not want large premises. It was to be more the size of the one in the Shambles in Worcester where she had started out all those years ago. In this new business venture she wanted to have priceless antiques and develop a clientele who would return to her regularly with their requests. This would be her personal concern which she would run herself with a view to keeping an eye on the others. All these thoughts were rampant when she snatched the telephone from its cradle.

'Hello,' her voice came abruptly down the line.

'Carenza. It's Hugh.'

'Yes,' she said suddenly brought down to earth by the realization that he had telephoned after all. That possibility had not even been considered.

'How are you?' he asked.

'I'm fine.' Her voice had softened and this had not gone unnoticed by Hugh.

'I shall be in the area on Saturday. Would you care to join me for lunch?'

'Yes,' she replied, even surprising herself.

After their first meeting she had thought about all the excuses she would make if he should telephone. Her main excuse had been that she was not over Tom. Anger had flared within her when she thought that Tom had left her widowed at such a young age with five young children to look after as well as all the problems which had been unleashed on them from Lorna's petty hatred. She had not felt such rage inside her in all these long months since Tom's death. If Spencer had found happiness she was entitled to some as well. To remarry had not been uppermost in her thoughts. There had been too much responsibility on her shoulders with the children, May and the business to keep her occupied. Marriage to Tom had not been an option all those years ago until she was ready to make a firm commitment to him. The happiness they had shared would be difficult to replace. The fact that she was not trying to replace it did not prevent her enjoying a mild flirtation occasionally or even a romance which did not have to be a true commitment.

'Shall I collect you at one o'clock? I have found a little bistro not far from the river.'

'That would be lovely. See you then.'

Sitting at the bottom of the stairs, she remained there for a few minutes contemplating the conversation. She was concerned about what she would wear on her first date in years. How would she cope with a man that she did not know very well? Student days were long gone when they had been carefree, now she came with baggage she thought, while Hugh was a free spirit to live his life as he wished. But this was just lunch, she suddenly chastised herself, without strings attached. Hugh did not control her life. The future was hers to control as much as was possible.

'Oh Tom,' she whispered. 'Why did you have to make my life so complicated?'

'Carenza. Is that you? Who are you talking to? Who was that on the telephone?' May's voice called from the sitting room.

'Well there's nothing wrong with your hearing May,' Carenza mused.

Carenza entered the sitting room and regarded her mother thoughtfully before she spoke.

'It was Hugh Groves, that university friend of Tom's. He has asked me out to lunch on Saturday.'

May smiled cherubically.

'Good,' she said. 'Can you pass me my knitting please?'

'Is that all you can say?' Carenza queried. 'It has left me with a dilemma. I said yes but I really meant no.'

'I told you to get out more. This is a wonderful opportunity for you. You don't have to marry the first man you set eyes on but it will break you into a new part of your life. So it is good.'

'I hope you are not matchmaking May.' Carenza stood with her hands on her hips regarding her mother sternly. She had seen this steely look in her mother's eyes before and was no longer fooled by her.

'Why would I do that Carenza. You need to get out more. You are becoming rather boring these days. What with all the children and the antiques you have nothing else to think or talk about. Stop yourself becoming a dusty, antique like me. It will do the children good not to take you for granted for once. They have everything they need and want except for their father. Any way you were made for marriage just as I wasn't.'

'What are you trying to tell me May?' Carenza suddenly felt on the defensive regarding her children.

'I'm trying to tell you that you spoil those children to try and compensate for what happened to Tom. You are right at the bottom of your list of priorities and it is time that you thought of yourself for once. My mother used to say that the onlooker sees most of the game. I am the onlooker and I do not like what I am seeing.'

'That's an odd expression.'

'But oh so true.' Carenza looked at May in a puzzled way. She had never heard her speak like that before.

'May, have you been drinking?' Carenza glanced at the sherry decanter but the level of the golden liquid in the bottom of the glass looked just the same.

'Just because I am speaking my mind for once does not mean that I have consumed alcohol.'

'Well you do sound a trifle odd.'

'Well that might be but I have always had your interests at heart. So you my girl go out,' May continued in the same vein, 'and enjoy yourself on Saturday without another thought for anybody else. I'm here, so are Dorothy and Anita. The children will come to no harm. Now then where's my knitting?'

Carenza contemplated her mother for a moment and then found the errant knitting by the side of the chair where May knew it was all along.

Carenza left May with her head too full of everyday events to sort out. Perhaps May was right that she did worry too much but it was her nature. Reaching back into the grey and distant areas of her childhood, she remembered the struggles of her grandparents even to put food on the table, the regular beatings that Hannah had been subjected to every night after Ray's return home from the local public house. Her children lived a privileged life of the well off, here within May's beautiful home. Their financial future was assured in so many ways. That was what good parents wanted for their own children so that they did not have to face a childhood of poverty like she had done.

It was strange to feel that part of that security was down to Lorna but it was still very difficult to think of her with any warmth. Carenza did not want her children to be so spoilt that they lost sight of values. They were spoilt but it was not possible to spoil a child with too much love. Frank and Doris had nothing to give but their endless love. Even May in latter years had not lavished her with material goods but her love had been unconditional. Perhaps she did over compensate for Tom's absence in their lives but single parenting was not easy. Over the years she had worked hard to build a comfortable lifestyle for them but her money had accrued into wealth. May in her wisdom had observed what she had missed since Tom's death.

'The onlooker sees most of the game,' the saying repeated itself in her mind. Thinking about all May had said she truly realized how wise her mother was.

'I will make it up to you May for thinking so badly. You are right as you are on most occasions.'

The children had to allow her some space and time to become an individual once more but it did not mean that she would ever remarry.

The week had been too busy and exhausting to dwell on May's pearls of wisdom but when Carenza woke up on Saturday morning she could feel her stomach turning summersaults. It was nerves, but she knew that she could not withdraw from the promise she had given to Hugh. Her absence from the breakfast table had been noticed by the children but Dorothy who was aware of what lay ahead for their mother that day brushed aside any comments with aplomb.

'Where is Mum?' Meredith said.

'Yes, where is she?' asked Georgia. 'She is usually down for breakfast.'

'Leave your mother alone,' Dorothy said sternly. 'She needs a lie in this morning because she has had a busy week. Now all of you eat up or you'll be confined to your rooms.'

The children looked at the nanny curiously wondering what was going on but they knew that she would do what she had threatened. Her word was law in the nursery world even with the older ones.

Carenza had stolen a banana from the fruit bowl but even that she found difficulty in digesting. By midday she was panicking about what she would wear. Lily and Georgia had sauntered into their mother's bedroom and observed the chaos that surrounded her. Clothes were strewn over the large bed and chairs. Their mother was the tidiest person they knew.

'Are you tidying out your wardrobe?' Lily asked.

Carenza was distracted by her problems.

'No,' she said with a sharpness that was unusual.

'What are you doing then?' Georgia was puzzled by this strange course of action. The whole morning had been unusual.

'I'm going out to lunch today.' Carenza kept her composure but wanted to scream at them to leave her alone.

'Out for lunch?' the twins chorused in unison.

Carenza never went anywhere except to work or on outings with the family. Stopping in her tracks, she glared at her beautiful daughters. All that May had said was true. Everyone took her for granted. She was their possession. All that she had ever wanted to do after Tom's death was to make her children secure and happy. That achievement had been accomplished but it looked as if she was not allowed a small vestige of independence or happiness of her own.

'Yes. I'm going out to lunch,' she repeated. 'It's my turn to go out to play.'

'But …'

'There are no buts,' she said firmly.

'Who are you going out with?'

Carenza turned her gaze on them. Her hands were placed firmly on her hips challenging her daughters to say more. She had made a stand against them and on this occasion she refused to be intimidated.

'Well, let's go and see Granny May. She will know,' the girls declared mutinously and vanished.

Carenza continued to rummage in her wardrobe and found a pair of classically cut trousers which she teamed with a red jumper and scarf. A mini skirt did not seem quite right on this occasion. The late October day was warm but she decided to top her outfit with a jacket to match. Promptly at one o'clock Hugh Groves parked his impressive vehicle outside the house. Carenza had been watching and waiting. Her anxiety to disappear without her daughters making inappropriate comments was etched on her face. Unbeknown to her, the twins had observed this activity from the retreat of their attic bedroom.

'Granny May,' the twins chorused. May looked up from reading her newspaper. As usual her glasses were strategically placed on the bridge of her nose for such an occasion as this.

'Hello,' she smiled at the girls. It amazed her how like their mother they looked when she had been a similar age. 'What can I do for you?'

'It is Mum,' said Georgia, always the more dominant of the sisters.

'What about her?' May was beginning to find this conversation rather hard work but she continued as patiently as she could.

'Well, we have just seen her get in a car with a man.'

'Yes. That's the man who was at your grandfather's wedding. He's called Hugh Groves and he was a friend of your father's at university. What about him?'

May had sensed what this was about and was prepared to play a cat and mouse game.

'Should Mummy be going out with another man?' Lily had found her tongue.

May fixed a stern look upon the girls. It was one that they had seen only a few times before. This look had been honed and developed over countless years during her time as the village headmistress. The girls took a step backwards suddenly unsure of what she would say.

'And why should she not go out with a friend, for that is all he is? Sometimes Mummy needs to enjoy herself. Just think how you would feel if you could not go out and have fun with your friends.'

The girls nodded but did not look too sure. May then fired both barrels of the shot gun at them.

'You and all the others have been spoilt by your mother. She attends to all your whims. You have everything her hard earned

345

money can buy. I think you should be kinder to your mother and give her time to be herself for once.'

There was a mutinous silence as they glanced at each other uncomfortably. They did not like May's tone of voice.

'It has been incredibly sad that you have lost Daddy,' she continued. 'We all miss him very much but did you know that your mother lost her own mother and grandmother in the Blitz. Do you know what that is?'

'Yes,' they replied soberly.

'When your mother came to live with me she had no living relatives and the war had taken so much from many people. Your mother kept going and rose above such trauma. And now you are trying to stop her having some pleasure. You are more selfish than I could ever imagine.'

The girls could hardly look May in the eye. She had hit the mark and they realized that they had been selfish. The greatest shock of all had been why Carenza loved her mother so much. May was everything to their mother.

'Go now and do something sensible.' May's voice had lost its severity. She watched the girls leave the room knowing that she had made her point.

Carenza and Hugh parked the car by the river in Upton and watched the boats bob up and down in the water. Some men were working on the boats completing last minute restoration tasks before the winter set in. Awkwardly they then turned towards the town walking side by side not feeling that they were a true couple. Carenza kept her hands tucked into the pockets of her jacket. If she had been with Tom he would have taken her hand in his as a matter of course but their relationship had been long established. They might have strolled amicably in silence or have chatted about family events or the children but there would have been none of the awkwardness that lay in this new invasion into uncharted waters. It was hard to even think of beginning another relationship. Did she even want another man in her life? It had occurred to her recently that as her children left home she might have a lonely future without someone but was that the right reason for a relationship. It was all so difficult.

Hugh had found Carenza still attractive after all these years. He had often thought that Tom had been lucky to find her for his own relationship with Pippa had been more turbulent but somehow it had matured into marriage which was not destined to last. Pippa had been flighty, having liaisons whenever it suited her. There was no question of producing a child which might ground his wife and cement their union. Pippa had decreed that she did not want children and he had had to capitulate. After Pippa's third affair Hugh had had enough of her antics and had advised her to stop what she was doing or leave. She left. After three years on his own Hugh wanted a more permanent woman in his life but any dalliance he might have had come to nothing. Meeting Carenza in her widowhood had set him thinking that it might turn out to his advantage. His good common sense told him that if this was to become a relationship it was one that had to grow slowly. Rushing her in her still delicate state would hinder any progress in the matter. So Hugh had done what he had promised by marking this as the beginning of a friendship. He had noticed Carenza's awkward body language but had made no attempt to put her at ease.

'The bistro is over there,' Hugh pointed across the road.

Carenza had noticed it before when she had made visits to the town looking for a suitable property for the new shop. Suddenly Hugh placed his hand under her elbow to help steer her across the road. She flinched slightly at the physical contact but Hugh made no reaction. They were welcomed at the door of the restaurant before being shown to their corner table which stood in the dark recesses of the bistro. A candle flickered on each table, even at this hour of the day. The restaurant was not full but couples lingered over a leisurely lunch. Nobody glanced up at the newcomers for they were engrossed in their own lives. Hugh, a gentleman of the old order, pulled out a chair for Carenza to be seated. The menus were placed in their hands to scrutinize at length before the maître d' came, pen poised to take their order. When he had departed Hugh and Carenza looked at each other and smiled. Both of them had not realized just how difficult an occasion like this could be.

'Is this the first time since Tom?' Hugh asked being almost sure of the answer.

'Yes. I didn't know how difficult the first time could be.'

'It always is. I have seen a few people since Pippa but it is never easy.'

'Tell me about Pippa,' she said.

'There's not a great deal to tell. Like a lot of people we became infatuated with each other at university and we were married almost straightaway afterwards. We were too young I think. After some time we were leading separate lives. My work took me abroad a lot and my wife started seeing other men. She did not want children. Funnily enough she has remarried and had a child very quickly.'

'That's sad,' said Carenza studying his face but he was resigned to his fate.

'Inevitable I would say. It was not a marriage made in Heaven.'

'And you?'

'Good,' she said smiling. 'We were happy. We did not rush into marriage. Five children later and it was still good. There were some problems like Tom's mother but we managed.'

'I had heard that she was not easy and her death was a shock I should imagine.'

'Yes, but again we have survived and are moving on. Spencer, as you know has found happiness and that is wonderful.'

'It really is. He is a different fellow from the one I remember. When I was at university I used to go and stay with Tom occasionally.

The food arrived and was delicious. As the lunch progressed the conversation became easier and then flowed. By the time the coffee arrived Hugh took one of Carenza's hands and caressed it with his fingers. She did not pull away. He looked directly into her eyes making her feel naked under such close scrutiny.

'I would like to see you again Carenza. I have enjoyed our time together more than I can say.'

'Yes,' she blushed. 'I have too.'

Chapter 49

The new business venture was proving a great success. As she had done many times before with new projects, Carenza had advertised in the local press and on her first day she had received many visits and sales had been profitable. This new part of her business empire was to sell more expensive antiques. There would be fewer items but the furniture took up more space. After a few weeks, it was made known to her that the upper floors of the building were also becoming empty. They had been used as office space in previous times but the company which had used them was now moving to a more convenient building which had been newly built. It had been May who had wondered if she was going to use the upper floors. At first Carenza expressed her doubt.

'I wanted this to be my own base so that I am nearer home most of the time instead of having to travel so much.'

'I know,' May had said,' but you could sublet it to other people who might also sell antiques, perhaps not as grand as the ones you sell.'

Carenza thought for a moment.

'It could be sublet in the form of small areas partitioned off.'

'Carenza's emporium,' May muttered.

'What a wonderful idea. May you are genius. How did you think of that one?'

'I have too much time on my hands now that I am old,' she said. 'You wait 'til you get to my age.'

Carenza rolled her eyes.

'How often have I heard that one,' she said.

Carenza felt excited. This venture had given her a new lease of life. Activity was a great aphrodisiac and she worked late planning what she would do. Again she advertised for people who were interested in selling antiques for themselves on a smaller scale. She believed that she could set up a nucleus of staff who would sell for the small businesses. The reaction was very positive. Carpenters were engaged to divide the rooms into smaller units. As the weeks passed all were sublet and then filled with small antiques. It all looked festive now that Christmas was approaching.

'I'm exhausted,' Carenza told Hugh on one of their now regular dates. 'I could sleep the clock round.'

He looked concerned for her. Exhaustion was etched on her face.

'You shouldn't work so hard,' he said. 'You could do with a weekend away.'

'I suppose I could,' she remarked in a casual manner.

'Would you like to?' he asked in more serious mode.

'Do you mean it? I thought you were just being flippant.'

'Of course I meant it. Not too far away. What about a nice quiet weekend in Gloucestershire? We could walk and wine and dine ourselves. It would be lovely.'

Carenza looked at him and grinned.

'I suppose it would. It would be lovely to be quiet. Am I getting too old for all this ambition?'

'Of course not,' he said generously. 'We all need to recharge the batteries some time.'

Carenza had enjoyed her dates with Hugh. He was kind and considerate and caring. It had been nearly two months since their first date. When she had time she analysed her feelings for him. She knew that she did not love him though she certainly liked him, but he was not Tom. Although the rawness of her emotion at losing Tom was beginning to dissipate she was not entirely over his death. He still remained with her in her heart and in the darkness of the night when she could not sleep she would lie thinking about him and wonder how he would cope with some of the problems that manifested themselves with the children. But she also knew that she must move her life forward as May had advised all those weeks ago. May had opened up about the grief that she had experienced when her young man as she called him had died during the Great War.

'You have to take life by the horns my girl and get on with it. Grief can sometimes be self indulgence. Move into the next phase.'

Carenza had taken that advice to heart and it was beginning to work but it also went hand in hand with time as the greatest healer of all. It was with pleasure that she had accepted Hugh's invitation to escape for a weekend. As he had promised he had found a luxurious hotel which had once been an old manor house but had been converted into somewhere fabulous but expensive. It had extensive grounds with a large lake and woods. He had stayed there before and knew that it was a wonderful place to unwind.

Carenza had only a few days' notice to prepare for her weekend away. One evening after supper she sat with May after the younger children had gone to bed.

'Hugh has asked me to go away for the weekend on Friday. He thinks I'm looking tired. Would you mind if I go?'

'You know what I think,' May was feeling excited for her daughter.

It was time her life moved forward. May had liked Hugh from the first time he had been introduced to her. She liked his old fashioned charm and gentle sense of humour. It was not in her nature to compare him to Tom but there was a certain similarity about them in manner but not in looks. As long as he was good to Carenza that was all that mattered and she felt that it was time she remarried. All that performance last time about her independence and then keeping Tom waiting for ages was in the past but she hoped that Carenza would be more decisive next time. She was sure that there would be a next time.

Carenza bent and kissed her mother.

'You're the best,' she said.

Georgia and Lily were not as impressed by their mother's absence. It was the weekend before Christmas and they were home for the holidays. They had hoped for some shopping trips. Fashionable clothes were now important to them. They wanted their hair cut in a more up to date style before they returned to school. There was fierce competition between all the school friends and two new families had moved into Nether Heydon in the more expensive houses near the vicarage. They had several teenage boys between them so they had been told. Their conversation had been relentless in its selfishness.

Dorothy had been doing some laundry checks in the cupboards on the top floor near their rooms. At one point she had stopped to listen. It was not in her nature to eavesdrop but the content of the conversation had annoyed her. Were all teenage girls so self centred? As she was only just beginning to experience this new breed of child she thought perhaps she should show patience. But when she heard Georgia say.

'Do you think that we have a stepfather in the making?' followed by a peel of malicious laughter. Dorothy made her presence felt.

'Is it any of your business young lady?' she said angrily. 'What would your mother say if she heard you talking like that?'

They turned and saw Dorothy leaning against the door post of Lily's bedroom. They had never seen her look so angry.

'May has told me what you two have been up to in recent weeks. It is not good enough girls. You are not learning any lessons.'

The girls looked at each other guiltily. They did not want Dorothy to tell their mother, who would be angry. It was not often that Carenza's temper exploded but it was not always wise to test her patience. As for May they knew that her tongue could be acerbic when she was riled.

'Please don't tell Mum or May,' they pleaded. 'We won't do it again.'

'Remember your mother would never do anything to make you unhappy but you must get used to her having a life of her own sometimes.'

Dorothy walked into the room and automatically began to collect clothes that had been strewn about.

'You are lucky to have a mother like that. Anyway how about tidying up this mess? That should keep you out of mischief for a while.'

The weekend away had gone well. Both Hugh and Carenza had enjoyed each other's company, without strings attached to a more permanent commitment. The weather had been clement although cold allowing them to walk in the extensive grounds of the hotel or to drive into the spectacular countryside looking for little rural inns where they could lunch in the peace and quiet that they both needed. They had held hands like any well established couple and had kissed romantically in the subdued light of the old fashioned restaurants. At night they had slept together making a new declaration that there was an intimate side to their burgeoning relationship. This had been something that Carenza had missed after Tom's death. But often too tired at night to even think of it, she had put all thoughts to the back of her mind of it ever happening again. But it had and at once she felt womanly and desirable. It was a delicious enough sensation which she had long forgotten.

Hugh had also enjoyed his weekend. His mind was filled with thoughts of marriage and commitment but Carenza had made it clear from the beginning of their relationship that it was too soon to make such serious decisions and so he had respected her wishes. They had just enjoyed each other's company. On the last afternoon they gave each other Christmas gifts. Carenza had found an antique book of Shakespeare's sonnets during her rounds of her shops. Hugh had confessed his love of Shakespeare but in return he had found her a beautiful cashmere jumper in her favourite colour of red. Both had been happy at the choices made.

Carenza did not know when she would see Hugh again. She had not invited him to their family Christmas knowing that the children were not yet ready to have a father figure thrust into their lives. Hugh had not minded for he usually stayed with his sister and her family in London. They would resume their lives in the New Year and see where Cupid's arrow landed.

Chapter 50

'You can put your clothes back on now Mrs Heston,' old Doctor Fulbrook said from his side of the screen. Carenza fiddled with the buttons and hooks and eyes on her outfit before picking up her shoes and reappearing into the main part of the surgery. The old doctor, his rheumy eyes fixed firmly on her face, looked serious. He had been her doctor ever since she had lived in Nether Heydon all those years ago. His son, known as young Doctor Fulbrook, had also joined the practice after he had finished his medical training to help his ageing father. Carenza still preferred the older doctor with whom she felt more comfortable.

'Sit down Mrs Heston,' he insisted.

'Carenza,' she said, but he was used to formalities and did not like to be over familiar.

'I would say that you are about seven weeks,' he said looking over his half moon spectacles.

Carrenza nodded. It confirmed what she had thought and she had done the maths as well.

'What number pregnancy is this,' he asked without attempting to look at her notes.

'It's my fourth pregnancy but sixth child.'

'Quite so. And where do you want this child to be born?'

'Well. I had hoped for a home birth this time,' she said. 'I know the midwife and have every confidence in her.'

'There were no complications before,' he said, this time looking at the notes in front of him.

'No. There were none,' Carenza confirmed.

'But you are becoming an older mother and sometimes that can cause some difficulties.'

Carenza did not like the term 'older mother'. Although Doctor Fulbrook had not said anything specific, she felt that he was judging the fact that she would be an unmarried mother. He was of that generation who did not move with the changing times and attitudes. Would May understand this brave new world?

'You will need to make an appointment for a month's time.'

'I will,' she said, 'and thank you.'

He looked down at her notes once more and began to write. She felt that she was being dismissed like a naughty school girl or was she being over sensitive about her situation. Closing the surgery door quietly behind her, she observed a full waiting room of patients who all appeared to be watching her. Her body felt hot and sticky under such close scrutiny as if they all knew that she was pregnant again but she knew that she was being ridiculous.

'Mrs West you may go in now,' the receptionist called as an ageing matron rose to her feet and waddled to the surgery door.

When this baby started to show, Carenza knew that net curtains would twitch as they had done over the years and the bush telegraph of village life would be ready and waiting to spread the scandal. Holding her head high, a fixed smile on her face she nodded to a few acquaintances and emerged into the gloom of a February morning. It was cold, but the brisk walking pace that she set herself warmed her extremities as she made for home.

The walk provided an opportunity to dwell on the problems that had to be overcome. It did not bother her that she was pregnant and unmarried. One more child would not make much difference to the family nursery but she wondered how Dorothy would accept another baby to look after. The reliable Dorothy had been with them for years now but it was not fair to take her for granted. The alternative would be to hire a young nanny to help with the workload of a young baby.

There were also the other children who had not taken easily to coping with the changes that had been brought to her life in the guise of Hugh. She knew Lily and Georgia would be disgusted with the way she had behaved. They still did not fully accept that she had an entitlement to her own life. Their acceptance of the new child was going to be one of life's greatest challenges. Josh had been the easiest of the older children. Now that he still saw Spencer regularly he was content with his life. Carenza had kept her promise to her son and his grandfather. The younger twins would love a new baby in the family and then there was May. What would she say? She had a feeling that May would understand in her own way but at heart she retained the Victorian values taught at her mother's knee. If Carenza was ever criticized May would make excuses about the decisions that had been made. May would always remain her champion.

Hugh would want to marry her. He wanted children and she knew that before long he would propose. The knowledge of a child on the way would accelerate that course of action. The signs were all there in black and white.

There was time before she was required to tell people about her condition but it was courtesy to confide in May. For the moment she did not extend such rights to Hugh although she knew that was an unfair course of action. There was no way that she wanted to marry him but she was happy to have his child. Carenza did not want to live with Hugh in May's house with all the children. This was their home and was not open to outsiders. Even Tom had never lived in this house for a great length of time.

May was sitting at the kitchen table which had been drawn to the old Aga to keep her warm. She was busy writing one of her letters but the numbers had dwindled over time as her friends began to die, a fact of which she was very aware. On entering the kitchen, Carenza placed her handbag on the table and sat down on a chair to face her mother. She looked at May who continued to write until she had completed her sentence. Glancing up she smiled at her daughter but observing her gloomy face, her expression turned to one of concern.

'What's the matter? What did the doctor say?' she asked. She had had no idea what was the matter with Carenza who remained quiet for a moment or two.

'I'm pregnant again.'

On her walk home from the surgery she had decided that the only way of telling May was to be straight forward about the whole affair.

'Oh!' May was lost for words.

'I knew you wouldn't be pleased,' Carenza blustered.

'It's not that,' May knew that she was lying, 'but you have so much responsibility as it is. I assume it is Hugh's.'

'Who else's would it be,' Carenza snapped.

May looked at her in surprise. It was out of character for Carenza to be so out of humour.

'I'm sorry,' she apologized. 'I don't know what to do. I want the baby but I don't want to get married. I like Hugh but don't love him and I don't want to live with him.'

'History repeating itself,' May mused.

Carenza looked at her.

'Perhaps but I did love Tom and the trouble is that I still do. I have no intention of getting married just for the sake of it and then getting divorced. You know that I run my own ship and always will.'

May looked at this daughter of hers and noted that time and experience had not mellowed her on such matters.

'Hugh will have to know and as the father he will have rights. What about Spencer?'

'I will tell Spencer in time and he will understand. He has moved on from Lorna and can't be hypercritical about my situation.'

'What about Dorothy? Will she want another baby to look after now that Meredith and Alexa are six?'

'I know. I know,' snapped Carenza. 'I have thought of all this and I will have to speak to Dorothy.'

May was alarmed at Carenza's mood. Obviously she was under a lot of pressure. She dropped the subject and resumed writing her letters indicating that the conversation had reached its conclusion.

Chapter 51

May did not raise the subject about the new baby for several weeks but left Carenza to sort the problems hoping that she would make the right decisions. The first person Carenza had spoken to had been Dorothy.

'Don't worry Carenza,' she had said. 'I love a baby in the nursery. Perhaps in a few years' time I won't want to be doing this but for now I am only too happy.'

'Are you sure?' she asked. 'I don't want to put on you. I can assure you that this one will be the last. I had said that to Tom after the twins were born but I took precautions then and nothing happened. When Tom died there was no pressure for me to do anything about it. It will be another visit to the doctor after this one is born, make no mistake about it.'

She patted her stomach but there was no bulge as yet to indicate the new baby's presence. Dorothy just laughed. She and Carenza had become such good friends over the years that they could discuss personal matters at length but she guessed that it was not going to be easy for Carenza over the next few months. Hugh would exert pressure over marriage, while Georgia and Lily would find it difficult to accept someone else's baby in the family.

'Well, I shall keep you to that,' she said. 'I will drag you to the doctor myself.' Both women laughed at the image that was conjured up but then Carenza's face clouded.

'What about Lily and Georgia? They are not going to like it when they know about the baby. I don't want bad relationships with them after all those years I had with Lorna.'

'They won't but they will need a good talking to. You are the one to do it as their mother but I am happy to be with you when you do. I think that they need to know where you stand with Hugh. But before that you need to thrash it out with him and make your stand.'

Carenza looked at the older woman and felt the wisdom of her words. There was no point in burying her head in the sand like an ostrich and think that all the problems would go away. It all needed to be tackled in a forthright manner. Carenza had never been known for evading a problem before.

She hugged Dorothy warmly.

'You're such a treasure. What would our family do without you? You are so much part of this family.'

Dorothy could not help feeling touched by what her employer had said. A stray tear glistened in her eye as emotion overcame her.

'I have never felt anything but part of this family since I first joined you all those years ago.'

'I'm so glad, Dorothy. If I had had a sister, I would have wanted her to be just like you.' They hugged again knowing for certain that their friendship would remain forever.

A few weeks later Hugh came to collect Carenza for a special dinner date. It was six months since they had first met. He came bearing flowers and chocolates and all the fussing had set alarm bells ringing in Carenza's head. There were other surprises in store for her. Although he was always smart on their outings Hugh had made a greater effort than usual to look his best. His efforts had not gone unnoticed by Carenza.

'You are looking very dapper tonight,' she had teased.

'And you are looking particularly lovely Mrs Heston,' he had retorted making them both laugh.

They returned to the bistro in Upton where they had first dated. This had become a favourite haunt of theirs over the time of their courtship. It was an early Saturday evening but the restaurant was bustling with conversation and laughter extending a heady ambiance to the interior. The bond between the couple had grown since the beginning of their relationship but Carenza had not changed her mind about marriage. It was difficult to deny that she was fond of Hugh but it was not the love that she had shared with Tom. Tom would always be her first love but she had begun to realize that love had many facets. She knew now that over time their relationship might turn to something special but as yet it was too soon to say. A baby was not going to coerce her into a union that she might regret but she could not guess how Hugh would react to such knowledge. Neither of them had youth on their side. She and Tom had been young and full of hope but life moved on at a fast pace and events and dramas took over when one was least expecting it to happen.

The food was a sumptuous feast followed by coffee and brandy which Carenza declined. The brandy had made Hugh loquacious and care free. Like Tom had all those years ago he reached across the table and took her hand in his. She did not pull it away from him but deep inside she sensed what might be happening.

'I love you,' he said. It was the first time that he had uttered those words. Carenza was no longer in unchartered waters. This had been part of her journey with Tom although that was where the similarities ended. She waited for the inevitable but dreaded what was going to be asked.

'I want to marry you,' Hugh's love shone like a beacon in the dark. 'Will you?'

Carenza felt the weight of guilt on her shoulders, like Atlas holding up the world. She knew that Hugh really did love her for he was in ignorance of the child growing inside her. He wanted to marry her for herself and not because he felt he had to with a child on the way.

'Hugh. Hear me,' she said slowing him down in his adrenalin rush. 'I am not ready to marry anyone. I love you in my own way, but Tom has taken a lot of getting over. He was my first love but I even made him wait.'

Hugh looked crestfallen in his disappointment.

'Please don't feel that way.' This time she reached for his hand. He looked at her with troubled eyes.

'I am very mixed up at the moment,' she continued to explain. 'I have something to tell you.'

He looked at her but was not really following her train of thought.

'Hugh, I am having your baby. I would have told you before but ...' her voice trailed off as he looked at her with renewed hope.

'My child,' he repeated incredulously. 'I have always wanted to be a father. I can't believe it.'

'Yes, it is yours Hugh,' but it came out as a whisper. 'It is a much wanted baby but our relationship has to grow deeper before I will think about marriage. I did not marry Tom for several years before I agreed to his proposal. I know that I can be difficult but it does not mean that sometime in the future that I won't marry you. I just need time to adjust to everything. You know how complicated my life is anyway.'

Hugh's demeanour changed. He held her hand tightly and brought it to his lips in a romantic gesture.

'You have to trust me Hugh. This is your child and you have every right to its future as well as I do. We will love it together. If you still want to marry me you must know that I come with baggage. My elder twins have hormones that fly in every direction. They don't like me at the moment and they don't like our relationship but other than that they are fine.' And she laughed. He had the good grace to laugh too.

'So there is hope then? Perhaps we can live together?' he asked trying to push the boundaries even further.

'Of course there is hope but patience is what I ask. I cannot live with you without marriage Hugh, and there would never be room for us all in Nether Heydon. May is old and becoming frailer and I couldn't leave her and I am like the woman in the shoe. I have so many children ...'

Hugh laughed with real humour.

'Oh and by the way,' she continued, 'our child moved today for the first time. He knew what is going on. He is beyond wise.'

'I do love you,' he reiterated, 'so hope is not dead?'

'No,' she said actually meaning it. 'But patience is a wonderful thing. And by the way there will be no more children for me now. My doctor could not bear the shame.'

Hugh was too happy to contradict her.

'Anything else while you are confessing everything?' he asked.

'Yes,' she said. 'Until I make up my mind the child will be known as Groves Heston. He will not be treated differently from his siblings.'

Hugh did not say a word. He had learned the full measure of Carenza and her personality. She had not refused his proposal but in the same instance he had learned he was to become a father. What was the world all about? They lapsed into silence for a few moments lost in their own thoughts. Carenza felt that she rather imposed her own will on the men who had passed through her life. First it was Tom and now Hugh. She wondered why they put up with it. It was still rather a male dominated era but slowly the world was changing. There was a moment of self doubt about her attitude but her distant past had moulded her into the way she was. Self forgiveness was a difficult thing but she had to be true to herself and responsibilities.

When Carenza saw May the next day she told her all the details of her evening with Hugh.

'I didn't completely reject him May. Do you think that I treat men badly?' she asked.

'Yes,' said May, 'but you are your own person Carenza like I was in my youth. It was worse to be like that in my time. But I'm glad that he has hope. Like Tom he is a good man. Don't keep him waiting too long or he might find someone else.'

Carenza made no comment. She did not know what to say. There was always something holding her back before she made a commitment.

A few weeks later Lily and Georgia returned home for a midterm break. They were aghast at the size of their mother who for all her forthrightness had avoided the issue of telling them about the new pregnancy. Now she regretted that decision. Georgia looked at her in a horrified way while Lily did her best to avoid her.

'It's disgusting,' Georgia said. 'How could she? We are nearly grown up and there is going to be a new baby and she's not married.'

Lily had the common sense to say nothing. Although she felt intimidated by her sister's attitude a new baby made her feel insecure. Georgia's obvious distaste at the whole proceedings was not shared by Lily in the same way. She did not want to offend her mother as vociferously as Georgia. She felt that they were beginning to miss out on family life by making themselves so detached from the rest of them. Her obvious insecurity made her feel that she craved more of her mother's affection and following her sister's lead had put them in limbo but it was difficult to slide away from her sister's dominance. The fact that they were twins and did most activities together did not help the matter. Lily knew that she allowed Georgia to dominate everything because she herself was more willing to capitulate to her older sibling. Georgia expected full loyalty from her twin on this matter but this time Lily held her nerve and was prepared to face her sister's ire.

'I bet you think it's all right,' Georgia spat spitefully. 'You are not fully supporting me on this.'

Lily knew that she would pay a price for her individuality. It was like stepping into the sun from the shadows.

'No, for once I don't agree with you Georgia,' she shouted at the top of her voice. 'I am beginning to see that Mum has a right to be herself, just as I do. So think about it.'

The argument echoed through the entire house. Carenza had been at her desk trying to concentrate on her paperwork which had once more been neglected for weeks. At the moment she did not feel that she was on top of anything. She was more tired than she had been during her other pregnancies. Perhaps Doctor Fulbrook was correct that it more difficult for an older mother to be pregnant. Life had been complicated with family, business and her relationship with Hugh. He was being rather demanding and fussing over her health like an old woman but after all it was his first child. May never fussed in that way so why should he?

Now this argument was something different. It was so unlike the twins to be at loggerheads. She had a fair idea what it might be about. If she ignored the implications of it, it might fizzle out or it could upset the other children who were not used to such disharmony. Besides that, May was asleep in the sitting room as she did for a while most afternoons and this could wake her. Leaving her desk she made her way upstairs. It was a slow and laborious task ascending the stairs with her bulky size and breathlessness. Dorothy was employed in the nursery putting away laundry while Meredith and Alexa played contentedly with their dolls in the playroom. The two women arrived almost simultaneously in the doorway of Georgia's bedroom. The argument had gathered momentum.

'Girls,' Dorothy's voice rose an octave higher than normal. 'Stop it at once.' The girls took no notice and the storm raged on.

Carenza, breathless from the climb, stood behind the nanny. As she entered the room her heart missed a beat as she regarded the distorted, enraged face of her oldest daughter. Reflected there was an image so strong that it almost made her gasp. It could have been Lorna Heston herself. Carenza felt a stab of fear that Lorna's genes could surface in all her children but at this moment they were physically etched on her daughter's angry face. The recent nastiness that she had suffered at her daughter's hands was reminiscent of a reincarnated Lorna. She knew that she could not suffer such torment again. This situation had to be resolved now and not left to haunt her into the future.

Lily was not copying with this newly unleashed turmoil. She recoiled to Georgia's unmade bed and curled into the foetal position sobbing her heart out. Dorothy glanced at Carenza but her face was inscrutable. She made her way to Lily and sat on the edge of the bed pulling the distraught child into her arms.

'Come with me Lily. I need some help to sort the laundry.' Her voice was kind but there was a firmness about it which made Lily respond immediately. Nanny's voice had always been law in the nursery even as the children grew older. There had been an unwritten rule that Nanny and Mummy were never played off one against the other. Carenza caught Dorothy's eye and nodded her agreement. The bedroom door closed softly behind the retreating figures allowing mother and daughter to confront each other in their animosity.

'Sit down,' Carenza's voice had a new edgy sharpness to it that Georgia had never heard before. This side of her mother was unknown territory. Carenza rarely lost her temper but her anger made her strong even though her hormones raged in the most mysterious ways see sawing her emotions like a pendulum. Georgia was not prepared to heed the warning signals and knew that she had to battle on regardless.

'I said sit down,' Carenza's eyes flashed dangerously.

Georgia's fortitude caved in under this new mood that she was experiencing. She flopped defiantly onto the unmade bed.

'I think that you need to hear a few things young lady. Making judgments on other people is a dangerous game. It can make you unpopular and you can be labelled as vindictive. You are way too young for such epithets.'

Georgia still looked mutinous.

'Grandma Lorna never liked me from the day I entered your father's life. It caused trouble with everybody in the family. Spencer and your dad at one point would have walked away from her but they were good people and battled on. Lorna never tried to change. I bore the brunt of her anger until the day she died. There were good people in my life. I had the love of the family members who were important; May, Spencer, your father, and my children. I have loved each and every one of them and you. Your dad is not here but I will always love him. He was my first love. He gave me my children who mean the world to me.'

Georgia started to cry softly. Carenza moved to sit beside her and put an arm around her shoulders. Her daughter did not attempt to move away.

Carenza continued

'You miss Daddy.' Georgia nodded, sobbing even louder. And you think Hugh will steal me away from Daddy and our family.'

Georgia nodded again and hiccupped loudly. They had reached the heart of the matter. Carenza marvelled how adults believed that older children were more like adults when at the end of the day they also found difficulty coping with the complexities of the grown up world.

'Do you want to hear the rest?'

'Yes,' came the pathetic reply.

'Well, when Daddy died I had to carry on when I would have liked to curl up in my misery but responsibilities didn't allow that to happen. Someone had to be strong. I haven't always been strong but over the years May has been my salvation. She has been a better mother to me than my natural mother who was called Hannah. That is the truth and I will never lie to you or the others.'

Georgia looked into her mother's face with large solemn eyes but made no comment.

'What I am about to tell you is between us and nobody else. I am treating you as an adult. We had agreed that Meredith and Georgia would be our last children. Our family was complete. But along came Hugh, who is a lovely man if you give him a chance. As I am only human this little one was conceived, not out of the great love I shared with your father but a night of pure passion which is not quite the same thing. You will understand that when you are older. I was unsure about wanting this baby at first but now I do. It will still be a brother or sister to you all even though you have different fathers. Even Spencer says that it will be his honorary grandchild even though there is no blood tie. Do you understand what I am saying?'

'Yes. I think so.'

Carenza continued.

'Hugh has asked me to marry him but I am not doing so at the moment. I have feelings for Hugh but I don't want to marry anybody just yet. I still love your father but in time I might want to remarry. The new baby will not take my love away from the rest of you. Parents love all their children. One's heart is very big. As for me being an unmarried mother, attitudes are changing. Remember the Summer of Love?'

Georgia had cuddled closer to her mother. She giggled through her deluge of tears and basked in the sunshine of her mother's undivided attention.

'This baby will be loved as much as you all. When he or she arrives I will promise you that there will be no more. I will be taking my pill again. I'm too old to be producing so many children.

You have to remember that I was an only child. So was your father. We wanted to create our own family. We had so much love to give. Remember you are my first born although it was just a few minutes ahead of Lily but there is that bond that can never be broken. Whatever you all do through life I will love you unconditionally for that is what a mother does.'

Georgia was now sobbing uncontrollably in the comfort of her mother's embrace. It occurred to Carenza that this was probably the first time that her daughter had truly mourned her father. It was a terrifying thought that her anguish had passed unrecognized. Lily might require similar counselling. Had she been negligent of the handling of her children in the midst of her own grief? She knew that Josh was fine and the smaller twins barely remembered their father.

'I miss Daddy so much. I'm sorry but I felt that Hugh was going to take you away from us Mummy.'

Carenza had not been called Mummy by this child for a long time. It had been Mother since Tom's death.

'You silly child; do you now understand that that will never happen? Hugh is not like that. Whatever I decide to do my heart is large enough to love you all. That will never change. Now Georgia, your heart must be large enough to make amends with Lily.'

'I know and I will,' she said. 'I love you Mummy.'
'And I love you Georgia more than words can say.'

Part 6: Journey's End

Chapter 52

A year had passed since the conversation between Georgia and Carenza had taken place. The bond between mother and daughter had never been closer and Dorothy was full of admiration at the way Carenza had handled the whole affair. Later Dorothy learned the full details of the conversation and could not believe the extent of the heartache that the child had concealed for so long after her father's death. The bond between the sisters had been strengthened and the best part of all lay in the fact that Lily now felt her sibling's equal and no longer remained in her shadow. They still did much together but they had developed individual friendships which had boosted their confidence. Carenza could not have been prouder of them and knew that if Tom was watching he would have been too.

The most momentous event of that year was the birth of the new baby who had been named Hugh Jonathan Groves Heston, but Jonty to the family. May felt sorry that he had been given such a cumbersome name but as was the norm these days she said nothing. It was the lesser of two evils to say and do nothing while life in general plodded on with its highs and lows. Old practicalities such as being able to spell such a mouthful remained with her from her teaching days. She had been rather surprised at Carenza allowing it to happen but she had long wanted a quiet life and had kept her own council. This new world was fast becoming an unfathomable thing even though she had tried to keep pace with it all.

Both parents had been overjoyed at Jonty's arrival. He had proved to be the most contented of all Carenza's brood allowing Dorothy to enjoy a happy nursery. Carenza's guilt at producing another child for the already overtaxed nanny had resulted in the employment of an extra pair of hands to relieve the burden. Life was a little easier now that Alexa and Meredith were at full time school. Harmony reigned once more in the Heston residence. Hugh and Carenza were no nearer making a decision to marry but they did love each other in their own way. Hugh spent as much time as he could in Nether Heydon with the whole family. He knew Jonty might be his only child unless he married someone else but his love for Carenza was too strong to contemplate such a course of action.

Hugh fought to break down the barricades that remained in place despite his endeavours. Like Tom he persisted in his pursuit of her hoping that one day he would win his trophy.

One Saturday afternoon May and Carenza found themselves together in the sitting room. The fire blazed brightly although the day outside remained bright. Jonty was taking his afternoon nap in the nursery where Dorothy remained in her element, caring for her new charge. The rest of the family had embarked on a long walk with Camilla and Spencer along the country lanes surrounding the village.

'Do you realize that I will be forty-two next week May,' Carenza declared slightly aghast at the march of time.

'Yes, I know. You're not hinting for a present are you? And I will be ninety soon,' her eyes glinted in merriment. Age and vanity meant little to her now.

'No. I'm not,' Carenza tried to look annoyed but she laughed instead.

'I was just thinking about my childhood.'

'Which part of it?'

'The years before I came to Nether Heydon.'

'Oh,' said May, 'is there still part of it that I don't know about after living with you for so long.'

'But it has just come back to me about Hannah and Ray. It seems strange to think of them as my birth parents after all this time. Hannah used to say that they had a dream to make the future brighter particularly for me.'

'Isn't that what all parents want for their children,' May said pragmatically.

'Yes of course. But she really believed at one time that it could happen, and then the war came of course.'

'Yes that upset everybody's apple cart.'

'But not mine. If there had never been a war May, I wouldn't have met you and I probably would be still living in the East End of London.'

'True,' said May looking wistful. How different her life would have been without this child who had changed her future completely. Over time she had felt fulfilled by her life after Carenza had occupied her latter years and then eventually her children, all six. She looked around at the walls of this familiar room which had seen so much life, good and bad over years and possibly centuries. The old house groaned under the weight of its occupants but it had been made for large families and the love and affection that emanated within its four walls.

'Oh by the way, the name Carenza,' she continued, 'I was teased relentlessly about my name at school. I think now that it was part of the dream. The kids used to say it was posh. They taunted me by saying that I thought I was above all of them. It doesn't seem to matter anymore.'

'It is not an unusual name any longer. The world changes, moves on; too fast sometimes.'

They fell silent.

'What are you thinking?' Carenza asked after a few minutes as she watched the mobility of her mother's face as the thoughts tumbled in her still agile mind.

'Oh that life is a journey , my dear and I think yours so far is one of the greatest of all but there is still a long way to go.'

'May.' Her arms reached out to enfold the older woman in the warmest of embraces.

'I love you May. Never doubt it.' Her eyes glazed with unshed tears.

'I love you too my child for that's what you will always be to me; my child.'